Rumble in a Village

Rumble in a Village

LUC LERUTH *with* JEAN DRÈZE

ALEPH BOOK COMPANY
An independent publishing firm
promoted by *Rupa Publications India*

First published in India in 2020
by Aleph Book Company
7/16 Ansari Road, Daryaganj
New Delhi 110 002

Copyright © Luc Leruth and Jean Drèze 2020

All rights reserved.

The authors have asserted their moral rights.

This is a work of fiction. Names, characters, places and incidents are either the product of the authors' imagination or are used fictitiously and any resemblance to any actual persons, living or dead, events or locales is entirely coincidental.

No part of this publication may be reproduced, transmitted, or stored in a retrieval system, in any form or by any means, without permission in writing from Aleph Book Company.

ISBN: 978-93-89836-12-7

1 3 5 7 9 10 8 6 4 2

For sale in the Indian subcontinent only.

Printed at Replika Press Pvt. Ltd, India

This book is sold subject to the condition that it shall not, by way of trade or otherwise, be lent, resold, hired out, or otherwise circulated without the publisher's prior consent in any form of binding or cover other than that in which it is published.

In fond memory of Rekha

To all our friends in Palanpur

I feel best in that little space between a smile and a tear.

—Toots Thielemans,
Belgian jazz musician

Contents

Preface / xi

Prologue / 1

Part I / 5

Part II / 117

Part III / 203

Epilogue / 288

Acknowledgements / 291

Preface

JEAN DRÈZE

At first sight, Palanpur is as dull a place as its name suggests. I'm not talking of the hill station called Palampur in Himachal Pradesh, or of the headquarters of Banaskantha District in Gujarat, but of a nondescript village in Moradabad District, western Uttar Pradesh. Briefly, Palanpur is a cluster of mud huts and brick houses nestled by the side of a tiny railway station known as Jargaon, the name of a larger village three kilometres away.

On an average day, life is fairly quiet in Palanpur. Farmers tend their fields, women look after babies and animals, children mill around, others commute to Chandausi—the nearest town—for work, others still play cards by the railway tracks or hang around at the tea shop. There are no newspapers, no sports, no cultural gatherings and (virtually) no love affairs. Thrill, beauty, pleasure, comfort, hope seem to lie in small mercies—the sunrise, a special dish, a good joke.

The passage of time, however, brings some variety. Events like marriages, festivals, elections, visitors, even the pranks of the dreaded monkeys somehow conjure some zest into the daily life of the village. Now and then, a game of kabaddi or a troupe of itinerant acrobats attracts a cheerful crowd. Once in a while, the monotony is dramatically broken by the odd quarrel, dacoity, rumour, accident, or even—yes—a daring love affair. And, of course, over generations, the village has gone through momentous changes, mirroring the historic transformation of independent India.

I kept detailed notes of these events, big and small, when I lived in Palanpur in 1983–84. I had just completed my PhD in Economics at the Indian Statistical Institute, and joined a research project that involved a field survey in Palanpur. I spent a year there, rarely leaving the village except for short forays to Chandausi, Moradabad and some of the surrounding villages. The survey team also included N. K. Sharma and S. S. Tyagi, both sharp observers, and our assistant, Om Prakash, a fountain of local knowledge and wisdom. Aside from learning a lot about the village from the survey work, I immersed myself in Palanpur's social life, making many friends, some enemies, and generally getting to know everyone. I also made a quixotic attempt to cultivate a small plot of land, seemingly successful at first (I had bought top-quality seeds from a renowned agricultural university), but later ruined by a poor monsoon. In my spare time, I updated my notes.

Many years later, I shared those notes and memories with my friend, Luc Leruth, an accomplished writer with considerable experience of India. Like me, he had studied at the Indian Statistical Institute, and tied the knot later on with his Indian sweetheart. He had also visited Palanpur a couple of times, for extended periods. With his fertile imagination, Luc thought that there was plenty of material—and inspiration—in my notes for a novel. Initially, I was a little sceptical, but I hope that the reader will agree, by the end of this book, that I have been proved wrong.

Much like *Raag Darbari* fifty years ago, *Rumble in a Village* adopts a light-hearted tone but leans in to what might be called the dark side of village life—jealousy, intrigue, corruption, violence, and such. That side is very real. For one thing, social life in Palanpur is a morass of class, caste, and gender divisions. I had not read Dr Ambedkar when I lived there, but during my visits to Palanpur in later years, the words he spoke in the Constituent Assembly on 4 November 1948 often came to mind: 'The love of the intellectual Indians for the village community is of course infinite if not pathetic.... What is a village but a sink of localism, a den of ignorance, narrow-mindedness and communalism?'

There is, no doubt, another side as well. In Palanpur, as everywhere, there is love, compassion, friendship, and more. At the individual level, I don't think these sentiments are in shorter supply there than anywhere else. But the social environment is not quite designed to help them flourish. Let's take love. At one level, love is a bit of an obsession among Indian youngsters. Popular songs, for one, have few other themes. If a future historian tries to understand today's India through the prism of popular films and songs, she will probably think that romantic love bloomed all around. The reality, however, is almost diametrically opposite, at least in Palanpur. Even as young boys and girls listen to love songs and dream of a sweetheart, the actual prospect of reciprocated love is virtually nil. In the conservative environment of Palanpur, where everyone is watching everyone else, a love adventure can be very risky, and should it be discovered, retribution is likely to be swift and brutal (especially if the love birds belong to different castes). Matrimonial arrangements, for their part, are business-like affairs that often turn sour on the very day of the marriage ceremony. Even in arranged marriages, some couples probably develop feelings of comfort and mutual respect that are as good as love. The fact remains that a young bride in Palanpur is a kind of glorified domestic servant.

Much of this, of course, is in the eye of the beholder. If Palanpur feels a little morose at times, so do the gloomier neighbourhoods of London or Wolverhampton. When I lived in Palanpur, I thought it was an exciting place. I was sad when I had to leave the village prematurely, after contracting tuberculosis. Anyone with a happy temperament and a curious mind could probably have a good time there. Still, it is doubtful that the residents of Palanpur include many happy-go-lucky types (though there are some, including at least one who has been immortalized in this novel). And if they are hit by tuberculosis, they are more likely to die than to get well and start a new life.

And then there is the grinding poverty. In 1983–84, Palanpur was not exceptionally poor by Indian standards, but it was poor enough. The poorest families in Palanpur lived on the margins of survival, never quite certain whether they would have enough to eat the next day or a blanket in the winter. That cannot be fun for anyone.

Caste, inevitably, runs through this novel. In Palanpur, everyone knows everyone else's caste and is conscious of it. Caste is like being branded at birth, forever. It would take much longer than a one-year stay to understand the subtleties of caste in a village like Palanpur, but some aspects do strike the observer fairly quickly. One is the absurd and cruel nature of the caste system—a trivial point, worth making only because the caste system is still regarded by many as a method for 'managing society in an orderly manner', as the current Chief Minister of Uttar Pradesh candidly put it in a recent interview with NDTV. Another glaring aspect is the wide divergence of norms, values, and ethics between different castes, in particular, between the Thakurs and the Muraos—the dominant castes in Palanpur.* Much as in Bollywood

---

*The term 'dominant caste' is often used in Indian sociology to refer to the caste, if any, that is numerically dominant in a particular village or area and also dominates in terms of economic and political power. In Palanpur, the dominant caste used to consist of Thakurs, but at the time of my stay in 1983–84, there was a budding struggle for dominance between the Thakurs and the

films, these contrasts are enhanced in the novel, but their essence is far from fictitious.

All this, of course, is changing over time. The main events in this novel take place in 1984, when the observations that inspired it were made. Thirty-six years later, the village is a different place in many ways. By and large, life in Palanpur is less harsh today than it used to be then. Thanks to televisions, scooters, and mobiles, it is also less insular and monotonous. Some of the earlier pathologies remain, including deep social divisions, and women's lives are much the same as before. But there is some hope at least, certainly for the younger generation.

It is also worth clarifying that the pathologies of social life in Palanpur are far from universal in India. In recent years, I have lived in an Adivasi hamlet on the outskirts of Ranchi in Jharkhand, and the contrast with Palanpur could not be sharper. Unlike Palanpur, this hamlet has a relatively egalitarian culture, much natural beauty, and plenty of fun. People often help each other, women move around freely, and on festival days everyone joins the circle dances with abandon. Sparks of liberty, equality, and solidarity—all scarce in Palanpur—can also be found in many other areas and communities of India. One reader told us that this book revived a flood of memories—good and bad—of her natal village in Bihar, suggesting that *Rumble in a Village* has a wider relevance, but how far it extends is hard to guess.

Most of the events and characters that inspired this novel have been fictionalized beyond recognition. Any attempt to separate fact from fiction is bound to be futile. In particular, the thoughts and actions of the narrator—Anil—bear no resemblance to my own. I know very little about cameras, let alone rifles and locomotives, and I certainly never had a girlfriend who attended transcendental meditation seminars. If you are an astute reader, you may notice the odd allusion to a real-life person. For the rest, it is best to read this story like the richly embroidered epics of yore.

Muraos. The growing economic and political powers of the Muraos were symptomatic of the rise of the Other Backward Classes (OBCs) in rural India at that time.

Prologue

Palanpur, one night of January 1984, around 11 p.m.

Rajendra Pratap Singh was running as fast as he could, trying to avoid potholes, stones, sleeping dogs, and other obstacles that littered the narrow lanes. There was a puddle of water: he could see it in spite of the new moon. He jumped and landed on the other side but his head hit a piece of metal sticking out of a wall. The shock was violent, and blood instantly gushed from the wound. Still, he continued running. They—whoever they were—were on his trail. He had to make it home. One more corner, a short, straight lane. He kicked a dog that had emerged from a dark corner to bark at him and tried to accelerate, holding his forehead and with blood pouring into his eye. He would have liked to stop and listen, but many dogs were barking now, and some cattle were rattling their chains. He turned left at the next corner, nervously took a key out of his pocket and miraculously managed to open the lock on the first try. He rushed inside, closed the door and leaned against it, desperately listening for any noise coming from outside. Except for the fading barks, there was none. His heartbeat slowed down a little and he decided to take care of his wound. He went to his room to look in the mirror. In fact, since his brother, Naresh Pratap Singh, had left in 1947, eager to make a more comfortable and respectable living overseas after their parents had died, all the rooms were his. To survive after the zamindari system was abolished, Rajendra Pratap had sold the house in Jargaon that was, once upon a time, a richly furnished and decorated residence. Then, he had sold the smaller properties, keeping only the Palanpur house—its location attracted few buyers—where he had settled. He was better off now but, living alone, he had not bothered to buy new furniture.

A sharp twinge shifted his focus to the pain radiating from his wound. He dabbed it with a wet piece of cloth and rinsed the wound. It looked nasty. He cleaned it as well as he could but was not very good at it. He cursed again: if that Neetu were here, she would be useful for once.

This was an unfair accusation: Neetu had been his faithful servant, dutifully cleaning the mess he always left behind. She had not complained much about the highly irregular pay, and barely objected to his lewd comments.

Damn that old piece of metallic junk on the wall. He had never noticed it. It must have been rusted. He took a bit of whisky from a bottle—one of the few things in abundant supply in the house. He applied it on the wound with a piece of cloth, biting down a scream. He looked again in the chipped mirror: the wound was deep, but it did not look too serious. Reassured, he gulped some whisky, then some more. Not a great vintage, but at least it had not been adulterated.

Rajendra Pratap took a deep breath. The combination of pain and alcohol, curiously, seemed to stimulate his brain. He considered the situation. The bullet had missed him by less than an inch. He had heard it very near his ear. A good shot! There had been several men. But sent by whom? He could not rule out anyone.

It must be about the loot. At that thought, Rajendra Pratap got angry. He had only taken his fair share, no matter what the boss had said. The boss! Who did he think he was? Or was it because of the little scheme with the cooperative? Or was it…

He shrugged his shoulders. Of course, he had always known that being involved in so many illegal activities—or even legal ones that meant taking advantage of some poor soul, of which there were many in Palanpur—could lead to retaliation. Could the brother or father of one of the many girls he'd molested have dared to take revenge? Unlikely, but these villagers could be hot-headed at times. All things considered, and although it had been a close call, he realized that he had escaped rather easily. Did it mean those who were after him did not want to kill him? Or that they did not know the village? Possibly. Then they would not have known where the loot was hidden. He would check the next day and make sure everything was in order. Could someone have heard about his hiding places inside the house? He had been very careful. In any case, that was easy to confirm. Still in shock, he looked at the corridor in front of him, littered with dirty, smelly items where the billy goat was tied up. He stood up and went to a corner in the corridor littered with old bidis, broken cups, dirty pieces of cloth, two pots of paint and other broken and dirty items. Slowly, he went to a large room where an old dowry chest was standing. He opened the small door in the middle, went on his knees, and twisted so that his right hand could reach a well-hidden small opening inside the chest. He opened it. Nothing had been touched. That meant that nobody had gone to the other hideouts either. Rajendra Pratap smiled—so much money hidden almost in plain sight and nobody ever noticed.

A little out of breath, he stood again, blood gushing painfully to the wound. He would go to bed after another swig of whisky, he decided. Suddenly, he heard a loud noise and the door was flung open. This was followed by a series of metallic sounds, quite discreet but easily recognizable: someone had just loaded a rifle. He turned slowly. The visitor spoke softly, 'Just tell me where it is…'

The barrel was aimed at his chest. Strangely, he felt no fear, just immense surprise, then anger. So much anger that he rushed towards the rifle, shouting 'What the… How dare you!'

Rajendra Pratap did not finish. Surprised by the attack, the intruder had pulled the trigger. He reloaded and shot again. Two large red spots appeared on Rajendra Pratap's kurta. The intruder realized quickly he had been a fool: he would not be able to interrogate his victim. In his last moments, Rajendra Pratap just thought it would be hard to disinfect the new wounds. Then, everything went dark.

A hand quickly explored the hideout inside the dowry chest and took what it contained. There wasn't much. The house was frantically searched but nothing found. The body of Rajendra Pratap was kicked out of frustration and shot at again for the third time. Then the murderer left.

Many in Palanpur heard the gunshots but nobody moved. Besides, Rajendra Pratap had not called for help. Someone saw what happened, though, and a very thin shadow followed the murderer until the edge of the village. It went unnoticed. In Palanpur, such shadows were seldom noticed.

PART I

Chapter 1

London, a few days later

'Anil! For you!'

I had decided decided long ago that anyone who needs to talk to me knows my extension. If they don't, what they must tell me cannot be important. Besides, I was busy going through some rather complicated calculations and did not want to be disturbed. It is amazing how the arrival of computers, which were supposed to make the lives of bankers easier—and the lives of others too—has backfired. Now we bankers were asked to do all sorts of simulations under the assumption that the computer will do them anyway. There is also the notion—especially among computer-illiterate bosses—that any additional request would only take five minutes, if that. My light brown—with a bit of orange—Tandberg computer is a top-of-the-line machine but I still have to feed it numbers and routinely check that what is displayed on the screen makes sense.

'Anil! Phone!'

That is the first step. The second step is that what I print must be what I want to show the boss. The problem is what you see on the screen is not always what you get on paper: the computer will occasionally do something wrong on its own. Mind you, it's often because you have accidentally keyed in something not quite right, but I always find it satisfying to blame the computer, especially—

'Anil!!!'

It seemed that I would not get away so easily. Still looking at the screen, I picked up the phone.

'Anil Singh.'

There were a lot of crackling noises before I heard a faraway voice…'Is it Mr Singh, the son of Mr Naresh Pratap Singh and Mrs Meena Singh?'

'Yes. The late Mrs Meena Singh and also the late Mr Naresh Pratap Singh, in fact. But yes, it is me.'

More crackling.

'Hello? I could not follow….'

'Yes, it is me.'

'This is Mr Kumar, Ashok Kumar…. Hello?'

'Yes, yes. But who are you? I mean…what can I do for you?'

'…Because you did not reply.'

'Sorry, but what are you talking about?'

There was a resigned sigh at the other end of the line and the person went on, 'I am Ashok Kumar, a lawyer in Chandausi. I sent a telegram informing you. But I have got no reply so far,' the voice added reproachfully.

I reflected quickly, trying to ignore the crackling and the desperate 'Hello, hello, can you hear me?' of my interlocutor. I had indeed received a telegram from India but had not paid it much attention.

'Yes, I remember. Vaguely. Can you refresh my memory? What was it about?'

'I'm calling from India and it is costly,' observed Ashok Kumar in a long-suffering tone.

'That is why you should quickly let me know what it is about,' I countered.

'Yes, but I had to make sure it was you. Hello?'

'It is me,' I confirmed, irritated. 'Please tell me what I can do for you.'

'Yes, as his lawyer, it is my solemn duty to inform you that your uncle, the late Sri Rajendra Pratap Singh, has passed away at his house in Palanpur, in Moradabad District, Uttar Pradesh. You are the sole survivor of the family. Kindly please come to Chandausi to discuss the inheritance.'

I was about to suggest that it was a joke…then…Palanpur…I knew that place. 'Hello? Hello?' Ashok Kumar insisted, possibly worried that I had been shocked into silence, a horrible prospect for his phone bill. I decided to explore the matter further while minimizing the cost to the lawyer.

'Can I have your phone number? I will call you back.'

As a banker, I am used to asking for phone numbers. I usually don't take them down because I have no intention of calling back. This time was different. Accurately extracting each digit was a painful and difficult affair that considerably added to the phone bill of Sri Ashok Kumar, but I sensed some relief at the other end of the line once it was done: the lawyer had completed his solemn duty and he would not be the one paying for the next phone call.

I hung up and reflected.

I knew my father had grown up in a village called Palanpur. I did not know much about it. Few people did, apparently. It is a small, remote place in the state of Uttar Pradesh in northern India, and not particularly exciting. I was told I'd visited the place when I was three or perhaps four years old, but I had no recollection whatsoever. If it had been exciting, I supposed I'd have remembered. I always had a good—if selective—memory.

For my parents, visiting Palanpur had been a nostalgic experience. They tried once or twice to discuss their visit with me. I must confess that, busy as I was with girls—a lot—programming my ZX81—a lot too—and my studies—a bit—I did not pay much attention to family stories. Still, I know that, as the Brits were leaving India in 1947, my father left with them for some mysterious family reasons. I say mysterious because their exact nature was never revealed to me in any detail. Even though I was not listening carefully, I am pretty sure of that. Be that as it may, my father left Palanpur for Bareilly as a young boy, and eventually managed to leave India. I suppose there were jobs in England for honest accountants. In London, he met Meena Singh, my mother, whose family had arrived long before the Second World War and married her. I vaguely remember my father had a brother, presumably the deceased uncle in question, but that is as much as I know about the family tree. My parents died a year ago, in a car crash, so they would no longer be able to tell me anything about Palanpur, my father's issues with the family, or the deceased Rajendra Pratap Singh. Pity I had not listened.

My mother had told me my father had typed some notes about Palanpur on his old Remington typewriter after they had visited the village in the early sixties. It was some sort of fiction, based on characters that he had heard about or knew when he was young. It was intended to become a novel, I suppose, but I do not believe that he worked much on it, at least not in recent years. He certainly never completed the book. The unfinished text was probably somewhere in the apartment, though. I decided I would take a look before returning Ashok Kumar's call.

My phone rang again. I often have the impression that, just from the tone of the ring, I can guess who is calling. This ring was suave, gentle, soft, not frantic, but with a touch of authority. It was close to noon also. It had to be…

'Hello, Pat,' I ventured.

'How did you guess?'

'Some tenderness in the ring.'

'So cute…'

'I know. I am very cute.'

'Cute for a banker,' she corrected.

Pat is a social worker and student specializing in cultural anthropology. She generally does not like bankers and has told me so on a number of occasions, insisting I was an exception. Her name is Jane but, as a true hippie of the seventies, she has chosen her own nickname: Patchouli. Patchouli became Pat. I'm not sure I am cute—even when compared only with other bankers—but Pat definitely is. She has long, curly dark hair held by a headband that usually features tropical flowers, enhanced by the occasional wide hat, even if not required on meteorological grounds. The rest of the hair takes care of itself, floating all over in a rather attractive way. She wears long necklaces made of just about anything provided it is big, includes a peace sign, and jingles as she moves around. The same goes for bangles, whether around the wrists or the ankles. Pat often wears long, colourful skirts from India: the ones with small mirrors sewn into the bright cloth and a simple blouse under a shawl. The shawls are often black, and I suspect she inherited a few when her very Victorian grandmother passed away.

She also wears large round spectacles, ostensibly needed to see at a distance. They certainly add to her overall cuteness, but many people have noticed that Pat looks over her glasses when she's looking at something far away. Since the glasses are large, it is a little difficult to do, but she looks even cuter when she does this. In any case, Janis Joplin and Yoko Ono used to wear such glasses, so the question of whether she needs them for correcting her eyesight is irrelevant.

Pat dreams of going to India—or perhaps Nepal—one day which might explain her interest in me even though I am a banker.

'Shall we have lunch at the Hare Krishna near St Paul's?' she asked.

This is not typically where my colleagues go for lunch, but Pat would never eat at a steakhouse. Still, she occasionally indulges in fish and chips soaked in vinegar and carefully wrapped in newspaper. But only when I insist.

'Would you not prefer a hamburger?' I enquired as a devoted meat-eater even though I knew the answer.

'Don't be silly. I'll see you at the Hare Krishna at 12.30!'

I like hamburgers, of course, but I like Pat more. So, I have hamburgers with my colleagues when Pat is not available or if she has been available too many times during the week.

I went back to my calculations, but my mind was wandering. The idea of going to India seemed unreal somehow. Besides, I found it difficult to imagine that in a lost little Indian village like Palanpur, there could be an inheritance worth my while. A small empty house with no running water and a bit of land, all worth nothing because I would not be allowed to repatriate the rupees. Some fake jewellery, perhaps. Why on earth should I go there? I was thinking deeply about this while my screen stubbornly kept asking me if I wanted to run another simulation.

'Anil, care for a hamburger?'

'Not today, I'm having lunch with Pat,' I answered, suddenly realizing it was quarter past noon. I grabbed my camera bag. I always keep a camera with me, you never know. I had to rush.

∽

'Are you crazy? Of course you will go. And I will come with you.'

Perhaps I have already mentioned that Pat is cute. She is even cuter when she is angry or disappointed. An opportunity to go to India should not be missed, she hammered at me. Besides, I, Anil, had family responsibilities to attend to and should take them seriously. It would be good for my karma.

My objection that the financial value of the inheritance was unlikely to exceed the cost of the ticket was met with contempt. Pat took her time to stir rice and dal with her right hand before pushing the mix into her mouth. She took a scornful look at the spoon I always insist on using and finally responded:

'How can somebody with an education refuse a chance to broaden his horizons? Improve his knowledge of human nature? Learn about another culture? Your culture, by the way!'

I always think that a banker knows quite a lot about human nature. But she had a point: maybe human nature was different in India. How would I know? There was one thing that irritated me about Pat though:

Rumble in a Village

her theoretical knowledge of the subcontinent. I am aware that she has read a lot about it: the Himalaya, the sadhus, the caste system, even the Vedas, and God knows what. When I can take no more, I argue that I am the one with the Indian blood. I add that, in addition to the trip to Palanpur when I was four, I saw the Taj Mahal when I was eight—I remember that—and I often saw my mother perform pujas at home in times of stress. I also had a three-hour stopover in New Delhi two years earlier. So there!

Nothing doing, though. Pat, who had never set a foot in India, is convinced she knows the place better than me. The truth is: neither of us knows much about it.

I ignored her attack on a banker's narrow horizons and adopted a firm stance, 'In any case, I don't have the time. I have a lot of work in the office with the new computers. Besides, that place, Palanpur, sounds awfully boring, and…'

Pat brushed aside the new computers and the risk of boredom, 'You've told me the bank owes you plenty of leave. As for being boring, you've said the same thing about your job for a while. Finally, I have a good reason to go with you to India, so you will not be bored.'

I managed not to point out that the statement implied my acceptance and looked at her enquiringly.

'I've decided to pursue a PhD in anthropology on rural India,' she revealed. 'I'm in touch with a professor in Delhi, a great scholar named Dr Subrahmanya Subramanian, who specializes in this field and I'm sure that a trip to your village will help me a great deal.'

Resigned, I finished my lassi and tried to gain time, 'Okay, let's talk about it tonight.'

She clapped her hands in a concerto of bangles and necklaces, 'Yes! How exciting. At my place at 7 p.m.!'

Pat left the table, leaving me to settle the modest bill. But she gave me a big smile and a passionate kiss. Once stabilized on her heavy Dutch-style black bicycle, she waved and yelled, 'Don't forget! Tonight, at my place'.

I took out the Nikon F that used to belong to my father and took a few pictures of Pat cycling away. Clever girl. She knew being at her place would put me at a disadvantage. After the death of my parents, I had inherited their flat in Wimbledon. Spacious, well lit…. Big for a modest banker, but I readily adjusted, helped by the cancellation of the large mortgage there was on it: my parents had wisely subscribed to a good insurance. I had the pleasure of discovering that my pay cheque was enough to take care of taxes, the utility bills, and the rest.

Pat lives in a cramped place in Arsenal. It is full of pictures of Indian gods, it smells of incense, and she listens to all sorts of music. Mostly meditation songs, but not only those. She also appreciates Herman's Hermits, Scott McKenzie, Mungo Jerry, and the Beatles and likes to play their songs on her guitar. I spend a lot of nights at her flat because of Pat and because it is conveniently located on the Piccadilly line. The incense and the meditation are why I also like to spend some nights and weekends on my own in Wimbledon. Especially weekends when Pat attends transcendental meditation seminars in some remote place where the menu consists of a few potatoes with a bit of cream. Once, she dragged me to a session, but I kept making common-sense remarks that did not please the audience. Furious, Pat told me that she would no longer take me along, which was really too bad. The next weekend, I was in Wimbledon listening to Men at Work, Phil Collins, or Eyeless in Gaza, feeling a bit sorry Pat could not see the world my way and reflecting on deep topics with 'You Can't Hurry Love' blasting on my great system composed of a Thorens turntable, a Kardon Citation 16, and two Tannoy Autograph speakers. Or rather, my late father's great system.

Back at work that afternoon, I found it hard to concentrate. It was true my job was boring. Still, I had to do it. I ran a few simulations but kept looking out the window. I was lucky enough to have been granted a small window with a view of a tiny corner of the sky. It never stimulated my photographic instincts, even though it had the same proportions as a camera viewfinder. There was not much to see: the occasional airplane and, that day, an accumulation of dark clouds. It was going to rain.

The computer beeped. I was asked to review the case of some dude who wanted to borrow money to buy an Aston Martin. I did not think it was a good idea—the gentleman was essentially broke—but the bank was eager to increase its overall lending. With a sigh, I approved the loan and went back to my spreadsheets. As I write these lines, I recall with considerable sadness that this was a time when second-hand Aston Martins—or Ferraris or E-Types—were dirt cheap.

As for Palanpur, it seemed clear that the financial arguments for and against a trip to India in the near future were tipping towards 'against'. Too bad for Pat's PhD. She could always go there alone to do her research.

When I came out of the office, it was 6 p.m. As I crossed the street, it started pouring. How fancy: a boring job with a wet commute! I took shelter under a nearby porch. It was a travel agency called Taj Travel. At first, I paid no attention to what was on display, focusing instead on the sorry reflection of a soaked Indian man of average height who seemed to be slowly disappearing into the background, like a ghost. Was it the effect of excessive boredom? I then realized that it was the growing fog on my glasses. I removed them and, unable to see far, focused on an appealing advert just in front of my eyes: a lovely beach with palm trees under the Kerala sun. I brushed the water off my clothes and decided that, even though Palanpur was not in Kerala, my arguments against the trip to India, like the case against purchasing an Aston Martin, could possibly be revisited. The rain had made me go in with a more flexible mind. An hour later, I came out. It was not raining any more but my mind remained flexible and I was even looking forward to the trip.

Needless to say, the evening with Pat went very well. She got very excited about the notes my father had left behind and—thank God—decided that we had to rush to Wimbledon to immediately explore them. The notes turned out to be a rather disorganized bunch of papers, all typed except for a handwritten and barely readable introduction. I glanced through them and read a few sentences here and there. I smiled. I recognized my father's style and I have repeatedly been told mine is similar.

It surprised me that the story of a small village could occupy so many pages. Pat felt the same. Lots of names, words that I had never heard. The narrative seemed to depict a place where the days were long and slow, with unexpected outbreaks of violence. These notes would presumably reveal a lot about Palanpur's past, and my mother, who had studied history, had told me that the past explains most if not all of the present and the future. Some of my colleagues who follow the stock market would have agreed with her.

'Can you lend them to me, pleaaaaase?' Pat asked.

I was not going to say no, was I?

I closed the file, telling her that she could take it away in the morning. She was obviously happy with me and demonstrated it to our mutual satisfaction.

I have been thoroughly well educated in matters related to such satisfaction and I would never turn my back and go off to sleep although I did not mind Pat doing so. Since I was not sleeping, I reflected a bit. Assuming—a fairly reasonable assumption by now—that I would go to Palanpur and spend some time there, how could I make the most of it? My eyes glanced from Pat to the rest of the room. The Nikon F was on a table. I used up the film with Pat as a sleeping model. I like everything about photography. Manipulating an F, a Leica M5 or a Hasselblad is such a pleasure. Then, one must choose the right lens, study the angles, analyse the light, and interact with the model if there is one. I counted that session with Pat as an interaction even though she was sleeping. Processing the film—I usually shoot in black-and-white, typically Ilford rolls—then printing the final product and watching it emerge in the developer is utterly satisfying. There is a bit of dish washing afterwards because you must clean the processing trays, but your pictures need to stay in the water for a while anyhow. I had often thought of producing a coffee-table book, but I lacked a subject. Maybe Palanpur would be good with a 'return-to-my-roots' kind of approach. Maybe Pat was right and there was scope for a broader purpose to my existence? Not more girls or more money, but better pictures. People like John Lennon and others had found inspiration over there. Maybe not in Palanpur but still! I could pretend to be a gentleman farmer in the vast plains of Uttar Pradesh. For fun, of course, just to give more substance to my book. Could it be worse than keying in numbers on a Tandberg computer? Worth a try, I thought. The bank would surely take me back if it did not work out. Or some other bank would. Besides, Pat had a point: I should give myself a bit of time to explore my roots. Dig them up, so to speak. It was a question of will power and a bit of organization. After a few months, I would come back rejuvenated, having discovered my true soul, my inner self, enriched by a deeper philosophy of life and a mountain of good pictures. A redemption of sorts.

A few days later, completely defeated by Pat and the prospect of better weather, I embarked on my book project. I had purchased a ticket to Delhi—via Bombay, which was cheaper—at Taj Travel and rang up Ashok Kumar to announce my arrival the following month. The lawyer did not seem particularly happy or surprised to hear the news. He probably believed that was my only possible course of action. I took down his address, which proved to be quite a challenge.

'By the way,' I asked, 'how did my uncle die?'

'He was murdered at his home, sir. Did I not mention that? But you should not worry,' he added hastily, 'the culprit has been arrested after the police enquiry.'

'Was it someone from the village?' I asked, shocked, as if that made any difference.

'Apparently, it was the cleaning lady. A Dalit,' he added with hesitation. 'The police say she confessed everything after thorough questioning.'

I remained silent for a little while and a rather practical thought crossed my mind, 'And how do I reach Palanpur?'

'You first go to Chandausi on the Bareilly Express from Delhi and then you come back a few miles on the local train. The express goes through Palanpur but does not stop there. And the station is called Jargaon, actually.'

I hung up. The visit to Palanpur might not be as boring as I had initially feared. It was my office and its grey corner of sky that suddenly looked even duller. I decided to register for a few Hindi classes. It was an accelerated course that essentially succeeded in convincing me I had not forgotten the little Hindi I had learned from my parents. It was the first good news on my way to redemption.

Three weeks passed, and then I was on my way to Heathrow with several cameras that included a Nikon F3, a Nikkormat FT2, together with a series of lenses, including a Novoflex 400mm, an 18mm Nikon, a 50mm f1.4, also a Nikon, and my preferred 135mm Tamron f2.5, plus a mountain of Ilford rolls. But I was travelling alone. Pat had some desk work to do on her thesis. She would join me later, after firming up her stay with Professor Subrahmanya Subramanian at the Social Research Centre for Rural India located in the heart of New Delhi. The professor was considering accompanying her to Palanpur, so she was very excited. With a beatific smile, Pat had returned my father's notes. She only had time to reorganize the lot and glance through it, but she assured me they were very interesting, starting as far back as 1869.

'When you get to your uncle's house, check near the bed,' she urged me.

Pat has always been particular about cleanliness. I shrugged, sceptical about the hygiene standards in Palanpur.

In exchange for the notes, I gave her the prints I had made of her sleeping in my bed. Pat looked at them, then looked up at me, her smile widening. Then she waved, her bangles jingling, and off I went. At least, during such a long trip, I would have time to go through the notes. I put aside the handwritten introduction and started reading the first chapter.

Chapter 2

Palanpur

For long, Palanpur remained unconnected from the few channels of communication that existed before the Raj. Nobody was too worried about this: Palanpur residents—limited, in the early days, to a few households—seldom ventured to other places that they considered foreign, hence without interest and somewhat dangerous. The feeling was reciprocated by the few outsiders who knew about Palanpur. It could have stayed that way: the village would then have been forgotten until the advent of telephones in the nineteen eighties, like so many other villages of the United Provinces of Agra and Oudh, as the region was then known.

But Palanpur had a grander destiny. Things started to change in an unexpected manner in 1859, soon after the end of the First War of Independence. The Commander-in-chief of the Indian Army had decided to put an end to the riots in Bareilly, a major city located to the south-east of Palanpur. Bareilly, the headquarters of a brigade in the 7th division of the Eastern Army, still hosts a military cantonment today. The proposed solution was to connect the troubled city to the fast-expanding Indian railways as early as possible.

Bareilly had been a thorn to British rule since 1810, when existing taxes were raised, and new ones introduced in order to reduce the arrears due to the East India Company. This was not appreciated by the locals, who failed to see the link between taxes and public services. At first, the big brass felt that the disturbances that occurred then, and those that followed in 1837 and 1842, did not really put peace at risk. The cost of punitive action had been calculated, and the lowest estimates were high enough to make the Commander break out in a cold sweat. He therefore made two key decisions: first, that such numbers should immediately be classified, and second, that the arguments of those against military action—

who had simply stated there was little to worry about—should not be disputed.

For a few years, things remained in an uneasy equilibrium. In 1857 that equilibrium became unstable. A revolt of the sepoys—as the native soldiers employed by the East India Company's army were called—degenerated because their strong views on the way they were treated were not shared by the hierarchy. The masters were indeed deaf to incomprehensible grievances such as perceived race-based injustices and inequities where they only saw fair race-based justice and equity.

It was decided that the benefits of British civilization should be imposed by Britain—using military power if needed—even when they were not fully understood by the locals. Half-witted people—so it was argued—would eventually see the light and be thankful. The operation took time and the scope of the rebellion made it a much costlier affair than had been envisaged at the time of the initial estimates. The main reason was the need to bring in soldiers from Britain and other corners of the Empire in order to ensure their loyalty. This was probably not necessary: once they heard about the plan to punish the sepoys, the Gurkhas, and especially the Sikhs, eagerly offered their services. Having suffered a great deal during the Punjab wars, the Sikhs were willing to slaughter as many sepoys as they possibly could, even without a pay increase. Still, one never knew, and the generals erred on the side of prudence and high costs.

In Bareilly, the revolt took an interesting turn: a prince called Khan Bahadur Khan—the grandson of Hafiz Rahmat Khan, a Pashtun famous for having honourably served several Mughal emperors—formed a government. As had been a tradition through centuries in Bareilly before the colonization, he decided to mint his own coins. Industrious and ambitious, Khan Bahadur Khan also proposed to mint coins for other aspiring regional rulers, eager to run their own independent states. Up until the Bareilly revolt, the British, sure of the almighty power of their rupee—and poorly trained in monetary and network economics—had not paid much attention to competition issues in the area of money supply. It was not a priority. These coins have now become highly valuable and today's numismatists from Britain and the rest of the world reap the benefits of that carelessness.

Once peace returned, a commission met to draw the lessons. An economist argued that the root of the city's unreasonable taste for independence lay in the deplorable habit of its past rulers to mint gold and silver. In his view, the first step to avoid further riots should be to make a spectacular example and hang the culprit. This seemed fair enough. The commission swiftly and unanimously endorsed the proposal. A court case was organized, and Khan Bahadur Khan was hanged in 1860. As predicted, this put a stop to the minting business in Bareilly and cooled, for several years, rebellious tendencies in the area.

The commission also decided to make Bareilly a crossing point of several train lines. This was quite a treat for a city where economic activity was limited to agriculture and the production of simple jewellery and glass ornaments. The tracks could bring loyal soldiers to replace or even fight those of the Bareilly Brigade if they were suspected of treason, argued the Commander. He went on to stress a second and worn-out argument: thanks to so many trains, locals would enjoy the benefits of British rule. Prudishly ignoring the first argument, the honourable members of the commission paraphrased the second at length. They proudly concluded that, with these tracks, Britain would indeed be in a better position to pursue the glorious objectives of its civilizing mission. Everyone realized that the same tracks could also help the rulers escape in times of need, but nobody mentioned it. Some things are better left unsaid.

The ambitious scheme of building a train network in India left a profound mark that would soon be noticeable on a 'macroscope'. The connection between Moradabad and Bareilly through Chandausi contributed to this. It also had a noticeable effect on a microscope focused on Palanpur because, on their way, the trains would pass through the village.

Palanpur, 1869–1872

The first sign that strategic plans conceived in London, Calcutta, and other important places by important people could have an impact on modest Palanpur went almost unnoticed. It was long ago but the situation is familiar enough: a young Palanpuri named Udaivir Singh had run away from home, following an unwise adventure with a village girl called Laila. His flight took him to Chandausi where he realized he had to find a way to survive. As is customary with teenagers everywhere, the boy had failed to properly anticipate the consequences of his actions. He discovered, with fear and considerable sadness, the misery of poor urban life. Kicked by some, cheated by most, and forced to fight for every morsel of food, he reflected on the sordid environment of slums and soon decided that a solid beating by his parents was preferable to such ongoing hardship. He also hoped—for distance often biases perceptions—that the beating would be softened by a lot of shouting and apologies on his part along with his parents' relief at his reappearance. Unfortunately, Udaivir's parents understood parental discipline as a process that needed to be inflicted without flinching. The family's relief was short-lived, and his shouting did not help: the correction was duly applied and in full. The culprit took it stoically, greatly helped by the tough training received on the streets of Chandausi.

After things settled, Udaivir decided to share the vast knowledge he had acquired abroad. He told tales of metallic monsters called trains, puffing, whistling, and moving at unbelievable speed. These contraptions had not yet come to Chandausi but they were very close and would soon arrive in the city. And then, Udaivir predicted, the terrifying trains would continue all the way to Palanpur and beyond.

Udaivir's father, Mahesh, looked at his son in dismay, wondering whether he had jeopardized the mental faculties of the young man by hitting him too hard. He gave strict instructions to Udaivir not to spread such fantastic stories. He also agreed with his wife that her unstable son—this was a rare instance where Mahesh was ready to delegate all responsibilities to his wife—needed to be married as fast as possible, preferably to the girl he had dishonoured. This would solve all problems at once.

As often happens with stories that ought not to be told, this one went around Palanpur and neighbouring villages faster than the trains that they were about. Initially, the villagers were excited. So much puffing and whistling, scary metallic monsters, massive clouds: it all sounded much more exciting than their usual topics endlessly dissected during the long summer and winter evenings. These old tales, thrilling as they were the first dozen times or so, inevitably ended up losing their novelty. The options ranged from the story of the fall of a calf in a pond—a favourite that could still generate a lot of mirth—to the one about a monkey who had been scared by a very small snake. To be fair, that last story had a twist as the snake had been duly killed by a heroic youngster before being 'killed' again several times by a crowd of villagers who felt a lot more courageous once the first execution had been accomplished. But the joke was still on the monkey.

Could metallic puffing machines provide new excitement? Alas, like Christopher Columbus telling fantastic stories of a vast and rich continent far away across the ocean, the prodigal son, after being heard a few times, faced incredulity and mockery. Sensing scepticism, Udaivir insisted a little too much and the train grew in size, as did the volume of smoke. The speed increased too. When the engine reached the size of ten elephants, and the train travelled so fast that it could barely be seen, all parties had to call it quits. The magnificent tale imploded at the cost of the narrator. Udaivir was laughed at by all and thus died the first sign of a railway in Palanpur.

Much to his relief in these extraordinary circumstances, Mahesh managed to marry his son to Laila. A scandal was avoided but not the monotony, as there were no new tales to renew the old stock.

Mahesh died two months after the wedding, swiftly, from an odd fever left untreated, the way so many Palanpuris had died before him and would continue to do so over the years. Nobody helped: everyone was busy staying alive. Sadly, he did not witness Udaivir being vindicated. That moment came a few weeks after Mahesh's death. It occurred in a spectacular manner that forced everybody to finally believe in the fantastic stories told by Udaivir.

It all started innocently enough. Udaivir was sitting in front of his house, smoking a bidi and enjoying the winter sun. A few dogs were lying on the ground, also enjoying the sun. There was no sense of urgency in the air. It was a peaceful morning, with nothing specific to do. Udaivir's eyes were skimming over the fields where wheat was slowly growing, although there were vast patches where no crop could be seen. To his left was a little pond with some trees close to the water. To his right, there were more small trees that had been planted along the path. There was also a large mango tree that provided shade to farmers at the hottest time of the day. Feeling comfortable under its coolness, they would take a nap, play chaupar, smoke, or just talk. It was under that tree that the barber would carefully place his set of shining instruments and slowly sharpen them before trimming the moustaches, beards, or hair—in that order of importance—of Palanpuri men. These sessions provided an opportunity to chat and update each other on important affairs in neighbouring villages, like Pipli or Jargaon. For a barber knows a lot and travels to faraway places. The tree also offered shelter to the monkeys, Palanpur's everlasting nuisance, mechanically chased away by annoyed but resigned villagers.

That day, Udaivir's mind was focused on the condition of women, or rather on the condition of his wife: Laila was pregnant. Maybe a son. Probably. Most likely. He would be named Ashok. Laila had prudently tried to lower expectations and had cautiously suggested that it could be a daughter. Udaivir was in no mood to entertain such sad ideas and he made that clear. Although he never articulated scientific or philosophical thoughts, he was, intuitively, a strong believer in the power of the mind and its ability to impact actual events. Udaivir would have been surprised to learn that the same idea was expressed in the most learned way in some holy books.

Udaivir was not prone to excessive imagination in spite of what Palanpuris, after the fiasco of the train story, had come to believe. But the forthcoming birth of Ashok stimulated his mind. He envisioned a charming future with his son helping him in the fields, doing more and more work as years passed until he, Udaivir, could retire. He would then live in perfect serenity and be fed by a dutiful son. Laila, of course, could also be there. That Udaivir himself had been rather stingy when taking care of his father did not upset the dream. Instead, carried away by the bidi and the increasing warmth of the sun, his mind ventured in another direction, a glorious one: maybe young Ashok would join the army. This was the dream of every Thakur—the ultimate achievement. He smiled. The boy would earn a salary every month without fail and, being properly educated, well trained and—above all—grateful, he would send quite a bit of it home. What was more, Ashok would sleep in proper quarters, put on a smart uniform and, as the crowning symbol of this glowing family success, carry a rifle.

Udaivir stretched, made himself more comfortable and focused on the martial dream of his yet unborn son as a future proud soldier.

He could have happily stayed there for the better part of the morning—Laila was busy with various chores that did not require his manly intervention—but the enchanting vision was disturbed by a bark. More barks followed. They were strange barks, concerned, more scared than angry. Udaivir immediately knew that something unusual was going on. A nilgai, perhaps? These voracious antelopes were a permanent plague. He listened carefully. The dogs now stood up. When Palanpur's canines stood up without a direct threat or the immediate prospect of food in sight, it was cause for great concern. The barking increased but it was now overwhelmed by a growing noise coming from the path to Akroli. Unfortunately, the view was blocked by trees. It was obviously not a nilgai, though, because the dogs, while still barking, had started a prudent retreat behind the kuccha house, apparently placing a lot of faith in the protective power of its frail walls. Udaivir could now distinctly hear the rumble of many horses and some voices too.

Then, they appeared.

Bombay, then Delhi, February 1984

I was not ready for that. Bombay Airport was a mess. It was worse outside the airport, with all sorts of people asking me whether I wanted to change money (no, I had followed the standard advice and done it at an official counter before coming out of the airport); a taxi (no, I would take the official bus); a hotel, I know very good hotel (no, I did not need a hotel, even a very good one). I still don't know how I managed to move through the crowd and resist all the marketing pressure but, suddenly, a bus was in front of me. The front door was flung open and the driver shouted, 'Domestic airport? You go to domestic airport?'

The bus looked old but official. I nodded and got in. At least I would make it to my connecting Indian Airlines flight on time. I found a miniscule seat between a respectable grey-haired Indian gentleman and a girl who looked a bit like Pat. I put my bag on my lap and tried to observe the scenery. I did not take out the camera. At 3 a.m., it was really too dark for that.

Things went smoothly at the domestic airport. My plane was fashionably late but that did not matter. I had planned to stay two nights in Delhi, having heard that keeping a buffer is essential in India. I would soon learn that it was even more important in Palanpur.

Once in Delhi, and blissfully unaware of the distance between Palam Airport and Connaught Place where the YMCA—the youth hostel where I had booked a room—was located, I decided to be adventurous. I ignored the taxis and buses and opted for a three-wheeler. The deal was rather unclear. The driver seemed willing to take me, swiftly pointing at the seat with his hand, but he shook his head in a way that seemed to say no. I moved to the next rickshaw: same thing. It took me some time to understand that Indians seldom shake their head up and down, preferring to shake it from left to right. Subtle variations in the movement differentiate yes from no. I finally reached an agreement with a chap who had a stiff neck.

I am pleased to report that we made it although I feared for my life at several instances and banged my head against the roof a few times. I checked in at the YMCA, organized my stuff in the room, and decided to explore the city. But, first, I needed to make a reservation on the train to Chandausi.

At the railway booking office, I found myself caught in a large crowd of people pressing up against a wall with a minuscule opening. A man was sitting serenely on the other side behind iron bars, seemingly jailed. The chaos on my side was caused by a long queue and the cool gentleman on the other side was selling tickets. It was not a queue like the ones you see at a bus stand in London. It was closer to a mob. My turn finally came after I had understood that, in order to reach the opening, I had to assert myself. I yelled my name, paid the required amount and got pushed aside by the crowd. The ticket was passed to me by the helping hands of would-be customers eager to progress towards the window. The piece of paper read: 'Old Delhi Railway Station—Chandausi Railway Station' on the Bareilly Express expected to leave at 5.30 a.m. two days later. My name was not readable. The coach number and my seat were not readable either but someone in the crowd assured me that my name had been correctly registered for coach 15, seat 37.

Cheered by this success, I ventured on a visit of Connaught Place—also known as CP—quickly acquiring the skills to navigate the crowd and continue moving in the desired direction in spite of the current. During my tour of CP, a reliable instinct led me to discover Nirula's—a joint that offered burgers. There, I chatted with a small group of tourists and joined them for a visit of Old Delhi. They had hired a strange-looking colourful vehicle composed of the front of what looked like an antique Harley Davidson while the back clearly came from a small open-air bus. The driver started the engine with a rope, like one starts an old lawnmower, and a deep 'potato' noise erupted that would make any Harley Davidson owner jealous. We finally departed, shaking with every explosion in the cylinder. We visited the Red Fort and Jama Masjid, marvelling at the architecture and the sense of peace they exuded. I briefly ventured into Chandni Chowk and took a few pictures of hand-painted movie posters before retreating: the crowd was suffocating. I also prudently avoided the 'bottled' water sold at the Red Fort, having observed the seller pretend to remove the cap from a seemingly new bottle with a spectacular gesture. He then discreetly passed the caps back to one of his aides while another was collecting the empty bottles from the thirsty customers. Then, the fist aide simply filled up the old bottles from a barrel and swiftly closed them with the old caps. The bottles were ready to be sold as new again.

In the evening, having experienced enough of Delhi for a first day, I decided to rest a bit. I opted for Chinese food—always a safe bet, I thought—at a place called Berco's. After the meal, I walked back to the YMCA to read and rest.

Palanpur, 1872

It was an impressive group—a dozen or so people, led by two tall white men perched on large horses, of a type never seen in Palanpur. They were followed by some Indians who were clearly important since they were also on horses, albeit smaller ones. Then came soldiers with rifles. For a confused second, Udaivir thought that these soldiers were the materialization of his vision of Ashok twenty years later. But the barks and the horses were real. Udaivir put his bidi out, briefly considered the possibility of getting up to greet the visitors, then rejected it. After his Chandausi escapade, he feared complications, and a large number of people led by two white men perched on such formidable horses could mean serious trouble. Udaivir decided to stay put, hoping the group would ignore him and pass him by. To increase the chances of this happening, he remained very quiet, looking straight in front of him without blinking.

The strategy did not work. And to Udaivir's dismay, the party came to a halt right in front of him. Unsure as to what to do, he continued to look straight ahead, which meant he could no longer pretend not to see the visitors. The white men were talking to each other. Udaivir had picked up a few words of English during his stay in Chandausi, proof that one learns a lot when travelling. Although he did not understand what they said, he knew it was English.

One of the important Indians climbed down from his horse and came to Udaivir. He was an engineer who was assisting the two Englishmen who were not quite so educated. He had already visited countless villages like Palanpur and had been tasked with explaining to the locals the mission of the team. He was a small man with intelligent eyes and a friendly smile. He assessed the attitude of the man who was still looking rigidly in front of him and correctly interpreted it as shyness. 'Namaste!' he said softly.

To the relief of his eyes that had started to ache, Udaivir blinked and looked at the man. He smiled back. The situation was getting complicated but Udaivir summoned all his courage, drew all he could from his overstretched mind and decided to impress, 'What, you too?' he asked.

In spite of long years of experience in dealing with villagers, the engineer was taken aback, but that was nothing compared to the surprise of the younger of the two foreigners, 'But you speak English!' the man said, delighted.

Before Udaivir could prove that he did not, the other white man intervened, 'Really? That would be amazing, would it not, Lieutenant?'

Red-faced with blue eyes, the old foreigner had a beautiful Oxbridge accent which was lost on Udaivir. What was not lost was the magnificent moustache turning grey in some places. After gently following the shape of the upper lip, it went on without interruption up to the whiskers where they merged with smooth, although bushy, continuity. This considerably impressed Udaivir whose own facial hair lacked substance.

'I can assure you this is the case, Colonel,' replied the young lieutenant with some pride: after all, he was the one who had recognized it.

'I always thought, Lieutenant, that you had a good ear for understanding English when it is so strangely spoken. Myself, I can never figure out what these people are saying, even those who have studied in Britain.'

'May I answer the question, sir?' the young man asked eagerly.

'Was it a question, then? I say! Pray do so,' the Colonel authorized magnanimously, 'but speak slowly.'

The Lieutenant came towards Udaivir who was now regretting his audacity. He stopped smiling or blinking and stared at the approaching moustache. Being well trimmed, that moustache was less impressive than the Colonel's, but it was still thick. It directly connected to the beard as well as the whiskers. It was reddish. Maybe henna, Udaivir thought vaguely, not being familiar with the famous English red hair. He feared for a minute that he would be the subject of some close physical investigation—these things happened, he knew—but was relieved when the young white man stopped and stood straight like the proud soldier that Ashok would hopefully become one day. The Lieutenant glanced at the surroundings and started a long speech that included all the key elements of his mission. He left no stone unturned, covering the background, the objectives, the current state of affairs, and the glorious prospects that would soon emerge for Palanpur. 'My man,' he started, 'we are here on behalf of His Majesty King Edward VII, King of Britain and Emperor of India, who has instructed the East Railway Company to complete the rail network of this country. We represent this powerful company and our team is in charge of the section linking Moradabad to Bareilly.'

The young man continued with increasing enthusiasm, thrilled by the future achievements of his colleagues and the glory of his own task. He was no longer looking at Udaivir but towards the sun, seeing a vision of steam engines proudly drawing grey clouds in the sky of this immaculate but poorly connected environment. He provided all the necessary details, and even some unnecessary ones. If only Udaivir had understood English, he would have learned that, soon after the tracks were built, carefully selected products of the British steam engine industry, the top of the line, would ride on them. He would have marvelled at the sophistication of these engines built by Sharp, Stewart and Company, of Leeds— 'yes, of Leeds, my man'—the very place where the best engines in the world were built. These machines would be of the 4-6-0 type, with three driving axles—'no less, I can assure you'—and these would be compensated, allowing for the highest speeds. Udaivir would have rejoiced at the thought that trains travelling at such high speeds could be halted thanks to powerful brakes. The Empire, having already done so much for this poor land, would, in an immense gesture of generosity, do even more and supply double bogies and double boiler engines. 'Can you imagine that?'

Briefly, the Lieutenant looked down and had a vague suspicion that the magnitude of the imperial generosity was eluding his audience. Quite natural, he thought, it would come with time. The speech had gone on for a while. The white man's face had turned red because the sun was high in a sky not yet obscured by powerful plumes of smoke. He wiped his forehead. It was time to conclude, 'These metropolitan blessings, these technical marvels, these gems on wheels, will soon be pulling numerous coaches loaded with people, food, and all sorts of merchandise. This will open up endless possibilities for rural as well as urban people. Thanks to the generosity of England, this land will prosper.... All that will be for the sole benefit of this land! And for yours too,' he uttered proudly, pointing at Udaivir but not looking at him. 'Yours too!'

The brief silence was soon interrupted.

'Bravo, bravo,' exclaimed the Colonel. 'That was brilliant!'

'Thank you, sir,' responded the Lieutenant, his face growing redder, 'always ready to oblige and serve our noble cause.'

For a short while, the men looked at each other, immensely proud to be among the architects of such a grandiose, welfare-enhancing scheme. Then, the young man bent forward to look down at Udaivir, expecting to detect in the eyes of his local audience the same flash of admiration he had just seen in those of his Colonel.

There was none of that, however, for Udaivir's wide-opened eyes had become really dry. Nevertheless, he had perceived the importance of the moment and that he, Udaivir, was somehow linked to it. He had to say something appropriate. Something very polite also, for one never knew. He frantically tried to connect some vague dots, desperately searched his mind for a suitable reaction. He had to please this Englishman! Finally, he knew what to say:

'Ji?' he enquired with a disarming smile.

The only person who was satisfied was the Indian engineer who sensed that, after an unusual turn, things had fallen back into place. Trying hard not to laugh, he suggested to his masters that he could, perhaps, relay in Hindi the information that had so brilliantly been conveyed in English. He received a disdainful nod authorizing him to do so.

In mysterious ways that have always baffled colonizers all over the world, the colonized could achieve results without using the more advanced techniques of their masters. Thus, everyone in Palanpur and neighbouring villages was already aware that two British people accompanied by a group of Indians had arrived in the village and that one of the white men was speaking to Udaivir in English. The first part of the news was correct and the speed at which it spread was remarkable considering the absence of telephones. The part concerning Udaivir's English skills lacked precision, but it helped repair his tainted reputation.

Many villagers from the neighbourhood had converged on Palanpur. Being shy, they had remained hidden in the background. But the replacement of the British lieutenant by a native had emboldened them and soon people started appearing. Strangely, they were all men. Even more strangely, precisely as their husbands had got ready to leave home to discover what was going on in Palanpur, their wives also felt a sudden urge to visit Laila and support her during her pregnancy. The husbands were quite sure the wives could not possibly have known the real reason for their trip—and it was no women's business in any case—but they were quite surprised at the number of couples also going to Palanpur. Such coincidences still baffle men to this day, and not only in

India.

Thus, it was to a small crowd of men sitting in front of him that the engineer conveyed once more the main points of the Lieutenant's message. He was also addressing an equally large but invisible female crowd observing the gathering through the small windows of Udaivir's house. That so many eyes could observe him through such a small opening was quite astonishing. Later, British train engineers would be amazed to discover that coaches designed to accommodate fifty British passengers could absorb two hundred Indians. Even later, proud owners of Ambassador cars would not hesitate to claim that the modest car, officially—and somewhat generously—labelled a five-seater by Morris Motors of the UK was able to accommodate up to fourteen passengers travelling in full comfort when built by Hindustan Motors of India.

Chapter 3

Somewhere in Uttar Pradesh, 1984

The sea is rough; I should not have taken the ferry to cross the Channel. I hold on to the rail but that does not stop the tossing. It is unpleasant. My face is drenched from the high waves. Still, I decide to stay where I am. The captain comes running and grabs me. I try to resist but he insists, 'Are you married?'

I open my eyes, confused.

The Captain was a big man with a thick moustache and impeccable white clothes. I was sitting in front of him on one of the two smaller seats that faced each other on one side of the corridor, the main berths being on the other side. The man looked at me with a benevolent smile, the hectic movements of the coach making his body oscillate although his head remained miraculously steady.

I stared at him for a while until I remembered I was not on a ferry; I had boarded the Bareilly Express at 5.30 a.m. from Old Delhi Railway Station. The taxi driver had warned me: careful, many pickpockets here. I did not see any, perhaps because I was holding my stuff tightly and swiftly moving away from anybody who came too close. I had gradually relaxed, though, and behaved like everybody else: wait for the train while watching the entertaining show of people moving hundreds of parcels in and out of old coaches dragged along by large steam engines. I had pulled out the F3 and taken pictures using the wide-angle lens—the super sharp 18mm Nikon. The best possible lens for a crowded train station.

As I was taking pictures, an empty train came to a slow stop at the platform. I discovered then one of the marvels of India. The name I had given earlier to the official of the Indian Railways was correctly printed on a small sheet of paper glued to coach 15 and my seat number was indeed 37. A man with an official jacket was checking the passengers. He checked my name. Even my age was correct, but I was surprised by the significant number of kids who were 11½ years old. Later, I learned that there was a discount for children below twelve.

As the train had started moving and people settled down, I had fallen asleep. When I woke up, I checked my camera bag by reflex. It was where I had left it and everything else was there too. I must have looked a bit silly.

'Are you married, then?' the Captain asked again while about ten pairs of eyes eagerly observed me.

'Err, no, I am not,' I answered truthfully, but with an embarrassed smile.

I started pretending to take pictures in the hope that this would put a stop to the questions or at least help change the topic. Suddenly, my face was squirted with water. The camera too. I withdrew in haste.

'Is it raining?' I asked.

The man found my question very funny and so did everybody else.

Annoyed, I tried to understand what was so funny and finally realized that the people in the next set of seats were throwing water through the window. With the speed of the train, the water was coming back into the coach through my window. I say water, but it could also be other things. I decided to sit a little distance away from the window after having wiped my face and the camera with a handkerchief.

Once things had quietened down, a lady shouted a question, 'Why are you not married?'

The man nodded approvingly.

So much for a change of topic. I smiled and meekly answered that I had not found the right person yet, mentally asking Pat for forgiveness.

'And how old are you?'

The whole compartment was in a state of disbelief on learning that I was twenty-five years old. There was a vigorous debate. I got the distinct feeling that a few people stood ready to assist me in these difficult circumstances by suggesting suitable brides. The moustachioed fellow, who seemed to carry some authority, took pity on me. He cut short the debate and resumed his questioning:

'What is your business?'

Before I could answer, he explained his at length. In essence, he was a retired captain from the Indian infantry, had been based all his life in Bareilly and had retired there. He was now a consultant working for various government agencies in the area.

I listened patiently, smiled stiffly and tried to bury myself in my father's papers instead of getting drawn into conversation.

Palanpur, 1872

As promised, the engineer explained in Hindi. To say that this made the message clear would be an exaggeration. It is not that Palanpuris were slow-witted, but entertainment was rare in the area and this was a very unusual event that they wanted to fully enjoy. Besides, they were not familiar with the concept of railways—except for what Udaivir had told them—and were anxious to obtain all possible clarifications. They asked many questions and not all, according to the engineer, were relevant.

The most serious difficulty was to convince the Palanpuris that they would have to pay to board the train. That was a great disappointment, debated at length. All had hoped that, to get them on board, the English would give them money. That was not to be. The dismayed villagers demanded an explanation. The engineer patiently explained that, thanks to the train, the villagers would be able to visit friends in Moradabad or Chandausi. Even that left the crowd unmoved. Few had friends in faraway Moradabad. Those who did seldom visited them. Occasionally, farmers needed to venture to the Chandausi market to sell their products and buy seeds or tools. Sometimes a kadai or other utensil needed to be replaced, having unexpectedly given up after decades of daily use. But did that require a train? As for carrying things, the villagers all agreed that they would certainly not risk losing their valuables on such a perilous journey. However, sensing that the engineer was disappointed and perhaps irritated, they pretended to agree. In truth, however, the explanation never sank in and, to this day, many Palanpuris reject the notion that they should pay to board a train.

UP, 1984

'So, what is your business, then?' my neighbour was smiling gently but looked determined, no doubt encouraged by the support of other passengers.

I decided to lose a battle—perhaps that would help me win a war, later on, after identifying the weakness of those invading my privacy—and explained that I was a banker. But a banker living in

London and that made the whole difference, the passengers seemed to think. They asked many questions. I answered most of them. I also spoke about my recent desire to explore my roots with the help of a camera and perhaps write a book. A few passengers asked if I would be willing to sell them the Nikon and one was ready to pay as much as 200 rupees. I grasped the opportunity to look offended and went back to my papers with the air of someone who is very busy.

Palanpur, 1872

The path to be followed by the railway tracks was less hotly debated. The engineer was firm: the tracks would pass through Udaivir's house, and that was it. Khatam!

At first, Udaivir felt this was quite an honour and he was a little surprised to see the engineer look at him sternly. Then he realized that in the process his house was going to disappear. He timidly raised the issue. That was unavoidable, insisted the engineer, a question of height of the land at that very spot. However, he added with a faint smile that Udaivir would not need to pay for the demolition. He could even get compensation by applying to the District Officer. These words did not reassure Udaivir who tried to argue that, instead of going through the house, the train could perhaps come up to it, take a sharp turn to the right, then two sharp turns to the left, then again a sharp right, thus going around the building. That failed to convince the engineer who categorically stated that trains were powerful and fast but unable to take sharp turns. They were a bit like crocodiles. The house would have to go.

Distressed, Udaivir reflected on this grand project that concerned the whole of India, involving very important people like the two Englishmen as well as important places like Bareilly and Moradabad. It essentially relied on one thin pair of tracks, not that far apart from each other. Why was it that these narrow tracks led to the destruction of his house and not, say, of the neighbours'? Of course Udaivir understood that some houses would need to be demolished to make room for so many tracks, but why his? He explained this to a neighbour and asked for his support to request that the tracks be rerouted. The neighbour showed little empathy and refused to oblige, as did all the other men in the crowd, only too happy that it was Udaivir's house that would be demolished and not theirs.

If other important people had thought through the same project, reflected an isolated Udaivir, would his house have been destroyed at all? But nobody seemed concerned.

UP, 1984

'Paani chahiye?' It was the lady who had propelled water on me from the next window. This time, she was pointing at her matka. I declined. I also declined a banana, a cup of tea, two sweets, a chapati with sabji, one without it, and an entertaining game of cards before finally closing my folder, fearing the scope for interruptions on board the Bareilly Express was unlimited. My opponents, it seemed, had no weakness. The seasoned soldier sensed victory and made himself comfortable. He lit a bidi. I let farmer Udaivir struggle with Bayesian reasoning and lit a cigar. I offered one to the Captain who threw away his bidi—it presumably came back in through another window—and gladly accepted the Romeo y Julieta. 'And what is it that you are reading?' the Captain asked engagingly.

'You mean, what I was trying to read?'

The irony was lost on the retired Captain. He nodded encouragingly, 'Yes, yes.'

I explained the story of my father and decided to make the most of it by asking questions rather than answering them.

'Have you heard about a murder in Palanpur? Recently? A certain Rajendra Pratap Singh?'

At first, the resulting cacophony had me thinking I had hit the jackpot. But I soon realized that I had not been wise. Most of the passengers knew someone who could have known or seen something. Others knew of murders that had taken place in other villages. Many acknowledged that they did not know anything but were eager to volunteer theories that might help. In any case, they were all talking, and I realized that nobody was paying much attention to me any longer. Well, almost nobody. The Captain had become silent and was observing me with keen eyes. I was not sure how to interpret his look but since he was no longer talking, I discreetly retrieved the folder and resumed my reading more or less peacefully up to Chandausi. Maybe I had been wise, after all.

Palanpur, 1872

A sad Udaivir consoled himself with some basic philosophy, finding comfort in the undeniable truth that it would not take long to rebuild his house. A realist, he assigned little weight to the probability of getting compensation from the District Officer.

The engineer then started explaining what trains were like and Udaivir lived his great moment of glory. Everything he had said after his Chandausi trip was true. He became a hero. The amazing machine would be large, quick, puff, and make loud noises, the engineer confirmed, opening his eyes and arms wide to emphasize the message.

'How fast is the monster? Like a horse?'
'Faster!'
'Like lightning?'
The engineer smiled.
'Like sound,' he responded as seriously as he could, well aware that this far exceeded what the robust 4-6-0 Sharp, Stewart and Company of Leeds could achieve, even with a double boiler.

'Are the tracks removed behind the train as it moves forward, and carried to the front so that it can continue its journey?' That question was raised by several people who found it hard to believe that all the steel needed to cover India with tracks could actually exist. The Indian engineer had given some sad thought to this, taking limited comfort in the notion that fixed assets could not, by definition, easily be moved. The colonizers would need to leave behind at least some of the instruments they used to exploit the natives. The same instruments could perhaps be used later for development? But these were sensitive considerations that were best avoided, even in Hindi.

Instead, he addressed some practical issues. In due course, he said, the train would need a pucca house next to the tracks. That house would be called a station. That would come in a few years. In the meantime, the train required a large amount of water and a stock of coal. Two containers would be built for this purpose, close to the big mango tree that was just next to him. He would mark the tree and the train would stop in front of it. The villagers looked at their mango tree with respect and asked the right question:

'Will that affect the quality of the mangoes?'

'Certainly not,' lied the engineer.

They believed him then but noticed, months later, that the mangoes tasted of smoke. Industrial pollution was making its way in India.

The two Englishmen coughed, which the engineer, familiar with the ways of both cultures, recognized as a sign of impatience. Nevertheless he religiously went through the list of stations between Moradabad and Chandausi. Even in those early days, the English had a passion for stations and timetables: he knew he would not be interrupted.

Once he was done, the engineer turned to his masters. The Lieutenant had deployed an instrument and calculated their position. Possibly stressed by the poor outcome of his great speech, he misread the result. Turning to the map, he saw a place called Jargaon and informed the Indian engineer that that was the name of the village they were in. Had he read the instrument correctly, his pencil would have pointed at an empty spot since Palanpur was not yet worthy of figuring on a map. The Indian engineer had some doubts: Were they in Jargaon? he asked around. There was a quick debate: Palanpuris never had much sympathy for the people of larger Jargaon, three kilometres away. But by then, they had concluded that, maybe, something good would come out of this train business. Except for Udaivir—who was concerned for his house—they all answered 'yes' looking utterly innocent. Not exactly fooled but pressed for time—the Englishmen had coughed twice already—the engineer wrote 'Jargaon' in big white letters on the mango tree. That would do. That is what the station is called to this day.

Finally, the group departed. The Indian engineer was later reprimanded for lacking concision and wasting the valuable time of the mission.

UP, 1984

I looked up. The train had stopped at a station and I heard some commotion along the platform. A poor soul had been kicked out of the next coach and his meagre belongings had been thrown after him.

One or two pots, a matka that broke as it hit the ground, releasing its water, and some old clothes. I reached for my camera, then decided not to take a picture.

'He was travelling without a ticket,' said the Captain, wistfully.

'That's no reason to treat him like that,' I objected, horrified.

'You are right,' he answered as the train departed. But Dalits are often more brutally punished than others when they are in the wrong.'

He then closed his eyes and I went back to my notes.

Palanpur, 1872

The visit of the two Englishmen and their Indian escort was followed a few weeks later by a row of carts heavily loaded with small stones, each pulled by a pair of sturdy bullocks. The line stretched as far as the eye could see. Strong men, their bodies sweating under the unforgiving sun, were pushing the carts to help the animals. A line of women was walking alongside. At a signal from a supervisor, the first cart would pull over to the side. The men would take their spades and load the stones into large shallow baskets. Helping each other, the women would lift the baskets, carefully place them on their heads and walk away with surprisingly light footsteps. They would drop the stones on the bed destined to receive the tracks. The women would then walk back to the cart, their saris billowing in the breeze, in a wave of bright, divine colours that contrasted with the dark, harsh reality. Once the cart was empty, it would move back, load more stones, and join the end of the line. The harsh ballet was moving smoothly, as if a masterful choreographer had made a desperate attempt to conceal the suffering of humans and animals. But the veil was not perfect and, occasionally, a buffalo, worn out, would fall to its knees. The cart driver, annoyed, would repeatedly hit the beast on the hip, close to its tail, precisely where the sharp stick had already left many marks that were constantly bleeding. Breathing heavily, the buffalo would finally stand up and painfully resume its slow walk. If unable to stand, it would die, be removed and replaced. Men and women were thus constantly reminded that any weakness would result in a similar fate. It was not cruelty. In this endeavour, men and animals were suffering together. All were trying to survive and earn a living. Many fell for good.

Train building was a costly exercise in lives and money. Later, as the English claimed they had donated the vast rail network to their colony, there were bitter smiles from those who had built it with their sweat and blood.

※

By the time the men, women, and buffaloes had moved on, leaving behind their dead, the ground had completely changed. Udaivir's house had been destroyed in the process: though forewarned he was shocked. A few other villagers were even more shocked as their houses had been destroyed without warning. They regretted not having supported Udaivir in his objections to the plan. Still, nobody bothered to lodge a complaint with the District Officer.

Finally, a train made its first spectacular appearance in Palanpur. It was pushing a bogie loaded with the tracks and beams needed for its own progression. There were several groups of people walking alongside the train. Only men this time. The first group was in charge of aligning, at regular intervals, the heavy wooden beams that had been covered with tar as protection against insects and rain. Each man of the second group held a long metallic hook. At the first signal from the supervisor, they would all place their hooks under the same rail. At the second signal, all would lift it together. They would then carry it up to the next empty space with quick small steps, their bodies very stiff. They would carefully place the rail on the beams, aligning it with the previous one. Some workers would fix it on one side to the previous rail while others were fixing it to the beams.

Working in the fields develops the body but lifting heavy rails every day builds it more. The women would naturally never notice—let alone comment on—this particular aspect of railway development. The married ones admired their husbands and those who were still single were patiently waiting for their parents to find a suitable boy. If they could not avoid passing by the workers on their way to some place, they would always put a hand in front of their face so as to protect their modesty. It was said that some left a gap between their fingers, but that was never proven. Still, nine months later, there was a little spike in the Palanpur birth rate, possibly a statistical anomaly.

The engine itself convinced everybody that they would never travel on such a thing, especially at the speed of sound. Little did they know that most of them would become masters at jumping from the train at the scary speed of eight miles per hour and often travel on top of the roof.

A little adjustment was needed in the natural behaviour of all those experiencing the massive technological breakthrough unfolding before their eyes. To assist them in making that adjustment, impressively armed soldiers explained that anybody who stole a piece of property from the railways would be shot. Examples from neighbouring cities were widely advertised. That limited stealing to the bare minimum of a few bags of coal every now and then. Palanpuris considered that the rule only applied to fixed assets that were cumbersome to remove in any case. A few accidents occurred, helping villagers learn to watch for the train. Some drunks were rescued at the last minute by obliging friends; other drunks who did not have sober friends were hit hard. Some dogs were also hit, as were a few buffaloes: the robustness of the 4-6-0 type engines built by Sharp, Stewart and Company, of Leeds, was not mere legend.

There was also a desperate—and later abundantly ridiculed—attempt by a henchman of Avnendra Pratap Singh, my ancestor, to demonstrate that his horse was faster than the train. The man was an unpleasant fellow, so the bets were on the train. Udaivir had been promoted head of the village—by consensus—soon after the death of his father. All agreed that he would give the starting signal. In a clamour of steel that easily covered the noise of the hoofs, animal and machine started, pushed to their limits by their respective conductors. At first, the train was indeed slower. Once they reached some distance, though, the horse appeared to have stopped while the train was gaining speed. Soon, it was evident that the train would win. Then the villagers lost sight of both, but the happy whistle of the train seemed to confirm its victory.

A little later, the henchman came back, boasting he would've won had it not been for the smoke that made the horse cough and fall. The horse was in bad shape and everyone felt sorry for it but not for the henchman. My ancestor, quick to make the best of that situation, punished the man on the spot—which greatly amused the Palanpuris. Overall, this episode did not make the henchman nicer, nor did it change the pace of technological progress.

Eventually, the villagers, their cattle, their dogs and the train learned to live in reasonable harmony. Plumes of smoke from huffs and puffs became a permanent feature of Palanpur and started punctuating the days and the sky. The train also brought a regular stock of new stories with each load of passengers. That is why, each time a train arrived in Palanpur, an eager crowd would be standing near the mango tree hoping to sell their goods, purchase or learn something, or simply watch the commotion and discuss it later.

The economic impact on the village was immediate. The travellers were happy to eat hot snacks, drink tea or have a banana. Once, a British supervisor wanted to have an elaborate chicken dish, for which he was reportedly ready to pay amounts never heard of in Palanpur. Others wanted to buy a shawl or a knife. There was a growing demand for goods and services. Prices rose quickly and, as a result, supply too. Palanpuris were quick at learning to offer what was in demand.

Palanpuris realized that the passing trains created some wealth that stayed in the village. They also observed that people coming by train did not always continue with it. Sensing a promising investment climate, some travellers decided to stay and settle. Among them were the Thakurs who had retired from the army to live on a property that the zamindar—under instructions from the British—would grant them. These Thakurs would martially climb down the stairs of the bogie and stop to caress their moustaches— for they all had one. Then, they would slowly take down their rifle, followed by large if less important parcels. They would call the porter with the thundering voice of someone who is used to giving orders and being obeyed. Once the belongings were off the train, the family would follow. Udaivir would always greet these retired soldiers and engage in small talk, sometimes drink a cup of tea— something he would never do with other visitors.

A few Dalits—mainly Chamars—who had helped build the tracks, also stayed. Muraos who were cultivating the land for the zamindar, witnessing the influx of migrants, invited some relatives to join them. The size of the village grew. Nevertheless, its structure remained much like in the old days: farming accounted for most of the economic activity and supported a few peripheral services. Agriculture was dominated by the Thakurs, many of them land owners; Muaros were farmers; and Dalits supplied labour when needed by others. The peripheral services were offered by one or two households each of Dhobi, Dhimar, Teli, Nai, Badhai and Kumhars. Some Muslims also settled in Palanpur. They built a small mosque and, by and large, lived in harmony with their Hindu neighbours.

This steady growth also had some disreputable aspects. It is not that husbands, wives, or young folk, or indeed older ones used to be more virtuous in the rural areas of UP than elsewhere. But in the old days, it was almost impossible to have an affair without getting caught. With walls so thin that everybody knew what was going on in their neighbour's house, dogs that would start barking at any unusual movement, and the eager eyes of people that were constantly on the lookout for gossip, the sins of the flesh would always be noticed. Over time, opportunities to stray increased, and so did the number of sinners. Beyond this, the train also offered a convenient mode of transport to thieves and dacoits. Crime in Palanpur became more common. In short, the village was entering the modern era.

One person was particularly happy. Although he was the zamindar of several villages around Palanpur, my ancestor Avnendra Pratap Singh had always struggled to fully exploit his land. Murao families lived in simple hamlets all over his domain, but there were too few of them. The train brought in people who could work the land and, as a result, its productivity increased.

There was another side to the blessing. Avnendra Pratap had no son, much to his regret, only two daughters named Gaitri and Savitri. Thanking the gods for the sudden increase of his wealth, the zamindar discovered that he could marry them off more easily: Gaitri to Gavendra Singh and Savitri to Rajendra Singh. Both ceremonies were celebrated during the summer of 1885 and each daughter received a substantial part of the land.

Chandausi station, 1984

The discussion about the murder was still going on when the train slowed down along the platform in Chandausi. I had passed the Jargaon station without noticing it. People realized I was about to leave when I started preparing my bags. They all wanted to have their picture taken even though I would never be able to send it to them. My foreign banker status, it seemed, had stimulated the matrimonial instincts of the crowd. I declined a number of offers including a convent-educated young lady of fair complexion; one equally fair and well-educated with the additional asset of an uncle who had been an IAS officer; one whose father had a scooter; one whose family did not have a gas connection yet but was expecting one soon; one who had breasts that could fill an intimidating DD bra displayed to me as proof, making some women look on with envy while a few men seemed to feel dizzy; one whose brother had a job in Delhi; one who had green eyes; one who had a green card; and a few others. Finally, I made it to the platform, still single.

The Captain waved at me. 'Actually, I have heard about the murder of your uncle. See you soon, my friend. We will meet again. But be careful.'

How right he was.

Chapter 4

Chandausi, 1984

Finding the office of Ashok Kumar in Chandausi turned out to be the first real challenge of my trip. I had an address, of course, but when I asked people at the station to help me, the answers lacked precision. Desperate, I hired a cycle rickshaw—no engine, just pedals—to take me to the post office of the lawyer's postal area. Prudently, I negotiated a rate for a three-hour ride, because after the visit to the lawyer, the rickshaw would need to take me back to the station. I would then retrace my steps towards Moradabad in a train that stopped in Jargaon as Ashok Kumar had told me to do. An employee at the station confirmed what I had read in my father's notes and what the lawyer had said: Palanpur station was called Jargaon.

At the post office, a rather enthusiastic junior postman read the address and seemed to recognize it. As soon as he started explaining, his boss intervened, deciding that, as a distinguished visitor from abroad, I should be talking to him. Not for the first time, I was annoyed to find that people in India infallibly detected my NRI status often before I could say a word despite my ordinary name and appearance. I tried to go back to the junior clerk, but the boss would not let him talk and insisted on monopolizing the conversation. Unfortunately, it was soon clear that he had no idea where the lawyer's office was. I gave up and took the opportunity to send a telegram to Pat, urging the junior clerk to keep safely any response that might come for me in the future. His boss promised to do so.

I suddenly felt hungry. The train had arrived a little before noon. It was now 1 p.m.—time for a snack. I decided to go to a tea shop I had spotted from the rickshaw: it was in the direction of the lawyer's office. At least, that was my impression from what the junior clerk had started explaining. Kallu Halwai was clean and proudly advertised a licence to sell Cream Bell ice cream. Interpreting that as a guarantee of quality, I ordered two samosas, a few barfis, and a cup of tea. Miraculously, the server knew the lawyer, who often had tea there.

The owner of the shop had the good sense not to intervene and he let the boy give instructions to the rickshaw-wallah. I relaxed a bit and ate my food facing a massive ad for a newly released movie—in Chandausi—featuring a robust woman in a pink sari happily dancing in the vast, flowery landscape of the Himalaya under the approving glance of her soon-to-be lover and the support of her many girlfriends.

We reached the office of Ashok Kumar without further difficulty and, after checking that he was there and ready to see me, I instructed the rickshaw to wait. We were still within the agreed three hours.

The lawyer and I got along very well. He was a nice and harmless fellow, though a little pompous and not very dynamic. When I entered, he was sitting behind an empty desk, drinking tea. He was expecting me: my file was lying on a table about three feet away from his desk. Ashok Kumar reached for his bell, a symbol of importance no doubt, and rang it—not too hard, just a distinguished little 'ding'. This discreet call exuded self-confidence: faint as it was, the lawyer knew that it would be answered without delay. Indeed, a peon rushed in, humbly enquired about the wishes of his master and correctly interpreted the casual movement of a hand that hung as if exhausted by the weight of several rings. The folder was moved to the desk.

Ashok Kumar made me sign a bunch of papers, countersigned them, stamped them all over, examined the result, and looked pleased. Then he opened another folder—also fetched by a ding—and pulled out maps and records indicating with amazing precision where my property was. The map of Palanpur, drawn on a rough cloth, was several decades old, and referenced each fragment of property with a number. A separate book contained a list of all these numbers, along with the number of the page on which they appeared in yet another book, together with their exact area and the name of their owner. These books were continuously updated, and the lawyer explained that my name would replace that of my uncle. It is astonishing to think—as I discovered later—that most of India is covered by documents of this sort. My uncle's property essentially consisted of a rather large house, it seemed. There was also a plot of land, but it looked quite small.

'It is only a few bighas,' revealed the lawyer, putting on spectacles with circular, thick glasses. 'It is all that is left.'

As is customary in that profession all over the world, he immediately added, 'Would you be interested in selling that land? It is not large enough to live off it and I may have a buyer...'

His brown eyes, immense behind the glasses, were looking innocently at me.

'It's a bit early for that,' I countered with a smile.

I wanted to negotiate, obviously, and I knew very well I would sell the property at the end of my stay. I explained my coffee-table book project to the lawyer. I felt that having a bit of land and trying my hand at modest agricultural activities would help me understand Palanpur and therefore improve the quality of my pictures.

Ashok Kumar was disappointed and seemed to have difficulties accepting that an interesting book could emerge from joining the ranks of farmers in a poor village in Uttar Pradesh. In any case, it was clear he would never consider farming in Palanpur as an activity worth pursuing, irrespective of the circumstances. He considered my plans from several angles and made a gesture with his hand, implying that the ways of foreigners were strange. His eyes darted back with some regret to the few bighas marked on the map, then to me again. I asked him about something that was bothering me, 'You said that this land was not large enough to live off. I shall essentially be a photographer, so it does not really matter to me. But how did my uncle manage, then?'

Ashok Kumar removed his glasses and coughed embarrassingly, 'I think that your uncle had some other sources of revenue. But...that is what I heard. I'm not sure...'

The lawyer stressed that my uncle had no debts which, in Palanpur, appeared to be an achievement. Some people owed my uncle money, however. The details were probably listed in some documents that should still be inside the house, but the lawyer had no such document in his custody. In any case, he warned me not to expect much furniture or any luxury in the house. Rajendra Pratap had the reputation of having...the lawyer hesitated again before finally uttering...'having money...but the house had always been quite bare. He lived simply.'

'Where did he keep his money, then, in a bank?' I asked, curious.

Ashok Kumar's hand made a quick gesture. 'People talk about gold, cash, jewellery, and a good rifle, but who knows?'

Then, he turned to a more immediate question, 'Where will you stay?'

'On my property, of course. You will give me the keys, right?'

Ashok Kumar smiled indulgently. 'As I told you, your late uncle was assassinated.... He was shot three times. People had heard another shot earlier, but not in the house. In the village. And it clearly missed your uncle since he made it home.'

He paused to let me digest the information, '...so, the keys are with the Superintendent of Police,' he continued.

'But I thought that the culprit had been caught.'

'Yes, yes,' agreed the lawyer, after another hesitation, 'but it is better if you go and sort out the details with the police. You should talk to the Superintendent directly. It is better. He is known as BKS. In any case, if there is any difficulty with the keys and you still want to go to Palanpur today, you can stay at the Seed Store, at the entrance of the village. The chowkidar is used to it and will let you in. That way, he makes a bit of money. The poor fellow: his salary is not paid very regularly. If you want, come back after you see the police people and I will take you on my scooter until Akroli, where the path to Palanpur starts. No need to take a train.'

I thanked the man: he was certainly helpful. But the trip to the police station sounded less promising and I thought it prudent to ask a few questions about the murder before leaving the lawyer. I only got vague replies, but I understood that BKS, the Superintendent, was not an easy chap to deal with. In fact, he sounded like a bastard.

However, having resisted the lawyer's advances on my land, I would not be defeated by a policeman. I went back to the rickshaw.

The police station was not far away. It was nicely located, under a large banyan tree and in front of an enormous castle-like residence which—I was told later—used to belong to a powerful zamindar. As I stepped down from the rickshaw, I immediately realized that police activity was far from intense. A sleepy policeman in uniform looked at me vaguely, stood up when I talked to him and seemed uncertain about what to do next. He scratched his nose, spat betel juice on the wall behind him in spite of a sign urging people not to do so, and informed me that his boss was not there. He added that it would not be possible to see him without a proper appointment. I told him that was perfectly understandable and proposed to make an appointment on the spot: for the next day, perhaps?

The policeman flattened his hair, looked at the phone, then at me, before brilliantly stating that an appointment could only be made for a date and time that the boss would agree to. In any case, the boss never came to the office on Wednesdays and never before 11 a.m. on any day. This made it clear that BKS was not only a bastard, he was also a lazy bastard.

I kept staring at his phone. The policeman hesitated but finally acted.

BKS picked up and the policeman started an uncomfortable ramble, struggling to explain my presence. With an engaging smile, I offered to talk directly to the Superintendent, which was accepted with gratitude and relief.

BKS had a rather unpleasant and authoritarian voice, sounding a bit like a tornado. In a nutshell, he said that the keys would be given to me a few days later. This was necessary although all the evidence had been collected, and the culprit placed behind bars. He regretted that I would not be able to go to Palanpur right away. Without giving me a chance to explain my plan to spend the night at the Seed Store, he instructed me to pass the phone back to his subordinate.

The constable, who had sat back down while I was talking to BKS, stood to attention when I handed over the phone. BKS barked a few orders to which he listened respectfully. He hung up but was so stressed that he forgot to sit again. That made it difficult for him to write my name on the register, but he finally managed it and I had an appointment for three days later at noon.

As I was about to leave the police station in the rickshaw, a shy-looking young man, very thin, entered the office, his head down, staying close to the entrance, his feeble body against the door frame: the attitude of someone who is not used to being welcomed. I did not really understand what he said but the guard obviously knew him and no longer looked friendly. He jumped from his chair, reached for a lathi and managed to hit the poor chap on the back a couple of times before the man could escape. I was petrified, but who was I to intervene? The policeman turned to me, all smiles, and disdainfully uttered, 'Chamar. Dirty Chamar.'

Shaken, I went back to the rickshaw and we departed. Back at the office of the lawyer, I let the rickshaw go. Ashok Kumar was sorry about the beating.

'There is too much permissiveness in India these days. Like others, some Dalits can be daring and probably need to be put in their place. But they are so often ill-treated.'

'It was horrible,' I said. 'I'm sure that the chap was hurt quite badly. He was not that strong either. Really an abuse.'

'They look thin,' conceded the fat lawyer. 'It is sad, and at the same time surprising, that they survive their ordeal. As I said, they are abused much too often. It is so convenient to blame them. Or if you want to know something,' he added mysteriously.

'I don't understand what you mean,' I confessed.

Ashok Kumar suddenly started shuffling through the stack of papers on his desk and asked if I was still planning to go to Palanpur that afternoon. Sensing there was no point insisting, I confirmed my plans and thanked him for agreeing to take me. We got ready and, to my amazement, both of us and my luggage managed to fit on his Bajaj scooter. More amazing still, Ashok Kumar sat very straight and dignified while skilfully avoiding cows, bulls, goats, rickshaws, pedestrians, trucks, buses, potholes, and other mobile or fixed landmarks that randomly threatened our progression. He also continued smoking his cigarette when we stopped to buy petrol, in spite of a large safety warning—'Tanks for not smoking'—displayed on each pump. However, since the petrol-pump workers themselves were smoking while filling the tank, I did not protest.

Ashok Kumar dropped me, safe and sound, in Akroli, and with a grand gesture, showed me a country track that led deep into the fields towards Palanpur. He wished me well, assured me that he was at my disposal, and reminded me that I should collect the remaining papers three days later, when I would come for the keys. He would expect me. Then he drove on, lighter and as straight and dignified as before, but with a new cigarette.

I piled my suitcases to build myself a comfortable seat. I was keen to observe the place, at least for a little while, before proceeding to Palanpur. I looked around. Though just off the main road between Moradabad and Chandausi, Akroli did not seem very developed at first sight. The houses did not look very clean and, although a few children were playing around, they looked undernourished. Since the lawyer had mentioned that Palanpur was even less developed, I started worrying. Slowly, a crowd gathered around me and asked all sorts of questions. I ignored the matrimonial ones and focused on my photography project. That triggered some vague interest. I slung the F3 fitted with the Tamron around my neck and let it hang for a while so that people would get used to it. In the meantime, I started chatting with the villagers and explained my plan to stay in Palanpur, and not in Akroli as some had thought. The reactions were lukewarm, and all gave me a sobering account of the plight of farmers in such places, which was even worse than their own in the moderately advanced Akroli. Many blamed the government for taking all their money. I tried to suggest that the government was surely helping in a number of ways, but the villagers did not think much of what the authorities had done for them. My City colleagues in London would certainly share this view. In fact, people in Akroli rarely saw government officials, who seemed to prefer to stay in their cosy houses in Chandausi or Moradabad. If that was the case in Akroli, on the main road, it seemed unlikely that I would be frequently bothered by the administration in Palanpur. While everyone was arguing, I had started shooting with the 135 mm. It is a good lens to avoid appearing intrusive. I promised to distribute copies of the pictures once they were developed.

The sun was going down, and while the photo shoot was a pleasant exercise, I needed to move on.

That is when Babu appeared in my life. He was a shy, dark shadow, with legs like sticks, wearing torn clothes of uncertain colour and riding a rather sad-looking antiquated bicycle. He could very well have passed unnoticed and was probably trying to do just that when, by cutting the corner of the track to Palanpur as far as possible from our group, he hit a stone and fell. Nobody moved as I ran to the rescue. He had hurt himself but also had other bruises on his back that could not possibly be due to this fall. I sought help but people had started leaving. Nobody seemed concerned. He was so light that his feet briefly hovered above the ground when I pulled him up.

'Are you alright?' I asked, worried.

The man did not answer. He was not looking at me either. He remained still, holding on to his cycle that I had also pulled upright.

'You need to see a doctor. Where are you going?' I insisted.

Finally, he uttered something:

'Palanpur,' he murmured.

'Maybe I could walk with you. You cannot pedal with your bruises; I will pay you if you agree to let me put my stuff on the cycle.'

'Ji,' he agreed after some hesitation, still not looking at me.

I turned and discovered that everybody had left. I lifted my luggage and secured it on the cycle. We departed.

My new friend gave me his name in such a low voice I had to make him repeat it: Babu Ram, but I should call him Babu. He looked like a young boy. His shy face looked familiar. I thought I had seen him before, but where? Then I remembered: the chap who had been beaten up at the police station. That also explained the bruises.

'I knew I had seen you…at the police station.'

Babu looked uncomfortable and did not respond. I was not so easily discouraged:

'You wanted to see someone, I think.'

A slight movement of the head seemed to indicate that the wall of silence would break soon. I smiled encouragingly:

'If you do not want to talk to me, that is fine. I will not talk either.'

After a short while, Babu could not take the psychological pressure, 'It's because of you,' he said.

I was ready for about anything, but not for that.

'What do you mean?' I replied, flabbergasted. 'I have just arrived here.'

'Not you, your uncle,' he corrected.

'Rajendra Pratap Singh?' I asked, as if I had another uncle in these parts.

'Yes, my mother did not kill him,' he said forcefully.

I took a minute to reflect on this extraordinary statement.

'You mean, it's your mother who was arrested by the police and is now in jail at the Chandausi police station?'

'Ji.'

'What is her name, by the way?'

'Neetu.'

'And you were trying to see her?'

Babu probably felt that I was a bit simple-minded. What else would he be doing in a police station? I decided that it was important to correct that poor impression before I set foot in Palanpur. But what do you tell the son of your uncle's murderer?

'How do you know your mother did not do it?' I asked.

'Because she was at home that night. And so was my old auntie.'

'Did you tell that to the police?'

That question did not improve my standing. Babu threw open his hands: of course he had told the police.

'They must have had a reason to suspect this Neetu…I mean, your mother.'

'Because it is easy and because your uncle was doing…sometimes did things to her.'

It took me a little while to realize what he meant. But that would have been a reason to put my uncle in jail, not the victim. Finally, it dawned on me that the police must have suspected revenge. I ventured that line of reasoning.

Babu listened, seemed to agree, and finally lifted his hands, 'And because it is easy, and they want to know things.'

After the lawyer, it was the second time that I heard something to that effect. However, prudent and eager to preserve what was left of my dignity, I refrained from asking more questions. I needed time to explore the matter further.

For a short while, we walked in silence. The lawyer had told me that the road between Akroli and Jargaon that went through Palanpur was under construction. Eventually it would become a pucca road but the work had hardly started. I thought it was a safe topic for discussion. Babu explained that the workers came from a village called Bhoori and were employed by some kind of contractor. They were paid piece-rate wages: five rupees per 'khandi' of earth dug. Babu said that anyone could get work there at that rate if he so wished, so I asked if he had considered it. He proudly answered that it was too little. That was why the contractor was rich. He, Babu, was a good farmer and could make a better living in Palanpur. He looked up, clearly expecting me to be impressed. I knew that look: shopkeepers who come to me have the same look when they stress how brilliantly they have managed their finances so far and ask for an urgent loan in the same breath. I displayed a diplomatic smile of admiration but did not comment.

As we were chatting, we heard loud breathing behind us. Very slowly, a bullock cart was getting closer. It was empty and the driver, at first ignoring me, questioned Babu about my presence. Once his curiosity was satisfied, he invited me to sit at the back of the cart with my luggage, but not Babu, who did not seem to expect anything else. He was a Murao, I learned, one of the two main castes in Palanpur, the other being the Thakurs. He seemed hard-working and expected the same from his bullocks, skilfully guiding them along the path and not letting them slow down. He was a rather interesting chap called Kishan Lal, not well educated, but who talked a lot about his farming activities. I finally interrupted:

'Do you like life in Palanpur?'

Kishan Lal shrugged his shoulders. Life meant work, whether in Palanpur or elsewhere. The place did not matter. He added that there was no peace for either rich or poor. The poor suffered and the rich aroused jealousy. The difference was that some rich people were skilled at hiding their goods. He added that those who were poor could not hide it. I reflected that, in my business, there were many poor people pretending that they were not and that seemed to be a big difference between Londoners and Palanpuris.

When we finally reached the village, the group that surrounded us included almost everyone who could walk. One man suggested that I could stay in his shed. I agreed and thanked him profusely. Then the generous would-be host, perhaps fearing that he had gone too far in extending hospitality, hastily added that there was a snake in the shed—I would need to be careful.

Not a fan of snakes, I put him at ease: the Seed Store would be a convenient place.

'Yes, the Seed Store,' agreed Kishan Lal. 'White men have stayed there, you will be comfortable. And Govindi is used to attending to foreigners.'

'And who were these foreigners?' I enquired with interest.

That triggered a lively but inconclusive discussion. Nobody was too sure. They were probably from Britain, at least some of them. Where else could they come from? They asked all sorts of odd questions and filled forms with the answers. Nice people, but very strange. Some had found bliss in Palanpur, but others remained stern.

'They often stayed during the harvest and kept interrupting our work,' observed Kishan Lal disapprovingly.

I concluded that they had been academics. So, we went to the Seed Store located at the entrance of the village, just as the lawyer had suggested.

That is how I met Govindi, the old and exhausted chowkidar of the Seed Store. Not quite a hundred years old as he claimed, but closer to sixty as his daughter—not keen to be the child of a century-old father—suggested. There were six members in his household: himself, his wife, his daughter, her husband, Prem, and two kids. Govindi earned 150 rupees per month, but only when his money came. The lawyer had been right about that: the pay was quite irregular. His wife took care of the animals. Govindi was the only breadwinner at that time but he said that Prem might work in a sugar mill after the sugarcane harvest. My arrival was a good thing: it would bring in some money as they were waiting for the elusive mill job. I smiled, unsure about how much he expected from me.

Before we visited my quarters, a proud Govindi showed me a pile of bags containing seeds that were stored in the rooms located on the ground floor. I understood that the bags had just arrived and would be distributed in the village in a few weeks. His job was to guard them. Then the chowkidar took me to my room on the first floor. He confirmed that white people had lived there and assured me that they had been very happy. Maybe. But, in order to get to my 'room', I had to climb a hazardous staircase with missing steps. The landing had also rotted away, except for a fragile edge, and I had to carefully negotiate a big hole in the floor. Then, without knocking my head against the frame where there might have been a door ages ago, I had to glide to the next space where the floor had not yet collapsed. The bed was an old charpoy, barely holding together, and probably used by Govindi's father when he was a teenager.

It was late but the evening was wonderful and breezy. I was not tired. I started my two-in-one with some Indian music. I had purchased new batteries and a few cassettes in Delhi after I had heard Reshma, a woman with an incredible voice, singing. That would create the perfect ambience in which to read my father's papers.

Chapter 5

Palanpur, 1906–1908

Udaivir had never considered it important to educate his son Ashok in matters of governance. Laila seldom ventured outside the house and had remained blissfully unaware of the tax collection practices of her husband. She had also been overly protective of her son. This, coupled with the natural innocence of young Ashok, resulted in a surprising lack of acumen in his approach to the position of head of the village. To some extent, it did not really matter. Most Palanpuri farmers were cultivating the land of Gavendra Singh, my great-grandfather. Most were also indebted to him and had been forced by ignorance to let him manage the accounts. At first, they appreciated being relieved of complex calculations. It seemed natural, simpler, that the person who could read and count should keep the accounts. The importance of checks and balances was yet to be felt in rural India and my great-grandfather was skilled at exploiting his farmers' ignorance.

A few people—those who sensed that they had been repaying their debt for too long—had objected from time to time. When indebted farmers complained, the zamindar was quick to pull mysterious papers out of a large box. He would shove them under their nose, explaining that these papers proved he was right. Most supplicants would then retreat. If they persisted, one or two henchmen would pay them a personal visit and assist them in appreciating the benevolence of their boss.

In his day, Avnendra Pratap Singh, the old zamindar of Palanpur, Pipli, and other places, had obtained his post and status by winning a highly contested auction arranged by the English masters. Strong believers in decentralization, the colonizers had organized this region into areas covering a few villages. The principle of the auction was simple: who could extract the largest amount of taxes from the farmers cultivating these lands? The organizers had thus relied on a purely competitive method and were pleased with the financial results. Since there were laws to prevent the exploitation of farmers, the approach was considered effective and fair. A prudish veil was drawn over the unscrupulous methods used by the zamindar to collect funds. In a highly simplified world, all that mattered was that a proper contract had been signed. If the farmer could not sign, which was usually the case, a thumbprint or a cross would do. In his day, despite his shortcomings, Avnendra Pratap had been a reasonably good man, often helping the farmers. That landed him in hot water a few times with the colonizers, but he wanted to earn the respect of the villagers, not the foreigners.

Having married off his daughters and given land to his two sons-in-law, he had had time to observe them in action. It soon became obvious that Gavendra, although brutal, was a hard-working man who took good care of Gaitri. It was equally obvious that Rajendra was a drunkard whose fits of anger had forced Savitri, severely beaten, to return to her father on many occasions. On his deathbed, Avnendra Pratap had chosen Gavendra as his successor. Rajendra insulted the old man and wanted to beat him up. Gavendra—who was physically stronger—intervened and gave his brother-in-law a few punches before offering him a substantial sum to keep quiet. Fuming, yelling insults at the whole world, Rajendra drank away a good portion of the money, went back home and would have harmed his wife if he had not fallen asleep at the entrance of the house. He never woke up. Savitri collected what was left of the money and went to her brother-in-law to seek refuge. Gavendra promised to take care of her, especially since she was pregnant. She had had other children, but they had all died. He knew she had money, so he insisted that she pay for her stay at his place. Soon, she gave birth to a boy, whom she named Sipahi. A year later, Savitri ran out of money. Magnanimously, Gavendra let her stay in a little kuccha house that he possessed in Palanpur. In time, the house began decaying. Much to Savitri's despair, Sipahi had inherited his father's character and temperament, and was considered a bad lot by the villagers.

Of course, the zamindar was not in possession of all the land in the village. Ashok, for example, had inherited a plot that rightfully belonged to him. His father, Udaivir, had been a very efficient collector of taxes on behalf of the zamindar and he had kept some of the money for himself. The zamindar had considered that an incentive and turned a blind eye.

A few other farmers had owned small plots but, at one time or another, faced financial difficulties, perhaps during the marriage of their daughter, or because of an illness or other contingencies. Desperate, they had borrowed from a moneylender, and when it became clear that they would not be able to repay the loan, they had turned to the zamindar. They soon discovered that Gavendra had a tougher approach to financial management than his father-in-law. At first, he spoke to them sweetly, explaining that of course, the late Avnendra Pratap Singh had always been ready to help, but times had changed and he, Gavendra, was facing difficult circumstances of his own, despite being so careful and leading a frugal life. By contrast, the farmer had been careless in borrowing so much from a moneylender. They were all rascals.

The farmer would then plead that he had not realized how kind the zamindar was.

'You should have known that,' the offended zamindar would shout. 'Have I not always looked after the interests of all?'

'Yes, yes,' the farmer would answer—surprised that the thought had not occurred to him before—'so please, please help me again.'

Touched by such despair, the zamindar would reluctantly—and exceptionally, my imprudent fellow, he would stress—show further empathy and agree to help. Of course, there would be costs and the benevolent zamindar needed to watch his money so that others could also benefit from his generosity.

'How big is your land?'

A little later, the farmer would leave, his debt with the moneylender settled, and a larger sum due to Gavendra Singh. Years later, bent under the implacable sun, his back aching, his hand desperately driving the plough across a field that was no longer his, he would sometimes stop his bullocks and wonder how marrying off his daughter had made him a slave of the zamindar. But there was no way out and he would chase that thought away with a click of the tongue. The bullocks knew the signal and would resume their slow, yet powerful walk.

With the bulk of the land belonging to the zamindar and most farmers working for him in one way or another, the role of head of the village—besides collecting taxes—essentially consisted of organizing long meetings under the mango tree with the elders. The hookah would go around, and the discussions would start. They rarely led to any major decisions, but they lasted long because nobody was in a hurry. In the old days, Avnendra Pratap would let these councils take place and hear from the head what had been decided. Sometimes, he would even take part, actually interested in what his farmers had to say. Under the new dispensation, when a decision was taken, it was because Gavendra had already made it. He would then instruct Ashok to make the village council adopt it: a diplomatic way of informing the village.

In 1906, the harvest was good. Taxes were collected with little resistance, if any, and there was no major crisis. As village chief, young Ashok did not face difficulties. He took his share with strict honesty and, in an equally honest manner, handed the rest to the zamindar. As Ashok had understood it, the zamindar would take his own share and the rest would go to the British. In what proportion exactly was not something the fresh and innocent village head cared much about. He had performed his duty and assumed others were doing the same.

The following year, the harvest was good again. Palanpur also benefited, unexpectedly, from an event taking place in faraway Bengal: railway employees went on strike and trains were stranded in Calcutta. This had repercussions in Bareilly because there was no point letting trains depart and get stuck in the middle of nowhere. This meant, in turn, that Chandausi and Moradabad stations were crowded and that one or two trains got stuck in Palanpur. By then, Palanpuris had mastered the skills needed to enter into a profitable exchange with passengers. On the shadier side, they also took the opportunity to steal from freight trains. This was a good year for Palanpur. Once again, all were ready to pay their taxes without fuss. Ashok shared the proceeds fairly, just like in 1906.

This time, the zamindar did not appear as delighted as the previous year. Having observed the abundance of the crop and the traffic around the stranded trains, he had assumed that Ashok, after one year on the job, had learned the trade. People usually suspect others of doing what they would themselves do. Accustomed to pocketing much more than his fair share before transferring the money to the English masters—exactly what was agreed under the contract—he suspected that Ashok was doing the same. Surely, the chief had collected more than he had admitted to.

Gavendra decided to send his men to Palanpur to ask the farmers a few pointed questions. This had to be done discreetly; there was no need to advertise that the zamindar had been cheated if that was indeed the case. Cheaters do not like to be cheated. His men came back to Jargaon with unexpected news: the headman had collected precisely the money that he was supposed to collect, from every single farmer.

'Has he not taken advantage of the good harvest?' the zamindar's tone was almost wistful, way beyond sarcasm.

His henchmen laughed heartily, hoping that the poor management practices would give them an opportunity to exercise severe punishment. But the zamindar lifted his hand to contain their enthusiasm:

'You and you,' he added, pointing to two of the henchmen, 'punish him. But do not hit too hard, do not break any bones, and explain what is expected from him.'

The two fellows waited for the right moment and performed well. It had been a good assignment, they felt. A bit frustrating, maybe, but good. They returned, job done, with a well-deserved sense of achievement.

As for Ashok, his skin covered in black and purple bruises for days after the beating, he felt more surprise than pain and failed to understand what it had been about. He gave it some thought but, not used to much thinking, concluded that it must have been a mistake: his surprise turned into anger. He decided to complain to the zamindar.

The next morning, he got up and set off. His walk was as brisk as the pain in his limbs allowed. Jargaon suddenly seemed very far from Palanpur. Upon reaching the zamindar's mansion, he slowed down a bit, surprised by his own audacity. Still, he called with a firm voice at the door. He was ushered in with the respect due to a village headman: the zamindar was very particular about this.

Heartened, he went in, vaguely noticing that everyone was smiling a bit too much, but unable to interpret its meaning.

He was asked to wait...and wait. Finally, my great-grandfather appeared, offering his regrets that he had only been informed of Ashok's presence at that very minute and asking about Ashok's bruises with great concern. Ashok reassured him: it was nothing, he would soon recover. He told his story and felt a little better when Gavendra assured him that his men would be severely punished. Gavendra also asked a series of questions about the taxes that year and explained the need to be strict: surely, the farmers had had it easy after two years of good harvest and a major railway strike. Surprised by the turn of the conversation, Ashok swore that the right amount had been collected. The zamindar made a pacifying gesture: he knew that was true. Still, it was good to put a little pressure on the villagers, he insisted. They could easily pay: it was just a question of finding the right approach, the right tone. He knew Ashok would not disappoint in the future.

'Haan ji,' replied Ashok, somewhat mechanically.

'I feel terrible about what you had to go through,' continued the zamindar. 'Let me fix this immediately.'

With these words, he called the two henchmen, wagging his finger at them. He told them that they had been very bad to beat the head of the village. They could go to jail for this—Ashok started smiling—but it would not be necessary as they were good men who, like Ashok, were able to understand their mistakes. They should consider themselves lucky that both he, the zamindar, and the headman—the two most important people of the region—were ready to forgive them.

Ashok stopped smiling, but agreed with Gavendra nevertheless. He also thanked him before going back to Palanpur, disgruntled, and still a little confused.

His wife was more astute. As she comforted him, she drew Ashok's attention to the simple fact that he had made too little money to maintain the standard of life that his parents had had. She concluded that Udaivir, in his days, must have been a more effective tax collector. She reminded Ashok that he had promised to take good care of her. With authority, she listed some other promises that Ashok did not remember making, but that she insisted had not been fulfilled either.

Stunned, the chief tried to set aside all the reproaches and focus on the main issue: on the one hand, he was reluctant to increase taxes on Palanpuris. On the other, he had not liked the beating. Above all, he hated being lectured by his wife. He resolved to be shrewder in business and to collect more taxes. Prudently, he also decided to share the additional income equally with the zamindar.

Two days later, having recovered from his injuries so that he could show himself without embarrassment, he toured the village. He tactfully stressed the need to raise tax rates to more reasonable levels, in line with those practised by his late father. This was not well received, but the reactions were not too negative: the farmers were still enjoying the good harvest and Udaivir's corrupt approach to tax collection belonged to a distant past. As is well known, the discount rate is high in rural India today and was much higher then. As far as Palanpuris were concerned, the next monsoon was very far away.

The next year, the farmers grumbled a bit, implored a lot, but paid anyway. Ashok had learned his first lesson in corruption. Two years later, he learned the second…

Palanpur, 1984

The noise of angry voices woke me up. Something was going on. I switched off the two-in-one and checked my watch: it was 1 a.m. I heard some loud bangs.

I listened more carefully. People were shouting outside the large gate of the Seed Store. Once in a while, I could hear the lamenting voice of Govindi, but I couldn't understand what he was saying. I switched on my torch and went down. I found the old chowkidar arguing meekly with a bunch of people who were outside but were obviously determined to enter. He kept repeating that there was a foreigner inside, but the people did not seem to believe him. I called the old man. He was uneasy, scared, and kept repeating, 'Dacoits, dacoits.'

That is when I had the first brilliant idea of my stay. I shouted, 'Hey guys, come, there are some thugs at the gate.'

I sensed a little hesitation on the other side of the gate, some whispering. Then the banging resumed. I rushed upstairs, almost fell through the hole in the floor, seized my two-in-one, inserted a cassette that Pat had asked me to carry and went down again. Govindi was literally shaking now and so was the gate. The men were still shouting. I shouted back, 'Hey friends, they seem to be after us.'

I played the cassette at full volume. It blared out a loud exchange between a group of noisy people arguing at one of Pat's transcendental meditation seminars. The dacoits, I reckoned, would not understand what was said, and would believe that there were many people inside. Mind you, even I found it very difficult to understand what was said at Pat's seminars. I assumed human nature was similar in both England and UP and so it turned out: the dacoits ran away just as I had run away from the seminar. Govindi stared at me, a little lost. He pointed at the storage space, full of bags, 'Dacoits. They wanted to steal the seeds.'

Then he went back to his charpoy, looking relieved. I went back to mine but did not open my father's notes again. I didn't think I would be able to take another blow to the reputation of my family tree that evening, even if I had never cared about it earlier. I also reflected that the benefits of knowledge and transparency could sometimes be elusive. At least, I understood better why my father had left. I blew out the candle and turned painfully on the charpoy. There was no other incident that night except my occasional bout of sneezing from the dust in the air.

Chapter 6

Palanpur, 1984

When I woke up the next morning, it took me a few seconds to realize where I was. I finally opened my eyes to a ceiling covered with brown spots of humidity. My body was aching, the ropes of the charpoy had left marks all over my back and arms, and my neck was stiff. The first decision I made that day was that I would never sleep on a charpoy again. I am happy to report that this is one of the few promises I have scrupulously kept throughout my life—after I left Palanpur, of course. I managed to get up, scratched the various places where I had been bitten by insects, and began the perilous journey downstairs, determined not to let physical discomfort stand in the way of a positive attitude.

Govindi's daughter, squatting in front of a small mud stove, swiftly covered her hair with the pallu of her sari. Remarkably, she managed to do that while slowly pushing a bundle of dried sugarcanes through an opening at the bottom of the stove, to keep the fire going. Tea was boiling on the stove in an old, battered saucepan. Milk was added to it, and tea was ready. The lady filled a metallic tumbler and then skilfully mixed the tea by rhythmically pouring it from one tumbler into another and back. I knew the method very well, but the movement was gracious, and a ray of sun that shone through a hole in the wall made it even more interesting. I pulled the camera out and took a few pictures. Satisfied with the tea, Govindi's daughter handed one of the tumblers to me without looking at me. This was a difficult affair because it required holding both the sari and the tumbler. She very nearly managed it but could not avoid letting the garment slip for a second.

There was also a bit of dough next to the stove. The lady took a fistful of it, put it on a large stone and turned it into a flat chapati with a rolling pin. Then she quickly enlarged the chapati by slapping it from hand to hand before laying it on a pan over the fire. Soon it was swelling like a balloon. Why was I so interested? My mother had often made chapatis at home. But there was the light and the surroundings. And the smell, too. These chapatis smelled better, I thought. Pity the camera could not capture the smell. The tea and chapatis, plus a banana I had kept from my Chandausi stopover: it was the perfect breakfast. I took all that on a plate and decided to settle in front of the iron gate with the Nikkormat Ft2 and the short Tamron tele.

Govindi appeared just before I could take my first sip of tea. He made an explicit sign: all these services were costing money and I needed to pay for it. That seemed fair enough and, after some hesitation, I gave him three rupees which seemed to satisfy the old man.

I was a bit tense and very distracted when I had arrived in the village, so I had not cared much for the scenery. That morning, I would truly discover Palanpur.

The day was warm, although there was a breeze from the north. There was a bit of fog over the fields and the pale light of the low sun was gently diffused in it. The wind was pushing the fog away, revealing a flat landscape on which, despite my poetic inclination at that moment, there was not much to say. I shot a few pictures, then decided that Palanpur was about people and focused on two passing women in bright saris. Great pictures: the women were carrying earthen pots on their head and chatting. Their movements were elegant, as if there were no potholes under their feet and no heavy pot on their heads. Try it and you will understand that this is quite an achievement. They glanced at me briefly, giggled a little, and moved on. In the distance, I could see some farmers heading for the fields on their bullock carts and others already busy chopping fodder while their buffalos were grazing. Palanpur was also about trains: the Seed Store was located near the railway tracks—actually, nothing was far from the tracks in Palanpur—and, since I had woken up, I had already heard the rumble of a train twice. This was the third one and its sound was soon followed by a distant plume of smoke. A train was coming from Chandausi. It was an old steam engine pulling a few coaches. It passed slowly in front of me but did not stop in Palanpur and went on to Moradabad. I caught some faces at the windows lit by a perfect ray of sun.

Overall, I had an impression of peace and serenity. How could it be that my uncle had been shot and killed in such a place? It was hard to believe. The scenery also seemed at odds with the dacoits' attack of the previous night. Palanpur was clearly a place of contrasts. Exciting at times, perhaps. Dangerous things could happen, and the place therefore carried more interest than met the eye at first glance.

On this promising note, I went back inside to ask for another cup of tea. When I returned, I found that the banana and a chapati had disappeared from my plate. I sighed: I'd been warned about the monkeys and should have been more careful. Too bad.

Resigned, I decided to organize my thoughts and replace the breakfast with a small Romeo y Julieta I pulled out of the cigar holder I always carry with me. Clearly, my interest in Palanpur should not lead to unrealistic expectations and I realized that a person must be of a certain disposition to convert from a city banker to rural photographer in a foreign place where murders happen. I was of that disposition. I took a puff: Pat was right, it had to be about people, and people, including myself, were hard to understand.

I was pointing the camera around, looking for good angles, when I noticed Babu arriving. He was eating a chapati with a banana. A remarkable coincidence, I thought. Perhaps I had been too quick to blame the monkeys, but I chose not to explore the matter further. Babu stood in front of me, his eyes trained on the ground and looking very hesitant: the attitude of a man who fears retribution after having stolen something. I smiled engagingly and asked him what he wanted. The answer lacked clarity, but I understood that Babu wanted a job. In spite of the pilfered breakfast, I liked the man. Besides, there would be no need to draft a complex contract.

I assigned him his first task. He had to take me to my uncle's house, then to my fields, but we would first take a closer look at the railway station.

'Chalo!'

Our group of two soon became a group of many. As I had suspected, the rest of the crowd pretty much ignored the presence of Babu. Somehow, that reinforced my decision to take him on board. The station was a small building without much interest, I thought. I decided to walk around a bit. A few men, their heads prudently covered by a shawl in spite of the rising sun, were playing cards on the deviation tracks, surrounded by several spectators. Some of them felt I would provide better entertainment and left the players to join our group. We set off in the direction of my uncle's house. On the way, I discovered a small opening in a wall pompously named 'Teashop'. It was locked. I walked on and came across a modest temple painted in pink. It too was closed but I was told that a Brahmin from Jargaon sometimes came to chant prayers and rest here. However, he did not come often, and even though the opening days, let alone the hours, of the tea shop remained a mystery throughout my stay in the village, it was open more frequently than the temple. I managed to find a brief moment to take a few pictures with only ten kids and five adults in the frame.

Finally, we arrived at my uncle's house.

I realize now that I should have anticipated what it would look like. Or perhaps I was basking in some kind of bliss the evening before. I had the impression—baseless as it turned out—that the house was in relatively good shape. The kind that qualifies as a fixer-upper: nothing seriously wrong. A good broom, a hammer, a few nails and it would be fine. The morning's discovery was anti-climactic. Wild grass had overgrown everything around the property, proving nobody had taken care of it in a long time. There were a few holes in the roof and the main door had cracks too. It was secured by a massive lock that physically prevented entry while a thin ribbon marked 'Police' was psychologically trying to do the same. As I went around the house from the outside, I saw Kishan Lal in his fields. He waved at me but was obviously hard at work. The other side of the house was not in better shape. Suddenly, Kishan Lal materialized behind me, all smiles. 'I have a lot of work, but I thought that I would say hello. Will you keep the house? It needs quite a bit of work,' he observed, still smiling.

'Is that why you're laughing?' I asked, irritated.

He pointed at Babu. 'No. It is because everybody knows now that you are some rich nephew of the old zamindar. And you are here to rebuild the glory of those days, including this house.'

I sighed. 'The zamindari regime was abolished long ago and my uncle was a zamindar for only a few years. Why should people remember that my grandfather was one?'

'I don't know, why don't you ask them?' Kishan Lal suggested.

I did. In the crowd, there was an old, half-blind man who had fought in Europe. He had an interesting, battered face. He also wanted to have his picture taken, much to the annoyance of others who—rightly—considered themselves better-looking. They tried to get into the frame, and I had a hard time keeping them out of it. Once I had taken a bunch of pictures, we settled down for a chat.

The former soldier believed that, at the time of the zamindars, there was more law and order and people were happier. The train sometimes stopped to let the English go hunting with my grandfather because he was an important person. Once the old man had helped one of them kill a nilgai and the Englishman had given him some coins. Nudged by Kishan Lal and clearly embarrassed by my prestigious lineage, the poor man reluctantly agreed that the zamindars had a bad side too. They exploited the farmers to the point of driving them to starvation. Another man agreed, adding that the zamindars sometimes prevented farmers from building wells. Nowadays there was irrigation. Still, the consensus remained that there was more safety in those days.

Babu saw an opportunity to express his opinion in front of a large gathering. He said that there were better prospects nowadays. For example, he had been hired that very day for a promising position. It took me a couple of seconds to realize I was the concerned employer. Clearly, Babu was determined to link his destiny to mine.

There was not much more to do in front of the house if I did not have access to it. As Babu was still talking, I heard a noise coming from the house.

'Is there a goat trapped inside?' I asked, surprised.

'A billy goat, yes,' replied Kishan Lal. 'And it is fine, do not worry. In fact, you should worry when it is not locked up. It is quite a nasty beast.'

'It is a strong billy goat,' Babu corrected. 'But it is better to feed it through a hole in the wall. I have been feeding it since your uncle's death.'

There seemed to be more to Babu than met the eye. Regarding the billy goat, we could not do much about it, so I asked Kishan Lal to accompany us to my uncle's fields. He hesitated, arguing that he had some pressing work to finish in his own fields, but finally agreed. The land was on the other side of the village, along the path to Jargaon. It was an opportunity to see more of Palanpur. The village consisted of about a hundred houses, mostly made of dried mud. Most, but not all. Some were made of real bricks—pucca houses—that belonged to the richer people, usually the land-owning Thakur families. But that was not always the case. Some of these families had been relatively affluent—hence the brick houses—but had fallen into debt. The debts explained the dilapidated roof and walls, like that of my uncle's house even though my uncle, according to the lawyer, did not have debts.

The houses were simple, sometimes bare. Yet, many of those of brick had beautifully carved doors painted in lively colours. Smoke had darkened the walls in places, but the contrast with the coloured portions of brick walls was fascinating and I took more pictures. The doors often led to a small courtyard where the main property of the occupants—one or two buffalos or bullocks—would be kept during the day. The houses usually had two rooms or sections. The one at the back was a no-go area for outsiders: it was where the women stayed, and the only place where they could uncover their faces. Except for a few small holes proudly called windows, the only substantial opening led to the front room, abutting the courtyard. The cattle were kept in the courtyard or inside the house when the weather turned cold. The warmth of the animals helped people cope. The cold in winter was as implacable as the heat in summer or the rains during the monsoon. The Himalaya were too far away to be seen but the winter wind that blew from Nepal, in the northeast, made everyone in the village shiver. Heavy shawls and several layers of blankets wrapped around the saris could only help so much. And the small fire painfully kept alive in the coldest nights only provided warmth to the hands held close to it, sometimes inflicting small burns. It was desperately ineffective a couple of feet away.

During my stay, I realized that life in Palanpur followed the rhythm of the seasons and the cycle of life and death. The inhabitants had adjusted their pace accordingly. Daily activities followed a slow, yet distinct pattern, with a designated time for each task. Each gender also had its own occupations. Men mostly worked in the fields or entertained themselves in one way or another. Women stayed at home where their husbands, eager to protect their modesty, allowed them to keep things clean, prepare food, look after the children, and take care of the animals. To be fair, most women were also allowed to collect firewood and fetch water, but only at appropriate times and places. In recent years, some husbands had become more permissive and would let their wife go to the weekly market near the railway station. But their masculine protective instinct was then on full alert as the stern look of the men in our group made it clear when this topic was discussed.

It occurred to me that confining Pat to one room would be very hard, even if I granted her permission to collect firewood and fetch water. I also reflected that there was no disco or library in Palanpur. But there was a murder to solve and pictures to take. We would surely have enough entertainment.

Determined to learn as much as I could about my new environment without wasting time, I repressed my cynical side. I did well: overall, I was struck by the thoughtfulness and open-mindedness of the people who surrounded me. Their hard work too.

On the way, we walked past an obviously healthy field that belonged to Kishan Lal. It was indeed a joy to look at, even for someone whose knowledge of farming was theoretical. The wheat was still green, but thick and dense and free of weeds. The sugarcane, also dark green, towered over us gloriously. Near his Persian wheel, Kishan Lal was growing a range of vegetables, healthy and well aligned. He was also experimenting with mint, which he had recently purchased after hearing about it on the radio.

I was surprised that he owned two plots of land so far apart, and that triggered another confused discussion on land consolidation. Some considered that they had been short-changed. Kishan Lal pointed out that those who complained had not worked hard enough and had lost to others who worked harder. He went on to educate me on farming matters and explained the calendar of agricultural activities. Though Kishan Lal seemed to know the basics of modern farming well, I immediately saw opportunities for improvement. I had indeed read two books on the topic before embarking on this venture: *An Integrated and Encompassing Approach to Agriculture and Farming in India in the 20th Century* and *The Art and Science of Agricultural Technology: Methodological Aspects of Indian Farming*, both published by scholars from international agencies. I pointed out, for example, that Kishan Lal took it for granted that fertilizer should be applied at the time of sowing. My books indicated that this was not a common practice ten years earlier. Kishan Lal dismissed the books. Farmers' knowledge had improved over the years and they knew what they were doing. Judging from the look of his fields, he was probably right, and during my time in Palanpur, I had many opportunities to appreciate the depth of his knowledge of agriculture. So much for my scholarly books.

We soon arrived in front of my fields. If my house was in a sad state, the fields were worse. That was no fixer-upper at all. It looked truly depressing. Still, I decided to face the challenge. I would buy the necessary tools and get going. Probably out of pity, Kishan Lal invited me for lunch. His house was also kuccha but well-furnished. The women served a very good meal with rice, dal, two vegetables and many chapatis. The elder women, married or widowed, talked very freely and quite sensibly, while Kishan Lal's young wife and sisters sat in silence or cooked. Since I obviously enjoyed the meal and had nothing to do in the evening, Kishan Lal also invited me for dinner. I was touched by the gesture.

I generally had a good impression of him, so I asked if he would be willing to help me fix the house and the fields together with Babu. He thought about it and finally agreed under the condition that he would be the supervisor of the workers I would hire, including Babu, who did not seem offended. Kishan Lal wanted to be sure that things would be well done. That was perfectly acceptable and Kishan Lal the Palanpuri became my Zorba the Greek.

It was around 5 p.m. when I reached the Seed Store. I found Govindi surrounded by three men. Two were policemen who were scolding him. I learned that a train robbery had taken place during the night, and the robbers had made away with coal as well as bags of rice and beans. While investigating, the policemen had learned about the incident at the Seed Store the previous evening and wanted to question the witnesses. They became suspicious when they discovered a bag of coal in the bushes between the Seed Store and the abandoned building next to it which, I learned, had once been the village school. Since they could not find the dacoits or the rest of the coal, they opted for the easy approach—scolding Govindi. Babu had told me that the police sometimes preferred to harass the weak rather than chase the bad guys. This approach to law and order is not necessarily limited to Moradabad district, to UP, or indeed to India. Still, I found the scolding excessive and intervened. I gave my own version, which was the same as Govindi's and this seemed to mollify the two policemen. They told me the thief they were after was from Palanpur and known to them. However, he had run away. As for the apparently unrelated incident at the Seed Store, I had been lucky to escape the dacoits and should perhaps leave the village altogether. I replied that I would not do that and had every intention of moving into my uncle's house two days later, after their boss, Superintendent BKS, gave me the keys. The policemen sulked a little and asked for some tea which Govindi's daughter prepared immediately. They lit a cigarette and sat in a corner, leaving the third man to take up his own matters.

That fellow was the accountant in charge of the Seed Store. He also screamed at Govindi. I was not directly concerned by the accounting aspects of the fracas but wanted to know more. Babu was observing the scene from a safe distance and I joined him.

I learned that a certain Ram Singh, who was perhaps one of my remote cousins, a hopeless drinker and gambler, also unfit for work—well, these things happen in the best families—had given large bribes to important people in order to become the chowkidar at the Seed Store. The bribes had been accepted and the accountant—according to Babu—was looking for some excuse to get rid of Govindi. He kept pointing at official papers, but the old man could not read and was therefore completely helpless. My presence seemed to have a cooling impact because, after a little while, the accountant joined the policemen, had tea and then left with them as the train was arriving.

That was a lot of emotional upheaval for the day and it was time for dinner. I was about to invite Babu to join but, remembering that Kishan Lal had not invited him, I abstained. Instead, I suggested that he accompany me to Chandausi two days later. I would of course pay for the ticket and offer him a meal. Babu accepted but said that it would be fun only if he were allowed to eat so much that his belly would become as round as a ball. Bankers deal with clients who have all sorts of ambitions. After all, this was understandable for a man who had often been hungry and arguably more so than a Londoner who already had a Bentley desiring a Lamborghini. I agreed, curious to see how round Babu's belly could get.

While eating my chapatis with chana masala at Kishan Lal's house, I heard the sound of some women singing elsewhere in the village. Curious, I asked Kishan Lal to accompany me. This was an opportunity to approach women a little closer and take pictures. Very discreetly, Babu—who had suddenly materialized next to us—told me he would come along but stay in the background. Surprised, I asked why.

'Because I will marry soon, and I want to know about women.'

'Oh, you are engaged,' I exclaimed. 'Congratulations!'

'Not yet, but now that I have a good job, I can also have a wife.'

I sighed, 'What I meant to ask is why should you stay in the background and not come in?'

He merely shrugged his meagre shoulders. He knew his place. Kishan Lal added that there would be too many 'bahus', but it would not be a problem for me because I was a foreigner.

Our arrival caused a gentle stir and tittering but the singing went on, under the enchanting lead of the dholak. With no other place to sit, we joined a group of women who were squatting on a big stone. That was a slightly daring move, but it seemed to be accepted by the hosts given their obligation to offer us a seat somewhere. A man lounging on a large charpoy did not find our gesture shocking enough to insist that we should share his space. Babu was nowhere to be seen but I knew that he was nearby, witnessing the scene and educating himself in matters related to the fair sex. We were surrounded by joyful kids and it was a great moment. An old woman next to me was not singing and we talked and joked quite freely. I took pictures and promised to give them copies soon. This was greatly appreciated, and I won the hearts of some villagers. Taking advantage of the friendly atmosphere, I asked a few questions about my uncle's murder. Everybody agreed that three gunshots had been heard that night from inside the house. The neighbors had said so. Two in rapid succession, then one more. Few gave credence to the police's conclusion that Neetu was the culprit, but they all claimed to have no idea who it could be. Was that true, I wondered? They seemed to know more but, sensing their reluctance, I dropped the subject. I needed time to process this.

After the singing, I went back to the Seed Store accompanied by Babu. He had enjoyed the evening and wanted to discuss his preferences in terms of women. I learned that he liked women who were in good health which, I came to understand, meant reasonably fat. Changing the subject, I asked him if he knew where I could get a tandem bicycle in Chandausi. It would be a nice way to travel around with Pat, I thought. Babu promised to take me to a good shop. Happy, I returned to my father's notes.

Palanpur, 1909

Ashok, impeccably dressed in a white kurta and wearing a bright red turban, both spotless, was guiding a pair of huge bullocks across his own sugarcane plantation. The field was vast, at least five bighas, and packed with healthy sugarcanes that Ashok and his men were harvesting. He was standing on the cart and several labourers were assisting him, rhythmically cutting the canes and throwing them on top of the already huge pile in the cart. Ashok had an eye on everything, but his natural authority was enough: everyone was working hard. Even the birds were loudly contributing to the general felicity. Ashok was happy. He twirled his thick moustache and looked around proudly. His attention was caught by charming giggles behind him. He turned around, pleased: but there was nothing. Then, he saw a blue shadow moving lightly between the canes before disappearing. There were more giggles. Ashok smiled, delighted. He smiled even more when the shadow materialized not far from him. The lady was beautiful and, undoubtedly impressed by his stature, she undulated between the canes and came close to the cart. The birds sang louder as if guided by the rhythmic noise of the machetes chopping the canes. One could have sworn that several tabla players were hiding in the field. No doubt inspired, the lady started dancing for Ashok. How beautiful! She was wearing small bells around her ankles and wrists, which were ringing gently. Strangely, Ashok did not wonder what she was doing there. There was no conceivable reason for her to be in his fields, but he was not surprised. She waved at him elegantly. He waved back and she called out. It was a deep and rather unpleasant voice. She called again and Ashok's dream ended abruptly: it was indeed an unpleasant voice, that of Bhupal, the ferocious Murao henchman hired by Gavendra to do his dirty work. He was a new recruit, and still a teenager. Bhupal was not very tall, but vicious-looking, strong and ruthless. He had been kicked out of the Murao clan following a brutal fight during which he had not followed even the most basic rules, resulting in severe injuries to his opponent, who was now a cripple. His mother was a Murao too, but some whispered that his father was some railway worker who had briefly stayed in the village. Nobody knew for sure.

Ashok opened his eyes and reluctantly invited the henchman to join him: Bhupal's presence could only mean trouble, but it was hard to guess what the matter was. It must be serious or he would not have come from Jargaon. Two years had passed since the beating. Ashok, true to his word, had collected more money from the farmers and shared it equally with the zamindar. Was that not enough? The zamindar, he thought, had looked pleased.

Ashok's greetings lacked warmth. Bhupal pretended not to notice and smiled eagerly. He sat next to the headman and they both smoked their bidis. Bhupal asked for a glass of fresh water and Ashok poured him one from a matka. After an uneasy silence, the chief observed that the sun had already set, hoping that would get rid of the importunate visitor. Bhupal did not take the hint. Ashok offered him some more water and another bidi. For the road, perhaps? But Bhupal stayed put, taking his time. Desperate, Ashok claimed that he had some work to do in his field. A poor excuse: there was not much to do at this time of the year.

Finally, Bhupal came to the point. A station would soon be built for the train, a pucca building to mark the halt of the machine. It would be bigger than a house, much like the stations in Chandausi and Moradabad, explained Bhupal. A bit smaller maybe, but not much. There would be a special room for prestigious guests. Bhupal paused to let the news sink in.

This was indeed a new and spectacular development. By this time, the Palanpuris had become used to the trains, but they still commanded a lot of respect. The presence of a room for prestigious guests—Bhupal's rather loose translation of a waiting room for the upper classes—appeared to imply an upgrade in the kind of people who would visit Palanpur. That could also be a positive development.

'It is good if important people stop here.'

'Indeed,' agreed the Murao who seized the opportunity to provide details about the first of these more prestigious visitors: an Englishman named Hemming who would get the work started and stay for a few days. Since the station was yet to be built, he would stay in a tent.

'Accha, not in the dharamsala?'

Bhupal gave a quick thought to the dilapidated shelter and ignored the question.

'...and we have to take care of this person...attend to his needs,' he continued.

'Ji,' answered Ashok, nodding vaguely.

'We have to show him that we appreciate the honour. After all, the building will become the main feature of the village. Of course, the zamindar will meet him…'

'Ji,' Ashok nodded again, his eyes fixed on the empty piece of land where the grandiose building had not yet been erected.

'…but it is not really an affair for the zamindar.'

Ashok waved his hand in vague agreement with a line of reasoning that he did not follow. The end of it took him by surprise: 'In fact, it is a matter for the chief.'

The confused headman did not find the energy to object.

'Yes?' he agreed, non-committal.

'In other words, you,' insisted Bhupal with a sadistic smile only veiled by the light smoke of the bidi.

'Accha?' Ashok said, overwhelmed and unable to comprehend the magnitude of looming responsibilities he had never sought.

'Yes. You will have to receive this Hemming and make sure his needs are satisfied,' added the Murao who sensed that there was no point being oblique any longer.

'Accha?' Ashok's voice was shakier now. He was slowly coming to terms with realities.

'He is a white man, so he has very specific needs.'

'We will get the best food we can cook,' promised Ashok before adding shrewdly, 'although the year has been bad as you know and we do not have that much, so…'

Bhupal brushed aside the mention of the meagre harvest. 'Of course, I expect you to provide good food, but the white man also wants to be serviced in other ways…'

'Accha,' replied Ashok, lost again.

'In more physical ways,' insisted the Murao.

'Ji,' Ashok agreed mechanically.

Bhupal sighed, then he bluntly added, 'He wants a woman in his bed for the nights that he will spend here.'

'Accha!' said Ashok, realization dawning.

He was surprised by the request. The chief had never given much thought to the sex life of white people and had certainly never envisaged that he could be involved in such a matter. Why did Bhupal not take care of that? After all, he was notoriously dissolute and known for suspicious trips to Moradabad. His girlfriend had been a prostitute. That had given her enough experience to satisfy Bhupal and the level of inner serenity necessary to tolerate his multiple affairs.

'Arey!'

'Ji!' insisted Bhupal. 'A woman from the village should be provided to that man. A beautiful woman.'

Ashok thought of Savitri at once. Although she was the sister-in-law of the zamindar, she lived in hardship. It was rumoured that she had occasionally accepted money for providing such services but…

'And not Savitri,' Bhupal added hastily. His job had taught him everything about Palanpuris and their lines of thought. 'She is ancient and ugly.'

He did not add that the zamindar would not like it, but that was understood.

'But, who then?' cried Ashok, overwhelmed.

Bhupal sighed. He knew who it should be but wanted Ashok to suggest the name himself. He gave a clue, 'White men do not care about the colour of the skin.'

Ashok nodded; he had always thought foreigners were odd.

'And they prefer them a little on the thin side,' revealed Bhupal.

Ashok nodded again—these white people were strange indeed. 'Can you bring a woman from Chandausi?' suggested Ashok, hinting at Bhupal's vast knowledge in such matters.

That was not the drift that Bhupal wanted. He cut it short: 'Too expensive! Unless you want to pay for it.'

Ashok waved his hands in horror. Still, the shock motivated his imagination and, without any warning, an idea sprung in his mind. 'What about Dukhi?'

'Haan,' approved Bhupal, relieved.

Dukhi was not a prostitute, but she was a Chamar. She was dark too but, as Bhupal had said, that was irrelevant to a white man. These factors aside, and even though neither man would care to admit it, Dukhi had fairly attractive features. The men of the village would occasionally run into each other near the faraway spot where she went to bathe. She was not allowed to take her baths where women of other castes were taking theirs. In a sense, it was funny to see so many men feel an urge to go so far without any obvious reason. It could also have been funny to observe the way everyone would pretend to be there by accident, not concerned in the least about the shapely limbs moving under the wet cloth wrapped around them. One could have smiled at the sight of these men greeting each other rather meekly, skirting around each other for the best possible view, and staying there for as long as possible. But in truth, the whole thing was horribly sad. Quite aware of these manoeuvres, Dukhi would sometimes utter words of disgust and either turn her back to the men—thus providing an alternative view that they also appreciated—or insult them loudly. Insults from a woman were always frowned upon by the male crowd and they would self-righteously disapprove of such excesses of language. The culprits would happily condemn the victim, concluding that they could expect nothing good from a Chamar.

Bhupal stood up. 'It is settled then,' he concluded. 'Just arrange this with her. No need to pay too much,' he added while leaving. 'The British chap has money, they all do, and he will surely give her some. Still, take this,' he added, generously holding out five rupees.

Ashok took the money. He would hide it next to his charpoy. One should never leave valuable things too far away, especially at night.

'Make sure all goes well, the zamindar is counting on you.'

Before Ashok could object, Bhupal added soothingly, 'The zamindar was thinking of claiming what you owe him, but he is a good man and he knows that you will soon have a child. If all goes well, he can delay the payment as a special favour, perhaps even cancel it. And if you need something else, say so.'

Overwhelmed, Ashok stared at the Murao as he left for Jargaon on his horse. His resentment for that man was almost unbearable. The main reason was the martial air—a Thakur privilege, in Ashok's eyes—that he undeniably had on his horse. Of course, the horse was frail, its legs twisted, and the rifle a little rusty, but still, that Murao looked soldierly. Ashok felt some sympathy for the village Muraos who disliked Bhupal so much. How right they had been to kick him out of their group. For a moment, Ashok entertained murderous thoughts. But he was not a violent man. He lit another bidi and started reflecting on what he had to do. The complexity of the task convinced him that he needed assistance. He climbed down from the roof and went inside his house.

Chapter 7

Palanpur, 1984

I spent the next day visiting the village and talking to people. I also made pictures. Essentially, I was getting acquainted with Palanpuris and their way of life, too busy to read my father's notes. It was Babu, no doubt looking forward to the meal I had promised him, who reminded me in the evening that we were going to Chandausi together the next day. My sleep was reasonably peaceful. One or two trains passed through the station, but they did not stop and there was therefore no train robbery in Palanpur that night. At some point, the dogs started barking but I had been told that nilgais abounded in this season, so I just painfully changed position on my charpoy, scratched myself and went back to sleep. In the morning, in exchange for three rupees that I gave to a depressed Govindi, I got the same breakfast as the day before, handed to me by his covered daughter. This time, I ate it immediately to avoid any theft. I took a quick bath and rushed out, hoping that my new employee would also be on time.

He was. I found him at the station, waiting for me with a goat. I had no time to ask how the goat would contribute to the trip because a loud whistle announced the train's arrival just then. In Palanpur, one waits to hear the train in the comfort of one's home before going to the station. There is no hurry and no chance to miss it, especially since purchasing a ticket is not perceived as compulsory. Feeling virtuous, I bought two tickets made of brownish cardboard—the goat did not need one—and got them just as the train slowly reached the platform. It was like in Delhi, except that a platform is an elusive concept in Jargaon Station. But just like in Delhi, there was a sudden surge in activity.

'Samosa, pakoda, chai, chai, chai...'

Some people were climbing onto to the train, others were jumping down. Sellers of tea, snacks and peanuts were yelling everywhere, and passengers were shouting, putting their hands between the metallic bars to give a rupee or collect their order. The more adventurous vendors climbed on board with their goods and miraculously managed to come out through another door without losing or breaking anything. I boarded the train with the camera, Babu followed with the goat and we found a small space where we managed to sit. The Moradabad-Chandausi Mail was more crowded than the Bareilly Express from Delhi, but the passengers were more accommodating. A lot of smoke, the smell of heated oil and burning coal, a big shock, followed by more shocks of declining intensity: we were on our way. We had barely departed when I heard a loud greeting, 'Wah, this is my friend the banker!'

That voice rang a bell. I looked up. 'Captain!' I exclaimed, not too sure whether I should be pleased.

'So, my friend, I had told you that we would meet again,' continued the ex-army man. Babu had swiftly vanished with his goat. 'Are you leaving Palanpur already?'

I told the Captain that I was determined to pursue my photographic project and would stay as long as necessary. Half the coach had managed, by then, to surround us. All heard a stentorian cry of disbelief, 'Are you still claiming that you would rather take pictures in Palanpur than be a banker in London?' he exclaimed.

All eyes moved back to me, expecting a denial. I stayed firm, 'Absolutely.'

There was a rare moment of relative silence on board the Moradabad-Chandausi Mail. The Captain reflected for a moment and looked at me with his piercing eyes. Then he murmured something to the effect that, after all, it may not be a bad thing. To spare me further embarrassment, or perhaps as a continuation of his own thoughts, he asked, 'So, who killed your uncle, then? Have you heard something?'

I confessed that I had not learned anything new and added that, apparently, the maid had shot him several times.

The Captain laughed heartily. 'Do you know how old she is?'

I did not know, and I could not ask Babu. 'Perhaps forty-five,' I ventured.

'You believe that that old woman went to her master's place in the middle of the night, broke open the door, took the rifle from your uncle, loaded it and shot him several times? Do you know if they have found the rifle?'

'No, I don't think so.'

He looked at me with pity, 'So, she did all that and also managed to take the rifle away and hide it afterwards?'

'That is what the police say.'

Everyone witnessed my discomfiture. Obviously, I had demonstrated a pathetic lack of judgement for the second time since boarding the train.

Once again, the Captain set his piercing eyes on me. 'What about you? Do you think she did it?'

Irritated, I shot back, 'I just reported what I have been told but I will form my own opinion. I'm going to the police station to collect my keys and I will try to see that lady. Besides, why do you assume that she stole my uncle's rifle? She could have brought her own,' I objected.

The Captain laughed so hard that I thought the train would derail. 'A widow, a Dalit woman with her own rifle!' he exclaimed.

The whole compartment relayed his laughter. After a little while, relative normality was restored, although my analysis was still being abundantly ridiculed in various corners of the coach. The Captain spoke calmly, 'You should see that lady in jail. Yes, that is a good idea. A good way to form an opinion. You should be prudent, though. What happened to you could happen again.'

'What are you talking about?' I asked, surprised.

The Captain leaned forward, 'You managed to chase away the dacoits the other night. That was smart, very smart. But they can always come back. Or there could be others.'

'How do you know about the dacoits?' I asked.

'People talk. It would be better to stay at your own place.'

'I know. As I told you, I may get the keys today,' I replied.

The Captain smiled. 'You will get your keys,' he said mysteriously.

Just then, someone who knew the Captain walked by and they started talking. That gave me some peace for the rest of the short trip.

We reached Chandausi at around 9.30 a.m. I had ample time before the meeting with BKS. Leaving his friend behind, the Captain got off the train with me and shook my hand. He added softly, 'Be careful at the police station. And you should talk to the Dalits,' he added. 'Nobody listens to them. Nobody notices them. But they see everything.'

'But I should be fine at the police station, no?' I asked, concerned.

'Of course,' answered the Captain. 'Still, it is always better to be careful.'

The Captain left. I walked along the platform and finally found Babu with his goat next to the very last exit of the station. I smiled and we walked to town.

On the way, I learned that it was market day: Babu had decided to sell his goat. He was hoping to be able to give a bit of money to his mother and keep the rest for his future wedding. We first stopped at the cycle shop where I found an affordable, old but robust-looking tandem. The mechanic would need some time to get it ready, and since it was still too soon to go to the police station, the three of us went to the photo studio where I dropped off the rolls of film.

Eager to broaden my horizons further, I decided to learn from Babu's marketing expertise. Could I accompany him to learn how the goat market worked? Pleased and looking important, Babu agreed but explained that a careful approach was crucial if one did not want to be cheated. First, he needed to explore the place discreetly. Could I keep his goat? This sounded very mysterious, but I agreed, especially because we had reached the vegetable section of the market and waiting there would give me an opportunity to learn about that trade. Babu handed over the rope and went off.

The goat and I watched the nearby watermelon sellers. They were selling pieces by weight, for immediate consumption. To start with, all of them were sitting next to each other, each displaying his watermelons on a push-cart. The first one was energetically shouting 'Rupaya der kilo, rupaya der kilo' (one-and-a-half kgs per rupee), and he did very good business. The second was more expensive, selling at one kg per rupee. He was also shouting less than his competitor. As a result, he was not doing very well. The third vendor wasn't even shouting. He was just sitting on his cart, smoking one bidi after another, presumably expecting that potential buyers would make their choice on the basis of their own assumptions. Being thirsty, I decided to scientifically sample the wares of all three sellers, and thus learned that the price charged by the third seller was one rupee per kg. I could not ascertain any difference in quality. The goat was thirsty too and I struggled to hold it away from the fruits. I gave her the skins and she did not seem to taste a difference in quality either. I had been there for about half an hour when the second seller decided to relocate his business out of reach of the first seller's voice, but the third stayed where he was. I decided to discuss the matter with him: 'Why don't you move your cart away like that guy just did?' I asked, pointing at the second seller.

'Why do that?'

I was taken aback but, as a good banker, decided to spell out the business case, 'If you attract more customers, your income will increase.'

'But I don't need that much money.'

'Then you could still go home earlier and rest.'

'But I am already resting,' he countered.

Impressed, I bought yet another slice of watermelon, which confirmed my earlier observation that the quality was uniform.

'You see,' said the seller, 'I just sold two pieces in the last few minutes, like the others, except that I sold it for more,' he added and then went back to his nap.

I decided to give up. I could have explored the market for good-looking potatoes. They were being sold at around 0.25 rupee per kg but would be less refreshing.

The market was not only for food. Everything that a household might need was available. Medicines were being sold in various forms: from pills of undetermined colour to live lizards that presumably needed some preparation before consumption and that the seller had a hard time bringing back onto the counter each time they ventured outside it. There were also injections. The price had been fixed uniformly at five rupees, including administration and irrespective of the colour of the liquid. These stands were well attended. While preventing the goat from eating the medicines and scaring the lizards, I tried to figure out what all these medicines were for. It probably did not matter. Kishan Lal had explained to me that Palanpuris did not trust government doctors who were costlier and not necessarily more successful than a random injection from the market. It was true that if one ran a calculation of the respective probabilities of surviving a doctor, a random injection and doing nothing, the second proposition would most likely emerge the winner.

I heard a shout. It was Babu. He informed me that, after carefully observing his competitors, he had crafted a strategy to sell his goat. He took the rope and we walked to the cattle market. It had drawn quite a big crowd, perhaps a thousand souls.

The cattle sellers were all sitting quietly next to their animals. I noticed very few people who looked like farmers among the buyers. Most of them seemed to be well-off butchers who bought several animals. Some would take them away to Moradabad or to another city, while others had brought their knives to kill them and sell the meat on the spot.

Babu's carefully crafted strategy was rather basic. He sat down with his goat among the other goat sellers but then seemed at a loss to get things going. The price of goat meat at the butcher's was around 16 to 18 rupees per kg. My own guess was that Babu's goat would yield around 12 to 13 kgs of meat. She also gave half a litre of milk per day but that would not matter if the buyer was a butcher. Taking the butcher's margin into account as well as the large number of sellers, something between 100 and 120 rupees seemed reasonable. I therefore found Babu's starting price of 180 rupees excessively ambitious. After an hour, he appeared to reach the same realization and brought the price down to 150 rupees. But the buyers had an ample array of options and were taking away other goats of the same size and quality for 100 or 110 rupees. Poor Babu was not taken seriously and was usually offered around 100 rupees.

While at the market, we saw several Palanpur farmers who were selling bullocks, buffaloes, and even a goat that went for 105 rupees.

Not overly impressed with Babu's marketing skills, I decided I would rely on Kishan Lal's expertise to buy my own bullocks. I left Babu there and went to the post office. There was a telegram for me:

> Arrive Delhi in 2 weeks Stop Stay few days Stop Then Bareilly Express Stop Anything near bed Stop Love you Stop Pat

This left me speechless. Insisting on cleaning behind the bed in a telegram was a bit too much. I decided to send an appropriate reply:

> Expecting you Palanpur Stop All fine Stop Bed clean Stop Me too Stop Anil

Then I went to see the lawyer. Ashok Kumar seemed rather pleased to see me but our meeting was brief. He gave me some important-looking documents and certified that everything was in order. As far as he knew, the seals could be removed, and I was officially entitled to take possession of my property.

On my way to the police station, I went through the market where Babu was sitting with his goat, still asking for 150 rupees. He promised that he would join me as soon as the goat was sold. Otherwise, there would be no point because he would have nothing to give to his mother. I left him there again and went to the police station.

I had not liked the voice of Superintendent BKS on the phone. I hated how he looked. A big, fat policeman, well over fifty, he had kept his dark sunglasses on but had unbelted his gun and placed it on his desk. This served a twin purpose: his belly was more at ease and his power was on display. The hair was oily as was his tone when he was talking to me. But otherwise, he yelled his orders around. He smiled, toad-like, and explained that Palanpur was not a safe place. Most people there were bad, and I should have drawn that obvious conclusion from what had happened to my uncle, who had clearly been killed for petty reasons. Of course, the police were efficient, but it was hard to prevent murders. They tended to happen in backward places like Palanpur. I had been lucky the other night at the Seed Store. It had not been a good idea to stay there. He had thought I would stay in Chandausi, not go to Palanpur before meeting him. But what was done was done. He hoped that I had realized by now that it would be best if I went back to London after selling the house and the land.

My ambition of writing a book on Palanpur did not seem to impress him. Of course, it was hard to argue against the dreariness of Palanpur. But I seized on the allusion to my uncle's death. 'You're keeping the murderer in this jail, aren't you?' I asked.

'Yes,' barked the arrogant mastiff.

'Maybe I could see that person,' I suggested softly. 'I have never seen a murderer.'

BKS looked surprised. 'Of course, of course. We are keeping her here, but...'

'It is a lady, right? Her name is Neetu, I think.'

He started laughing loudly, his wide mouth opening to display pathetic teeth, 'A lady! What lady?'

'Is it not a lady?' I asked, surprised.

'How could it be a lady? She is a Chamar. These people will do anything. They are less than dirt.'

I ignored the comment. 'But why would she have killed my uncle?'

BKS became serious again. He removed his sunglasses, uncovering small and mean black eyes.

'She is denying everything, of course, but she did it for the money, obviously. Maybe she was also upset because he did not pay her enough attention. Or too much, although I would doubt that. And even if he did, she should have been honoured. These people are just dirt,' he repeated.

'How did she kill him?'

'With his rifle, but we could not find it,' he added with obvious regret.

I guessed he must have been salivating at the thought of confiscating a rifle to display in the collection that decorated the wall behind him.

'So, may I see her?'

BKS looked at me inquisitively, then put his sunglasses back on. 'Why would you want to see her?'

For once, his voice was soft. Dangerously so.

'To put a face on the murderer of my beloved uncle,' I said, adding a tremolo.

So much love between family members was something BKS had never personally experienced, but he had heard about it and seen it in Bollywood movies. Besides, the British were strange people, even those of Indian origin, everybody knew that. He reluctantly accepted the argument.

'Come,' he ordered.

We went into a dirty corridor where a few cells were occupied by people with the face of well-established ruffians. Then came the sorry sight of a frail old woman wrapped in a dirty, torn piece of cloth. The Captain was right: there was no way on earth this woman could have loaded a rifle, shot my uncle and hidden the rifle afterwards.

'Careful,' said BKS, as if he had read my mind. 'She could be dangerous.'

With his lathi, he hit the poor soul who lifted a devastated face: one of her eyes was all black and closed. Blood had dried on her skin, but her lips were still bleeding.

'This is the nephew of the man you killed,' yelled BKS.

The lips barely moved, 'No!'

BKS laughed and turned to me. 'I told you, she is still denying it but we will make her confess. Not true, you Chamar?'

He hit her again with the lathi, triggering a low howl from her and some moans from prisoners in neighbouring cells. Just then, a policeman called BKS and he left me alone in front of the cell.

'Neetu!' I whispered.

She hesitated, then looked at me. I quickly pulled out a couple of coins and threw them to the poor woman.

'From your son, Babu,' I said. 'But do you know where the rifle is? And the money?'

She shook her head and I could see her hand swiftly burying the coins in the earth of the cell. BKS was returning and there was no point insisting.

'Did she say anything?' he enquired suspiciously as we were going back to his office.

'Nothing,' I answered, trying to look innocent.

'If you find the rifle, you must give it back to the authorities,' insisted BKS.

'Where exactly?'

'To me.'

'Ah, to you.'

'Yes, to the authorities.'

'Ah, to them,' I replied.

BKS, annoyed, looked at me again and pointed a threatening finger, 'And if you find anything else, you must give it to me,' he urged, while opening his drawer. 'Your uncle was supposed to have money, and none has been found.'

After I promised to do so, he handed over the keys.

We left each other with that fragile understanding. The Captain was right: a police station could be a dangerous place. Especially for Dalits.

On the way, I picked up the tandem and went back to the market which, by now, was almost empty. The expert goat seller was there, still quoting 150 rupees. When I appeared, he told me that he was giving up, hinting that he was more interested in a good meal. I reassured him about his mother. Chatting away, we walked to Kallu Halwai's sweetshop, Babu pulling his goat and I pushing the tandem.

Babu was talking all the while, arguing that he had not been able to sell the goat for a number of reasons that were somehow exceptional. It would work better another time, when the conditions were more favourable. For example, there were too many sellers, not enough buyers. And the buyers were ignorant about what made a good goat. He looked resentfully at the small animal, possibly seeing it bigger than it actually was.

Our arrival at the sweet shop interrupted his flow because Babu started salivating at the sight of the food. We ordered lunch—a very substantial lunch. I had two samosas, Babu had eight. Then he ordered some dal and sabji accompanied by two butter naans. He ended his meal with four barfis and six gulab jamuns. As he was stuffing himself and indeed gaining a round belly, regularly contemplating it with an air of pure bliss, I mentioned that I had given two rupees to his mother on his behalf. Babu painfully swallowed half a samosa in one gulp and agreed that he would have given the same amount if he had had the money: she did not need more since the police were feeding her.

'Do you know who killed my uncle?' I asked out of the blue.

'How would I know?' he replied after swallowing another big bite.

'You could have heard or seen something,' I suggested.

'Yes,' he agreed, 'I could have seen and heard everything.'

'Indeed.'

'But I stayed home that night, with my mother and my old aunt. That's why I know that my mother did not do it.'

And that gave him an alibi too. So much for questioning Babu. Was he telling the truth?

Once it was clear that Babu would be unable to ingest any more food, we left Chandausi on the tandem, with me in the front, driving and pedalling, and Babu sitting behind, doing neither but pulling the goat along. He explained that he could not pedal because he was feeling heavy from the meal and sad.

'For your mother?' I asked with empathy.

'And for the goat. I could not sell it.'

When I complained that I was the only one pedalling, he argued that if I was trying to be nice to him by buying a real meal, I should not spoil it by making him pedal. That was bad for health. After a while, he suggested that he should take the goat onto his lap because if it ran too much, it would lose weight and value. Surely, I would not jeopardize his chance to win a suitable bride. I grumbled a bit and Babu replied that we, rich people, were always in a hurry and relied on faulty logic. Once the goat was on his lap, he argued, I could pedal as hard or as slowly as I wanted. The goat and he would not bother me. I sighed, let him take the goat onto his lap, and pedalled on.

Soon after we left Akroli, we caught up with the cart of the village head, a farmer called Rampal Singh, who was about fifty years old. He was coming back from the sugarcane mill in Baroli, with a jar full of juice. I was exhausted and decided to stop cycling and walk along. Rampal was guiding his bullocks with one hand while holding a rifle in the other. He invited me to climb next to him on the 'dunlop'—named after the brand of tyres used for bullock carts in the area—but it was clear that Babu was not welcome. Resigned, he pushed the tandem and pulled the goat, leaving a safe distance between him and Rampal's cart.

I had already seen Rampal a couple of times in Palanpur, once carrying a rifle, another time accompanied by men holding rifles. He was a Thakur. I had asked about him. Babu and Kishan Lal had told me that his ancestors had been rich but had gambled away their money as well as some land over the generations. There were rumours that he had some connection with the dacoits of the area, but that was not really confirmed. What was confirmed was that his house could do with a coat of paint and his clothes with some mending. Still, he sometimes seemed to have a lot of money and sometimes didn't have any. He must have been an impressive man once upon a time though, and he still had a convincing moustache. He had had a job in Moradabad when he was young but had to give it up when it became clear that his brother—a guy called Phool Singh whom I had spoken to once and who had called me Sir sahib—would not be able to manage the farm after their father's death.

Rampal was in a chatty mood. He explained that his brother Phool Singh was considered a useless farmer, possibly because he had studied too much, Rampal thought. Indeed, he had a college degree and had taught at the primary school in Palanpur. What Phool Singh was doing now was not clear and I did not probe. I already knew there was some mysterious family story about Phool Singh and Rampal's father, a fellow called Pitamber. But neither an embarrassed Kishan Lal nor a blushing Babu had wanted to discuss it any further. Rampal then discussed his son, Hukum, who was a great disappointment: far from joining the army as had been expected, he had studied to become a primary school teacher. Rampal showed his disgust by spitting betel juice, and I changed the topic.

'You have a nice gun,' I observed.

Rampal looked proudly at his treasure.

'It is a rifle, actually,' he said sternly.

'Did my uncle also have a rifle?'

'He had a beautiful rifle,' agreed Rampal. 'A Lee-Enfield, almost like mine. That Chamar woman must have taken it away after she killed your uncle.'

'It could also be that she killed him with her own rifle, if she is indeed the one who did it,' I observed.

As had been the case with the Captain, my suggestion made him guffaw loudly. He briefly lost control of his bullocks and they had to be brought back in line. There was only one conclusion to draw and Rampal did it for me. 'A Chamar does not have a rifle. It is a Thakur privilege,' laughed Rampal. 'For men, of course.'

Clearly, nobody seriously considered the possibility that Neetu could have used, let alone owned, a rifle.

'I did not know, I am sorry,' I said, looking confused.

Rampal gave me a magnanimous smile. 'You could not possibly know. But you should not spend so much time with Chamars'—he looked at Babu—'they are no good.'

I refrained from asking why, and remembered that the Captain had suggested just the opposite. Instead I claimed to be interested in learning the practical aspects of farming from an expert like him. It would make me more aware of the way things were done in these parts, and it would increase the 'resonance' of my pictures. Would he be willing to hire me as a casual labourer for one day?

Rampal caressed his moustache to hide a smile, and finally nodded. Very CEO-like, he explained that he was always looking for good workers. I would have to perform like the others. Seven rupees plus a meal for the day—that was the going rate and there would be no preferential treatment. That sounded fair and we agreed I would start the next day.

I asked if he would be present. He laughed, 'I never do anything, except guide the cart and give orders if there's something important going on. I do not even fetch a glass of water. People do it for me. Of course, I chop sugarcane from time to time.'

But he would have never worked in a potato field. I wondered why it was considered humiliating to work in a potato field, but not in a sugarcane field. There was a similar hierarchy among domestic animals—cows were loved, goats were tolerated, pigs despised. Anyhow, what mattered was that I had a job for the next day and would hopefully learn a few things. Quite happy, I dashed to the Seed Store to collect my belongings. I didn't have very much, but that was fine since I expected to find some basic furniture at my uncle's place. I loaded my stuff on the tandem and Babu helped me to my uncle's house. My house, rather! I was now looking forward to this stay in the heart of Palanpur.

We made a startling discovery as we arrived at the house: the seals had been broken, the locks torn apart and the main door left wide open. Clearly, someone had been in the house. I heard a noise inside and rushed in. A young boy was picking up something from the floor. He saw me and ran out. I tried running after him, but he had already climbed a wall that was too high for me. I went back in to discover that the house had been thoroughly searched. It was also bare: two charpoys, a sad table, two chairs, a couple of chests and a chipped mirror. Hearing a noise, I looked inside a kind of corridor and then quickly jumped back. The billy goat had charged at me before retreating to a corner full of junk. The place was stinking. There were also two old pots of paint and a few saucepans that had been left to rot in that corner where nobody had gone in a long time and for good reason. The billy goat seemed determined to prevent any intrusion and kept rushing at us at regular intervals. Fortunately, the rope that tethered it to the wall looked strong. I asked Babu to find something to feed it and wondered what I would do with that smelly animal.

Babu and I asked the neighbours what had happened to the door, but nobody had seen anything. All they knew was that it had happened during the night because the door was already broken in the morning. I noted that nobody had bothered to inform me. The dogs had barked during the night—I knew that, I had also heard them—and it must have been because of the thieves. As for the kid...he was the son of Chunni, one of my new neighbours. He had definitely taken something but was obviously not responsible for ransacking the house. He was also half-naked, like all the kids in Palanpur, and there could not have been much in his pockets. I visited Chunni and discovered him and his wife in tears: their son had run away from home.

I went back home, lit a candle, secured the door as well as I could, tried to make myself comfortable on the more robust charpoy, and immersed myself in my father's notes. The story was getting closer to contemporary Palanpur. Was I going to learn something relevant to this murder?

Palanpur, 1909

Radha, her belly slightly bloated with the new life of a son—like his father, Ashok had decided the gender of the child and it was now beyond debate—was attending to various household duties. She had an unusual lack of focus that should have sent a warning to a discerning husband. But Ashok was too absorbed to pay attention to such details, and he had never been discerning. Unable to admit that he was lost, he started a long preamble that Radha cut short, 'I will speak to Dukhi about this,' she said to his surprise and relief.

She opened her hand, 'Give me the rupees,'—not knowing the exact amount, she was hesitant to venture a number—'and I will convince her.'

Since the beating, there were matters that Ashok grasped more quickly. He sensed the hesitation and correctly interpreted the nature of the thoughts running in his wife's mind.

He frowned, 'What do you mean, rupees? One rupee will do. I need the other rupee for other matters,' he added cunningly.

Radha said nothing and closed her hand on the rupee, happy to take the money, determined to use it wisely, and equally determined to extract another rupee from her husband before he could use it unwisely.

She knew Dukhi very well. Being an upper-caste woman, Radha was not allowed to go out unless it was under Ashok's close supervision. Even private acts that low-caste women would perform outside on a daily basis, Radha had to do at home. This situation had created the demeaning occupation of the removal of the traces of these acts. Dukhi was one of those who did that. Thus, every day, the two women would meet and, both conscious that their difference in status was somewhat blurred by nature, they would enter into general gossip.

Naively thinking that he had won the argument, happy to be able to keep four rupees without much hassle and eager to extract the most out of the single rupee he had let go, Ashok turned to the question of the dance show.

'That will be easy,' decided Radha who had made her plans.

'But how?' asked Ashok, impressed.

Radha raised her hand again, palm up. It was empty as she had already hidden the first rupee in a fold of her sari. Ashok sighed and gave a second rupee.

'Dukhi will dance,' answered Radha simply. 'And the women of the village will take part. Just ask the zamindar to get his band.'

Radha was decidedly clever, thought Ashok. Indeed, the zamindar liked music and periodically hired a little band for his entertainment. To demonstrate his generosity, Gavendra often invited villagers from Jargaon and Pipli, sometimes even from Palanpur. He would certainly agree to make the band available. I remember listening to the little band, as a kid, at my grandfather's place. It consisted of three or four musicians from Pipli. Were they good? Hard to tell, but in those days, they represented the ultimate luxury.

Then there was the issue of food. Ashok could handle that on his own: all the farmers should contribute milk, lassi and vegetables. After all, this building was an honour for the entire village. If need be, Ashok would draw on Palanpur's meagre reserves. As for the chicken, he would ask the zamindar.

A relieved Ashok went back to his roof to reflect further. He needed some time to absorb the emotions of the day and go through the list of things to do. It seemed like a lot of work, but all doable. What he feared most was that he, Ashok, might not be as successful as his father in handling such a delicate situation. The collective memory of villages like Palanpur, definitely in those days and until quite recently, essentially relied on the ear to mouth method to channel historical facts through generations. It would be an exaggeration to describe this process as neutral and balanced. A serious chronicler would immediately detect the poetic licence of overexcited storytellers eager to impress their audience. It was through this collective memory that Ashok had learnt that his famous father had welcomed the legions of white men who had directed those building the railways. The son admired how brilliantly Udaivir had guided them, how he had helped them select the best possible spot, going as far as sacrificing his own pucca house for the welfare of the village and the greater good of the Northern Railway. Finally, how could Ashok not admire his father's mastery of the English language that had stunned visitors to

Palanpur and greatly facilitated oral and rail communications?

Having a famous family member is intimidating. Ashok feared that he might not measure up to the ancestral yardstick. Would his mind be agile enough to build a relationship with the Englishman? Ashok yawned. This was getting complicated and a bit scary. Time to go to bed.

When Dukhi arrived the next morning to perform her daily routine, Radha was very sweet to her. As usual, Dukhi entered, keeping her head covered with the pallu of her sari, her eyes downcast, and her back respectfully bent. Once inside, she picked up the short, old broom made of strong straw and started her work. The hard broom first. The softer one would come later and that would be a good time to talk. Dukhi's skin was dark, her demeanour humble and subdued. But she also had big eyes, a straight nose and lovely lips, thought Radha, who had never considered Dukhi with much attention. Indoors, the back was bent. Outside, Radha had heard about the men running to watch her take a bath. She'd also heard that, when she felt unobserved, Dukhi's waist would become suppler and that she walked elegantly. Radha suspected that was true and did not like Dukhi any more for it.

A little later, Radha introduced the matter in simple words and in her own way. Essentially, Dukhi would need to dance for an Englishman named Hemming who would then invite her inside his tent if she performed well enough. Remembering how wisely the father had helped the British in the early days of the village, the white man had contacted her husband through the zamindar to arrange a marriage. She, Radha, was not getting anything out of this, but she cared so much for Dukhi that she had immediately thought of her. Radha simply expected—as a just return for her efforts, but later, there was no hurry—that Dukhi would contribute a little money. For the village, of course. In the meantime, out of the goodness of her heart, Radha would lend a few annas to Dukhi. No hurry there either, she could return the money—with interest, obviously—after the harvest. She added that, should Dukhi not be interested, there were other women between Bareilly and Moradabad who would be willing to marry the white man. As was customary for Englishmen looking for a wife, it was essential that Dukhi agree to dance in front of him. The

Palanpuris would support her by dancing too.

Dukhi was no fool but she was poor and her husband—a brutal man—had just been killed in a brawl. The culprit's identity had eluded a police investigation team reduced to the bare minimum of a junior official who did not exude much energy. Dukhi was now destined to marry her brother-in-law. She had nothing against him as such, but did not find the prospect appealing. So, even though all her instincts were telling her that Radha's story was suspicious, Dukhi wanted to believe it. She still made the effort of raising objections. Not many, just a few. Just to give Radha a chance to dispel some of her misgivings, not necessarily all. Just enough to live with that little dream.

Radha sensed that she had won and uttered all the soothing words Dukhi needed to hear. When they left each other, Radha sat more comfortably on the charpoy, a smile on her face. Dukhi was heading home, her back straight, her fist clinging to the anna, walking a bit more briskly than usual. Just a bit. She had probably never looked so beautiful.

Chapter 8

Palanpur, 1984

The house needed a thorough cleaning, at least the space not occupied by the ferocious billy goat. That corner would be dealt with later on, after deciding what to do with the beast. Cleaning up would be the first task for my two new recruits. To my surprise, Kishan Lal flatly refused. He had better things to do. It was not that he considered the job beneath him, but if that was all I had to offer, he preferred to work in his own fields. Since the sun was rapidly going down, I let Kishan Lal go without arguing and stayed with Babu. In a corner, we found two grass brooms and two hard brooms that had seen better days. Babu explained that the hard brooms were better suited for a first clean-up while the softer ones were designed for final touches. I had just learned that from my father's notes but pretended to have learned something new. Babu looked pleased.

We set to work. I found that Babu was unusually focused and hard-working. By hard-working, I mean that, as a result of his energetic movements, dust was flying all over before gently coming down and settling again on the floor in a more uniform manner. Still, the scene was interesting. I took the camera out. Babu had no idea that he was photogenic. And, yet, squatting on the floor and vigorously sweeping it, surrounded by particles of dust that reflected the light of the sun, he painted an interesting picture of Palanpur, and I was confident that the camera had captured it well. But Babu was not only moving dust. He was also collecting anything of value that he could find. I saw him put in his pyjama's pockets a broken sewing pin, some bits of old newspapers, one little unidentified piece of cloth, a nail or two, a five-paisa coin, and a few other things. I even caught some of this on camera. After reflecting a bit, I put the Nikon F3 aside and went back to my broom without commenting.

At the same time, I felt that this was an excellent opportunity to teach Babu a lesson in good housekeeping. After all, Pat had done that for me many times and there was no reason why I should be the only one to get lectured. After giving Babu enough time to discreetly put aside yet another bright little object, I explained to him the basic ideas of interior maintenance. Babu did not seem interested but agreed to listen and watch my demonstration.

I obliged. By that, I mean that I swept even more energetically than Babu, which resulted in even more dust flying all over. That would certainly never have made a good picture, but I would not have trusted Babu with the Nikon in any case. While I was actively destroying the mud floor, a little piece of metal appeared. The shell of a cartridge... I picked it up. It reminded me that...

'Babu,' I demanded, 'did you not pick up one like this from the floor just now?'

His innocent look would not have fooled a four-year-old. I held out my hand.

With a sigh, he explored his pyjama pockets and gave me the other cartridge. Could they be the cartridges from the bullets that killed my uncle? That was the most likely explanation.

I returned to my demonstration with a typically British sense of rectitude. After more sweeping, I took the better of the grass brooms and started carefully pushing the dust towards the billy goat, who did not seem to appreciate it. I would have to find a way to retrieve the old pots of paint which could be used to make the house look better. Meanwhile Babu, sitting on the charpoy, was quietly observing me and presumably learning from my approach. I carried on, proud to make a valuable point and, finally, ended up with a pile of dust.

Babu did not look particularly impressed. I expected words of praise, so I insisted,

'What do you say?'

Babu shook his head, 'Can I take the papers home? And the other things that I found?'

Defeated, I agreed, hoping that, at least, the lesson had been learned. Babu opened the door to go and a brief but powerful blast of wind dispersed all the dust that I had so carefully gathered.

Babu looked at me; I at him. We laughed.

'Babu,' I said. 'We must clean this stinky corner.'

I was pointing at the billy goat, who was still defiantly protecting the pile of garbage. He flatly refused and angrily explained that being a Chamar did not necessarily imply being willing to clean stuff that smelled like shit because a billy goat had lived there for too long. Even my uncle had understood that, and he had never asked Neetu to clean that corner. Since he would not have cleaned it himself but wanted to keep the billy goat, it had always stayed that way. Would I behave worse than my uncle?

I sighed and agreed to leave that corner untouched for the time being. Before he went though, I thought I should propose an addendum to the contract: Babu would paint the house over the next few days while I purchased the necessary farming equipment with Kishan Lal's help and learnt farming. At first he refused, arguing that he feared getting a cold. I increased the wage to 10 rupees per day—three more than the going rate—a proposal he also refused because that job would take a week and required skills. After a long discussion, I finally offered 60 rupees for the whole job, an offer he reluctantly accepted. I told him that he should start with the two pots of yellow paint that were in the smelly corner. I would bring some more later, after a visit to Chandausi.

He finally left and I went back to my father's notes.

Palanpur, 1909

The big day finally arrived. The zamindar appeared in all his glory, in a white kurta and red turban and surrounded by his men, equally well dressed. Gavendra Singh was smiling but was in truth quite worried that the ten rupees he had given to Bhupal, out of the twenty he had got from the District Officer to make the arrangements, might not suffice. The most concerned of all was Dukhi: would the white man like her dance? These white people were supposed to be odd. Still, she had practised. As requested by Radha through Ashok, the zamindar had assembled his band and insisted that Dukhi carefully rehearse at his place. He had observed her gracious movements, and—since he could not be caught looking at her bathing—had discovered on that occasion that the rumours about her beauty were correct.

Finally, the train arrived, pulling the usual three coaches. But one of the coaches was different. Simply put, no Palanpuri had ever conceived that so much wealth—in a coach, moreover, not a permanent house—could exist for the benefit of a few persons. The body was pure white with no traces of grease. The brass handles were shining in the sun and there were no obvious fingerprints on or around them. The windows were perfectly clean and, at three places—the back, the front and the middle—stairs had been installed so that passengers could conveniently disembark.

Once the train came to a halt, this excess of stairs created a difficulty: eager to please, the zamindar's men moved the carpet to the middle of the coach and unrolled it. Summoning all his courage, the zamindar followed with slow dignified steps, wondering whether he should walk on the carpet or leave it all for the Englishman. He decided to step on it. At that moment, two formidable guards, obviously Sikhs, armed with long rifles and their heads wrapped in turbans that made the poor zamindar look quite small and under-dressed, came out through the door at the back. The henchmen considered moving the carpet but were unwilling to do so because Gavendra was standing on it. They were also hesitant to come close to the ferocious-looking guards who now stood on either side of the back door.

Then came the Englishman. He was a bit of an anti-climax. The man was short and pudgy. Even though he was still in the doorway while the Sikh guards were standing on the ground, the top of his head reached below their turbans. He seemed surprised to see the zamindar proudly standing in front of another door, waited a bit and, since nothing was happening, came down the steps, his fat body clumsily oscillating with every movement. Once he had landed carefully—for he had to jump: the last step was a bit high for his short legs—on Palanpur soil, his eyes wandered vaguely over the crowd. The zamindar finally reacted and moved back, instructing his men to move the carpet. They rushed and the Englishman stepped on the carpet as soon as it reached him. Annoyed that his polished shoes were covered with dust, he bent down to wipe them. By then, the zamindar had joined him with the intention of greeting the important visitor of whom he could only see the back. He hesitated a little but went ahead and delivered the key message: He, the zamindar, in the name of the village, was happy to welcome the visitor; it was a great honour for Palanpur, etc., etc.

The back did not react much, except for small movements

caused by the dusting of the shoes.

Surprised by the lack of interest, the zamindar stopped. Instinctively, he turned to the son of the hero for help. How should one behave in this situation? But Ashok, who had indeed inherited the genes of his father, did not pay attention to the signal of distress: still in front of the middle door of the coach, he was looking straight ahead without blinking.

The Englishman finally stood up. He brushed some dust off his right sleeve. He carefully did the same with the other sleeve and finally considered his host.

Perplexed, and without any help coming from Ashok, the zamindar decided to display his good manners and deep understanding of foreign cultures: he also bent down to brush his feet before carefully taking the dust off his sleeves.

That was not appreciated: 'What the…!'

The Englishman turned back and climbed into the train, 'Prepare my tent! If this fellow does not know how to behave, there is not much point my talking to him or to the rest of this lot. And get me some dinner.'

He rushed back inside the coach while everyone in the crowd remained petrified. The immobility did not last, however, as the bodyguards firmly told the villagers to go away.

People dispersed, including the distressed zamindar, but Ashok remained immobile. The Sikhs were surprised by a level of passive resistance that was not yet the norm in India. No doubt this was an unflinching warrior like them. Courageous, they thought, very courageous! The presence of a single man did not seem to pose much threat, however, and the guards needed information about where to erect the tent and how to get food, so they came to him and offered him a bidi. Ashok blinked and then readily engaged in conversation, revealing unexpected diplomatic qualities. First, the zamindar had not meant to offend the important white man: that did nothing to impress. Then, he explained the arrangements that had been made for dinner: this seemed to raise more interest. Finally, he touched upon the main event and the performance of the gorgeous Dukhi: that triggered a stronger reaction. One of the guards asked for more details that Ashok—who'd often go past the faraway pond—eagerly provided. The most senior guard decided that the situation deserved a second examination by his boss, and he climbed back into the coach. A few minutes later, he returned with the news that the Englishman had magnanimously decided to forgive the zamindar—he would attend the dinner and the party. He hoped that the food would be good and Dukhi too.

Ashok happily took the news back to the zamindar who, displeased with his own performance and jealous of Ashok's skills, scolded him. He concluded by warning Ashok that things had better go well from then on, or else.

Since he had never worked in an administration, Ashok tried once again to understand how he could be held responsible for what had happened but finally gave up. Nevertheless, he was aware that he'd been scolded for no reason and, like all weak people, decided to inflict the same treatment to someone else. He went back to the village and scolded Dukhi—all dressed up already—making it clear that she would need to do really well in the evening and fix that dress to start with.

India is a place for non-cooperative games but, in case of difficulty, there are solidarity mechanisms that foster cooperation. The villagers realized that their honour was at stake. If Dukhi was expected to dance well, it was important to create the right atmosphere. They convinced a reluctant Ashok to hold an emergency meeting. For once, something came out of it that had not been planted by the zamindar. The whole village agreed that it would lend its full support to Dukhi. They would cheer, clap their hands, and the women would dance. Everyone should do their best and be well dressed. Ashok agreed with these demands and shrewdly assumed ownership, thus adding to his brand-new reputation of a courageous saviour that of a decisive, yet benevolent chief.

Palanpur, 1984

Before blowing out the candle, I examined the two cartridges. It was hard to figure out what the police had been looking for if they had left such an important clue behind. A lousy job to say the least. They were probably happy to accuse Neetu and leave it at that. Holding two shells of the bullets that killed my uncle made me somewhat uncomfortable. It was a strange feeling. Without the third shell, there was always the possibility that the last shot had been fired by someone else with another rifle. As for the earlier shot, it could have been fired by someone else and the shell was somewhere in the village, lost for good. What mattered was the third shot. It had been heard long after the first two and the shooter could have carefully taken away the shell. So, where was it? With the young thief, surely. The only thing I could do was wait for his return, hoping it would not take too long.

It was late and I went to sleep after wishing the billy goat good night.

Chapter 9

Palanpur, 1984

I got up at dawn and, after the by-now usual tea at the Seed Store, I rushed to Rampal's field. He had delegated the supervision of work to his older brother Phool Singh—the former absentee teacher—who greeted me with a smirk and a loud, 'Namaste, Sir sahib.'

I joined a group composed of a few adults expert at chopping sugarcane and several children who would strip them of their leaves. Phool Singh cheated me roundly by laying at my feet a big pile of canes with hardly any leaves. This was not fair play since the workers get the leaves as part of their wage, and it did not help me build trust in labour relations in Palanpur. Phool Singh also seemed to enjoy scolding me for the poor quality of my work. That is how I learned that some people who normally make a show of respect start pushing you around the moment you indulge in manual work or the minute they think that they have an edge—even if they know that it will be brief.

I found the work quite hard, though this was obviously due in part to my lack of experience. Carrying stuff on the head is a task that bankers are not well trained for, and when Phool Singh loaded me with my share of the fodder, I thought my neck would crack.

At lunch time, I decided to run back to the village in the midday sun to have a quick dip in the stream of water flowing out of a borewell; it was one of those delightful moments when I certainly did not miss London.

Refreshed, I went back to the field and had lunch with the other workers, except Phool Singh who had gone home. I knew that the wages included a meal. It consisted of a few chapatis, a mountain of rice and an onion or two. Rampal understood the concept of efficiency wages: we could eat as much rice as we wanted. This meal was brought to us by Jagpal, the youngest son of the household, who struggled under its weight.

A lunch break is a great time to chat and take pictures. People concentrate on their food and do not really care about a camera. While shooting, I asked a few questions about my uncle. At first, everybody was embarrassed, but then they started talking. I soon understood that Rajendra Pratap had a finger in every pie. He was cheating anywhere he could make money. He also liked to drink, occasionally visited houses of ill repute in Moradabad, and was a bit of a gambler as well. So, if he earned money, he had probably spent a lot of it. As for who might have killed him, nobody had anything to say. However, observing my co-workers suspiciously focused on their rice, I sensed that they knew. Regarding Neetu as the possible culprit, I heard the usual laughs and a few coughs, all confirming what I already suspected: she had nothing to do with it. When Phool Singh returned, everybody started talking about something else. Clearly, he and probably Rampal had some shady dealings with my uncle. I would explore that more systematically when circumstances allowed.

Lunch was interrupted by a wandering monkey who jumped from a tree next to me, swiftly grabbed the chapatis from my hand and ran away before I could attempt the slightest resistance. Then, the stupid animal peed on me. Everybody laughed and I suppose I was completely adopted by the Palanpuris that day. Baptized, in a way. In the process, I also acquired a deeper understanding of Palanpur's sense of humour.

In the early afternoon, the young Jagpal arrived. He told me that his father had gone to Moradabad and that Shakuntala, his mother, wanted me to help collect fodder for the buffaloes. Unconvinced by my performance, Phool Singh had probably engineered this. I went with his little nephew, and we had a lovely time in the fields while the sun was slowly setting on a beautiful harvest scene. As Shakuntala came out to inspect the fodder young Jagpal and I had collected, she started lecturing me against spending time with the Chamars in general and Babu in particular. I tried to understand her motives, but couldn't get any clarity on that. Not much wiser but aware that my attitude was creating trouble in the village—I did not care—I listened politely and went back to my work in the sunset.

But realities hit hard and soon in Palanpur, and in all sorts of ways. A little later, the work day ended and I witnessed Jagpal struggling to carry his bundle of fodder back home on the narrow paths through the sugarcane fields. He kept straying off the path and getting stuck in the sugarcane, his vision obstructed by the leaves. The bundle was also too heavy and Phool Singh only allowed me to help after the kid started crying. He eventually reached home. These kids must learn very early in life how to fend for themselves. Even before school-age, they are often seen carrying a younger brother or sister in their arms and constantly looking after them.

I went back to the Seed Store to collect a candle I had left behind and walked past the tea shop, just in case it was open. It was not, and nor was the Seed Store. Govindi had gone to Chandausi, I learned, and his daughter was either not in or did not care to open the door to me. Since I had walked all the way, I went further and visited the dilapidated school building.

Standing in front of it was a family, looking very sad. They were the Bhatnagars: two women, three or four children and a man. What struck me was that the women were talking quite freely. They were clearly well educated and proud of it. When I commented on that, the man said that it was better to die than to live illiterate. To live was to study, just like, for Kishan Lal, as a true Murao, to live was to work. The Bhatnagars also seemed to be rather well off. Education and money were perhaps why they kept aloof from the rest of the village. But their sadness was plain to see. They explained that educational facilities had deteriorated badly. The school had closed down years earlier. Over one hundred children had been enrolled at one time, but hardly any attended now since the teachers seldom came. Phool Singh, for example, was supposed to be a teacher then, but he had never attended although he probably still drew a salary. I asked them to explain why this was happening and they said that corruption was the main reason, along with carelessness and repeated thefts. Except for them and a few other families, most Palanpuris had a passive attitude towards education. What was needed was a few committed teachers and, before that, some money from the government to repair the school.

'How does one get that money?' I asked, interested.

They thought one would have to meet the Administrative Development Officer, also known as the ADO, to apply for funds. One would then need to contact the BDO for starting the process, before going to the CDO, the EDO, the FDO and others for the necessary clearances. Every year, money was budgeted for the repair of school buildings in the district, but it ended being used for something else.

I promised that since I had to go to Chandausi very soon, I would take up the matter with the ADO and then left the Bhatnagar family to their sorrow.

A little later, I had a long and at times tense argument with Kishan Lal. He was devastated by the illness of one of his bullocks. Less so about his wife who had taken to bed since our dinner a few days ago. I found the contrast shocking and argued about her treatment. The day before, Kishan Lal had asked me for a few rupees to buy medicine, and I had given him the money. The argument started when he made the same request again, having spent everything on a visit to some obscure private doctor. I criticized him for doing that rather than go to the government hospital. He dryly replied that Palanpuris did not go to government hospitals and that the 'system' in Palanpur was that one went from private doctor to private doctor, first in the village when available, then to Bilari or even Chandausi, spending a lot of money. When one could spend no more money, one just left it to God. If I was not happy about the way he spent my money, I should not have given it to him—he could just as well have let things take their course. His stubbornness made me furious. I was sure that simple tests at the district hospital in Moradabad would have helped to diagnose and cure his wife's mysterious illness. Finally, I capitulated—after all, my teachers at LSE had always insisted on the importance of ownership—and agreed to cycle to Chandausi in the evening to purchase the medicine. He needed to arrange for a cycle however, because the tandem had a puncture. But that evening, no cycle was available, and Kishan Lal told me that since the medicines had had no effect so far, he would let things follow their own course.

I tried to read before going to bed, but I was too agitated and tired to do so. I woke up a little after midnight. I had heard an explosion. I went out and saw that a small hut next to the railway tracks and close to the temple was on fire. I knew nothing about that place, but the intensity of the flames took me by surprise. Since no other house seemed threatened by the fire, I went back home. Nobody was outside and I had to fight off a few dogs on my way back.

In the morning, my back was aching. This time at least, it was from work and not because of the charpoy, which I was finally getting used to. Then there were loud screams and a banging on the door. I rushed out, thinking that people wanted to discuss the fire, but it was something else far more dramatic. I found Kishan Lal in a panic at my doorstep. His sick bullock had died, and the cause was unknown. This was bad news because other animals had also died recently: Hari Om's buffalo-calf, Hira Lal's buffalo and Mannu's bullock. Ten minutes later, another farmer came running: his buffalo-calf was sick. Yet another farmer appeared, whose buffalo-calf was in agony. A veterinary doctor was urgently needed.

A little later, Kishan Lal and I set off on cycle to Jargaon to call the veterinary doctor. No cycle had been available to get medicine for his wife, but two had miraculously turned up for the sick buffalos the next morning. We were equipped with a letter from Rampal in his capacity as village headman. The letter was rather clumsy and included a sort of threat that he would complain to the highest authorities if the doctor didn't act immediately. I showed the letter to the doctor, but, as anticipated, it antagonized him, and he decided not to come. He sent us instead to Narainpur, where there was a small veterinary hospital. There, after two or three questions about the symptoms of the disease, the doctor made a diagnosis and said he would send someone to Jargaon with the appropriate vaccine. The doctor in Jargaon would then proceed to Palanpur to administer it. So, we went back, stopping only in Jargaon to impress upon the local doctor the urgency of the case. He grudgingly promised to come, and indeed turned up later in the afternoon. He went around Palanpur, injecting every head of cattle with a vaccine for a small fee of 50 paisa each. Meanwhile, two young buffaloes died, causing another collection of sad faces and wet eyes. That day, Kishan Lal's wife died too, but it was the death of the bullock that was putting the whole family in financial precarity.

In any case, all this made me forget the strange fire at night. It had also delayed my trip to buy the equipment necessary for my farm. I decided to use the rest of the day to ask questions and settle some scores. I went to see Rampal. He was obviously in a bad mood, but laughed heartily when I complained about how Phool Singh had treated me. 'At least, my good-for-nothing brother has managed something as he was supposed to do,' he said.

That was how my attempt to invite compassion ended. I also wanted to discuss something else. 'Do you know who killed my uncle?' I asked abruptly.

Rampal stopped laughing and looked at me with anger in his

eyes, 'No!'

'There was a fire last night,' I continued. 'That little hut next to the temple. What happened? And what was that place? I have sometimes seen a light on there at night.'

'No idea,' he replied dryly. 'I think it is a place where some people keep stuff. Nothing important. And if you will excuse me, I have more important things to do, about the cattle. You may not care, but I do.'

The drastic change in tone made me think there was much more to this fire than met the eye. And who were these mysterious 'people' keeping stuff there? I took my leave and noticed that Rampal's young daughter was listening. She was perhaps sixteen or seventeen years old, a little boyish looking, obviously intelligent. I learned that her name was Veena. I smiled at her and she smiled too.

On the way back, I went past the charred hut. The place had been left unattended and I saw bits of glass that looked like they came from broken bottles. There was very little, though. In Palanpur, anything of value left abandoned was swiftly recycled. I passed in front of the tea shop and—miracle!—it was open, so I drank a cup of tea and listened to what people were saying. It was all about the mysterious illness affecting the cattle. Nothing about the fire.

After tea, I went back home, hoping that the work on the house had progressed in my absence. Not pleased and not really surprised, I discovered Babu was yet to start the painting job. I went to question him. His hut was at the fringe of the Dalit area, in a part of the village I had never explored. Babu gave me a complicated set of reasons. First, he argued that he could not do it because my house was too tall for him. Next, he felt that the remuneration offered was insufficient. The work involved painting the outside and the inside, so it was worth at least one hundred rupees. He, Babu, a man of experience, had worked on much better whitewashing jobs the previous year. He had been given one hundred rupees after refusing sixty, and it appeared he was hoping for a better bargain once again. Finally, the weather was still cold, and he could not afford to be sick and miss out on other important jobs that had just come his way. He shrewdly added that he could not be held responsible for the fact that I had not yet purchased the necessary farm equipment, could he? As for cleaning the mess in the smelly corner of the house, he had already told me what he thought about it. I had agreed to postpone the clean-up and that was fine but, for the painting job, I needed to offer more. Reluctantly, I offered a hundred rupees, but on the understanding that he should start as soon as possible. Reluctantly too, Babu agreed.

Then I went to Kishan Lal's place. He was still mourning his bullock and his wife. We agreed to go to the market the next day to buy two bullocks for me and one for him. Back home, I immediately settled into bed, reflecting on the various events of the day. Soon I reached for my father's notes.

Chapter 10

Palanpur, 1909

The area near the mango tree was being prepared for the party in honour of the important visitor. Soon, the zamindar himself arrived and sat on a nice carpet, surrounded by his guards. Not that he feared for his life but, wisely, he sensed that having his guards around would reduce the scope for errors. He also chose to send Ashok to guide the white man from his tent to the mango tree.

Ashok had been impressed by the speed at which the tent destined to accommodate Hemming had been built. He was even more impressed by its size. It had a small roof at the front, to protect visitors from the sun or the rain: this tent, like the train coach, was a piece of luxury. Ashok hesitated a little when he reached the entrance, but one of the Sikhs he had befriended came out, followed by Hemming. The white man almost bumped into Ashok and hurried to the mango tree so that, far from showing the visitor the way, the chief ended up following him. They walked in silence, a situation that made neither feel too uncomfortable. The Englishman easily guessed where he was expected to sit and went straight to the chair prepared for him. It was high enough so that all the others, who were sitting on the floor, were at a lower level than him. This arrangement put him in a good mood.

Hemming had come equipped with a plate, a knife, a fork and a spoon. He had an instinctive horror of eating with his fingers off a banana leaf. He ate the food and found it good. He said so. That pleased the villagers, who had struggled to meet the rather unspecified demands relayed by Ashok. A chicken had been sacrificed, as requested, and prepared by a cook who had faced the extraordinary difficulty—being a vegetarian—of preparing a dish that he could not taste. Miraculously, the meat turned out perfect. The vegetables were naturally tasty and the lassi was fresh. The zamindar's henchmen, thoroughly briefed by their boss, policed the food distribution: the village should not be shamed because the Englishman was short of something. They took especially good care of this since, by doing so, they were also maximizing their own share.

Some music could be heard coming from the village. As Ashok had requested, Dukhi was accompanied by a small group of women who could dance and by men who could play the dholak, the tabla, and other instruments. Children were also part of the group, some were clapping their hands, while others were holding candles. The group arrived at the mango tree and that is when, in one of these rare moments in a village more used to curses than blessings, all the elements came together to make the event a success. The transition from the basic beats of the procession to the elaborate music of the band appointed by the zamindar was smooth, as if they had been part of the same raga. Dukhi, uplifted by the music that had accompanied her from her home, was quick to get into action. She reached the centre of the space in swift, nimble movements that jingled the little bells tied around her ankles. Her feet were flying, with sudden accelerations and stops. It seemed that the foot, coming from so high, would hit the floor. But at the very last second, it would remain suspended a bare inch from the ground before finally landing in a violent explosion of bells. It was amazing how such gracious movements, inherently musical, could at the same time carry her body and move it around so beautifully.

Dukhi was undulating, spinning, clapping her hands. It was all happening so fast that, sometimes, her kurti would fly up, revealing pants that tightly hugged her strong legs. It was just a glimpse, but of considerable interest to the spectators, including the very important white man. Soon, too soon, the spin would slow and the kurti would come down. Her hands moved briskly, violently even. Yet, the movements were sensuous, smooth, sometimes disdainful, but always conveying seduction. While the movements were mesmerizing, Dukhi's eyes, perhaps, did most of the work—they went left and right, up and down, now shy and now shameless. Overall, Dukhi gave a magnificent performance of movement, light and sound.

Hemming had enjoyed the meal but had looked distant and

slightly bored in a dignified way: something he was very skilled at. As was his habit, he had brought, in addition to the cutlery, a little flask of whisky. Careful not to offend the locals by displaying the alcohol, he took a discreet sip from time to time. This habit had helped him cope with his job, the hot curry, the weather, and, more generally, with the ordeal of being far away from home. He suspected that, in Palanpur or elsewhere, he would have offended only a few. Still, it was better to be discreet.

When Dukhi appeared, his interest grew and he drank less, his eyes riveted on her dance. His mouth fell open, he gradually lost his dignified posture. Dukhi was beautiful and, as Gavendra had anticipated, her rather dark complexion did not bother the pale Englishman. Having been posted in India for some time already, he had been invited to many parties featuring Indian dances. These shows were usually organized in the large mansion of some important official where food and drinks were liberally served. Hemming, who had a large appetite, would load his plate with food and throw back the drinks with enthusiasm, neglecting the artistic side of the party. The people he liked to talk with usually shared his preferences and considered it fashionable to talk disparagingly of the artistic endeavours of the locals. It would have taken a brave soul to acknowledge talent, even when it was obvious. There were such brave souls, of course, but Hemming was not one of them. Forced to sit and stay quiet, he made an artistic discovery in Palanpur. For the first time, he let himself be drawn in by the show. Too soon, and to his surprise—for he was not acquainted with the musical ways of the colonized—the show came to an end. In a last, brisk movement, Dukhi tapped the floor with her pretty feet and swiftly disappeared.

Palanpur, 1984

I had trouble sleeping. My father's notes and the recent events in the village had depressed me.

In the morning, I felt better. This would be a big day, the day when everything would happen: the house would be painted by Babu—at least he would have started—and I would come back from Chandausi with two bullocks, thanks to Kishan Lal who would guide me in this venture. I would get the photo prints, perhaps a telegram from Pat announcing her imminent arrival, and I would pave the way for a new school with the ADO. The sky was the limit.

The train left at 9 a.m. with a fair load of Palanpur farmers. Kishan Lal and I found ourselves with a group of Thakurs, including Khem Pal Singh who was hoping to sell some paddy, Ganga Singh, busy with the preparations for his sister's marriage, Kumar Pal Singh, who needed to see a mechanic about his pump set, and a few others. Most had tickets.

'My friend!' exclaimed the Captain. 'It seems you are adjusting well to your new life. Are you getting good pictures?'

I did not show any emotion, and, in truth, I was not really surprised to see him there. The Captain was in a good mood and I reassured him about the state of my project. I also explained that I was going to buy bullocks and that was proof, was it not, of how serious I was?

'Any interesting discoveries? I understand that you have cleaned up your uncle's place.'

'You know a lot for someone who only passes by Palanpur without stopping,' I answered, annoyed.

The Captain laughed heartily. 'That is because I speak to people. You should do the same. That would also be good for your book project. Any idea about the fire the other night? Scary, no?'

'I don't know anything about it. It just seemed to be a big fire for such a small hut.'

'Yes, the hut probably contained things that burn well,' suggested the Captain. 'That is the only explanation.'

'You really know a lot. I wish I knew that much. I do talk to a lot of people, as you suggested. It's just that they do not talk to me that much.'

'Of course, of course, but the key is to ask the right questions to the right people.'

'That is a bit mysterious,' I complained.

The Captain made a pacifying gesture and we talked about other things for the rest of the journey. But, in the back of my mind, I was thinking of the three shots fired inside the house—the earlier one did not really matter—with only two shells. Could I trust the Captain with that? I decided not to talk about it then. Perhaps later. But he had made an important suggestion earlier that I had overlooked: I should move beyond Babu's place and explore the Dalit quarters.

Once in Chandausi, Kishan Lal and I first escorted Khem Pal Singh to a rice dealer, on a rickshaw pulled by the son of a Dalit. He knew Babu very well who, apparently, was a distant cousin. The man told us that he came to the station every day and leased the rickshaw for six rupees per day. The rice dealers were cartoon figures, very fat with spotless white kurta-pyjamas, pens and thick notebooks in their pockets.

Then we wandered for a while in the busy Chandausi lanes, buying spices and vegetables.

After a pause at a bookshop where I bought an English reader, we went to talk to the ADO about the possibility of financing a school project. Unfortunately, he was in Moradabad, but the BDO was there. He was a grey-haired, official-looking man with a friendly smile. He confirmed that, under certain conditions, funds could be provided to repair the school. With this vague promise, we carried on as Kishan Lal was impatient to buy the bullocks so that he could go back to Palanpur and continue the work in his fields. Still, he stopped to get his watch repaired for one rupee, then suggested that I get some tea and snacks. That cost me three rupees. I bought some aerograms for 2.80 rupees and observed that, as often happens with these trips downtown—whether in London or Chandausi—the total cost could be quite high. I spent fifty rupees that morning, including twenty-one for the English textbook. At several places we came across Palanpur villagers going about various businesses. We also met Buddh Sen Mathur, a farmer from Pipli. His son had contracted tetanus and had been treated for fourteen days in a local private 'clinic'. We visited him briefly—Kishan Lal getting increasingly nervous about wasting valuable time—and it was a sorry sight. He was very thin and weak. In his pocket, wrapped carefully in a piece of cloth, he kept the tiny wooden speck that had entered his foot two weeks earlier. The treatment was expensive, but he was expected to survive, an achievement of sorts.

It was now time to go to the cattle market, so I skipped a visit to the studio. After three hours of searching and bargaining, assisted by Kishan Lal—he was clearly wiser than Babu in these matters—I walked back to Palanpur behind two good-looking bullocks with Kishan Lal walking behind the one he had purchased. It had been hard to decide between buffaloes and bullocks. Bullocks seemed better in this case: a good pair of buffaloes would have cost roughly the same, but bullocks were better for ploughing, especially in the heat. Buffaloes were better for pulling heavy carts. It was agreed among Palanpur farmers that buffaloes proliferated in the village only after sugarcane became a significant crop, so that the demand for transport services had rapidly increased. In my case, that was irrelevant.

Trading in the cattle market was straightforward, at least more so than Babu had implied. Prospective sellers sit in front of their animals, be it bullocks, buffaloes or cows while prospective buyers roam around inspecting the merchandise. When they find a beast to their liking, they ask for the price. The owner then quotes an exaggerated price, say 50 per cent above the highest reasonable amount. Although grossly inflated, the starting price gives an idea of the bargain one might be able to strike. If the buyer feels that he has a chance of driving down the price below his own maximum price, he settles next to the animal. Often, a few friends help him by squatting around the seller. They examine the animal closely and make disparaging comments: the legs are too short, the tail is too long, the backside is not round enough, and so on. Serious negotiations have started. At the beginning of the day, sellers keep quoting very high prices to take a chance and observe the market. There are only a few transactions. By the end of the day, the over-optimistic sellers and buyers go home without having made a transaction. Farmers routinely attend several markets before actually buying or selling an animal. I did not have that luxury and, after the five hours it took to make the seller more flexible, I bought two bullocks of medium size and price: a red one, well built but fairly old, for 627 rupees and a white one, younger—perhaps three or four years old—and good-looking, for 750 rupees. The price seemed fair. My Palanpur friends liked them. So did I. Kishan Lal paid 710 rupees for his bullock.

As we were returning to Palanpur, I realized that I had forgotten to go by the post office to check if Pat had sent a telegram. I would send Babu the next day to collect the pictures and the telegram, if any, as a reward for having started painting the house.

PART II

Moradabad, 1984

The little wooden horse-cart had been fitted with a poor roof made from an old piece of cloth. It was supposed to protect the lady in a red sari from the sun and was doing a shoddy job of it. The lady was young, but the sari was old. The little horse was old too and very thin. But it was pulling the cart happily. A few joyful bells were attached around its neck, the type dancing girls wore around their ankles. The hoofs lifted the dust from the road, creating a golden halo. The old cart pulled by an old horse made a pretty sight, but neither the lady nor the driver thought of that. The driver was a man in white kurta wearing thick glasses and one of the lenses was chipped. It had happened many years earlier, but he continued using the same pair of glasses. Next to him was a whip, but he wasn't using it. There was no need. He and his horse had been a good team for many years: the man had learned to keep his horse going without ever brutalizing it.

He did not really know the young lady. She would come to him, about once a week, and ask to be driven here and there. The first time they had met, she had caressed the horse who had gently pressed its nostrils against her. She had smiled. That had won the heart of the old man who trusted the instinct of his only partner.

'What is its name? she had asked.

'Faizan,' he had answered, 'and me, I am Faisal.'

She wanted to go to the other side of Moradabad. He quoted a reasonable price. She did not argue. She never bargained with him and he never took advantage of it. At the end of the journey, she would pay, thank him and flatter the horse. Even when she did not need him, she would say hello if they met, and always caress the horse. A gentle beauty, all smiles. Bless the parents, the man had thought. There was a young man interested in her. Actually, there were several, but she obviously preferred one of them. He was a student, like her. The young man was probably a nice chap, although not worthy of her, he thought. But that was none of his business.

He was not too sure what they were studying. If he had known how to read, he would have understood that it was a school that trained primary school teachers. But he did not know how to read. Once, the old man had found a book, abandoned by some tourist. He had given it to the girl. She had thanked him profusely and taken the book away as if it were a precious treasure.

A few days earlier, the young lady had asked him whether he would be willing to take her all the way to Palanpur. The man had been surprised. Palanpur was an obscure, sleepy village and he somehow did not think that the girl belonged there. She was a Dalit. He did not care but he knew that her life in such a small place would not be easy. In a city, she would be less vulnerable. He asked if she really wanted to go there. Nobody had books in Palanpur. He was sure of that. But she was equally sure, 'That is why I'm going,' she had answered with a smile.

Then she asked if her little suitcase and a small box of books would be too heavy for the horse. He laughed and they agreed that they would go two days later. And now, there they were, happily moving along the dusty path that followed the railway tracks. He knew that the young lady was not well protected from the sun but there was not much he could do about that. She probably did not mind.

The young lady was not talking. From her seat at the back, she was looking around. Once in a while she would pull back her hair that had been messed up by the wind. She looked happy, but also determined. The old man got the impression that she was embarking on a mission. He was right: that mission was to educate the children of Palanpur. Her own childhood had been rather unhappy, and she could have been called Dukhi, like her great-grandmother. But she felt that many girls and boys had been even less fortunate than her because they had not benefitted from the help of a rich relative. It was only by Palanpur's miserable standards that George, her uncle, was rich, but that had made all the difference: it had enabled Smita to bloom. Not only because of the money. When she was born, George uncle had decided that the baby girl should be given a name with a positive ring. Maybe that would help her in life. Just maybe. Nobody had really believed that, starting with her parents, but there was no point disagreeing with the inconsequential wish of an old uncle who had always been generous. Since the girl was intelligent, her uncle had also insisted that she should study. So at a very young age, she had gone to Moradabad where George had settled after retiring from his job as a train driver. He had no children and had never married. Those of his kind never did. Smita became like a granddaughter to him and she studied as he had insisted.

One day, she announced that she wanted to go back to Palanpur. George had been very sad. He knew that she would leave one day, but he had hoped that Smita would move on to Bareilly or Kanpur maybe. Even Delhi, why not? And what about simply staying in Moradabad? The house would be hers after he was gone. That would be soon as he was very old. Smita had smiled. She had heard these plans many times and seen that they made her uncle happy. But she had always known that her life was elsewhere.

George tried another approach. Smita was considered very pretty in spite of her dark skin, and she could perhaps marry someone important. He would pay the dowry. But Smita had resisted. Laying her thin hand on the muscular arm of her uncle, she had gently insisted: she was very thankful for all he had done, but it was her life and she had a duty. In Bareilly, there were plenty of school teachers. In Delhi, even more. Not in Palanpur. She, Smita, had been lucky, thanks to him. She wanted to pass on a bit of that luck to the kids of Palanpur. Uncle George reluctantly agreed to let her go. By then, he was old and sick.

As they approached Palanpur, the young lady asked the old man to slow down. The horse must be tired, she said. The old man smiled. The horse was not tired, but he slowed down nonetheless, sensing that the girl wanted to savour the rest of the journey. Smita was not only enjoying the ride. She was also gathering all her courage. Things would be difficult, she knew it.

Coming out of nowhere, kids were now surrounding the cart, running, screaming, shouting and, above all, smiling. The old man wanted to scold them, but she told him not to. She returned the smiles. They were the reason she was there. Soon, however, an adult scolded the kids for getting too close. Another appeared who said the same thing. Smita stopped smiling: the realities of Palanpur were catching up with her. Then Smita noticed a young man on the side of the road. He was different—that was the word that came to her mind—and completely overpowered by his two bullocks. With his mouth open and eyes that could not look away from her, he looked rather silly. She giggled.

Chapter 11

Palanpur, 1984

I almost let my bullocks escape for the first time since Chandausi. Who on earth was this? I must have remained immobile for a while because Kishan Lal—whose bullock had placidly continued its slow, straight walk—enquired about my well-being, 'Are you alright?'

'Who is that?' I managed to ask.

Kishan Lal shrugged his shoulders, 'Who? Ah, that girl? No idea. Someone's relative, I guess,' he answered as if this young woman could just be the cousin of a Palanpuri and not an angel straight from heaven.

'But who could she possibly want to meet here?' I insisted. 'The headman, Rampal? The Brahmin who is never there? She looks nice and intelligent.'

'She is dark,' noted Kishan Lal. 'She looks like a Dalit.'

It was my turn to shrug my shoulders. Troubled by this dazzling sight, I reached home in a kind of daze. There, realities hit me—Babu had once again failed to start the painting job. I was furious. After tying up the bullocks and agreeing with Kishan Lal that he would use them the next day to clear my fields, I dashed to Babu's place.

I found him having tea with his old aunt whom I had seen once or twice before. Irritated as I was by his laziness, I almost collapsed when he gave me a new set of reasons for not even starting the work. He argued—with his old aunt's support—that the following month, after Holi, he would earn a lot of money. There would be plenty of work: harvesting, repairing and especially construction, because bricks would be available again. He could earn good wages and mentioned a figure of ten rupees per day. The old aunt claimed that even she would make that much. While waiting for abundance, he knew there would be scarcity, a time without dal or sabji, when one would go hungry. In view of that, he had just borrowed fifty rupees from some moneylender to buy food. This was to be repaid after the harvest with 50 per cent interest. Babu brazenly added that the loan had been easy to get because he had boasted of a good deal he'd made with a foreigner for a painting job. Although this deal was taking time to come through, the lender assumed that it would eventually work out and that Babu would be able to repay his debt. Finally, a highly successful and well-established family member had promised to help them soon. The old aunt vigorously agreed with everything. What could I do?

I sighed and decided to give up on the painting job until Babu felt hungry. Dryly, I told him that he would need to go to Chandausi the next day since, busy with the purchase of the bullocks, I had forgotten to collect my telegram and the photo prints. In the morning, I would give him money for the ticket and the rest.

On my way back, I saw the cart pulled by the little horse leave the village. The girl was not on it. Nor were her belongings. She had stayed in Palanpur! And presumably for several days. I was foxed: a beauty like her is seldom alone. Whether in Palanpur or in a British village she was supposed to be surrounded by a crowd of admirers. Who could she possibly know in Palanpur?

I didn't have enough information to pursue my investigation and tried to chase away the vision. If the girl was here for a few days, I would catch up with her sooner or later. Anyway, it was time to go to Rampal Singh's house where—owning bullocks had improved my social status—I had been invited for dinner. Maybe the young woman would be there.

She was not, but the party was nonetheless well attended, and everybody was in a good mood. I—almost—forgot the enchanting vision. After about one hour, a strange character appeared at the door. He was a small man, dressed like a sadhu, a little plump. Rampal made quite a fuss over him: obviously, this was an important guest. I learned that his name was Brahmachari, and that he was the elusive Brahmin who lived in Jargaon and was supposed to take care of the temple. The man who, once upon a time, had run the school. Phool Singh had been a teacher then, so the connection with his brother Rampal was clear. That the school had been severely mismanaged did not seem to have humbled the newcomer. He accepted Rampal's homage with the air of a king receiving that of a vassal. Was the earlier vision connected to this man's arrival? He did not look particularly impressive. But who knew? When my turn came, Brahmachari looked at me with interest and said that he knew my uncle very well. He was sad about his fate but tried to remember the good times they had together. He would cherish the memory of a proud, well-off man. Of course, he, Brahmachari, was not concerned with material matters, but poor Rajendra Pratap had often expressed the desire to donate to the temple. His death had come too soon. Should I discover where he had kept his money, the holy person hoped that I would contribute to his good deeds. I promised I would and the Brahmin released me. Once all had greeted him, he looked around with satisfaction and offered his wise words, 'What thou shall give to the priest will be an eternal blessing.'

Rampal looked a little uncertain, so the holy person elaborated, 'The mind is fed by scriptures and deep thoughts. However, the body of a Brahmin also requires its own, lesser, earthly nourishment.'

'Ah, you want food!' exclaimed Rampal, happy to have decoded the wise words.

The Brahmin looked offended, but unopposed to the idea. Soon, the fat man was seated in front of a large leaf supporting a pile of the earthly food required by his body to sustain the deep thoughts of his holy mind.

As Brahmachari, focused on his meal, was clearly not in a mood to be disturbed, Rampal came to talk to me. I learned that the holy person was planning to restart the school because educational levels were low in Palanpur. I applauded the idea and mentioned that the Bhatnagar family would undoubtedly support the project. Rampal agreed but added a caveat, 'Of course, the school will be selective. It will teach the scriptures and there will also be a bit of arithmetic, but just what is required to run a farm. Naturally, it will be for boys only. Girls do not need schooling.'

'But, don't you think that it would be good to include as many kids as possible, and certainly the girls? I think it is the law!' I countered.

Before Rampal could answer, Hukum, his son, who had recently returned from Moradabad with a degree of primary-school teacher, intervened, 'Yes, I also think so.'

I had already seen Hukum once or twice from a distance, but he had remained unnoticed in the small crowd attending this dinner. He was the chap people were making fun of because he was not at all like his father. He was more like his uncle Phool Singh, people said, an accusation both had vigorously objected to.

For a few seconds Rampal remained silent, then he erupted into a fury, almost hitting his son. I think it was my presence and perhaps

Brahmachari's that stopped his hand. However, we failed to stop a kick to the backside of the young man who, thus motivated, left the room. Rampal's daughter, the boyish Veena, followed her brother with tears in her eyes.

The Brahmin was upset, 'Earthly necessities are of secondary importance, but they should nevertheless be performed with serenity.'

Rampal was too irritated to tolerate much, even from the Brahmin. His glare drove everyone back to the food. The headman turned to me, 'This boy is hopeless. He studied too much and that has put stupid ideas in his mind. He even claims that Chamars should be allowed to study.'

'Should they not?'

The chief did not bother to answer directly and spat on the floor instead, 'The government never comes here to help us poor farmers. Why should we do what they say, especially if it is not useful. If we ever reopen the school, he will help Brahmachari.'

'Does Hukum agree with this?' I asked foolishly.

Rampal had no patience for this irrelevant argument. I dropped the matter and became worried about education prospects in Palanpur. Nevertheless, I continued to enjoy the food and had a pleasant chat with several guests. As I was looking for Rampal before leaving, I saw him and Brahmachari talking in a corner. They seemed to be quite agitated. Adopting a Palanpur approach, I came closer, curious to know what was going on. I heard Brahmachari say:

'Are you sure? Why? It would be against our interest.'

'...no common interest. This fire was a declaration of war,' answered Rampal before spotting me.

Feigning innocence, I thanked the headman for the invitation, gratefully received Brahmachari's blessings and took my leave.

Later, lying on my charpoy, I tried to figure out what the conversation could have meant. Of course, the fire referred to the incident of a few nights earlier, but the conversation had not revealed much. One thing was certain though: Brahmachari, Rampal, and presumably my uncle were partners in crime. And others were involved too. Who and in what crimes? I did not have enough information to draw a conclusion. Instead, I focused on something concrete—as opposed to holy thoughts, education policy or lovely persons on the back of a cart—and read my father's notes.

Palanpur, 1909

'Where has she gone?' enquired the Englishman.

The question was translated and conveyed to the zamindar who seized the moment, 'She has gone home but she can come back to your tent later if you so wish. For a private show,' he added with an innocent look.

For a moment, the zamindar thought of asking for some money but then he decided not to push his luck. It was just as well: Hemming had been informed by the deputy head of the railways that two hundred rupees had been given to the section head in Moradabad who had been asked to relay the money—he had kept one hundred rupees for himself—to the District Magistrate to cover all the expenses of his stay in Palanpur. The District Magistrate had given fifty rupees to the zamindar.

Hemming hesitated. Accustomed to a prudish, strict life in Britain, raised by parents who believed in the virtues of an encompassing conservatism, he had been slow to adopt the rather more relaxed habits of the colonial service and had looked down on the occasional misconduct of his colleagues. As years passed, he started to secretly envy their way of life. Timorous, he would probably never have dared to imitate them and would have continued to seek physical relief in an occasional affair with some young maid freshly arrived from the British countryside. But here, in Palanpur, why refrain from readily available pleasures? Who would know, except for a few hundred Indians who did not matter? He nodded.

Ashok, the henchman, and the zamindar sighed in relief. There only remained one key question: would Dukhi perform the second part of her mission as brilliantly as the first?

Shyly, Dukhi approached the tent later that night. She was wearing the same dress for lack of a better one. She had taken time to freshen up and apply kohl around her eyes, using an old, broken and spotted mirror that she had found near the tracks one day. Her face was too dark, she thought, but quite nice, so she had smiled, and the white teeth had flashed beautifully in the old, worn-out glass. Pleased, she had pursued her preparations and perfumed her body with some good oil. As she left her humble house, she felt ready. It was just that she wasn't quite sure what she was ready for.

As Dukhi arrived at the entrance of the tent, she realized that she was expected. One of the guards immediately lifted the curtain to let her in. Had she doubted how good she looked, the eyes of the guard would have reassured her. She did not notice though and, ill at ease, she remained apprehensive. Hemming was also apprehensive—a lingering guilt not totally overridden by a sentiment of impunity—and he was not very experienced in certain matters. In the few encounters he had had with British maids, he had managed to keep an aloof attitude. It had worked because that was what they expected. With Dukhi, he felt uneasy. If she had looked at him with defiance, he would have kicked her out. But there was a touch of fear in her large, exotic eyes made even bigger by the kohl. That reassured Hemming, and motivated him.

In the morning, she went back home. The guards let her go with salacious smiles. Dukhi spent the next few nights in the tent of the Englishman.

Work on the station progressed. Soon, it was time for Hemming to go. He would come back, so there was no need to organize a farewell. Feeling generous, he wanted to give ten rupees to Dukhi. She accepted the money and a ring, a small ring that Hemming had found in a corner of his room, in Delhi, after one of his brief encounters with a maid. He was also leaving Dukhi pregnant with George, a child of mixed blood who, like all others of his sort, would be rejected by both races.

A few months later, Hemming came back to Palanpur to inspect the work. He saw that the sign 'Jargaon' had been duly painted on the front wall. He examined the quality of the building, scolded some of the workers, and did not say anything to the others. This was interpreted as a great compliment. Being alone for months had made him miss Dukhi. He enquired about her. She came, blushing, and revealed that she was pregnant with his child. The thought of being a father had never occurred to Hemming. He laughed, which Dukhi did not know how to interpret. All things considered, he did not dislike the idea and was perhaps proud of it.

He thought a little. If it was a girl, who cared? For mixed girls, there were limited options: they often looked quite pretty and a key criterion of beauty in these parts was the degree of fairness. This attenuated their ordeal and, if the dowry was right, they could find a husband.

For boys, things were more difficult. The English had undertaken a little sociological study. There was no reason to accept these young men in English society—they would simply not fit—but the scholars had been surprised that the Indians did not accept them either. That had been debated in scientific articles: after all, there was superior blood in these boys and the assumption had been that acceptance, or even gratitude, would be the norm. Statistically speaking, however, that was clearly not the case. These young men were unable to find a bride, even with little or no dowry demand. Was there a way to solve the problem while serving the Empire? The studies had not exactly concluded that these people were of higher intelligence than the natives, but there was no need to prove the obvious. Since they could not marry another local or, God forbid, a white woman... The Empire was growing and getting richer from improved exploitation of new territories. Surely, there had to be some use for these people. The colonizers thought about it a lot and came up with a brilliant answer: these boys would be married to steam engines. Thus, a large number of steam-engine drivers were Anglo-Indians whose loyalty would not be with Indians and could be redirected. Instead of looking after a family, they would care for their machine throughout their careers in the railway. They knew every bolt and understood the meaning of every possible puff. The engine was theirs. The bond was stronger than any marriage and one never heard of a driver being unfaithful to his machine. Over the decades, Palanpur supplied several train drivers to the Indian railways, thus contributing to the vast effort of the colonizer and to the pleasure of some of its male representatives who happened to stay a few nights in the village.

Hemming knew all this, and he decided to do something for Britain: he wrote a letter acknowledging the child as his. This wouldn't create any problem for him and there was of course no question of bringing that kid to England. He showed the letter to the confused Dukhi who did not understand his explanation except that the letter should be shown to the railways. A great admirer of the royal family, he insisted that the child, if it was a boy, should be named George. If it was a girl, she could have any name. Dukhi understood and carefully kept the ring together with the letter that would shape the life of her child.

Palanpur, 1984

That was enough for the day. The Dukhi mentioned in the notes was possibly related to Neetu, Babu's mother. I would find out, but the time had come to switch off the lights.

Chapter 12

Palanpur, 1984

In the morning, it occurred to me that my years of abstinence—I had left Pat three weeks earlier but it felt like years—might have clouded my judgement and made me see Romina Power in any decent-looking young woman. Or Lena Olin, Dimple Kapadia, Joanna Lumley, Shabana Azmi, Kate Bush, Smita Patil, Susanna Hoffs, to name just a few. Not likely, but possible. Still, I recalled her beautiful eyes; her shapely figure; the exquisitely carved lips... Stop! I urged myself. I had important business to attend to. I got up and wolfed down a quick breakfast composed of a banana, a sad bite of Cadbury Fruit and Nut chocolate that had become whitish and dusty, and a pathetic Nescafe instant coffee. Then it was time to get going. First, I had to take the bullocks to my fields, where Kishan Lal was waiting for them, along with a few labourers hired for the day to accelerate the clearing up. Then, I would need to find Babu and give him the money to go to the post office and to the studio. Afterwards, I would go back to the field to take bucolic pictures of the men working.

I took the bullocks and guided them towards the field as well as I could. A more experienced farmer would have followed a straighter line, but I managed reasonably well in spite of my lack of experience. I was walking behind the beasts, adjusting to their slow pace and taking the occasional picture when I heard a woman singing. It was coming from the most unlikely place: the old, dilapidated school. The voice was pure, like crystal. A beautiful deep voice, unlike the odd high-pitched tone I had heard in some Bollywood movies. I stopped the bullocks near a tree and tied them up. Slowly, I moved towards the building. The girl had stopped singing. She was talking now. On my knees, I peeked through what could have been a window but was only an opening in an old wall. Then I saw her. The girl on the cart!

She was addressing someone I couldn't see, earnestly explaining the need to be careful when one wanted to live with someone. That walking together was sometimes easier than walking alone but it had its pitfalls too. There were times of difficulties when one needed the support of a solid partner. The person she was thinking of would be a good partner, but even then, there would be times when problems would arise.

Who was she talking to? I could only see the feet of the man. Not big and clearly not carefully looked after. It was not Brahmachari though, whose feet I had seen the previous night. The man was silent. Was he a kind of local Casanova gone unnoticed? Or one who had also come to Palanpur to meet the intriguing visitor? Perhaps one of these young Palanpuris working in Moradabad or Bareilly, or even in Delhi, who would have come by train. Some kind of yet undiscovered Palanpuri intellectual? From the feet, it could hardly be the Nizam of Hyderabad, for sure.

The enchanting speaker continued, insisting on the importance of a mix of qualities. The girl she had chosen—that surprised me, but that was what she said—had weaknesses too. That was only natural. Nobody was strong and right in all circumstances. What mattered was that one would be strong if the other faltered a bit.

She was sweeping the floor as she talked. The task was simple, but her movements were rather attractive. This has always surprised me: simple things can actually be sexier than complicated ones. Pat, for example, would sometimes buy lovely nightdresses that she was eager to show me. I always preferred her without or, if she really wanted to wear something, I recommended a (short) T-shirt. She never liked me saying this. Or pretended not to like it.

That was beside the point. The point was that this young lady was mesmerizing.

I decided to interrupt. I absolutely wanted to know who the Palanpuri Casanova was. Besides, I should not be caught in that ridiculous position.

Before I could move, however, the man jumped on his feet, 'I knew there was somebody there,' exclaimed Babu. 'So, you have come to give me the money. But why are you hiding?'

Hunched over on the other side of the opening, I looked like a teenager peeping at girls, which was precisely what I was doing. Embarrassed, I managed to put on a brave smile while trying to regain my composure. 'Well, I was not hiding...just kneeling...lost something... my bullocks...'

'You should not hide,' Babu insisted. 'She knows all about you and her name is Smita.'

The young woman giggled, 'Yes, my cousin has told me about you. How generous of you. And I have already seen you, I think.'

Of course, she remembered me looking silly with my bullocks. And Babu was her cousin! Oh, gosh.... And why was I so generous? At least when it came to the painting job, Babu had seemed to find me too stingy.

'And I can assure you that I have found the right person,' continued the young lady.

'For the painting job?' I asked, flabbergasted.

'No,' she laughed, shaking her head, 'a good bride for Babu.' The situation was becoming murky. Of course, I knew that Babu wanted to get married, but how could this possibly be linked to my supposed generosity?

'And you need not worry,' continued Smita. 'Thanks to your help, he will have a nice ceremony—nothing excessive, of course—and enough money to settle down. It is so nice of you,' she repeated. 'I was ready to help financially as well, but my salary as a teacher is not very much. It is good, of course, but not enough to pay for a whole wedding. Besides, with Neetu aunty unjustly in jail, Babu has already suffered a lot. Still, he managed to give her some money a week ago. I am so proud of him. He is such a great person.'

Well, I thought to myself, this clarifies many things. I turned to Babu with a question in my eyes. The subtlety was perhaps not lost on Babu, but he continued putting on an innocent face.

'This really makes me happy,' she continued. Perhaps she had not noticed my uneasiness or had preferred to skilfully ignore it.

Could I disappoint her? I adopted the attitude of the guy who, embarrassed by public praise, prefers to change the topic. 'It is only natural. Err...I would really love to discuss the future of this school.'

'Yes, it is in a terrible state. We would need some funds, but I am told it is very difficult. I know somebody who could possibly help me, but he is poor. He is really a good person though, and...' she blushed.

'I can help you,' I said, eager to rescue a damsel in distress.

'Really? That would be incredibly nice of you,' she said, looking at me with a flash of admiration.

'But, first, I must give some instructions to Babu.'

I dragged my employee over to where I had tied the bullocks. 'Why did you say that I would help you for the wedding?' I asked sternly.

'Because you will,' he answered.

'But I never promised such a thing.'

'You just did, in front of my cousin.'

I sighed. 'And what is this nonsense that you gave money to your mother? I did!'

'Well, if I had had the money, I would have given it to her. And, besides, you told her that it was from me, right?'

I gave up and sent Babu off with the bullocks to my field where Kishan Lal was waiting. I also gave him the money for the trip to Chandausi. Once Babu and the bullocks had disappeared from my sight, they also quickly disappeared from my mind. There was someone else I had to attend to.

Inviting Smita to my house would not be proper in Palanpur and would have been considered excessively bold even in London. Helping her with the school building would be a virtuous, useful, and inconspicuous first step. So, I offered my help in the noble task of increasing the level of education by helping to raise funds and, in the more immediate future, by cleaning the place with her. She blushed a bit, looked left and right, then modestly agreed although she pointed out that I would then help her while I was her cousin's employer. She giggled a bit more.

'Babu has told me you can sometimes be strict as an employer. Of course, he likes working for you, but you are a little demanding. That is not unexpected,' she hastily added, 'as you are so generous.'

I understood in that moment why people can sometimes strangle others.

That is how I found myself sweeping the floor of the school while Babu was taking care of a telegram sent by my girlfriend and Kishan Lal of my fields with workers hired by him and paid by me at the daily wage of seven rupees plus food prepared by his mother.

But all this gave me some time with Smita. The only annoying aspect was that children kept popping in to observe what was going on. Since she did not seem to mind, I gave a few forced smiles that were enthusiastically interpreted, 'You like children too,' she exclaimed, overjoyed, while I was discreetly trying to sweep one of the little darlings out with the broom.

I told her that the headman was eager to help with the educational facilities and that Brahmachari would be an advisor. Smita did not think much of that approach, 'Then the school will only be for boys and it will not teach all the necessary things.'

'You could focus on the girls, then,' I argued, annoyed that she had immediately raised the critical objections.

'It is better if boys and girls are mixed. I am not sure about that project. In the past, it was not well managed. But maybe I should not say that...'

She stopped, blushing again, and resumed her sweeping. I waited to see if she would add something. She did not.

'Maybe you could collaborate?' I suggested.

Smita looked at me. Tears were welling in her eyes and she gave me a forced smile, 'Do you think the Brahmin will want that? The truth is that they already want my project to fail.'

I did not respond and there was no point asking who 'they' were. She was probably right: that Brahmachari chap and Rampal would not collaborate with Smita. They might even be up to some mischief, like restarting with the young Hukum the scheme implemented years earlier with Phool Singh. After all, Rampal had hinted at that. There was no point insisting. The cleaning went on smoothly and I learned a few more things. Importantly, she was single. The link with the person called Dukhi in the notes was also established: Dukhi was her great-grandmother. Smita was the grandniece of George, the fellow who indeed ended up driving steam engines as suggested in my father's notes. George, not yet born in the notes, was now very old. He'd always cared for the family. Smita had been poor but was now better off and she wanted to help young Palanpuris.

Time for lunch was quickly approaching. I suggested that we ask Govindi's daughter to prepare something. I would of course pay for both meals. Smita did not like the idea and said that she needed to eat with her mother. I asked if it was the old lady I had seen at Babu's place. It was. Her name was Ramkali.

Smita also asked me many questions during the course of our work. Not surprising. Pat would have done the same. I have often thought that women have more genetic variety than men, but there are certain things they all do. Guys too, I suppose. For example, since Smita was single, I made it a point to share my own marital status. Most guys would have done that. She was surprised and wanted to understand my sad circumstances better. I stressed the difficulty of finding the right person who would be able to live with a banker who had an artistic side. Talking of which...I showed her the Nikon F3, 'Would you mind posing for me?'

She hesitated and raised the usual objections. I'm not ready, I should first take a bath, my sari is too old, my hair is not done, etc.

'You are perfect the way you are,' I assured her truthfully. 'Please do not mind if I tell you that you are very beautiful, it is the way we, photographers, speak,' I added as professionally as I could.

'I will not believe you anyway, I am so dark,' she replied.

'Well, that is fine, then,' I concluded.

'And you have to let me continue cleaning.'

'Even better,' I assured her, truthfully again.

The wide angle gave me an excuse to be close to my model. I showed her how cameras worked, helped her hold the Nikon. She smelt amazing. Once or twice we brushed against each other.

Time had passed very quickly. As promised, I kept telling her that she was beautiful. After a while, she had relaxed and the pictures, I knew, would be good. It was time for lunch and we both went home with the understanding that we would meet later in the afternoon. I picked up my lunch at the Seed Store and, since my father's notes had reached the point where I could clearly make a connection with today's Palanpur, I skipped checking on Kishan Lal and rushed home. I settled on the roof and opened the notes while smoking a cigar and listening to 'Selling England by the Pound' by Genesis on my two-in-one.

Palanpur, 1910

Several births contributed to the growth of Palanpur's population in the early twentieth century. Some of them are particularly important for my story.

The first one concerned the Thakurs. Radha, whose pregnancy had progressed without incident—a rare occurrence in those days—gave birth to a son, as Ashok had decided. He had given a lot of thought to the future of his first boy—for there would doubtless be many more—and that included finding a suitable name, no easy matter. Ashok, for example, was certainly a great name. He was a village chief and had performed brilliantly when Hemming had visited the village. There was also the Great Emperor, of course. Ashok was not entirely sure when the Great Emperor had lived or what he had done, but he had undoubtedly been an important man. Still, one had to face the sad truth: no Ashok Singh from Palanpur or its surroundings had ever become a soldier. Mahesh would be a good name, but Ashok somehow did not think it was a proper name for a soldier. He had to find something better.

He decided to think out of the box: the stakes were high and deserved a proper effort. It bore fruit: the name would be Pitamber. He remembered that a distant cousin from Moradabad called Pitamber had made it into the army. He now lived in Bareilly, in proper barracks. Maybe young Pitamber would emulate the career of this cousin. This was ambitious of course, but at least, the name would give the boy a good start.

Ashok did not know much about that name and, aware of his own limitations, he prudently decided to consult Lakshminarayan, the young Brahmin who also taught in neighbouring schools but only when his other occupations allowed him to do so. He found the holy man in the courtyard of his house, slamming his clothes forcefully on the washing stone after dipping them in soapy water. Greetings were exchanged and the sweets Ashok had brought were accepted with suitable disdain. The chief asked his question. Lakshminarayan listened benevolently, without interrupting his laundry, which gave him time to reflect. He was better at it than Ashok but not all that much and his ability to think had been used mostly to find ways of earning money. He was quite good at that as the plump belly, gently bouncing under the janeu, testified. But a human mind cannot do everything, and he had had less time to penetrate the meaning of the Vedas. Still, he had some education and that name, Pitamber, rang a bell. He washed the garment some more, although it didn't really need it, and bought more time by stating the obvious, 'Pitamber is indeed a glorious name,' he said emphatically, 'and it means yellow garment.'

Ashok already knew that but, since it came from a Brahmin, it carried more weight, 'Thank you, thank you,' he said, humbly.

'It's alright,' answered the holy person, as he continued washing his clothes.

A long silence followed, only broken by the tap-tap of the clothes.

'But maybe you can tell me more. Is Pitamber a great god?'

'I can tell you more,' nodded Lakshminarayan, looking carefully at a portion of the cloth that was desperately white.

'Thank you,' said a relieved Ashok.

Lakshminarayan did not immediately continue. He first spat some paan on the wall, adding a bright but short-lived red line to a large and old brownish spot. He cleared his throat loudly, spat again and, all obstacles removed, uttered, 'Yes, I can tell you more. But I am hungry now,' added the holy serenity, 'and it is hot.'

As already indicated, the generally slow Ashok was less slow in certain matters since the pedagogical beating he had received from the henchmen. He had anticipated this possible situation. He took out a few annas from his dhoti and stretched out his hand. The Brahmin accepted the coins but said nothing.

Ashok gave him a few more annas very slowly—the message was clear, Ashok was ready to part with this, but there would be no more until substantial information were supplied. The discerning Brahmin took the hint and thanked Ashok on behalf of the gods. Ashok nodded devoutly.

Desperately squeezing from his mind particles of knowledge that might be worth a handful of annas, Lakshminarayan correctly revealed to Ashok that Pitamber was another name for Vishnu, and that a famous Pitamber had once been a king somewhere—it was in Manipur—several hundred years earlier. Knowing Ashok, he added more adventurously that people called Pitamber were great soldiers. Delighted at this vindication, Ashok gave more annas to Lakshminarayan who piously accepted.

The chief returned home to inform his wife of his decision, already designing plans for festivities commensurate not so much with Ashok's current status as with Pitamber's brilliant future. Dukhi would dance as she had done so brilliantly for the Englishman, an exalted Ashok continued. There would be a big meal for everyone, ending with sweets and...

Ashok's voice trailed off. Radha had raised her hand. She agreed with the name but had the poor taste of disagreeing with the rest, in particular with the need for a grand party. Just to deflate his enthusiasm, she asked a pointed question, 'Why throw money away to look at Dukhi?'

Like the other wives in Palanpur, Radha had come to resent the enthusiasm for Dukhi's performance and its lasting impression on the male community. But Dukhi, after enjoying her heroine status briefly, had gradually returned where she belonged.

Of course, there would be some expenses, Ashok acknowledged to pacify his wife, but that would be compensated by a little tax increase—not much, just the minimum necessary—in the form of a higher share of the harvest.

'The zamindar will not like it and that will not be enough anyway,' Radha had replied with authority, for she knew how to count if not how to read.

'I will borrow money, then,' responded Ashok, 'how does it matter? Everybody does it.'

'From whom?'

'The zamindar! We are friends, now.'

'Promise that you will not do it,' an alarmed Radha warned, instinctively holding her belly.

Reluctantly, Ashok promised, but he was not a man to feel constrained by unreasonable promises made in a moment of weakness. Especially to his wife. Besides, for the birth of a son, Ashok was ready to bend rules. He went straight to Gavendra.

When it came to money, my great-grandfather had a reliable instinct and a ready-made speech that could be adapted to the specific circumstances of the borrower. Ashok was a village chief. He received a warm welcome, worthy of his high status. Yes, of course, Gavendra was ready to lend the money at a moderate rate in line with the creditworthiness of the chief. Important persons had to assist each other, and the arrival of a son had to be celebrated with pomp. This was a must. If money was not spent for the arrival of the first son of a chief or for his wedding, then what—tell me!—should it be spent on? the zamindar argued. He rested his hand on Ashok's shoulder, who was immediately overwhelmed by this new testimony of his friendship with a powerful zamindar.

Ashok asked for twenty rupees. The zamindar prepared

a document that indicated he had lent thirty rupees at 75 per cent interest. He assured the chief that it was 25 per cent. Ashok received ten rupees only, the rest went towards paying off the previous debt. Ashok should have argued that, since the party had gone well, there was an implicit promise to cancel at least a part of that debt. He preferred not to raise the issue, eager not to upset the zamindar and ruin the nascent friendship. Ashok went back, happy with his ten rupees in cash and blissfully unaware that his debt had now reached thirty rupees for which he would have to pay an interest of twenty-two rupees just after the harvest.

Ashok used the money to purchase shawls, sweets and cartridges that would allow his fellow Thakurs to use their rifles and celebrate the important event with adequate fire-power.

A few days after his birth, baby Pitamber was blessed by Lakshminarayan for a modest fee. Then, the party was held. The proud father got a little carried away and was rather lavish with the coins. Being generous on such an occasion would surely bring good luck to Pitamber, a factor that his financially conservative wife had failed to grasp. The ceremony was spectacular even though, as a concession to Radha, Dukhi had not been asked to dance. It was a small concession: Dukhi was several months pregnant.

By contrast, the birth of Rajesh, a Murao baby born a couple of months later, went almost unnoticed. Rajesh's parents had arrived in Palanpur by train a year earlier. Their Palanpur cousins had talked about work opportunities and told them of a train to conveniently reach the place. They settled in Palanpur with a lot of resignation and a little hope. Very little: there or elsewhere... Life would in any case be an endless succession of days in the field. That was how it had to be, of course, and the couple was proud of its hard work. Still, a life of incessant work and hardship is not particularly appealing. It makes boredom something to look forward to.

Beyond boredom, there was also the slim hope that has always motivated entrepreneurial minds. Rajesh's father had offered his services as a labourer and, being a good worker, he was often hired. After working for others, he would work for himself, determined to build some sort of house that would become the starting place of his own little farm. He dreamed of having children, preferably sons who would be able to help in the fields. His wife shared that dream. Rajesh was the first of a series of young contributors to the survival—and future prosperity—of the household. The parents immediately sensed that the child was a rebel by nature. He had been born a little later than the expected due date, as if reluctant to embrace the world. He had also refused to cry, and a lot of prodding had been necessary.

Like most other babies in Palanpur, he remained unnamed for several days: a reasonable period of time for fate to decide whether it would allow the child to live or not. In the case of the little girl born ten months earlier, fate and some neglect had decided against. Meanwhile, the father went to work, and the mother joined him the day after the birth, leaving the boy in the care of his old and half-senile grandmother. The father could not afford to forgo a day's wages and the mother had to attend to a young calf in which all the savings of the family had been invested. After a week, fate seemed to have made up its mind. Rajesh got his name. Although tired after a long day's work, the parents looked at each other with some pride. Then, they forgot their exhaustion: more children were needed. At the prevailing infant mortality rate, it was important to maximize their chances, even at the risk of increasing an already high mortality rate for mothers at childbirth. For the next decade, almost every year that passed gave Rajesh a brother or a sister. Several survived.

The birthday ceremony was limited to the bare minimum. A few sweets would do, the father had reasoned. In any case, he had no time to waste in partying. Even less money to spend carelessly. Thus, the young Murao started an austere life that would be shaped by tough love. It made him strong enough to face the sequence of dramas that would soon unfold. It also nurtured his rebellious nature.

Elsewhere on the social ladder of Palanpur there were other births. A few months after Rajesh was born, Dukhi gave birth to a son, alone in her house. Dutifully, she called him George. She could have died, and nobody would have helped her: the village had been happy with her performance for the Englishman but that was some time ago and she had to suffer the consequences on her own. Feeling miserable and lacking the resources to take care of the baby, she agreed to marry her brother-in-law. Her pregnancy out of wedlock could have been an obstacle, but the issue was not raised. Overall, it was a peaceful marriage, if not a happy one. Still, there had been enough passion to give George a little sister who died too soon to have a name, followed by a brother called Chhote Ram. Then twin sisters were conceived just before Dukhi's second husband died.

For George, there was little joy at home and misery outside. The misery increased when the baby girl died, although that was one less mouth to feed. Chhote Ram survived the ordeal but the lack of food and recurrent illnesses kept him short and frail. He made up for this by being mischievous, aware that honesty would not bring him much good anyhow. Fortunately, George—arguably like many little boys all over the world—found it more appealing to drive a steam engine than to get married. This gave him something to look forward to, unlike most young people in Palanpur. Dukhi never talked badly of Hemming but her eyes were sad whenever she looked at her son and he found it hard to take. George always sensed that his mother's unhappiness had been caused by that white man of whom he only knew the name and the fact that he was chubby.

Palanpur, 1984

So, that was George. Sadly, the notes painted a decidedly unflattering picture of my ancestor... I certainly understood better why my father had left Palanpur. It was a strange feeling. I grew up without knowing much about my father's side of the family. And the grandparents on my mother's side were really from London in spite of their Indian looks. My great-grandfather, that Gavendra fellow, was a crook and I was in one of his houses, the house he seldom used because it was in Palanpur where he did not want to be. Was there something left of him? I looked around. Just the atmosphere, I guessed. I shrugged my shoulders: I was feeling the influence of the bad smell coming from that corner. I gave some food to the billy goat, just managing to avoid an attack. It was time to go back to the school and help Smita.

She was at work decorating the classrooms. I tried to convince her to resume the photo shoot but she said that there was too much to do. I was about to insist, betting on my charm, when Babu made an untimely appearance. Or maybe he had entered some time earlier and watched us. Who could tell?

'I have done what you asked for,' he announced proudly.

'Good,' I said, slowly detaching myself from a joint examination of the lens. 'Can you show me the photos?'

'I left them at the station. People wanted to see them. They are very nice but, on one of them, Rampal bares his teeth. We all laughed a lot.'

Smita giggled and I sighed, opening my hand, 'Can I have the telegram at least?'

'I left it at the station as well. But I know what it says,' he added helpfully.

'Do you mean to say...?'

Then I remembered Smita's presence and played it cool.

'Good. What does it say?'

'You dumbass. Stop. Coming soon. Stop. Kisses. Stop. Pat'

'You have a friend coming?' asked Smita. 'What does he do?'

'She. She's a woman,' I admitted without enthusiasm.

'Ooh, of course, she said "kisses." Is she your fiancée, then?'

'Well, not quite... I don't know yet... I'm too young.'

'But you are not too young. And she said "kisses",' Smita stressed, cheekily.

That is when the very guy who had sabotaged the possibility of a closer friendship with Smita took another shot at me, 'Pat is his girlfriend,' explained Babu. 'She thinks he's an idiot. Dumb ass means idiot. A man at the post office told me when I asked.'

There was an awkward silence. Smita was looking at me strangely. But I would not let myself be defeated by Babu and found something to say, 'Pat is a close friend,' I meekly countered, 'and "dumbass" is a private joke.'

That convinced nobody. Myself, I have never been convinced by the 'private joke' argument. Still, it was a brave attempt to protect my dignity. I added that it was high time to go and look at my field. I left my new friend and dragged Babu along.

We first tried to collect the pictures. Fortunately a few of them had been left behind, although not the one with Rampal's teeth that had caused such mirth. Someone must have kept it to laugh leisurely at home. The telegram, now looking like an old over-read newspaper, was on the floor. Babu had accurately conveyed its contents.

We proceeded to my fields. As we approached, I immediately realized that the work had progressed well. A few bighas had been cleared. All the wild grass, old rubbish, and some big stones had been removed. Suddenly, I heard the angry voice of Kishan Lal shouting orders. I rushed to see what was going on. Sitting on a stone, my employee was abusing—in foul language—those who were unable to keep up with the pace of the group. The way he was talking was a disgrace. I was about to intervene when Kishan Lal, seeing me, stopped screaming and made a welcoming gesture. He was imitated by the workers who all seemed to be in reasonably good mood, even those who had just been scolded. I nevertheless felt the need to act. I decided to keep the matter private and took my partner aside. Babu followed us, all ears. Sternly, I told Kishan Lal I would not tolerate abuses in my field. This was simply not on.

He looked surprised, even pained, but remained defiant. This was the way things had to be done if the work had to be completed on time. All these labourers were paid for the day, not for a task. If their individual pace differed, the work would progress unevenly and gradually slow down.

'Still, that is not the way,' I insisted, quoting the principles of good management I had learned at the university, 'you should demonstrate, show that it is possible. Like this.'

I took a khurpi and joined the labourers who were weeding out the grass. Babu sat on the stone next to Kishan Lal to observe my novel approach. A few minutes later, sweating in the heat, surrounded by insects and dust, I had considerably slowed down the whole team's pace and my status in Palanpur had taken another dip. I stopped my experiment in applied strategic management and sent everybody home.

After the workers had left, there was an embarrassed moment when I wondered how I could regain some authority. Fortunately, Babu could not take the uneasiness and started talking. He agreed with Kishan Lal. He had himself been scolded on a routine basis by supervisors and he readily accepted it when deserved. Not when it was undeserved. For example, I could scold him for sitting all day, as I had done the day before, but not Kishan Lal for making people work harder. That field was good but required a lot of work.

'Besides,' added Kishan Lal, more concerned about my attitude than offended by my intervention, 'you were treated the same way when you worked for Rampal. This is the way things work here and what people expect.'

It was hard to disagree, but Kishan Lal's comment had given me an opportunity to change the topic, 'Things do not always work, here,' I countered. 'Take the school next to the Seed Store. The lady we saw yesterday—you know, Babu's cousin—is the new school teacher. How can she work there?'

'That building is empty and rotten,' said Kishan Lal.

'Exactly,' I replied, 'but she can hardly be blamed for that. I saw her clean the place.'

'And he helped her a lot,' interjected Babu, annoyingly.

Kishan Lal shrugged his shoulders, 'There are reasons why this school is in bad shape. It's all in the blood,' he added mysteriously. 'And, if you want my opinion, it would be a good thing if the elections could be won by someone honest for a change...'

To my surprise, Babu butted in and asserted that when it came to elections, the Muraos had no lessons to teach anybody. Even more surprisingly, Kishan Lal did not respond and, instead, went to the field to collect a few tools he had left behind. I tried to take the opportunity to understand this election story by asking Babu, but he did not wish to elaborate. Clearly, the two of them had reached a strange and mysterious truce.

I left my colleagues, instructing Babu to bring the bullocks back home, and decided to pay a visit to Rampal. Smita's presence was an additional reason to seek funds from the authorities and revive that school while steering it away from Brahmachari's plans. I stressed that a meaningful collaboration with Smita would be very useful. At first, the headman did not seem to like the idea—indeed he looked quite irritated—but as I explained the plan, he warmed up to it. I prudently mentioned the concerns raised by Smita, about corruption and mismanagement, but Rampal proudly answered that he would personally handle the matter.

'Naturally,' he added, 'the use of the funds will be decided by the village council, the gram panchayat. But since the school is a priority, the project will most likely be accepted.'

I promised to abide by the decisions of the gram panchayat. We were lucky, Rampal added, because a meeting was scheduled for the next day and it would be attended by the BDO whom I had already met in Chandausi. He might know whether a government subsidy would be available. In any case the school project could be debated and its merits examined. The meeting would be held at 10 a.m. and I should attend. If the gram panchayat agreed in principle, Rampal continued, he and I could draft a letter to the ADO. We thus agreed to meet the next day after the village council meeting to work on it.

I thanked Rampal for his unexpectedly strong support. Just before leaving, I mentioned the exchange between Kishan Lal and Babu. He laughed and explained that, before him, a Chamar had been elected head of the village following a major fight between the Thakurs and Muraos. That man, now dead, had been a crook unanimously held responsible for finishing off the village school. He had stolen every remaining piece of furniture that the previous headman had left behind. He also became quite rich in the process, notably by demanding a share of the teacher's salary to forgive his chronic absenteeism. That had suited the teacher. Rampal did not mention that the teacher was his brother Phool Singh and that the scheme had been hatched by his friend Brahmachari.

'Teachers like that do not deserve their degree,' a voice suddenly interjected.

It was Hukum who had strong views on education.

'Of course, of course,' agreed Rampal, even though his eyes were lambasting his son.

'But that does not explain why Kishan Lal fell silent,' I objected.

'That,' laughed Rampal, 'is because the headman before the corrupt Chamar headman was a corrupt Murao. They also had their turn at running the village. That was the year when the cooperative was restarted. And there were difficulties. Major difficulties.'

'All village heads are corrupt, then!' I observed. 'Power corrupts, apparently. I guess it has nothing to do with caste.'

'I beg your pardon,' an offended Rampal shot back. 'I just talked about Muraos and Chamars. Me, I'm a Thakur and I am not corrupt.'

Suppressing a laugh, I took my leave. On the way back home, my enthusiasm dipped, and reality took over. It dawned on me that Rampal's enthusiastic support would require close monitoring. As if to help me come back to earth, my neighbour Chunni appeared. He was pulling his son by the ear—the boy who had pinched something from the floor of my uncle's house the day I had moved in. The boy—named Rakesh—had run away to Moradabad and had finally decided to come back. Chunni told me that Rakesh would be severely punished. I felt pity for the boy, despite my eagerness to retrieve the third shell.

'Do you have what you stole from sahib's house?' asked the father.
'Noooo,' answered the boy, wincing in pain.
The father twisted the boy's ear a little further, 'Really?'
With a smile, Chunni turned to me, 'The boy will talk,' my neighbour assured me.
'Don't be too harsh,' I begged. 'I am sure Rakesh regrets his deeds.'
'Of course,' said the father. 'He will regret.'
'You should make peace with him,' I urged.
'Yes, I shall make pieces with him,' agreed the father, leaving me with a promise that could be shattering for Rakesh, or simply reflect Chunni's poor grammar. Or both.

It was still early. Remembering the Captain's advice, I decided to venture into the Dalit quarters with the camera and try to strike up conversation. As I entered the area, my usual little band of followers suddenly waved me away as if I were crossing a border post. I realized then that none of them were Dalits. I continued, alone perhaps for the first time since I had arrived in Palanpur. I pulled the camera out but, to my surprise, people paid no attention. After being constantly examined whenever I was moving around the village, this was quite a relief.

Once I came across a picture taken in a bar in Kinshasa. The picture was perfect: the angle, the contrasts, everything. It was of a man sitting in a bar, smoking and watching a dancing girl in a white dress. It was very real. Yet, that man and I had nothing in common. I just sensed it. He was not better, or worse. He simply belonged to another world. The photographer had masterfully conveyed all that in a single shot and had allowed me to take a glimpse at that world. I had a similar impression among the Dalits. It was different from the rest of Palanpur. Much poorer, certainly. But there was something else. And it was not that people did anything unusual: men were quietly coming back from work, women were cooking dinner, children were playing around. I was not sure what to make of it. Suddenly, Smita appeared next to me. 'It is different, is it not?' she asked.

I nodded. She talked briefly with some young chap and he invited us to have tea. I bent as I entered his hut. There were holes in the roof and the floor was made of dried mud. The wife was preparing tea.

Moved at the sight of this bare hovel, the children in rags, and their hospitality, I handed a fifty-rupee note to the young man, adding, 'Use that money wisely. Maybe you should invest it in fixing the house, because…'

Before I could finish, Smita jumped to her feet, furious, 'Who are you to tell these people what they should do? Even with the little money you give them?'

I was at a loss for words, but Smita went on, 'How would you possibly know what is best for him? Every day he wonders whether he and his family will have enough to eat. And you want him to invest?'

Then she cooled down a bit, 'I know you meant well. But the truth is that none of us has a nice house or a nice job like you, let alone fancy cameras. And people's scorn weighs on our lives. It is misery with no silver lining. Our children have names like Bhukhan and Dukhi. If he invests fifty rupees on fixing the roof, will it make him feel better? No! He will still be miserable on a daily basis.'

Cautiously, I interrupted, 'What will he spend the money on, then?'

'On whatever he wants,' Smita replied dryly. 'He may well have fun with it. I do not mean buy alcohol: we do not drink much. Maybe buy food and eat a lot for once. Or even purchase firecrackers. His life will be fun for a few minutes at least, and everybody in the community will have something good to remember. Can you understand that?'

I blushed behind my cup of tea and nodded. Then I stood up, thanked the man and we continued our tour.

The Dalits came across as industrious people, cowed by centuries of subjugation. They were keeping a low profile as they had always done. At the same time, they were certainly not lifeless.

'This has been an interesting visit,' I said. 'Babu, it seems, is the odd one out.'

'He is. He firmly believes that we, Dalits, must not be content with having our own systems. We should be better integrated in the community. That is the only way we will get out of our condition. Staying among ourselves is not enough. He wants us to be part of the larger world, equally. Not everybody here believes it is a good approach, but that is why he came to you.'

So much for me picking Babu. He was the one who had picked me.

'And what do you think?'

'He and I see eye to eye on this. I want kids to have a better education for the same reasons. The children should all be in the same classroom together. Maybe they will learn to appreciate each other more. But there is opposition among the Dalits and that is why he could not easily find a wife, even though he is such a nice man. I helped him find someone who thinks like him.'

'I hope it happens, I really do.'

I would need time to absorb all that I had seen, but it suddenly occurred to me that if the Captain had wanted me to visit the area, there was another motive, so I changed the subject, 'I have another question: does Babu know who killed my uncle?'

Smita sighed, 'We all do. But it is not our business, you see, except for Neetu aunty. In fact, we would prefer that you find out for yourself. Don't worry, Babu will help you. I don't want to say more.'

I took my leave, unable to find comfort in the notion that Babu would give me his support. As I came out of the Dalit quarters, I met again with my band of followers who looked at me disapprovingly. I had known all along that spending so much time in that area would be frowned upon. I continued not to care and went home to sleep. Chunni would interrogate his son and the boy would confess having stolen something from my place, presumably the third cartridge. That would complete the evidence and at least clarify one important matter.

Chapter 13

Palanpur, 1984

Soon after falling asleep, I woke up. It was not the bedbugs or the mosquitoes: I could hear loud screams from the upstairs room in Chunni's house. I got up and climbed to the roof. From there, I could hear and see what was going on. Rakesh's ordeal was not a pretty sight. He was punished not only for running away and for taking something from my house, but also for stealing twenty rupees from his parents before leaving. A severe beating was on the cards. The parents had tied the poor boy's hands with a thick rope, stretched them upwards and tied the other end of the rope to the roof of the veranda. They threatened to leave him there the whole night. Then they sat inside and started discussing his transgressions, constantly shouting at him. After about an hour, Chunni told his wife to start questioning Rakesh. She did it with the help of a rod: What had he done for so long? Where was the money? What had he taken from my house? The questions were punctuated with heavy blows. I was not sure whether I should intervene or not. I decided to keep quiet, at least temporarily. At some point, Chunni's wife seemed to feel tired and told Chunni to continue, but he would have none of it. After a short quarrel between husband and wife, during which Chunni's authority seemed in jeopardy, she resumed her task, making Rakesh promise that he would never do this again. The boy promised and I left the roof, hoping that that would be the end of it.

Back on my charpoy, I found it hard to sleep as the promise was being sealed with a few more blows. The beating finally stopped. The parents untied the boy at last and gently told him to have some dinner. In England, the boy would have been sent to bed without dinner instead of being roughed up, but such a harsh punishment was evidently unthinkable in Palanpur.

The beating did not yield what I had expected. The son had screamed his confession in a way that left no doubt in my mind: he was telling the truth. What he had pinched from my house was a little golden star—not made of gold, much to Chunni's regret—of the sort one sees on police and army uniforms. At least, that was what Chunni thought. It would not be surprising: the police had searched my place several times. I was left with only two shells for three shots. It was not clear what I could do with that.

I turned on my charpoy but, in spite of the silence, I could not sleep. Too many things on my mind. Of course, there was the missing third shell. But Pat's insistence was also odd. Had I looked behind the bed? What a strange question! Why come up with that all the time—when I had left for the airport, and then in the telegrams. She could not have known more than me about the place especially since, at least at the time of my departure, she could not possibly have read my father's notes in full. Unless…

Unless, of course, she had read the prologue. I never read prologues. Pat always does. That was it: she must have read the handwritten introduction. I retrieved the notes and quickly found what I was looking for:

> There is a little hideout next to the bed I used when in Palanpur. One brick can easily be removed and put back, without anyone noticing it. This hideout was probably made when the house was built and forgotten later. I found it by chance one evening. That is where I have hidden the drafts of these texts until my departure for the UK.

So, that was it. I moved the charpoy and it took me only a few minutes to find the brick. The hideout contained a packet, carefully wrapped in a brown paper. I would look at it the next day. I put the brick back and had no problem falling asleep.

In the morning, I had a quick breakfast and then went to meet Chunni, who gave me the little golden star while lamenting that the boy had spent the twenty rupees he had stolen. I enquired about Rakesh and learned that he had been sent to the field, from which I concluded that the punishment had not damaged him too badly.

'He is limping a bit and has a few scars, but he will recover,' Chunni told me.

Reassured somewhat, I went back home, put on 'Money' by Pink Floyd, and checked the packet I had found the previous night. It was clearly hot stuff. The brown bag contained several books of accounts with financial records stretching back over decades. They itemized all the shady deals that my uncle had made. It was clearly a running document. The last booklet referred to financial transactions that started at the beginning of this year and the last entry was made two days before my uncle's death. I decided to start with that one. Aware of the way information circulated in Palanpur, I had to be cautious. I carefully checked that all the windows were closed and that the door was bolted. Then I lit a candle, placed it on the little table and immersed myself in the accounts. At last, I was in my element.

In Palanpur, however, spending a few hours on your own to analyse documents—or do anything for that matter—in full serenity is an elusive enterprise. People are concerned about your whereabouts. It is not mere curiosity. They care for your well-being; they want to make sure that you are not desperate to indulge in a little gossip; and they may need gossip material themselves, so as not to appear uninformed, disconnected, or out of touch. Sure enough, a little after I started, I heard a light knock on the door. More like a discreet scratch. I ventured a guess, 'I'm busy, Babu.'

'It is me, Babu.'

'Yes, Babu, I know. I will see you later. I am busy.'

A pause, then a slightly more assertive knock, but on the shutter this time. Babu's amused voice echoed inside the house, 'You are not busy, you're looking at a picture.'

This was a short but revealing statement. First, for Babu, being busy meant working in the fields or stirring a kadai. Writing or reading was not real work. To be fair, there are people in the UK who feel the same way. Second, I realized there was a hole in the shutter.

I sighed, shooed Babu away, found the hole and blocked it. Then I went back to the accounts.

I quickly realized that the rumours about my uncle having a finger in every pie were true. A glance through the other books proved that this had been going on for a long time. He was not necessarily the instigator of everything, but he was certainly involved in many corrupt schemes. My uncle was actually running a kind of informal racket, with interest in just about anything that involved money in Palanpur and the neighbouring villages. He took cuts from the farmers' cooperative on seeds, loans, and fertilizer. He kept some of the money and transferred the rest to mysterious individuals. The same individuals would transfer him money from other activities. The scope for corruption in Moradabad District seemed endless. It had also evolved over time as new opportunities popped up while others disappeared: the construction of a road, repairing a school or temple, even organizing elections. Anything valuable stimulated the creative mind of my uncle and his partners in crime.

The loans to farmers were typically recorded as follows:

Amount outstanding Farmer A: Rs 10,000
Amount due this year: amortization + interest: Rs 1,000 + Rs 1,500 = Rs 2,500
Amount paid by Farmer A: Rs 500 (recorded, plus Rs 1,000 unrecorded)
New amount outstanding: Rs 10,000 + (Rs 2,500—Rs 500) = Rs 12,000

A neat little trick, enabling the crooks to collect 1,000 rupees for every 10,000 rupees of outstanding debt every year. Meanwhile, the victims' debts increased at a compound rate of 20 per cent per year. These helpless Palanpur farmers must have borrowed sums as small as fifty rupees at the time of the zamindars and were still struggling now against galloping indebtedness. Below this, there was another line:

Misc. Rs 1,000 o/w Rs 100 fee, Rs 250 to B, Rs 150 to R

And, presumably, 500 rupees to my uncle—half of the entire loot.

The 'fee' must have been the amount kept by the manager of the cooperative, assuming that the farmer had not paid more than the 1,000 rupees reported to my uncle. Earlier in the books, it had been C, G, and others. My uncle was a survivor. But who were these people, like B and R? Hard to tell. I would need to think about it and investigate.

There were also transactions that involved bigger amounts, although they were less frequent.

I found, for example:

Seeds. Sale Chandausi one tonne minus purchase common seeds 800 kgs. Net Rs 30,000
Rs 5,000 fee to B, to D, and to P; Rs 500 to two supervisors
Fertilizers. Purchase Moradabad. Net Rs 1 lakh
Rs 10,000 fee to B and to D, Rs 1,500 to two supervisors

I sighed. I had heard many times that cooperatives in rural India were tampering with seed and fertilizer sales and had always done so. What was annoying was my uncle's involvement.

It was clear that the motive of his murder was related in one way or another to the activities recorded in these documents. It did not matter which: it was all about money. The books also made my life easier in an unexpected way: if I wanted to do something for the village, I could donate money in proportion to the harm done by my uncle and his predecessors to the villagers. There was enough material to do this fairly. Enough material indeed, but—and that was frustrating—I had not found any money yet. Where was it? I had looked everywhere, and there were not so many places to hide things within these old walls. In addition, all this convincingly exonerated Neetu, if further proof of her innocence were needed. It would have been nice to find the third shell, though.

Just as I had started reflecting on all this, there was a martial knock on the door.

'Anil sahib, are you there?'

'Err, yes.'

'It is Rampal here. Are you sleeping?'

'I was, but no longer,' I said.

'Good,' said Rampal. 'I could not see what you were doing because someone has blocked the hole in the shutter.'

'Really?' I asked. 'Well, I am very busy, can I see you later?'

'Have you prepared the letter for the ADO?'

'Not yet. We agreed to do it after the village council.'

'Yes, yes, but I heard that you were not doing much. Do you want to go to my field and take a picture of me with my rifle?'

I decided to negotiate. 'No, but I can take a few pictures here. Then I will need to rest,' I said firmly, 'and you should get ready for the gram panchayat.'

Resting was something that Rampal understood. Reluctantly, he agreed to my terms. I came out without giving him a chance to look inside, and took a series of pictures with the 50 mm. He gave me a little lecture on his Lee-Enfield rifle. He had inherited it from Pitamber, his grandfather. It was an old piece. The barrel was covered in wood that made a sort of nice protective case. That was as well because the wood was badly chipped in several places. I was delighted to learn that his original .303 had been modified to a .22 calibre, whereas my uncle's rifle had not been modified and would therefore be more interesting. Rampal was a generous man and he invited me to try the weapon. I agreed to try it sometime but not right then and sent him off, barely managing to divert his attempts to enter the house. I realized later that I should have accepted his offer: the mystery would perhaps have been solved faster.

Door safely bolted again, I returned to the accounts. All the books contained lines similar to those I just reproduced. But on the last page, just before his death, my uncle had written something unusual:

P getting greedy and aggressive. Could become dangerous. Has threatened me. B too.

That was very interesting. Who was P? Or B for that matter?

My thoughts were interrupted by an odd noise. Not a knock, more like a kind of cry or lament. I pretended not to hear. It grew louder, 'Anil sahib, Anil sahib!'

This was followed by a scratching on the shutter. Apparently, that hole at the window was quite a popular spot in Palanpur.

'I cannot see you,' complained the faint voice.

'What can I do for you, Govindi?'

'I need to buy food and I don't have any money.'

'Nor do I.'

The claim would not be easily accepted. Rightly so. But negotiating is in my nature, 'Why don't you ask your daughter to prepare some chapatis, a cup of tea and two kelas for my lunch? I will give you some money afterwards.'

'I need an advance,' replied the lamenting voice.

'How much?'

'Five rupees?' risked Govindi.

That was a tall order. I sighed, 'Why five rupees?'

'Can you give me two rupees, plus three rupees for your food? That would be five rupees in total.'

My thoughts went to the thousands of rupees plundered by my uncle. Perhaps my redistribution scheme could start with Govindi. More so since Rajendra Pratap had been involved in that bribe to replace Govindi with a new chowkidar as I had also found out. I came out and gave three rupees to the old man, promising to hand over two more after the lunch was delivered. Govindi stopped his lament and immediately rushed back to the Seed Store to give instructions to his daughter.

A little later, lunch in hand, I gave the two rupees to Govindi. I cannot say he thanked me profusely, but that is not a Palanpuri habit. Afterwards, I decided to help my meditation with a Romeo y Julieta cigar and smoke it on the roof just like Udaivir must have smoked his bidis some 130 years earlier. In a few days, Pat would arrive, and my life would change. She would look at things differently and meet Smita. There too, she would look at her differently, I presumed. How could I best use the reasonably peaceful days ahead?

Conditions in Palanpur were decidedly more complex than a Londoner would have thought, and information flowed within the village as efficiently as in the City. That hole in the shutters, for example! Everybody knew about it. People must have been looking through it forever. I got up and went back to examine it more carefully. Just above it, there was a nail. I remembered that, without looking for it, Babu had hung his gamchha there when he had come to help me with the cleaning. He obviously knew that the nail was there. If Babu knew that, everybody knew it. My uncle too. Perhaps he had even made the hole himself. That had two implications. One was that he knew people could see him and had decided to let them spy on him at times of his choosing—a clever trick for someone involved in shady deals. Nobody would have much to report when the hole was open and that was possibly the best alibi a crook could have. Clever!

The other implication was even more interesting. There was nothing hanging on the nail when I had arrived the first day. Quite likely, therefore, nothing was hanging from it when my uncle was killed. If the hole was unobstructed, it's possible that someone had seen the murder and knew who did it. Quite possible, in fact. That was food for thought.

Time had passed. It was 9.30 a.m. I needed to attend the gram panchayat meeting and the BDO should have arrived with the train I had just heard. When I reached the old mango tree, there were only a few people there and no BDO. I suggested that Babu, who was sitting idle, could go around the village to remind the council members that they were expected. He objected. He could do it, of course, but he already had a job with me whereas his friend Roshan was in desperate need of a little income. Babu's remark shamed me. I had seen Roshan

Ali once or twice since I had arrived in Palanpur. He was a poor wretch, and looked sick and weak. I had honestly thought that he had died.

'Never,' replied Babu, looking offended, 'I take care of him.'

This is how I learned that I was certainly not the only one helping people in Palanpur. Babu, deemed rather useless by most, was helping someone whose existence I had overlooked, busy as I was with my own worries. A good lesson. As I now look back at my stay, I am embarrassed by my preconceived ideas about how my presence would help the villagers of Palanpur. We travel with our bag of prejudices, even when we travel light. This does not mean that I was not occasionally used by one Palanpuri or another. I was. But being used and directly helping are two different things. In addition, there was my simplified view of the village. A lot of things were happening that I simply had no clue about. Like it or not, I was never really part of Palanpur's life despite my family connection. How do you help in these circumstances? The reality was that throughout my stay in Palanpur, I had been a catalyst and that was a far cry from the highly satisfying belief held by so many visitors that they are the ones making a difference. Perhaps more than a pure catalyst—a catalyst makes the reaction happen but comes out unscathed—because the Palanpur experience changed me.

Roshan was sent around to announce the meeting and I went for a walk. At 10.15 a.m., I met Kumar Singh outside the school—it was empty, Smita was not there—and, realizing what time it was, I told him we should hurry. He quietly replied that the meeting was scheduled 'Indian time,' and that anyway the BDO had not yet turned up. At 10.30, we reached the tree with another farmer called Sundar Singh who joined us on the way. There were only two other persons near the tree, both complaining about the lack of interest in this meeting. After a little discussion, we decided to come back when the BDO turned up, which he did just as we were going away at 11. The grey-haired man recognized me and was quite courteous. Roshan was sent again to round up the council members. Tea was served as more villagers joined, and by 11.30, the meeting started, with about ten villagers present: Bhagpal, Sundar Singh, Kumar Singh, Kishan Lal, Basant, Nand Lal, and a few more. Babu was also there, of course. The discussion proceeded rather smoothly, especially because the BDO announced that government subsidies were available to repair the school if the villagers were ready to contribute matching funds. The gram panchayat decided to take advantage of this and collect the necessary matching contributions from the villagers. That was the tricky part. After discussion, it was more or less agreed—although not firmly decided—that each household would pay ten rupees; fifteen if they possessed a plough; and twenty-five rupees if they were a member of the gram panchayat. Under strong pressure from everybody, headman Rampal reluctantly agreed to contribute one hundred rupees, but after that, he remained silent for quite a while, looking like a man who has lost his last bullock. Except for that, there was no major argument. In principle, the contributions would add up to 2,500 rupees. I asked whether the poor members of the gram panchayat would be able to pay the twenty-five rupees, but one member exclaimed that if they were poor, they would not be members in the first place! I volunteered to add another 2,500 rupees as a donation. People were quite thankful. Another source of income was found in the form of a big tree, called the panchayat tree because meetings used to be held there. It was due to be felled, after a long life, and its value was estimated at about 2,500 rupees.

Funnily, and much to my surprise, Rampal insisted that I should take charge of the accounts, arguing that the villagers did not trust him, for reasons that he did not fully comprehend and therefore preferred not to elaborate upon. I agreed, but on the condition that no wage labour would be employed from outside Palanpur on this scheme. After all, I had been trained at the LSE in labour economics and I had learned about the ills of market distortions. Rampal argued—and all agreed—that there should be an exception for a few skilled masons who would come from outside because there were none in Palanpur. I reluctantly agreed: these skilled workers were probably needed and would not excessively disturb the village economy or create jealousy. Could my focus on distortions be misplaced?

Once this was over, the BDO announced that a recent government order required the gram panchayat to have at least one female member. Since the Palanpur panchayat had no Muslim member either, someone suggested inducting Barkatiya, a witty Muslim woman. She was also illiterate, which Rampal felt was a good thing. Barkatiya was called at once and the BDO gave her a rather confused briefing about her responsibilities, made even more confusing by constant interruptions from other members. Barkatiya was nevertheless convinced and put her thumb impression in the gram panchayat register. Finally, the council decided to convene a gram sabha at 7 p.m. that night to decide on the exact nature of the work to be done on the school. For such an important business, the whole village had to be invited. That would help make the proposal more relevant.

Everybody was in a good mood. I felt happy, too. Things had gone very well and the village residents had kindly agreed to contribute amounts commensurate with their means. These amounts, so it had been decided, would be collected within two days and the BDO had been adamant that official counterpart funds would come quickly from the ADO after approval from the CDO, the DDO, and perhaps a few others. The ball was in the court of the village, but I was hopeful that Smita would soon be able to teach in a well-refurbished school. What a nice day! The BDO took this opportunity to walk around the village while farmers returned to their fields. He left by the 3 p.m. train.

At 7 p.m. most people were still in the fields. By 8, only a few had come back, so Rampal and I decided to part and reconvene at 9. We sent Roshan door to door to announce the new time. Around 8.45, there was a big sandstorm. I concluded that the meeting was cancelled and, after the storm subsided, I had dinner. At 10, Rampal knocked at my door, saying that people were waiting. That was a nice surprise and I rushed to the spot. I found eight or nine villagers sitting there with more coming in. We all waited for another half hour. By then, we were about fifty and Rampal felt that this was good enough to start. The expectation that meetings are likely to be cancelled or start hours late is naturally self-fulfilling and rounding people up at a given time seemed more challenging than convincing them to contribute funds.

Much to my annoyance, just as Rampal was about to start, Brahmachari appeared. I did not expect him at all. I expected even less to hear Rampal ask Brahmachari to make the case for repairing the school. I was furious and argued that Smita should at least be part of the discussion. Rampal replied in a dignified tone that Smita had just arrived in the village and she had no reason to participate in the gram sabha.

'But Brahmachari is not from here either,' I exclaimed, 'and neither am I!'

That argument did not get any traction. I decided to keep quiet and tried to take comfort in the thought that, if the school project went ahead, I had no reason to object. Brahmachari spoke pompously, stressing the importance of the sacred texts and the need to educate boys in such matters.

I was shocked again when Rampal asked if the temple did not need fixing. Still, I managed to remain calm.

Brahmachari agreed with a pious look. The gods would be thankful and bless the village. A bit of money spent on the temple would surely be auspicious for the harvest and deflect calamities which, members of the gram panchayat acknowledged, was an important side benefit.

I soon realized that the audience would not disagree with Rampal and his partner. That was how it was and how it had always been. A very long discussion followed, but I never sensed much support for my views. Once again, I did not feel that I should go on objecting. In fact, the discussion led to nothing constructive. Many were talking but nobody listened. Phool Singh, Net Singh, and Bhoore Singh made passionate but useless and—worse—endless speeches about the need to be careful. Just as I was hoping the attention would return to Smita's school, Rampal brought up the possibility of financing a road from the pond to the temple. I could not resist pointing out that the road would mostly provide him with a convenient access to his fields. He looked deeply offended and stressed the need for drainage: everybody could use that road and drainage was important. The discussion resumed and, step by step, people started agreeing that the funds should be used first for the temple, and second for the road. Finally, after the Bhatnagar family made a strong case for it, the council remembered to include the school as a third item, and to allow girls to attend.

Enraged, I threatened to withdraw my offer of Rs 2,500, but Rampal reminded me that this offer had been recorded in the minutes of the gram panchayat and that I had promised to draft a letter to the ADO based on the decisions of the council.

Grudgingly, I nodded.

At night, I felt discouraged and tempted to give up. Only a few hours had passed since the BDO had left after what I thought had been an excellent meeting. In this short period of time, things had become very murky. My banker's instincts were telling me there would be nothing left for Smita's school. On reflection, however, I thought of an alternative approach. I would advance another Rs 2,000 on behalf of the village, to be reimbursed after the sale of the old panchayat tree. Or never, who could know? This would raise the contribution of the village to a total of Rs 5,000 + Rs 2,000, and if we were lucky, the government would provide a matching grant of about Rs 20,000 at least, as the BDO had indicated. With careful use of Rs 27,000, it would be possible to fix the school and build the new temple as well as a little road that would start from the pond. I had to admit that drainage was important and that I should not let myself be biased because of Smita. Maybe things would not be that bad. Overall, I probably had to accept that the plan made by the village council had its own rationale. One of its positive aspects was that undertaking these various projects would likely minimize frictions among Palanpuris while preserving the chances of approval by the ADO.

The next day, I drafted the proposal, discussed it with just about everyone I met and started collecting the money and signatures. People tended to agree with the proposal but less so with the need to give money. And where were the 100 rupees promised by the chief? After a lot of coaxing, I managed to collect only a few contributions. I decided to tackle the problem and went to Rampal with my proposal document and arguments for the swift deposit of his own contribution. He too was more inclined to discuss the former than the latter.

Nevertheless, he promised to pay very soon and expressed his own despair at the lack of enthusiasm on the part of the panchayat members, except the newly appointed Barkatiya, who had paid in full. He promised he would talk to the other members. I should at least get their endorsement—if not the money—early enough to catch the train for Chandausi the next morning. Unfortunately, he would be busy at the market. I could find him there if his signature was required, but, regretfully, he would not be able to accompany me to the ADO due to unavoidable reasons and would take a later train.

Chapter 14

Palanpur, 1984

The next morning, I went to see Kishan Lal and requested him to accompany me to the ADO. Most of my fields had been cleared and Babu would take care of the final touches. Since headman Rampal was not available, I wanted to have a witness with me—one never knew—as well as someone familiar with Indian administrative procedures.

Kishan Lal did not like the idea, but I insisted, 'Please buy two tickets and wait for me on the platform, I may be a little late.'

I resumed my round of the village, asking for contributions to the fund and the endorsement of the panchayat members. Again, realities took over: in spite of Rampal's genuine efforts—psychological more than financial at this stage—it was very difficult to get the money and the signatures. Each person required an increasingly shorter yet firmer argument. As for the money, I ended up with 750 rupees instead of the target of 2,500 rupees. The Bhatnagar family had paid up but most of the other contributions came from the Dalits and the Muraos, although they too—like everybody else—wondered why they should pay if Rampal did not. I had anticipated this situation, so I had enough cash with me to compensate for the Thakurs' stinginess. Time spent arguing passes quickly and, when I heard the train's whistle, I was at the other end of the village. I ran back to the station but would have missed the train had a helpful hand not helped me aboard. It was not Kishan Lal's hand, though, I could see his worried face at the window of the next coach. I jumped in.

'My friend, what a pleasure,' exclaimed the Good Samaritan.

'Good morning, Captain,' I said, resigned. 'Thank you for helping me.'

The Captain lifted his right hand to convey that it was only natural, waved the left one to shoo away the person sitting in front of him, and invited me to sit down.

'I hear that you are involved in construction projects in Palanpur. I would not have expected that from you.'

I gave him an annoyed look that was correctly interpreted by the Captain, but he shook his head in a casual gesture indicating that things were very simple. 'The BDO is a friend of mine and he told me about his meeting here. He was surprised to see you but understood that you were eager to support—how shall I put it?—infrastructure development in Palanpur. It is very nice of you. I also heard from someone that you wanted to go to Chandausi this morning to initiate the application for the government grant. I looked for you on the platform. You were late. I was quite concerned that you would not make it.'

'I'm really touched. But it is not one project for the village. There are three, actually.'

The Captain nodded and smiled, 'I know. You are very quick and quite efficient. Collecting so much money from poor villagers so quickly is unheard of.'

How could he possibly know that? The BDO had left when the decision had been taken. Reluctant to ask, I decided to bluff and retorted, happy to nail him for once, 'It is the Palanpuris who are efficient, Captain, not me. The three projects include repairing the school and the temple and building a road.'

The Captain raised his eyebrows, then smiled. Obviously, he did not think much of Palanpuri efficiency, 'One temple, one school and a road. This is amazing. And to think nobody had thought about doing all this before. In fact, it is unheard of in the whole of Moradabad District. Maybe in the whole of UP. This is very good. I am sure these projects will soon be completed. Things are usually slower in Palanpur. Even when they hire professional masons from the outside.'

I preferred to look elsewhere. It was true that there was something odd about this sudden outburst of construction plans. And he was right: the clause about masons had been included. Rampal had insisted a bit too much and now that I thought about it, it sounded strange. I would have preferred to be left in peace but the Captain was in a talkative mood, 'How is your photography project progressing? I hear you finally decided to visit the Dalit area. Did you find what you were looking for?'

I assured the Captain about the state of my project, showing him the rolls that I intended to leave at the studio in Chandausi. The Captain looked pleased but doubtful. I could not resist asking, 'You seem to know a lot. Who are you exactly?'

'What I told you. A retired Captain. But I still work for...the authorities. Let us talk a bit in Chandausi.'

I looked at the Captain. All traces of sarcasm had disappeared. He was looking concerned. We remained silent until Chandausi where we both climbed down and had tea while Kishan Lal waited impatiently outside the station. He would wait a bit longer. I learned that the Captain had been tasked by the authorities with identifying and bringing to justice a gang that had been operating between Chandausi and Moradabad for many years. They were involved in various criminal activities and he was accumulating the evidence necessary for a trial. The murder of my uncle was related to all this and, he regretted to inform me, my uncle was a member of that gang.

This was certainly true and I had found an undisputable proof of it. However, I decided to listen without revealing—for now—what I had discovered. For all I knew, the Captain could also be part of the gang. I preferred to test the waters, 'This Dalit lady, Neetu, did not commit the murder, then. And you know it.'

The Captain laughed. A sad laugh, 'Of course I know it. Everybody knows it. But there is no way to prove that she did not, unless...'

'Unless?'

'Unless we find the real culprit.'

'If we could find the shells of the bullets that killed my uncle, it would be helpful, right?' I asked.

The Captain smiled a bit, 'Yes, especially if your uncle's rifle is also found. I think everything is still in the house, well hidden.'

'The house has been searched thoroughly and nothing was found.'

'Nobody looked for the shells. If the police saw them, they did not care. They were looking for'—the Captain counted—'(thumb) money; (index) documents; and (middle finger) the rifle. They did not find anything. They argued that the old woman found the rifle at your uncle's house and shot him out of revenge. Then, she ran with it and hid it somewhere. Stupid! Some people must hope that she knows where he was hiding his money.'

'I found nothing, though.'

I had a feeling that the Captain did not quite take me seriously, but he simply replied, 'The point is if the rifle is found hidden at your uncle's home or nearby—in a place not accessible to Neetu, say—and if the cartridges do not correspond to the rifle, it will prove that she could not have done it. But, really, we should not worry about that. What matters is finding the real culprit and the rifle that killed your uncle.'

'And you are sure it could not have been my uncle's rifle?'

'People think that your grandfather had a very good but very old rifle. He apparently acquired it in strange and violent circumstances, years ago. There were plenty of bitter fights at that time and even a murder. Having said that, there is a very good chance that the bullets that killed your uncle will not fit his rifle. If that is the case, BKS will have to release Neetu. So you are right, if the shells and the rifle are found, it will be useful.'

'I have not found the rifle,' I admitted. 'And why should people be interested in an old rifle anyway?'

'Believe me, there should be interesting documents and some money too somewhere in the house. Mostly, it is the money, I think. Some people are also fascinated by rifles in these parts. Maybe you will find that rifle. And maybe you already found the shells,' he added with a smile that made me uneasy.

I pretended to ignore the smile, 'Okay, I will look again. In the meantime, what else do I do?'

'Keep taking pictures. And since you are in charge of keeping the purse for the construction projects, make sure at least that the people who contribute get something out of it. And be careful,' he warned.

We parted on these words. It was becoming increasingly clear I was being used. For a good purpose? A bad one? Some good and some bad? I would need to disentangle all this and, in doing so, be very careful indeed. I did well to keep the shells to myself.

I found Kishan Lal waiting for me outside the station, quite irritated at all this time wasted. I tried to pacify him, and we rushed to the court area in order to get the letter addressed to the ADO typed up. This was done by an important-looking fat man with a huge drooping moustache, dressed in an impeccably white dhoti and kurta. At first, I thought his thick fingers would not be able to slip the three sheets of paper separated by two carbons into the old Remington typewriter, but he managed it. Then I feared that he would struggle to hit the narrow keys, but he managed that too. The final product, consisting of one original and two carbon copies, was very good.

We then looked for Rampal. We found him buying a large ready-made plastic sheet. He explained that his youngest child, Jagpal, was wetting the bed at night. He would spread the sheet on the boy's bed so that it didn't get wet. After the scene with Chunni and his son Rakesh the previous day, I realized that such sheets might be needed in some other houses as well. Rampal signed the letter and accompanied us to the bank to deposit the money into the panchayat account—that was done very quickly. He asked if I could sign the document, allowing me to withdraw the money if need be, so that he would not have to come back to Chandausi later on for this. This seemed practical—I signed. As announced earlier, Rampal needed to go back to the market and return early, so he did not accompany us to the ADO. We would brief him on our return. Armed with the receipt, the letter, and our high morale, Kishan Lal and I continued our courageous expedition through UP's administrative labyrinth.

We reached the ADO's office. He was not there but was expected soon. In the meantime, we had another chat with the BDO. He reassured us that, as soon as the proposal reached him, he would pass it on. The ADO would surely sanction the project and construction could start within days. That sounded very promising, but we waited for one hour and the ADO was yet to arrive.

I decided to leave Kishan Lal there and went to the studio. Its owner and I were becoming friends. As I handed over my latest rolls, he proudly showed me the brand-new Paterson tanks he had received and the various chemical solutions that were necessary to develop black-and-white negatives. This was great news. I could develop my rolls myself. But it would not be possible to make the prints because that would require a whole darkroom with an enlarger, so I asked to see his equipment. He had a cigar-shaped Krokus for medium-format negatives and a more modest looking Meopta for 35 mm. The Soviet influence had extended its grip all the way down to deep UP. The lenses were excellent, made by Schneider Kreuznach, respectively a 105 mm and a 50 mm. I was surprised that people in Chandausi would use medium-format cameras like Hasselblad or Bronica for their family pictures, but he explained that the Krokus was mostly used for shots taken with an old British Kershaw or a Soho Myna. I figured that I probably had a bit of time before the ADO came back—and Kishan Lal was there anyway—so I offered to help him reprint the pictures that Babu had given away at the station. He agreed and we did a good job together. The machines were good. I asked if he would let me use them if I still paid the normal rate. That would free him up for his other clients. Not that he had that many, but he liked to go out and shoot people with his camera, so he accepted. I took my pictures, purchased a Paterson with the chemicals and went back to the ADO's office.

Kishan Lal was waiting stoically. Just as I arrived, the BDO informed us that the ADO, unfortunately, would not be available that day and would only return to his office two days later due to unavoidable circumstances. I would need to come then. Meanwhile, I could leave the documents on the BDO's desk so that everything would be ready for the ADO, should he unexpectedly come to his office.'

On the way back, I had a difficult discussion with Kishan Lal. It had started on a promising note, though. He explained that the Muraos, unlike the Thakurs, did not resent my friendship with the Chamars. The Chamars had unclean habits like keeping pigs, and I had gone as far as accepting food from Babu. But still, the Muraos were not so perturbed about it. I learned that—it was absurd, obviously, Kishan Lal hastily added—there were two different suppositions: I was after Babu's recently arrived cousin; or after Roshan's wife. I preferred not to comment on Smita but answered—truthfully—that I did not know Roshan was married. Later, I tried to find out whether these rumours were really floating around or simply a creation of Kishan Lal's mind. His deep-rooted honestly made me think that they were real. It could have been jealousy, perhaps because of my recent purchase of two bullocks.

Kishan Lal had a real issue though, one that was hurting him deeply. I had not been vigilant with money that did not belong to me. I had made the Muraos and the Dalits pay for the construction of a temple and a road, de facto subsidizing the rich Thakurs who did not pay. Did I understand that the funds would benefit not the poor but the rich, mostly the corrupt members of the village council? If I really wanted to spend money, my fields needed attention. Investing in them would have given a job to some poor labourers and would have been more useful. Or perhaps I liked to throw money away, but farmers in Palanpur could not afford to do so. Nor could they afford to go for several days without work. And poor farmers should never pay for rich ones.

'Well,' I countered, 'at least you agree that repairing the school will be useful.'

'Useful for whom? It will be repaired by masons working for shady contractors.'

He was talking like the Captain and also like Babu when he and I had first walked to Palanpur from Akroli. They all had a point and I promised to make sure, just like the Captain had urged, that the money would be well used. Meanwhile, lacking counter-arguments, I changed the topic. Since the best way to find out about someone in Palanpur was to ask someone else, I asked Kishan Lal, the Murao, about the mysterious Pitamber, the Thakur. I learned that he had been a bold headman who had been a colonel in the army and therefore become a celebrity in the village. He was known for liking—Kishan Lal blushed and hesitated—women. Rampal and Phool Singh were his sons. My uncle himself used to call the current headman Pitamber from time to time, because he was also seen in places of ill repute, squandering money. Of all the sins that could be committed in such houses, wasting money appeared to horrify Kishan Lal the most.

Then, there was the way Pitamber died. That topic was taboo and Kishan Lal would not give me details. However, I deduced that it had happened in shameful circumstances that had something to do with women of ill repute as well.

Kishan Lal had more sympathy for Phool Singh, lazy as he was. In spite of having studied, he was considered intellectually and physically weak. There had been some hope that he would join the army, but he could not manage it in spite of his superior education. And I already knew that Phool Singh had not taught much when he was in charge of the village school with Brahmachari, although he was the appointed teacher. This revived my fears that things could go wrong with the school project. Kishan Lal continued, explaining that when Pitamber had died, it was clear that only Rampal had the stomach to take charge of the farm. He later became headman himself. Rampal would have loved to join the army, but circumstances had not permitted it.

'Is Rampal corrupt like all the other village heads, then, or more?'

Kishan Lal frowned, 'Many headmen have been corrupt but, as for Rampal, how would I know? Not more than others, I would say. At least, not much more.'

He then echoed my own views, 'When they become heads, they forget their values.'

The conversation then turned to Hukum. Kishan Lal confirmed he had the same character as Phool Singh. A little more determined and honest, though. He was weak but had studied to become a teacher. Rampal had placed a lot of hope in him, especially after the boy had managed to learn how to read and write in spite of the poor learning environment created by Brahmachari and Phool Singh in Palanpur.

'Hope for what?' I asked.

'Hope that he would join the army, of course. Rampal has many friends in the army and the police. Hukum might have become a sergeant.'

I smiled. 'Is Rampal friends with BKS, then?'

'Best of friends. BKS's father was from Palanpur. But he was not a Thakur, nor a Murao. He was...'

Kishan Lal fell silent. I filled the gaps, 'a dangerous man.'

I looked at Kishan Lal. That was not what he was planning to say, so I dug a little deeper.

Reluctantly, and speaking very softly, Kishan Lal finally uttered, 'BKS's father was a guy called Bhupal. People say that he is the one who murdered my father, Rajesh.'

Who said that Palanpur was boring? Shocked by the casual tone of the accusation, I resumed the probe, 'Why would Bhupal have done that?'

'It was very complicated. There was the story of a rifle that had disappeared and my father had also caused some harm to that man, so he took his revenge.'

I tried to find out more, but to no avail. In Kishan Lal's view, his father, though hard-working, had often tried to do things that were not for people like him. He had aspirations that were not proper. God's hand had punished him for that and Bhupal had only been his instrument.

I gave up. Hopefully, my father's notes would shed some light on these past events. As soon as we got down from the train in Palanpur, Kishan Lal ran to his farm while I walked to my field. Surprise! Babu had done the work and, as I discovered a little later, my bullocks were quietly waiting for me at home. That, in addition to the promise of speedy action by the ADO and the time spent developing film in the studio, had put me in a good mood and I decided to shelve my suspicions about Rampal and Brahmachari's intentions. Later, I briefed Rampal and we agreed that I would go to Chandausi two days later to push the proposal through. Then, we went together to

Rajinder Singh's house, where Brahmachari had come with a friend of his, a sadhu from Haridwar. He was telling stories from the epics, interspersed with short chants. Neighbours and relatives had joined in large numbers. We were enthralled for the whole evening, thanks to simple and harmless activities, without any kind of stimulants, or even cigarettes. This admirable and harmonious scene revealed yet another side of Palanpur.

After this excitement, I found it difficult to sleep and went back to my father's notes.

Palanpur, 1914

For a few years, everything went as smoothly as one could hope for: no railway strike, no unrest in the province, no famine, no disease, flood or drought of significant magnitude. These were years of abundance, so the zamindar made no serious attempt to recover the principal of his loans. He was quite happy to collect the interest year after year without hassle.

The only loan that created an issue was the couple of annas received by Dukhi at the time of her performance. Radha had insisted that Dukhi should repay, with interest and in full. His heart objecting to this, Ashok had managed to delay the recovery for one reason or another. To be fair, the main reason was practical: the money rightfully—or so he thought—belonged to him, but he knew that it would go to his wife. Helped by the lukewarm support of the chief, Dukhi was resisting.

Things changed for the worse after Dukhi's new husband was killed. The loss of a second husband after the birth of a mixed-race child clearly demonstrated that she was a source of bad luck. Left with no resources and two children to feed, Dukhi needed money. She first approached her principal employer. Radha explained that as a proper wife she was leaving such matters in the hands of her more capable husband. However, Radha reminded Dukhi that she still owed the two annas plus interest and that the debt was growing. She also mused that she could hardly be held responsible if Hemming had not proposed to marry Dukhi. Everything had been perfectly planned. Did Dukhi fail in some way? Dukhi had also been disappointed but, used to a life where good things were few and far between, she had tried to forget her nights with Hemming. She made some apologetic noises and retired. Radha later warned her husband: under no circumstances should he lend money to Dukhi. If he had extra money, she, Radha, could use it quite well on herself or their lovely Pitamber. If that was too much to ask from a father, Ashok could also use any extra money to pay back a portion of that silly debt to the zamindar that seemed to keep growing.

Impressed with his wife's logic and feeling a trifle guilty as a father, Ashok agreed. It was true that the small debt to Gavendra seemed to be growing as fast as Pitamber. He decided to complain to the lender himself, his friend the zamindar. Gavendra received Ashok but looked important, somehow less friendly, perhaps because the henchmen were watching closely. He reminded the chief that he had been late with his payments and it was only because the zamindar was of the caring type that he did not make a big issue of it.

Swiftly the zamindar became friendly again. He took the chief by the arm, 'Do you think I would cheat you, my brother?'

That manoeuvre upgraded their friendship. Impressed and pleased, Ashok agreed to everything that the zamindar demanded and went back home. It was Radha who pointed out that he came back empty-handed. She made it forcefully clear, so, when Dukhi approached Ashok a few days later for a few annas, he rebuffed her and suggested that she try her luck with his friend—almost his brother, he added—Gavendra.

Desperate, Dukhi went to the zamindar. The important man was very sweet to her. Of course, he had appreciated her successful efforts with the Englishman. The whole village—the zamindar first and foremost—was still very thankful. Of course, he regretted that she had borrowed money from Radha and needed more for the family. He understood the difficult position she was in. But she had been paid very well at the time of Hemming's visit and had probably been careless. Dukhi was telling him that none of the money had reached her, while both Ashok and the henchman had assured him that the money had reached the intended recipients at all steps of the chain. Ashok—almost a brother—was a chief who would not lie, would he? And Gavendra had complete trust in Bhupal. On the other hand, Dukhi had a poor reputation—undeserved, certainly—that did not speak in her favour. Besides, how could he lend money to someone who, by her own account, was without resources?

Desperate, Dukhi started crying, burying her face in her hands. Then the zamindar showed some empathy. He came close, very close, and put his arm around her shoulders. He whispered in her lovely ears. She should forget his role as Gavendra the zamindar. He was a man too, a good and understanding person. But the understanding should be mutual. Was Dukhi ready to understand the needs of a man who sometimes felt so lonely? Just like Dukhi. Was she not lonely as well? The difference was that he was, after all, an old man, who would do no great harm. At the most, he might get a bit of pleasure, if at all. And give some too, perhaps.

Dukhi was taken aback. She realized that the henchmen had disappeared, discreetly sent away by their boss. She was alone with the old man who was pressing his body against hers. She stood up like a furious cat, spitting her anger.

The zamindar knew how to handle furious borrowers and still extract the most from them. He felt furthermore that he was offering a fair deal: he had the money and Dukhi the body. Gavendra looked very sad, hurt. How could his empathy, his deep concern for a fellow human being in distress be so misinterpreted?

Dukhi cooled down a little. Maybe she had misread his intentions. The zamindar went on. His voice was a little drier. In order to give a loan, he would need collateral.

All along, Dukhi had expected and feared that moment. Very reluctantly, she pulled out the small ring Hemming had given her. Would that do?

My grandfather took a look at the ring. It would fetch fifteen or twenty rupees in Moradabad. He calculated quickly. Too small a loan and Dukhi would perhaps manage to repay: he would lose the ring. Too high and it would be a waste of money. He offered five rupees. Quite a profit and there was no way Dukhi would ever be able to repay it. A perfect deal, he thought. He prepared the document. It stated that Dukhi had received ten rupees and left a ring as a deposit. She would have to repay sixteen rupees after the harvest—he told her she would have to repay eight. Should she fail to do so, the same rate would apply, and she would owe him twenty-five rupees and sixty paisa after the following harvest. That would exceed the value of the ring and he would keep it.

Although not a man to neglect the smallest business opportunity, Gavendra would have preferred a good time with Dukhi rather than a small profit on the ring. Looking straight at Dukhi, he placed the ring near him and five rupees in coins. Did she want five rupees out of this ring? Or keep the ring and the five rupees? He said no more, letting her options sink in.

On the way back with her ring, Dukhi's walk was mechanical. Had she been the suicidal type, and without two kids to take care of, she would very well have jumped for good into the pond where she bathed. She did not. The money gave a bit of relief. Just a bit. George noticed a new, persistent sadness in the eyes of his mother.

In 1914, Pitamber, Rajesh, and George were about four years old, although nobody knew their age for sure. They were living reasonably peaceful lives by Palanpur standards, but that was about to change because a lunatic killed an archduke somewhere in Europe.

Soon, the word went around that the British were fighting against other white people. That caused a great deal of surprise, but the villagers soon observed the effect of the war. Ashok, during a meeting of impressed elders, revealed that about one lakh soldiers had left Bareilly and gone to cold places in Europe to help the British. He had heard that from Gavendra and had seen many soldiers huddled in the passing trains, more scared of crossing the black waters than of fighting the Germans. One lakh was probably an exaggeration. This was also a meaningless number for most farmers in Palanpur, but it helped them, including Ashok, to grasp the scale of the problem. India as a whole had sent ten lakh men. Many did not come back.

One of the Palanpur elders asked a brilliant question that was regretfully not given its due importance: Why do the British need us? They are so powerful. And if their enemy is even more powerful, what can we do? Ashok, who did not know the answer, ignored the question as all skilful politicians routinely do. And since nobody could answer it, the question was brushed aside, at least in Palanpur. But the same question was asked in other circles, less loudly, but more forcefully. It introduced the germ of an illness that would eventually undermine the British rule a few years later, as it did for Belgian and French rule—and indeed English rule—in Africa years later, at the time of the Second World War.

The First World War left another dramatic trace in India, including in Palanpur. Beyond the deaths in the battlefield, those who survived the trenches brought back with them a disease that killed many more.

'One lakh,' a horrified Ashok cried again, overwhelmed at the thought of the Palanpuris who died in their fields or at home and the many bodies, all twisted, the skin blackened by the disease, unceremoniously thrown from moving trains.

This was an exaggeration again. Many died of the Spanish influenza, but one cannot really know the number and Palanpuris did not keep a count of their own dead. Then, one day, people stopped dying of influenza. No horrible dead bodies were thrown from the trains anymore. It was over. Palanpuris continued to die, but at the usual rhythm and from other causes. Life went on.

Chapter 15

Palanpur, 1984

I got up early and took stock of the situation over breakfast. The letter to the ADO was in the right hands and there was nothing more to do there. Pat would arrive in two days, and she would help with the murder investigation. I knew she would. She often saw things that I did not see. The Captain—he seemed to be genuine—wanted me to find the cartridges and the rifle. I had two of the shells, not the third one. And neither the money nor the rifle, even though I had the book of accounts. I had to admit that I was a bit lost.

To give myself a break, I decided to spend the day working on the 'nature' aspects of my photography project: the flowers, the fields, some wild animals maybe. I would go around the village with my camera, shooting everything that appealed to me, and hoping that Kishan Lal and Babu were taking care of my field. I was also hoping to take pictures of nilgais roaming the fields. Preferably from a distance—they were dangerous—so I selected the powerful 400 mm Novoflex. That lens has a pistol grip that changes the focus on squeezing. It is unbelievably fast. I also took the Tamron and, thus loaded, I departed. I had been walking for five minutes or so and was coming out of the village when, behind me, loud cries attracted my attention. I turned around, aimed the camera and took a few pictures of a ferocious-looking Jagpal, the incontinent eight-year-old son of Rampal. He was brandishing a khurpi, probably trying to imitate one of the heroes he had seen in a movie. After a few shots, I turned my lens slightly to the right and discovered that the kid was actually threatening a young girl. Letting the camera dangle on my chest, I rushed to the scene and took great pains to remove the khurpi from Jagpal's hands. I had to be careful: the boy was resisting and a khurpi can be sharp. I gave the khurpi to a woman who was standing nearby and went away while the kids began pulling each other's hair, something less life-threatening. Soon, I heard alarming noises again. I rushed back: the khurpi was in Jagpal's hands for the second time and he was being even more aggressive. The mother of the girl suddenly turned up like a typhoon. She rushed at Jagpal, took the khurpi, and started beating him ruthlessly. This enraged the boy, who tried to retaliate by throwing stones. He was not strong enough though and, realizing this, ran away crying and cursing aloud. At least, the situation was under control.

It was written somewhere that the day would not be peaceful. A little later, I witnessed another scary scene. A Murao farmer called Mullo was about to be trampled by his own furious bullock. He barely escaped by grasping the beast by the nostrils and hanging from them with all his weight. I thought Mullo had the upper hand and I took a few pictures. Then, I realized that both man and beast were stuck in that position. It was a very uneasy equilibrium. Once again, I let the camera down and went closer. I prudently grabbed the rope attached to the neck of the animal and managed to tie it to a tree. Mullo immediately jumped to his feet, grabbed a rod and started beating the animal mercilessly. Palanpuris are used to a tough environment. Their general kindness and hospitality should leave one with no illusion that they can be quite ruthless too. It is not for me to judge. My banking environment is also ruthless, although not in that raw way. But then, a banker's smile should not give the client any illusion that he has a friend.

The wheat harvest was now in full swing and kept people busy. Not far from my uncle's fields, a whole family of Muraos was busy harvesting and threshing. They thresh by beating thick bundles of wheat three or four times against a heavy wooden beam, a method that seemed effective. They had been there since early morning, would presumably have their lunch on the spot, and go back home at dusk. Threshing in that way generates clouds of dust that look different depending on the position of the sun. I stayed there for a while and did not regret it. The family had brought a she-buffalo who was expecting. I had the good fortune of seeing the calf being born right there in the midday sun.

The birth of the calf had taken quite a bit of time. I got up and realized that it was too late to shoot a nilgai. It was better to go back to the village. At the Seed Store, I would fix up my dinner with Govindi. As I walked on the path towards the building, my attention was caught by a Mahindra police jeep parked in front of the school. I had seen the same vehicle at the Chandausi police station and recognized it because the little pole holding the official flag was slightly bent. There was no one around, but I could hear some voices coming from inside the school. I moved a little closer, very carefully, and peered in using the Novoflex like a telescope.

I discovered BKS in a heated discussion with Smita. He seemed to object to her presence in Palanpur and was threatening her. I could only hear a few words.

'...repair. This building does not need repair. Good enough for Chamar kids...'

'...trying to help...kids...read and write...'

'Chamar kids do not need to read or write. The others.... Who needs a Chamar teacher?'

Smita was trying to put on a brave front but I could see that she was scared. The bully was insisting, pushing her as he moved around the room. I was about to intervene when I noticed that someone else was also observing the scene. From the distance, I could not recognize the man. I withdrew discreetly and went around the building. High grass kept me invisible. I settled in a convenient spot and observed what was going on, taking pictures with the telelens of the increasingly violent argument. I was cursing—mentally—the noise made by the camera, but everyone was too busy to hear it. I finished the roll and loaded another as quickly as I could. At one point, BKS pushed Smita against a table and started unbuckling his pants. I was already putting my camera down to run when the man who had been watching the scene stood up and rushed inside. Taking pictures was the best thing I could do, so I quickly refocused the lens and started shooting again. The newcomer was Hukum, the son of Rampal Singh—I could see him clearly by then—the one who had studied useless things according to his father. This time, he did not look meek at all. He was rushing, holding a wooden stick that did not look very strong to me. No surprise, wood was in short supply in Palanpur.

BKS, his fat behind exposed, suddenly realized someone was behind him. He tried to turn around but, with his pants around his ankles, he tripped. It was too late in any case. With a swift movement, Hukum brought the stick down on his head. The stick broke. BKS was stunned but he did not fall. He tried to move towards his aggressor but finally stumbled to the floor. Hukum helped Smita up and would have hit BKS again if she had not stopped him. BKS was struggling to get off the floor and his erection was quickly waning. It was rather modest, I thought. A modest erection in a big fat bully like BKS is very satisfying, so I took a few extra pictures for future use. Finally, BKS stood up and buckled his belt. Then, the struggle quickly turned in his favour. He grabbed Hukum and punched him. Hukum fell. Smita, enraged, rushed towards the policeman, but he pushed her aside with a single blow. Even more furious, BKS kicked Hukum again and dragged him to his vehicle. Soon, the Mahindra left. I had gone on taking pictures: once developed, the prints would be proof of what had happened in the absence of other witnesses. That is when I felt a gentle touch on my shoulder. Babu was next to me. 'It is often like that with the police,' he said, sadly.

'I will get these photos printed, and BKS will go to jail,' I said, furious, as we rushed to Smita.

'Now, it is Hukum who is in jail for attacking a policeman,' observed Babu, 'not only my mother. They will give him hell, even though he is Rampal's son.'

We had entered the school. Smita was in tears. I had naturally thought that she would run to me for comfort, but she held Babu instead and sobbed in his arms.

That was how I learned that Hukum was a friend of Smita's. They had studied together in Moradabad and shared the common goal of improving standards of education in the village. It was not clear why BKS had come to the old Palanpur school. Maybe because there had been another train robbery and he suspected that some of the loot had been hidden near the school, as sometimes happened.

'I heard a few things about this BKS bastard in Palanpur,' I said loudly.

'Of course,' said Babu, confirming what Kishan Lal had already told me. 'We all know about him. He is the grandson of a prostitute and another bastard from the village who was called Bhupal. A Murao, but a corrupt one. People say BKS is close to the dacoits. They are his friends.'

I had suspected that, and it added another dimension: perhaps BKS had come because the proposal to repair the school could deprive his dacoit friends of a hideout for shady activities.

'I'll get these pictures developed and they will be proof of what happened,' I repeated firmly. 'We will get him that way.'

Smita looked at me with her wet eyes. 'The studio will never give you these pictures. The photographer will claim something happened and that they got spoiled. Too dangerous for him. And for you too.'

That was indeed a problem, but it could perhaps be dealt with.

'Of course,' she continued, 'if we could get these pictures it would be helpful. But don't get involved in this. If you do get those pictures developed, just give them to Babu. He will know what to do and when. It is our fight.'

She was probably right, although her faith in Babu seemed exaggerated. Still, there were a few things that I could do, 'Let us keep the existence of these pictures secret for the time being. I will get them developed and nobody will know about it. We shall see what to do with them later.'

As I should have expected, Rampal already knew about his son. That was obvious from the commotion that was happening at his house. I peeked from outside and saw him furiously waving his rifle while other household members kept a safe distance. He was screaming at everybody and rambling against BKS, Hukum, the Chamars, the school, and what not. Brahmachari was there and seemed worried. I also saw young Veena silently holding her crying mother in a corner. Poor Shakuntala was devastated. I withdrew quietly. This was not the time to discuss anything.

On the way back, I learned that Mahipal Singh's little daughter had died. A few days earlier, I had noticed her extreme weakness and dehydration. I'd thought she would recover. She had not.

Back home, I put another cassette of Pink Floyd in the two-in-one: *The Wall*. Ironic! I was in a place where kids should not be left alone and really needed an education. Then I lay down on the charpoy and lit a cigar. At least, it dispelled the smell of that junk in the corner. And the music covered the noise made by the billy goat. The day had been eventful. The more I learned about Palanpur, the more I had to agree with Smita and even with the Captain: my place was elsewhere. The Captain! He was right. If I could find the rifle, it would be so helpful. Even with only two shells out of three. Perhaps I was the only one who could find it. But where on earth could it be?

I observed the evolving shapes created by the grey smoke of the cigar. Talk to the Dalits, the Captain had said. I had done that and learned a few things. I had talked to the others too. Rampal, for example. What would he do now that his son had been put in jail by his friend BKS? And what was Brahmachari up to, really?

I took a few more puffs of the cigar. I had settled in this second room, preferring not to sleep where my uncle had been killed. That room had become my office. The hideout was behind the charpoy in my bedroom. The charpoy for guests, in a way. I took another deep puff and it suddenly dawned on me that I should take a closer look at the other room. The one where my uncle had been staying. If there was a hideout next to the charpoy on which I was lying, was it not likely...

I got up. I searched a little and soon discovered another hideout, much larger than the one in my room. In it—somehow, I already knew—there was an old rifle, a sealed box presumably containing cartridges, about two lakhs in cash, some gold—not much—and some more documents. I reflected a bit, then took the gold, the cash and the papers, and put them in the other hideout next to my charpoy. They fit easily. As for the rifle, it was a beautiful piece. The wood surrounding the barrel was superbly polished and the movements of the breech were smooth. I quickly checked whether the two shells I had found fit it. They were much too small. Rampal had said something about the cartridges: his rifle was a smaller calibre. That was it. I put the rifle where I had found them. I needed to think a little more about the best course of action.

Things were not getting much clearer, but I had more facts at my disposal. Another element was the photos, but it was better to develop the negatives later, when it was darker and with fewer people around.

I stood in front of the billy goat—at a safe distance—and looked around. In this bare environment, in this dilapidated house, there were three hiding places that I had only discovered by chance: two in the walls, and one—empty—in the furniture. Was there a fourth one? Possibly, since I had not found the gold that my uncle was rumoured to possess. It could also be hidden outside the property, but I did not think so. He kept his belongings near him. I gave some fodder to the billy goat, managing to avoid being hit, and reached for my father's notes.

Palanpur, 1917–1925

Rajesh's life was a model of austerity: he was expected to help his parents as soon as he grew up and the demands increased as he advanced in age. Playing with kids who were not Muraos was not encouraged and, even among Muraos, playing was considered a waste of time. He had better things to do. When he was young, he was told to eat and sleep. Later, he learned not to waste. He should also have learned not to take excessive risks or question the established order, but he was a rebel and the parents failed to curb his nature. Although hard-working—nobody denied that—he openly resented authority and objected increasingly strongly to his father's preferred answer: keep quiet, you should know your place! He thus earned the un-Muraolike reputation of being a trouble-maker. Rajesh, fortunately, had the good taste of muffling his screams when disciplined and the neighbours interpreted the sounds as normal and healthy punishment, earning his father a reputation of wisdom and restraint in the face of teenage disobedience.

To better understand the concerns of Rajesh's parents, it is necessary to relate a story that could have had disastrous implications for his family. One day, he took advantage of his father's absence to sneak back home from the fields. Straight-faced and looking important, he explained that the buffalo was needed in the field, an explanation that was accepted without discussion. Off they went, but not to the field. Rajesh wanted to take part in a buffalo race organized by other kids. He climbed on the animal—the family's main asset, fattened by years of tender loving care—and proudly joined them. During the race, Rajesh fell, viciously pushed by Pitamber who went on to win. Rajesh's buffalo—lighter without Rajesh—finished second but, no longer guided, kept running. Used to a path that it knew well, the animal ended, out of breath and traumatized, in the field where Rajesh's dad was working. A rapid check reassured the alarmed owner about the health of his treasured buffalo. A rapid check at home led him to the truth. Rajesh was punished without mercy for putting the family's financial future at risk. He was used to it, but the punishment was commensurate with the crime and he screamed a lot, amusing the neighbours.

His life soon took a turn for the worse, but for no fault of his this time. When the Spanish influenza epidemic broke out, Rajesh, decidedly a rebel, resisted. His father was less lucky: he fell in his field, one day of 1918, as he was trying to plough in spite of a persistent fever. The financial situation of the family soon became precarious. A distant cousin helped once or twice, but he was busy with his own work and was short of cash owing to some old debt. The mother had to face the situation alone. She was not prepared for that and had to rely on Rajesh for the bulk of the work. By the age of eight, a huge load of responsibilities fell on his frail shoulders. One learns quickly in such circumstances but not without making the odd mistake.

One such mistake almost wiped out the family. Rajesh knew that gambling was bad. He had been told many times but was fascinated by the game of chaupar. The players, surrounded by numerous advisors, used to sit near the deviation track. They would carefully spread the small carpet where squares had been beautifully embroidered to form a cross. The tokens would move from square to square, depending on the roll of the dice and the strategy of the players. Dice and tokens were kept in an old, nicely crafted wooden box carefully looked after by one of the players. They were usually Thakurs, those who had land and could afford to play. Bhupal, the Murao henchman, also took part from time to time. His participation was tolerated because he often acted as a banker and advanced money to the losers. The players were immersed in the game, always fighting, sometimes screaming. Rajesh loved the suspense. An intelligent boy, he had mastered the game and never hesitated to join the chorus of bystanders offering their views and comments. He was therefore considered a pest. One day, however, instead of threatening him, the players suggested that he join the game. Rajesh should have suspected that something was amiss, if only because Bhupal was among the players. Bhupal was still in open confrontation with the Muraos. Naively, Rajesh joined the game.

When four persons play chaupar, they form two teams of two. Unsuspecting Rajesh teamed up with one of the men—who he knew was a good player—against the other team that included Bhupal. Rajesh was given a few beans and the game started. Soon Rajesh grew irritated by the numerous mistakes made by his partner. He got really angry when he realized that his stock of beans had vanished.

'Don't worry,' interjected Bhupal with a benevolent smile, 'here are a few more.'

Those too were soon lost. Furious, Rajesh stood up and left. But he was soon caught by Bhupal who had run after him, 'Where is the money, boy?'

Rajesh understood in that minute two things that had escaped him about chaupar: the beans stood for real money and the players could cheat. He owed five rupees, Bhupal informed him while twisting his arm. A fortune! The other players joined Bhupal and started beating Rajesh. So did Rajesh's partner at chaupar, revealing that the invitation had been a trap.

Badly bruised, Rajesh went back home after promising to pay his debt the next day. After castigating her son, the mother courageously called on chief Ashok. He listened carefully: he had no sympathy for Bhupal and saw an opportunity to take revenge. He called the council of elders. It was clear that Rajesh had been framed. It also became clear that Bhupal had overdone it in the past, when lending money to the losers—including some elders who had kept a grudge. Ashok went to the zamindar with both pieces of information. One thing Gavendra hated was being cheated and not even knowing it was happening. That Bhupal, in the course of his missions for the zamindar, would keep some of the money he made was perfectly understandable. Natural, even. But this was another matter. The zamindar thought that there could possibly be some money for him in that chaupar business. It would be his in the future. Not Bhupal's, who needed to be taught a lesson. That saved Rajesh. A compromise was found: Rajesh would repay one rupee to the zamindar who knew he had no assets, and nothing to Bhupal who would leave Rajesh in peace. Ashok went back to the council of elders and informed them about the verdict. That day, he consolidated his reputation as a severe but fair judge, a true chief.

Rajesh sighed in relief but resented the contempt in Ashok's voice when he said that the young Murao was too poor to honour his obligations. He promised himself that, one day, he would be as rich as these arrogant elders. The other person who was not pleased was Bhupal. He brooded for a while and decided to settle scores by punishing, if not Rajesh, then one of the family members.

A few days later, sure that Rajesh's mother was alone at home, Bhupal sneaked in, shoved her to the floor and pushed her sari up. A few seconds later, he felt an excruciating pain in his backside. Alerted by a friend, Rajesh had rushed back and planted a knife in the most obvious—although moving—target. Swearing and bleeding, Bhupal ran away, yelling threats at Muraos in general without attracting any sympathy from anyone. Bhupal knew that the other henchmen would not help him: the zamindar had left strict instructions.

A few years passed. Having learned a valuable lesson about the evils of gambling, the turbulent Rajesh was ready for another. This one nearly cost him his life. Settlement regulations in Palanpur being nil, people built houses wherever they wanted. Rajesh's family had constructed its house at the very end of the Murao quarters of the village. The next house belonged to Sipahi Singh, my uncle who had been exiled to Palanpur. Most of the time, Sipahi was absent and the whole village suspected him of being involved in shady deals, and of having landed himself in jail. Or perhaps he was drunk somewhere. Rajendra Singh had died of alcoholism and Sipahi would undoubtedly share the same fate or be killed by someone. Savitri was living in reduced circumstances, with her son, daughter-in-law Lata, and their two girls, barely older than Rajesh: Radhika and Mallika. Gavendra had passed away some years earlier. His son, my father, Tikam Singh, who inherited the title of zamindar in 1923, decided to do nothing for his cousin. He was comfortable in Jargaon and preferred to keep Sipahi in Palanpur.

Lata, Mallika, and Radhika were petrified when Sipahi was away on dangerous errands, fearing for their future and livelihood. They were also terrified when he was at home because the evening would always end in a drinking binge. Sipahi would then beat up everybody, usually accusing Lata of being unable to produce a son. She would reply that she had produced a son already and that he should have cared for him like fathers normally do, instead of beating him senseless at the age of two, causing his death. And from there, the discussion would deteriorate.

In Rajesh's eyes, Sipahi had one redeeming quality. Her name was Mallika. Rajesh had always been aware of the girls next door, although he had paid no attention at first. One day, this dramatically changed. He had decided to chase a monkey who had stolen his mango. Ready for a duel, Rajesh carefully sneaked to the roof where the animal was enjoying the fruit. Just as he was about to strike, the monkey saw him and bounded away. Rajesh looked down but, instead of the monkey, discovered the most beautiful profile he had ever seen. In spite of the racket that Rajesh and the monkey had made, Mallika had not noticed Rajesh, only the monkey, so she had gone on with her own activities. Rajesh remained perfectly still, tantalized by the beautiful vision. Mallika suddenly lifted her eyes and saw Rajesh. The sun was high, blinding her. That gave time for Rajesh to smile rather awkwardly. She smiled back, then realized that the situation was embarrassing. She pulled her sari to cover her head and ran inside.

The next day, Rajesh climbed on the roof again, pretending to chase another monkey. The courtyard of the neighbours was empty, but soon Mallika came out. Rajesh overheard her explain that a particular vessel needed to be cleaned. He was delighted at the coincidence. Even when he heard the mother explain that that particular vessel did not require cleaning since it had not been used, he naively saw luck where there was strategy. It became routine: upon hearing a noise on the roof, Mallika would go out on one pretext or another and let herself be watched by Rajesh.

Rajesh saw a chance to deepen this relationship the day Radhika and Lata left to visit some relatives. Savitri had remained at home, but she was so old that it did not matter, thought Rajesh, who regarded anyone aged fifty or more as ancient. His own mother and the kids were busy. He jumped from the roof and landed in the courtyard. Mallika did not shout. On the contrary, she dragged Rajesh into a corner. In some matters, even when they do not have practical experience, girls know better than boys. They just brag less about it. Rajesh learnt about natural things that occur between men and women and enjoyed them. Prudent, he jumped back home as soon as it was over, which seemed to annoy Mallika.

The next day, since the rest of the family was still away, Rajesh jumped into their courtyard again. When he was about to leave, Mallika tried to hold him back. Surprised, Rajesh banged into a kadai that fell with a bang. Horrified, Mallika pushed Rajesh out.

Naked, his clothes in his hands, he climbed to the roof. Savitri came out but, with her poor eyesight, she was not sure what she had seen. Still, suspicious and protective of the girl's virtue, she felt compelled to report the matter to Sipahi. Mallika was duly interrogated by her father, and almost killed in the process, but she kept denying that anything had happened. It was just as well—Sipahi would have shot Rajesh's whole family.

Palanpur, 1984

I now knew more about Rajesh, and understood better Kishan Lal's comment about his father's character. It was late, very late. I listened carefully. There was no noise outside. I made sure that the holes were blocked. Slowly, I opened the back of the camera, took out the film, removed one cap of the metallic container, and loaded the film on the white spiral of the Paterson in complete darkness. I added the second exposed roll on a second spiral and screwed the top of the tank. I lit a few candles: light did not matter anymore. I poured the diluted Rodinal and waited, periodically shaking the tank. After a while, I rinsed, then poured in the stop bath, rinsed again, then poured in the fixer. Ten minutes later, I rinsed everything again. It was all good. Once both rolls were dry, I carefully tucked the negatives into plastic boxes and put them in the hideout.

Going past the mirror, I smiled at myself. Everything was set but put on hold. The next day, I would simply go to Chandausi to clinch the school project and I would be back in time to welcome Pat who would arrive on the afternoon train. It was time to sleep, but I found it rather strange to live, and soon sleep, in the very place where Rajesh, Kishan Lal's father, had…not slept.

Chapter 16

Palanpur, 1984

On my way to the station, I stopped at Rampal's house. He was quieter than the night before but had obviously not slept. I listened to what he had to say. It was not very enlightening, and he still seemed to veer between resentment towards BKS, Smita, and his son. This, fortunately, diluted his anger. Nevertheless, he asked me if I could do something to help Hukum. I didn't promise much and firmly informed the headman that I wanted to first see some progress with the proposal submitted to the ADO. As I was leaving, I felt a finger on my arm, 'Please do something. Hukum is a good person,' Veena urged me, her eyes wet. 'The best in this household. He should not be in jail.'

'I will try. I promise I will try,' I answered, 'but it will take a few days.'

I resumed my journey, shaken by this: indeed, Hukum was probably the most honest man in that household. A little further, I ran into Babu who was going to my fields.

'I thought that I should perhaps meet Smita,' I said. 'Do you know if she is at the school? I hope she is doing well.'

'I'm taking care of her,' said Babu with a reassuring gesture, 'so there will be no problem.'

'Maybe I will see her in the school later, after I return.'

'She will be there,' Babu assured me.

Not fully convinced, I proceeded and reached the station well on time. Kishan Lal had flatly refused to accompany me this time: there was too much work to do, including in my fields. The Captain was not in the train and, somehow, that did not surprise me. Other passengers were not particularly familiar to me, so I went back to my father's notes.

Palanpur, 1925–1932

While one young man was making the pleasurable discoveries of his age, another was being prepared for an unusual life with his assigned partner. When George turned fifteen—more or less—Dukhi, who had saved for the occasion, took all her money and bought two tickets for Bareilly. She was almost trembling, full of hope and apprehension. Would her son be hired by the railways? A relative, as a precaution, had checked with one or two train station masters whether that was a possibility. To his amazement, he had learned that it was. George should go to Bareilly and he would get a job.

Dukhi accompanied her son, but she was ill at ease. She had already felt out of place in the train. It was even worse when they reached Bareilly. There, Dukhi was completely lost. She had never imagined that such a huge place, with so many people, could exist. She stood still on the platform, unsure of what to do. People, avoiding the mother and son as they rushed about, were scolding them. It was George who rose to the occasion. Holding his mother's hand, he moved towards the station, a building several times higher and longer than the one in Palanpur. Then, things began to go smoothly.

At the office of the station master, gentleness was in short supply, but so were mixed-blood young men available for training. The station master looked at the letter signed by Hemming. He did not pay any attention to the ring, which surprised Dukhi, and asked his staff to take care of George. The station master even reimbursed Dukhi for the ticket. She sat in the train back to Palanpur, full of pride, horribly sad, but also hopeful that George would soon reappear in Palanpur, this time driving an engine. Such a leap forward. Later, clinging to the modest ring, in her even more modest home, she could not believe she had achieved so much.

In 1932, in his early twenties, George officially became a train driver—based in Moradabad—after a brief theoretical training, and many miles covered as a helper on various engines all over the province. Thus, George regularly passed through Palanpur. Although officially a resident of Moradabad, he became a permanent feature of the village, and even one of its important citizens.

Palanpur, 1984

I was first in line at the ADO's office and, miraculously, he arrived early. I was introduced by the BDO who made all the right noises about the project. His boss was sitting in a leather chair. He was rather thin and tall but had a round belly that seemed to be a separate piece attached to his body. He appeared less enthusiastic than his colleague. He looked at the proposal rather casually, deplored that it had been drafted in English, and recommended that the CDO get the proposal translated into Hindi. It was better if the request came from that office. I could then bring it back to him and he would see what he could do. So, off I went to the CDO to get the translation done. It was a lengthy process but, at least, it gave me an opportunity to continue reading the notes.

Palanpur, 1926

There was also some drama in Pitamber's life. Duly protected by Radha from any excessive paternal authority, he was quite aware of his high status from a very early age. He also learned who to play with, and George and Rajesh were soon off the list. His destiny seemed to be to become another Ashok and rule Palanpur under the strict supervision of a zamindar. This suited Radha but was not compatible with Ashok's dreams. For once, the chief resisted to the bitter end all the womanly manoeuvring of his wife. His success was due to two independent factors. First, Ashok was convinced that Pitamber would become a soldier and he simply could not conceive that Radha might think otherwise. Second, Radha was pregnant again, this time with a girl who would be called Shobha, then with another boy who was a bit sickly and required all her attention.

The word went around that the army was recruiting. It was George who heard the news in Bareilly and informed the Palanpuris during one of his visits. Ashok decided to seize the opportunity. A few days later, he and Pitamber went to Moradabad where there was a recruitment centre. Pitamber, less tense than his father, waited in queue for a few hours. Finally, it was his turn to go into a big tent carrying the 'Indian Army' sign. He stopped at the entrance and was guided to a corner where a stern sergeant told him to remove his clothes. He stripped and carefully placed his clothes in a little pile without being told to do so. That was appreciated. He was then examined by a doctor. There again, he submitted to the various tests without fuss. That also made a good impression, especially since he masterfully passed the physical. He was less impressive in the basic test of intellectual capacity, but that was considered less crucial. The recruiter suggested that things had gone well but Pitamber did not seem to take the hint. That further contributed to a decidedly excellent impression. The stern sergeant closed the interview by looking less stern, 'Well done, young man.'

He then informed Pitamber that an official telegram would confirm whether he had made it or not.

Pitamber informed his anxious father that a telegram would come soon, but he had no clue how things had gone. An odd couple composed of a placid Pitamber and his agitated father walked back to the station to catch the next train back to Palanpur. From that day on, Ashok slept badly. Pitamber continued to sleep well.

Ashok almost fainted when the official telegram arrived. Chhote Ram, duly informed by his half-brother George, had initially considered calling on Pitamber, but thought better of it and instead ran to Ashok. The chief gave one anna to Chhote Ram who, cleverly observing the trembling hand, decided to follow Ashok, hoping that this munificence would be repeated in the event of good news. Both ran back to the station where the telegram, already opened by helping hands and passed around many others, finally reached Ashok. He looked at it closely, trying to guess. Nothing doing, the telegram remained obscure. This was a rare moment when the chief and all those who had already seen the document regretted their lack of education. They all decided to wait until Lakshminarayan returned to the village from one of his errands. Ashok's mood was oscillating from ecstasy to despair at an alarming rate. Commenting that the Brahmin was never at home when needed, he sent everybody to look for the holy man but without success. Fortunately, as if the gods had decided to spare Ashok further angst, the Brahmin made his appearance. In truth, he too took some time to fully understand the content of the telegram: short as it was, there were plenty of letters in it. Finally, he gave a loud cry: a mixture of joy, poorly disguised jealousy, and shared pride in the achievements of a son of the village. Pitamber remained composed but seemed surprised by a display of fatherly affection he was not used to.

That evening, Ashok offered another anna to Chhote Ram and batasas to the whole village. He also gave some money to Lakshminarayan, mostly for being the bearer of good news since his contribution to Pitamber's education had been limited. The Brahmin accepted the gift with a short speech where he claimed just the opposite.

A few days later, Pitamber left for his new life. He loved the uniforms, the rifles, the parades and, in general, all aspects of his time in service. The English were the masters and Pitamber, not a rebel by nature, never questioned this state of affairs. That was the time when, for economic reasons, the English in the lower ranks were gradually being replaced by natives. Pitamber was unconcerned. He would sometimes lament that discipline had deteriorated since the reform, but that was to please those of his colleagues who felt that way. He could equally have joined the chorus of others, who resented the foreign presence and were arguing for Indianization of higher ranks. Simply put, Pitamber was a good soldier who dutifully obeyed orders yelled at him, irrespective of the identity of the yeller. His role in the army was not one that revolutionized organizations and he was therefore well regarded.

In Palanpur, Ashok was overjoyed. Finally, there was a soldier in the family. Unfortunately, much to the regret of Ashok and Radha, this high achievement did not really translate into important or even regular transfers of money by the poster boy to his old parents. Ashok managed to send a few letters to Pitamber to remind him of his filial duties, at least their financial aspects—he had sent them using a letter-writer based in more discreet Chandausi—but to little avail.

Palanpuris discussed Pitamber's uniform and his rifle. Although no one had yet seen him wearing one or carrying the other, Ashok was very proud of both. His pride ran so high that it started clouding his judgement and straining relations between him and the zamindar. In truth, resentment about zamindars was gaining ground all over India. By 1927, the ideas behind the Kisan Sabha were spreading everywhere, including in Palanpur. Feeling directly concerned, Radha supported, if not the movement, at least its ideas, and she reminded her husband that, chief or not, he had been financially oppressed by the zamindar and physically abused by his henchmen. Now with a son in the army, Ashok felt that he was in a position to challenge Tikam Singh, my father, who had taken over the role of zamindar from his father, Gavendra, when he had passed away.

One day, Ashok refused to relay the tax money, convinced that the rifles of the almighty Indian Army—or at least one of them—were on his side. Not pleased, the zamindar sent his henchmen from Jargaon. Ashok tried to resist and soon discovered that Pitamber would not intervene. The rifles of the Indian Army were still on the side of Tikam Singh. That distressed the chief a great deal, especially after Bhupal vandalized his home with the blessings of his boss and found the tax money in a hole.

The zamindar had re-established his authority but at high cost. When the relationship between the chief and the zamindar came under stress, a general sense of uneasiness emerged in the village. It led to bad blood everywhere within Palanpur's complex social network. For once, Dukhi was less affected: George would often give her a bit of money and that was enough to meet the needs of her family.

Yet, for a while, all could live with the illusion that things had returned to normal.

Palanpur, 1984

The translation was ready and had been stamped all over by the CDO, making the document look impressively official. At the bottom of it, the ADO had finally signed and applied one last stamp—for good measure—on top of his signature. He assured me that all the required stamps were there. The document was not quite final, though. The ADO would need to see it again, but later, after I took it to the DDO who would review the key features of the project and take whatever action he deemed necessary. I was asked to rush there as soon as possible.

The DDO carefully examined the stamps and the signature. Then, he got hold of his bell. Unlike Ashok Kumar, the lawyer, he rang it with energy. A peon appeared. The DDO pointed at a huge book sitting on top of a shelf. The peon took a stool, climbed on it, struggled with the heavy book, and managed to place it on the table without falling. A cloud of dust spread through the office, making us sneeze. Obviously, the book had not been touched in years. The DDO opened it like the Archbishop of Canterbury opens the Bible during a service. His finger went through the numerous columns and stopped in front of a title: ADO. There was a name and a signature, 'The signatures do not match,' the DDO said, looking at me suspiciously.

I had not expected that. I sighed and looked at the file, 'This is not the name of the current ADO,' I argued. 'You know that. Besides, this signature dates back to 1975, nine years ago. How long do government officers stay in the same job?'

'Four or five years,' the DDO acknowledged.

'So, this must be the signature of an earlier ADO. How could it match?'

'Be that as it may, this must be fixed before we can proceed. And I need a legal opinion on the matter.'

'But how long will it take? I can't be held responsible for the fact that the files of the UP administration are not in order,' I cried. 'Besides, you know the ADO. He is just down the road.'

The DDO closed his eyes, put his hands on his protruding belly and reflected for a moment, 'Naturally, things can proceed while this is being sorted out. Show me the receipt proving that the money has been deposited into the gram panchayat account. That way, we will not waste time. Work should be started on a priority basis; it is of the utmost importance for rural development,' he added unctuously.

Fortunately, I had the receipt with me. He looked at it again and again. I was wondering what the next trap would be. The DDO returned the receipt.

'This money will need to be deposited in a special State Bank of India account. After this is done and certified by the EDO, please come back to discuss the rest of the procedure.'

Reluctantly, I set off to the bank and waited there while the money was moved to the special account.

Palanpur, 1930

A few years passed in that fragile equilibrium. Ashok and Radha's main concern was to get Pitamber married. Somewhat naively,

Ashok had thought that Pitamber's admission in the army and posting in Bareilly entitled him to a bride of the highest possible status. He soon faced disenchantment. Pitamber's high position was appreciated, but his humble origins were frowned upon. After short negotiations with prestigious families that did not lead anywhere, the determined parents thought they would be successful with Gulabo. Her family was vaguely related to them and proudly based in the outskirts of Moradabad. The city was small and its outskirts were rather dilapidated, but it was still an urban environment. That greatly enhanced Gulabo's value but also—as had happened with other possible brides—the parents' reluctance to marry their daughter to a Palanpuri, even if he had made it to the army. The negotiations made some headway but the main obstacle this time was Pitamber's parents' view that the marriage required an appropriate dowry. Gulabo's parents felt the same way but their definition of 'appropriate' went in the opposite direction. Weeks passed without a breakthrough.

To complicate matters, the chief fell ill during the negotiations. He shivered and, soon, could no longer move. When his resources were exhausted, he sent Radha to borrow some wheat and money from the zamindar. With great difficulty, she obtained a fistful of wheat and a few rupees. For Ashok, it had been too little too late and, when it became clear that no amount of food would help the ailing old man, Radha no longer reduced her own rations to feed him. The last hope was that the money promised by Pitamber would arrive.

It arrived the day after Ashok died. Had it arrived a few days earlier, it could have saved the old man but Pitamber, although saddened by his father's death, did not realize the result of his carelessness and nobody told him.

Palanpur, 1984

The transfer of money to the special account had been successful, but I needed to get it certified by the EDO, so I went to his office and waited. And waited.

Palanpur, 1931

While Palanpuris were mourning the death of their chief, another event was about to rattle the village. As George was getting ready to climb into his engine at Chandausi station, he was informed that an additional coach would be attached in Moradabad for the return journey. An old and seemingly important Englishman would travel in that coach. The Chandausi station master handed over the papers that would be necessary to complete the formalities in Moradabad. George was not a good reader, but he had learned. It was useful in his job. He took a look at the papers. He was putting them aside because the train was about to depart when something caught his eye. He picked them up again. He had read correctly: a certain Mr Hemming, fifty-nine, would be travelling with his young wife. The final destination was Bareilly. George looked at the paper in sheer amazement. Was it possible? Hemming, fifty-nine, Bareilly… His mother had described Hemming a few times. How could he be sure? He turned back to the station master, 'Who is this fellow?'

'Some ageing British guy who used to live in Bareilly. He is taking his young wife to India to show her the place. Apparently, he had been in charge of building some stations on this line. That's all I know. Rush now, or you will be late.'

George, his heart beating faster, climbed into the engine, blew the whistle a few times, gently applied power to the wheel to avoid spinning excessively in front of his superior, and the Chandausi–Moradabad Mail commenced its journey. George accelerated and the train soon reached fifteen miles an hour. He blew the whistle again once or twice and since there would be nothing for him to do for a little while, he took another look at the paper. It clearly said 'Hemming'! What should George do? He thought a bit. That was it! He blew the whistle again, out of sheer excitement. The plan required a bit of luck, skill, and Rajesh's cooperation. Would he go along? Chhote Ram would also be required, but that would not be a problem.

Shortly before arriving at Jargaon, George saw Chhote Ram waiting for him near the tracks, as he usually did. He stretched his hand out and helped his half-brother onto the train. He gave him strict instructions, then slowed down and let him jump out: Jargaon station was fast approaching. Once the train had stopped, George jumped down. He took his official hammer and went around the engine, tapping here and there with a worried look. He explained to the station master that there was an issue with some important mechanical part that would need to be fixed, but the train would be able to continue. He tried to sound reassuring, 'If things really go wrong, I will repair this in Moradabad.'

Not quite reassured, the station master gave the departure signal. The stopover had been a little longer than usual, but that was fine. George started the train, feeling happy. Hemming would pay for his sins. In Moradabad, George hooked the extra coach, handed over the necessary papers, and examined the important person, a chubby old Englishman with a young Englishwoman at his side. It was the right man, surely. Smiling to himself, George inspected his machine one last time, checking that everything was in place, and started.

Just before Jargaon, George briskly turned a few of the many wheels controlling the engine. He also moved some of the levers forwards and backwards. The train started jolting. George pushed another handle and a huge plume of smoke emerged from the front of the engine. The train slowed down but still managed to reach Jargaon station where it stopped, more smoke spewing. A crowd had already gathered around the ailing machine.

A very agitated George jumped out of his cabin with the big, official hammer. He again banged everywhere, went between the wheels, banged a lot more, and came back looking very upset. The worried station master followed George but had no idea of what he should look for. He got sprayed with oil, drenched in hot water, a piece of burning coal burnt a hole in his uniform, while he struggled to stay behind George who was more at ease in the mechanical maze. Finally, George stood up with a doubtful pout, 'Khatam,' he said with authority and precision.

'What do you mean, khatam?' insisted the station master, thinking of the important passenger.

'Khatam,' clarified George.

Close to despair, the station master, who knew George was a responsible driver, took him by the arm, 'You must do something.'

'Nothing can be done,' George replied.

The station master looked close to tears, 'Do something please…'

'Unless…' added George, then he frowned doubtfully.

'Unless what?' cried the station master.

'No, it won't work,' said George.

The station master shook the driver 'Unless what?' he demanded. 'Tell me!'

George put his hand on his chin and looked lost in deep mechanical thoughts, 'I can repair it but first I must empty the coal and the water. Once it's repaired, I will need help in reloading the coal and reigniting the fire. Then water will have to be put back in the tank and heated. All this will take two or three hours.'

'Good,' sighed the station master who could see an end to the problem and a way to send the important man up to the next station at least.

'I want everybody away from the train. It is too dangerous.'

'Okay,' agreed the station master.

'No one should stay inside,' insisted George, 'certainly not the Englishman.'

'Okay, okay!' the station master agreed desperately.

'I will unload the water and the coal now. This will create a lot of smoke.'

'Accha. Go on, then.'

Once everybody including Hemming was evacuated, George went around the train, opened the outlet for the water and the burnt coal. Everything fell out at the same time, creating an immense cloud of smoke that engulfed the whole station.

Duly briefed by George, Rajesh and Chhote Ram were waiting. They rushed to the fancy coach and took all the valuables they could find, making sure all the bags and suitcases looked untouched. Meanwhile, some members of Rajesh's family jumped into the train and took away as many bags of coal as they could carry.

After the smoke dissipated in the wind, everything seemed normal, except for the huge pile of burnt coal between the tracks.

George was very busy. He used his hammer quite freely, installed a new part, making sure to smash the old one so that it looked damaged. Then he announced that everything was in order, it was simply a question of restarting the fire and heating the water. Meanwhile, he would be happy to play chaupar with the esteemed guest. His friend, Rajesh, and his half-brother, Chhote Ram, could make up the rest of the foursome.

Hemming had not been unhappy to stop in Palanpur. He remembered the village well, learned that the chief had sadly died and that the zamindar—not eager to speak to Hemming without assistance—would not be able to come from Jargaon to meet him. He refrained from asking about Dukhi, wisely anticipating that he would be disappointed, as growing old in rural India was an unforgiving ordeal. It also risked provoking uncomfortable questions from his young wife. Better avoid that.

Hemming gladly accepted George's invitation and decided to learn the game, pairing up with Rajesh. In the process, he lost the few rupees he had in his pocket, blissfully unaware that the rest of his money had already been stolen.

In Chandausi, where the robbery was discovered, an enquiry was ordered. It was never completed but Rajesh, Chhote Ram and George, who had been with Hemming all along, were cleared of all suspicions at the behest of Hemming himself.

Soon after, Dukhi repaid her debts, explaining that George had given her the money. She died a week later, worn out by life but relieved about her son. As for Rajesh and his family, they had coal to last the entire winter and a bit of money to spare.

Palanpur, 1984

Finally, the EDO received me. He signed several documents certifying that the ADO was indeed the correct one and warned me not to go to the FDO or, God forbid, to the GDO before going back to the DDO and having him approve the documents. I went back, armed with all the required forms duly signed and stamped. Unfortunately, the DDO was no longer there, but his secretary volunteered to keep the pile of forms for his boss's perusal. He also said that he had taken charge of preparing the letters that would need to accompany the proposal so that it could move on to the FDO and then the GDO without delay. That was remarkable and I thanked the man profusely. He modestly accepted my praise but reminded me that the ADO would need to sign again at the end of the process. Then the document would go to the HDO. Still, he felt that the work could start within a month and that we were likely to obtain a matching grant of 15,000 rupees.

That was rather good news, so I set off to Palanpur in a cheerful mood. The project would soon be sanctioned, and Pat was arriving. Things were going well. In the train, I had more time to read.

Palanpur, 1932

Another year passed without Pitamber's career taking off. Nobody was upset: in Palanpur, climbing the career ladder was a remote concept. Pitamber himself did not mind, content as he was with his situation. Since Ashok's death, he had sent money home more regularly than before. Things could have stayed that way but, as Indians were being promoted to fill the vacuum left at the top by the accelerating departure of the English, Pitamber benefitted from the ripples of a wave that was losing much of its force as it was progressing down the ranks.

He had shown his mettle in 1930 soon after the Salt March which led to civil disobedience all over India. Pitamber's battalion was told to keep law and order in Meerut. A little intimidated by the scale of the riots but, like all simple souls, placing trust in his bosses, he obeyed orders as he had always done. He methodically fractured the skulls, arms, and legs that came his way. Not that he particularly enjoyed it, but it was his duty. He performed very well and, much to his surprise, received his first chevron, symbol of his promotion to the grade of lance naik after four years of service.

On that occasion, he was granted an exceptional leave to visit his family. He was also graced with a speech that had been carefully crafted: always strategic, the British were determined to convince underpaid soldiers that the honour of a promotion was infinitely more important than an increase in salary. Money was just icing on a cake that was already rich. Pitamber profusely thanked his superior for the chevron and almost told him that there was no need to raise his salary. Fortunately, his peasant roots stopped him on that slope and he accepted the chevron, the pay raise, and the exceptional leave.

Delighted, beaming with pride and sweat, basking in the sun and in his newly earned military glory, Pitamber arrived three days later in Palanpur, wearing his uniform and making a considerable impression. Palanpuris looked at the chevron with immense respect, then at the sweating face of the man carrying it. He seemed transfigured, certainly enlightened. He was another Pitamber, at least a lieutenant or a commander, perhaps a general. Pitamber allowed Palanpuris to call him lieutenant, wisely refusing higher titles with which he was less familiar. Few failed to honour the bearer of Palanpur's pride and Rajesh, who ventured to ask whether he could touch the chevron, received the stare he deserved from the important lance naik. The other Thakurs, shocked but not really surprised, looked at Rajesh with disdain: these pathetic Muraos only thought of their fields and had no respect for loftier matters. Working was all they could do. Rajesh was scolded—but not beaten, as Lieutenant Pitamber magnanimously interfered, a move that earned him the reputation of a truly gentle, forgiving person. Chhote Ram, who had actually touched the uniform, got badly beaten—of course Pitamber would not intervene for a Chamar.

Ashok's death had put a halt to the protracted negotiations for a possible marriage between Pitamber and Gulabo. This had hurt Palanpuris beyond the close family circle: they had felt snubbed. The chevron opened a new, more hopeful chapter for the aspiring groom. Surely, it would squash any doubts that Gulabo's parents had.

It did. During his leave, Lance Naik Pitamber went to Moradabad accompanied by his mother and an uncle, in order to display the uniform with the chevron. After the usual salutations and small talk, as the reluctant bride's family members were eyeing the symbol of military prestige flaunted by Pitamber at every opportunity, a respectful silence settled. The achievements of Gulabo's second uncle, who had once worked as a clerk in a ghee factory, paled in comparison. Those of a distant cousin, who had left the army under murky circumstances and now worked as a chowkidar in a sugarcane factory, paled even further. An urban residence would not impress a seasoned and decorated military man living in Bareilly. Defeated by the chevron, Gulabo's family threw in the towel and accepted a major upward revision of the dowry. The marriage took place a month later, this time hurried by Gulabo's family who feared the devastating financial impact of a second chevron.

The ceremony was spectacular, and everything went smoothly, an unusual combination. There was music, plenty of food, dances, and laughter. Zamindar Tikam Singh made an appearance and blessed the couple as part of a strategy to rebuild ties with the family of an important person. This was applauded and all agreed that the Lance Naik and his distinguished bride from Moradabad formed a beautiful couple. Even the steam engine had seemed happy: although still saddened by his mother's death, George had blown his whistle as he drove past the ceremony and everybody had favourably commented on the gesture.

Pitamber had a rude awakening the next morning, which had nothing to do with Gulabo. He had just remembered that his rifle was no longer with him. He started a frantic search for it. He asked his wife to help him, then the neighbours. Soon, however, it became clear that the precious army rifle had disappeared.

Pitamber tried to calm down and reconstruct what might have happened. The army had allowed him to take his rifle for the wedding. The exceptional nature of this permission had been emphasized. Over-emphasized, actually: the antique Lee-Enfield .303 bolt-action MLE, known as 'Emily', should have been replaced several years earlier by the superior SMLE known as 'Smelly'. Pitamber had used the rifle rather liberally to spice up the celebrations, allowing others to fire it as well. Towards the end of the ceremony, 'Emily' had passed from hand to hand, even among non-Thakurs: Rajesh and Bhupal had tried it. Actually, Bhupal had commented that if Rajesh had been allowed to try the rifle, should George—whose train had just passed by at that moment—and Chhote Ram not try it as well? Everybody had laughed and Rajesh, annoyed, had left, carelessly leaving the rifle in a dark corner. He announced that he had to leave anyway because he was planning to go to Chandausi early. What happened afterwards? That is what Pitamber could not remember.

While he was desperately racking his memory, he heard a shot followed by a scream in the distance. His heart sank. It was his own rifle, he recognized the sound. And that scream, he could have sworn...

Rajesh had departed very early to go to the station, as was his habit when travelling. He never made it. Halfway there, he was shot in the back. In the commotion that followed, with so many villagers running to the spot and the arrival of the train, nobody saw anything. There was no rifle nearby, no culprit, just a man lying dead in a pool of blood. The station master stopped the train until the police arrived.

Towards the end of the festivities, when Rajesh had left the rifle, Bhupal had jumped on the opportunity to steal it and vanish into the night. Everybody had forgotten about him. But all remembered that Rajesh had tried the rifle, especially after Bhupal's joke. At the scene of the crime, a crowd had rapidly gathered. Bhupal made sure that he was not the most conservative in expressing his sorrow.

The police finally arrived. Before they could deal with the crime, Pitamber lodged a complaint about the stolen rifle. He added that, to his knowledge, a Murao named Rajesh was last seen with it and the last one to use it as well. The policemen took note and proceeded to examine the body. They observed that he had been shot. Unfortunately this eliminated the only name on their list of suspects. They were told by an obliging Bhupal that he had heard the rifle from the train driven by a man of ill repute named George. The henchman had thought it wise to deflect suspicions towards the train. The police took note even though nobody else could say where the shot had come from. The police also learned that the victim was planning to take the train that morning.

That seemed to strengthen the case against the new suspect. Armed with the information, and although they could not find the rifle, the police noted the strong presumptions against George, a half-Chamar whom they had not yet met. Since the train was arriving, they proceeded to do so.

A few minutes later, and despite his vehement denials, George was removed from the train that was still waiting at the station. He was taken into custody by the two policemen, who were proud of having served justice and solving the mystery so quickly. They decided to brush aside several niggling aspects of the case: if Rajesh had been shot in the back from the train, it meant that he was facing the wrong way. It was also hard to understand how the rifle had ended up in the train since there had been no train movement at the time the rifle had been stolen. Finally, the rifle was nowhere to be found and none of the passengers had heard the shot. The detectives ignored all of this: small details should not prevent justice from following its course. George would eventually speak, with the assistance of the police. Unfortunately, he never confessed. These Chamars were decidedly stubborn!

Still, George was jailed. Three days later, he was freed: the Indian railways could not do without their drivers. An important official pointed out the inconsistencies and was very angry. The affair was classified.

Pitamber went back to his barracks a married man but a soldier without his rifle. He was punished and forced to purchase a new weapon. It was costly—the Indian Army was always making money off careless soldiers—but, at least, it was a new Lee-Enfield of the SMLE type.

Palanpur is not a place where secrets can be kept. True, Bhupal had not been seen with the rifle. But, somehow, suspicions started spreading. Did Bhupal talk too much one drunk evening? Did he threaten somebody? Did someone see him? Did the Murao community learn something? One thing was certain: after the shooting, there had been a major showdown between Bhupal and the zamindar, followed by another between both of them and Pitamber. As for the rifle, it was never found.

Palanpur, 1984

My train was slowing down as we were approaching Jargaon. I put down the notes. I had found that rifle. It was that rifle that everybody was after! As the Captain had said, some people loved weapons beyond reason in this part of UP. Phool Singh and Rampal could have killed my uncle simply because they felt that the weapon belonged to them. And the notes had revealed a few things about Kishan Lal's father. Could Kishan Lal have killed my uncle to retrieve the rifle that killed his father? Unlikely, but how could I know?

I reached the station around 4 p.m. which left me with an hour to kill before Pat's arrival. I took the opportunity to visit Kishan Lal, who was busy working in my fields. In fact, I had so many things on my mind that I had become increasingly uninterested in the agricultural side of my stay. But Kishan Lal was taking it very seriously, so I suffered in silence as he gave me a lecture on all the good work he had done. I expressed my gratitude, paid him, and escaped to report to Rampal on my efforts with the proposal for the school. The headman was no longer shouting. Instead, there was a touch of desperation in him—the same desperation I had seen in Veena's eyes earlier in the day. I tried to comfort him but, since I could not reveal the existence of the pictures, my soothing words were ineffective. As I was talking pointlessly, I heard Pat's train arriving. I excused myself—although Rampal did not seem to care much—and ran to the station.

PART III

Wolverhampton, then London, 1968–1984

Jane was never satisfied. Her parents always said so, even before she was called Pat. There was some truth there. She had hated seeing her father leave everyday for a job he disliked, in part because his own dissatisfaction could be felt at home. Her mother seemed more content, but Jane always wondered how a life limited to staying at home, cleaning, cooking, and managing the scarce resources of the household could be satisfying. And if there was a special event one day, like a modest dinner for some guest—a rare occurrence—the end of the month became a painful challenge. It was a life where any little extra was necessarily followed by a painful struggle. Sundays were dull beyond the tolerable. She would sometimes lift a corner of the grey curtain and investigate the street. Usually, it was empty. Just the same boring dark houses in a straight line under the grey sky. Sometimes, another curtain would be lifted across the street. A pale face would appear, but the sad curtain would soon go down. Later, when Anil had suggested that, coming from Wolverhampton, she should watch Slade in Flame because the music was great and because Slade came from there, she thought that some scenes could have been shot in her street.

'I don't understand,' her mother said one day. 'When you're here, you pull a long face. When you go see Aunt Clara, you pull a long face...'

Jane looked up. Her Aunt Clara was a grumpy old lady who served soggy biscuits. She had not particularly disliked her husband but thoroughly enjoyed the attention she was receiving after his death. A very respectable widow with a mean streak that was universally excused, she lived in a similar kind of place as Pat's parents. A bit smaller and a bit greyer, perhaps.

Unfazed by Pat's silence, her mother had continued, '...of course, the poor thing has not been very happy. But when you see your grandmother you also pull a long face.'

Jane looked up again. The grandmother had more money than them and took pleasure in rubbing it in. Her short-lived husband had worked in India during the time of the Empire—the wife had prudently stayed in Britain—and the couple had lived comfortably, at least from a financial point of view. He had caught some disease there and died. His widow had cried a lot when she learned the news, but her sorrow had been attenuated by a good lump sum payment and a regular pension for life. That pension was enough for the old lady but apparently did not suffice to help her son. With the lump sum, she had purchased a dark house and a dark set of rococo furniture that was as dull as could be. The good thing was that the furniture was usually covered with a sheet so that they would be spotless in case an important person visited. But Jane's family was not considered important enough to remove the sheets. It wasn't all bad though. It was at her grandmother's house that Jane had discovered India. She did not know exactly what her grandfather had been doing there. That didn't matter. He had taken many pictures with an old Leica Rangefinder that was in the attic. The pictures were all in black-and-white obviously, but even so, Jane could sense all the colour of the place. She had decided as a young girl that she would go there one day.

She had tried to learn more, asking her grandmother for details. The old lady did not like these questions because she didn't know much about her husband's life—not an easy thing to admit—and did not care much. She had let Jane explore the attic, happy that the child was keeping herself busy. The grandmother would simply yell from downstairs, 'Don't make a mess up there!'

Once, Jane had pinched a photograph. It showed her grandfather next to a bare-chested native with thin legs and a strange hat. Behind them was a flat landscape with a few trees, and one or two buffaloes that looked formidable even from far away. There was also a lady in a sari whom Jane found incredibly elegant. One day, she would see a lady in a sari for real, she had decided. And she would wear a sari as well. Not in the streets of a British city, but for real, in India, under the sun. Her mother had demanded, 'Jane, I'm talking to you. What do you want, exactly?'

'I want to go to India.'

The mother had shrugged her shoulders. Nonsense! India was no longer a British colony, so there would be no future there for Jane's husband when she got married. It was a dangerous place in any case and Jane knew what had happened to her grandfather. As for tourism, the parents could not afford a trip to India, nor could Jane. So, there was only one thing to say to close that chapter, 'Don't be silly.'

Jane had not closed the chapter. She was good at school, so the parents let her study and that eventually took her to London where she met Anil. In London, she had briefly joined a Hare Krishna band, impressed at the way the girls, all dressed in white—perhaps looking a bit disembodied—would suddenly break into a little dance or bang their tambourines. They seemed ecstatic. A bit too ecstatic, perhaps, so after a while, she stopped going. At university, where she was studying sociology, Jane befriended a girl in the Oriental Studies department. The friend had invited her to join a group researching transcendental meditation under the guidance of a young guru. Shortly after, Jane had become Pat—she had chosen patchouli as her preferred scent because everybody in the group seemed to like it—and had lost a few kilos. Her grades had gone down, but she still managed to pass. She liked the transcendental meetings, but some aspects made her uneasy at times. Once, she had invited Anil. He had embarrassed her by asking for a sausage or a steak when everyone was vegetarian. She had been shocked, as had the other participants, but thinking of it later—and it had been hard to admit—she accepted that Anil had a point. She left the group the day she saw her guru riding a fancy green Kawasaki. Somehow, a Kawasaki was not the right mode of transport for a wise and detached guru. She had not told Anil but had written off the experience as another fiasco: neither the seminars, nor the incense, nor other stuff aimed at looking in the sky with diamonds had been satisfying. Something was missing. And why was she called Pat, after all? But how do you tell everybody that you have changed your name yet again?

Pat confided in her friend, who showed her a book written by a young French lady who had travelled to India. In the introduction, she said:

> I have seen Devi, Shiva's consort, wash her blouse in the fountains of Kathmandu; Kali, the dark, remove her lice...

That was it! Pat decided she would go to India and experience it first-hand. The friend had laughed and shown her, a few lines down:

> I thought they were mine, all these Scheherazades of my smelly one thousand and one nights, I tried to hold them back by the edge of their star-studded saris, I felt them flutter like trapped butterflies, I opened my hands and there was nothing left but specks of dust.[*]

---

[*]Inspired by M. Cerf, L'Antivoyage, Mercure de France, 1974.

'Even so, I will go,' Pat had firmly replied. 'And I will see Devi wash her blouse. If not in the fountains of Kathmandu, then in some Indian river.' As a first step, she decided to learn a bit of Hindi but never really mastered the language.

When Anil mentioned what had happened to his uncle, she realized this was her chance. She would prepare for the trip seriously. Pat had long thought of working on a thesis but she had not been sure what the topic should be. Something about women, India and the rural environment. Fortunately, one of her professors had contacts in India and she introduced her to Professor Subrahmanya Subramanian, an eminent scholar also known as Subbu. That would surely work. Pat felt ready.

Pat's experience in Delhi had been mixed. The Professor had been helpful, hinting that he would be interested in collaborating, but Pat had sensed that his idea of collaboration required her to be a bit too close. Fortunately, the city was a lovely, permanent chaos, with its smells, colours, noise, heat, dust, and everything else she had hoped for. She had also hit it off with the other students, and that facilitated her integration. After having selected a topic, 'Sociological Barriers to Women's Employment in Rural India: The Case of Palanpur', and clarified the approach with her supervisor, she had departed to test her hypothesis and join her boyfriend.

Chapter 17

Palanpur, 1984

I was expecting her to come out of the AC coach, but Pat came out of the unreserved compartment, clearly cheerful. She was not exactly travelling light, and her attire created quite a stir. A large crowd of men, women and children had suddenly appeared on the platform. They had probably been alerted by Babu. Pat did not disappoint: complete with her floating hair, multiple bangles on each arm, a long, floaty purple skirt, and huge earrings, she was ready to discover rural India for real after having studied its theoretical aspects for a few years in London and a few days in Delhi.

She waved at the crowd before throwing herself against me, which was not very conservative and, I imagined, abundantly commented upon later in Palanpur.

While I was responding to Pat's display of affection, I heard a voice from the coach, 'A very nice lady. Intelligent, also. Congratulations. I knew that you were engaged. It was not possible otherwise.'

With a tight smile to the Captain, I managed to pass on some of Pat's luggage to Babu, took the rest, and off we went, followed by a whole procession. As we approached the house, I pointed towards my bullocks but failed to elicit much enthusiasm from her. Then I opened the door to let her in. I briefly let Babu in too because of the luggage, blocked other people, and barely managed to get Babu out. Then I bolted the door to the dismay of hundreds of interested eyes.

'So, that is where it happened, huh?'

She looked around with keen interest, smiled indulgently at my clumsy explanations about the hideouts behind the beds and started asking me lots of questions about the village and its people. My detailed explanations were frequently interrupted by kisses aimed at demonstrating that she had missed me very badly. The lack of running water briefly upset her, but she would talk to the women of the village and find out how they managed. She did not like the smelly corner with the junk, and complained that I had not cleaned it up. I sighed. She did not seem to be too scared of the billy goat, though. Overall, she reacted positively to the house. At one point, I suggested that she should talk to Smita.

Pat looked at me, amused, 'Do you mean the pretty school teacher?'

'How do you know that she is a teacher and how on earth could you possibly know that she is pretty?' I asked, surprised.

'Simple. The nice gentleman in the train—the one who knows you—mentioned her. She ran into some serious problems though, poor thing.... He also said that the school would hopefully be functional soon, thanks to that lady. And to you! It seems you two are collaborating very well...'

That Captain, really! But I strategically decided to remain silent.

'You even volunteered to help her clean the building I hear. The Captain disapproves. Not because she is pretty, but because you are not attending to your fields. And you are also helping to build a temple and a road. The Captain said that you should watch out because the money could get diverted. I told him that he should not worry: when it comes to money, you comprehend the incomprehensible.'

I remained committed to my silent strategy. Pat wagged her finger at me, 'But he was surprised that you didn't mention me to him.'

I felt a little embarrassed, tried to change tack, failed, and offered a rather confused explanation...

'No need to explain,' continued Pat, smiling, 'I told him about your shy nature. That you like to keep such things to yourself, especially in front of other women. But I was a bit surprised that you exercised the same restraint in front of a retired Captain.'

I smiled meekly and focused on opening Pat's boxes and suitcases.

'I cannot believe that you brought your guitar,' I said. 'Such a hassle.'

'Not at all,' Pat replied. 'People were quite understanding and happy to help. The Captain, for example. He got in at some station, about one hour before Moradabad and when he saw me with the guitar, he immediately helped, making space for all my things. That is how we started talking. He knew about the murder of your uncle.'

Curse that Captain. Fortunately, there was no need for me to say much. Pat was holding the floor and had every intention of continuing, 'Besides, you seemed to find evenings long here, so I wanted to provide some entertainment. Unless, of course, you have found some other, more interesting entertainment elsewhere...'

'There is very little entertainment here,' I said dryly. 'Do you want to see the village?'

'That is an excellent idea, but I think that, right now, we have something better to do.'

We did these better things because, when a pretty woman like Pat asks sweetly and displays her arguments, you eagerly accede to the request. I did not resist. An hour later, Pat decided that the absence of bathroom was really a problem. She shrugged her shoulders and put her clothes on, 'That's okay. I will ask the women. Let's go.'

Immediately after we crossed the door, we were followed by Babu, tons of kids and other villagers who had come out of nowhere. Kishan Lal had continued to work in his fields, so we first went to say hello to him. Then, we went to Rampal's house. Pat found a few nice words in Hindi to say to the depressed headman and his wife, Shakuntala, who was understandably quite low. She also took time to talk to Veena, and the two young women seemed to get along. We saw Jagpal, but he must have been scolded rather badly because he stayed far from us in spite of our encouragements. As we came out, Pat had tears in her eyes, 'What a sad household! Expect more drama soon! Such a tense atmosphere. That girl, Veena, she is nice, though. I wish I could have talked to her a bit more. She's unhappy. And that small boy...'

'Jagpal?'

'He looked terrorized. The mother doesn't seem too happy either. What a mess. I hope the son gets out of jail soon.'

As we were talking, we reached my fields. Pat displayed a lot of enthusiasm, commenting on the peaceful atmosphere and saying that she really wanted to see more of the village. So, we went around the village, followed by another procession. We went past the shop. It was miraculously open, and Pat bought a few things. Then we went to the Seed Store. Govindi, who had obviously been informed about our visit, had asked his daughter to prepare tea. Pat went in and drank tea with the daughter, leaving me with Govindi, Babu and about half of the village. The other half stayed with Pat. After tea, she came out, 'I will go to the school. It's next door, I believe. Would you like to come along and introduce me to your good friend Smita? She is there, apparently. Or you stay at the Seed Store and enjoy your tea.'

I opted to go back home and read a bit. As I was walking—alone, the crowd had preferred the novelty offered by Pat—it occurred to me that, in my hurry to welcome my girlfriend, I had forgotten to hang something in front of the holes in the shutters. It followed that most of the village knew quite a bit more about Pat and I than we wanted to share. I decided to pretend that everything was fine and hung an old piece of cloth to protect our privacy in the future.

Palanpur, 1932–1933

Gulabo had settled with her belongings in the small kuccha house of her mother-in-law. Thanks to modest improvements hastily made by her husband—using the dowry money—it soon became very comfortable, perhaps one of the best houses in Palanpur.

Gulabo found herself mostly alone at home. Still, thanks to her husband's periodic visits—and let it be known that Gulabo was always a faithful wife, although the same could not be said of Pitamber—she soon became pregnant. Pitamber was happy. It was a girl. He smiled at Gulabo and they immediately thought of having another child. About nine months later, Gulabo delivered a second daughter. Pitamber smiled less. Quite alarmed and prompted by his wife, he decided to sacrifice a few coins and consult Lakshminarayan. The Brahmin welcomed Pitamber and his money. He consulted the gods who apparently felt that Pitamber's problem could only be solved with a more substantial offering. That distressed Pitamber, who went back home to discuss the matter in spite of the Brahmin's insistence that he part with another rupee—at least—as a starter. Gulabo suggested consulting a doctor. A doubtful Pitamber, resigned to sacrifice more coins, left home again.

'It is because you are not at home enough,' Prasad, the Palanpur doctor, explained scientifically. He had assumed this important responsibility by popular demand, because he had been hospitalized for two weeks at the Moradabad hospital and then stayed on for two years to work there as a compounder. Puzzled, the Lance Naik revealed the diagnosis to his wife. Gulabo heartily agreed with the doctor. Chhote Ram later claimed that she had dictated the doctor's diagnosis in exchange for some ghee. True or not, Gulabo intelligently mixed a lot of nagging with two other ingredients: energetic speeches on the need for a man to be at home to take care of things, including the emotional needs of his wife; and some more intimate arguments related to these needs. Pitamber was surprised and happy, as well as exhausted and thoughtful. After long reflections, skilfully guided by Gulabo, he came to the conclusion that having a son after two daughters was of paramount importance and that he should therefore leave the army as soon as possible. Gulabo also tickled the soldier's sense of pride: Rajesh, a mere Murao, had got married a few months before them and managed to have a son, named Kishan Lal, before dying. Surely, Pitamber and Gulabo could do as much. Of course, mused a devious Gulabo, Rajesh was home every night...

Upset, Pitamber went back to the army camp and decided to talk to his chief. In those days, the army granted land to deserving soldiers who had put in their time. India was large and hands were needed to cultivate. In addition, and conveniently, that noble reason happened to be compatible with a more economic rationale: giving a bit of land to retiring soldiers was cheaper than granting them a costly pension.

'There is some land available in Palanpur,' revealed the chief after checking the records, 'and I will make sure that you get a fine piece of it.'

Of course, he would miss Pitamber, who was a good soldier, but he also understood that leading another life was a natural reward that even the best recruits should look forward to.

The Lance Naik thanked his chief and, genuinely worried expressed concerns about the future of the battalion after his departure.

'Don't worry,' the chief assured him with a smile, 'the battalion will function very well.'

'And could I keep my rifle and the turban?' Pitamber asked meekly as it started dawning on him that his days in the army were numbered.

The chief made a quick mental estimate of the residual value of the Lee-Enfield .303 Bolt-action SMLE that Pitamber had acquired after losing 'Emily' and that had been modified to accept .22 cartridges. He granted the request in exchange for a substantial reduction in the severance benefits. Perhaps feeling a little guilty, he let Pitamber take the turban for free. As was customary, another chevron was added to the package. That propelled Pitamber to the rank of lance daffadar (rtd.) in the Indian Army.

It was with some regret and unexpected apprehension that Pitamber signed—with a cross—the formal request reducing him to a mere civilian. Still, the discharge had to be celebrated. A friend suggested that they visit The Perfumed Garden. The ladies of the house—for there were only ladies, at least in residence—knew how to take care of the needs of their guests in more ways than one, explained the interested friend. Pitamber discovered that the ladies indeed had many qualities. One was that they laughed heartily at Pitamber's jokes. They also provided a charming atmosphere where guests could play cards or gamble without feeling too bad about their losses. They were strong too, happily drinking with the guests while miraculously remaining sober themselves. Finally—the informed friend was right about this—the ladies could also take care of their more special needs. These more special needs came at a price, but Pitamber felt that he could afford it and he even treated the obliging friend. This experience was a revelation for Pitamber. He felt at once strong, appreciated, relieved and ecstatic. Later in the night, the ladies persuaded him to try his luck a little more. He lost heavily.

The next morning, his chief gave Pitamber another paper to sign and asked him to confirm that he wanted to purchase his old rifle for 200 rupees, a sum that would be deducted from the departure grant of 600 rupees. Thinking of the financial debacle at The Perfumed Garden the previous day, Pitamber hesitated but he simply could not abandon his cherished rifle. Of the remaining 400 rupees, he used 300 rupees to pay off his debts.

The next day, Pitamber was back in Palanpur for good, with his second chevron, the rifle, 100 rupees and twenty bighas of land, of which one part was conveniently located near his almost-pucca house. The 100 rupees were enough to turn it into a fully pucca house and buy two bullocks as well as essential farm equipment.

All this wealth and the second chevron made a strong impression on Palanpuris who promoted the lance daffadar (rtd.) from lieutenant to colonel by consensus. This time, Pitamber accepted the title without fuss. It also changed the behaviour of the henchmen towards him. After all, he was now also a land owner. Not quite a zamindar, because he was not collecting taxes for the English, but still. And he had a gun at home.

The position of village chief had remained vacant since Ashok's death. It seemed natural that the great man should replace his father. Elections were clearly not required in view of the immense respect of the villagers for Pitamber's two chevrons, his rank of colonel, his caste, and his experience. There were a few discordant views, of course. Two or three villagers did not seem to care much about Pitamber's great achievements. They did not count: just a few Muraos who should focus on their work—which, to be fair, they were already doing—and Chhote Ram, the only Dalit to have an opinion about village matters that didn't concern him. This insignificant opposition carried little weight in the local scheme of governance. For the sake of due process, the elders consulted Lakshminarayan who, reluctantly, confirmed the general opinion, aware that there was no point objecting.

Pitamber had another reason to be happy. Gulabo—possibly more at ease with her husband around, undoubtedly pleased by the uniform with the chevrons, and also reassured by the unexpected wealth of a household now protected by pucca walls and a gun—had become pregnant again. They quickly agreed on the name: the boy would be called Phool Singh. Doctor Prasad had certified that it would be a boy, simply on hearing the news. That it turned out to be true a few months later greatly enhanced his reputation as a discerning physician.

Of course, like all Palanpuris, Pitamber—fortunate as he was—had experienced his share of unhappy events. His two daughters died of fever in spite of the potions provided by Doctor Prasad for a modest sum of fifty paisa each. Keen to hedge his bets, Pitamber had also sought the help of the Brahmin. Fearing the competition, Lakshminarayan offered suitable prayers at a discount: one rupee and a plate of laddoos. But this was to no avail either. Those had been sad days for the parents. Over the years, the couple had also lost some buffaloes, and their crops had been successively ruined by drought, untimely rains, insects and nilgais. Despite his chiefly status, Pitamber was a villager like the others, and he experienced the same recurrent, dull pain. The courage with which the pain was accepted should have been called resignation. Unlike most other villagers, however, Pitamber's small capital allowed him to absorb the shocks. After Phool Singh, in 1935, another child was born. He was called Rampal but Gulabo died in labour. In spite of his sadness, Pitamber organized a party. It was a bit costly, but he thought that it was necessary and that it would help him cope. Later, alone in the vast house, with too many obligations to attend to, Pitamber called on his sister, Shobha. A widow herself and childless, she lived in misery in a kuccha house in Samastipur, a village close to Palanpur. Once in a while, Pitamber had sent her a bit of money, but not as often as he thought he had, and not enough to ensure a decent living to Shobha. Resigned, she had lived from hand to mouth.

Shobha arrived in Palanpur one night, on a cart pulled by powerful bullocks that had been sent by the Colonel. Thankful for an invitation that meant shelter and food for many years to come, she took good care of Phool Singh and Rampal who both became very attached to her. So much so that Pitamber, difficult as he had found it to accept a lonely life, decided against remarrying. His days became rather quiet and gently followed the rhythm of his daily walks: one as landlord to check the work done in his fields— he considered manual labour to be below his dignity, so he had hired labourers and a supervisor; one as chief to check what was going on in the village; and one at night for a friendly chat with the villagers who had gathered under the mango tree.

The only detours in Pitamber's life were his mysterious trips to Moradabad. When asked about these, Pitamber would immediately put on a martial expression but remain silent. The truth was that, within a year or two of Gulabo's death, Pitamber had reacquainted himself with some old friends in the city. Serving together in the army creates bonds. Pitamber and his friends had visited each other a few times but they preferred to meet in Moradabad to share tea, biscuits, bidis and, occasionally, some liquor. One day, they discovered that one Ms Padma had opened a branch of The Perfumed Garden in Moradabad. Delighted, they decided to hold their meetings there from then on. They also held them more frequently and, as a result, started spending much more money.

Palanpur, 1984

Pat entered the house, smiling, 'This Smita is very nice. And verrry pretty. You have good taste...'

I tried to look unconcerned. She smiled wider, '...but I already knew that. I must also commend you for your devotion to rural education.'

I tried to look modest.

'Of course, now that I'm here, there's no need to leave your fields in the hands of Kishan Lal or Babu all the time. And I will help Smita with the building, the teaching material and the rest of it. We will get along. The girls looking after children and the boys busy with more important stuff.'

She laughed and caressed my hair. As she was talking, she had taken out two T-shirts from her bag. She went straight to the windows and hung them to replace the old rags I had placed there. Information moved very efficiently in Palanpur.

'I think that this will be better for what we have to do. The only witness will be the billy goat and I can tolerate that.'

'And what we have to say,' I added. 'But let us do first.'

After a while, we talked.

'What happened to Smita is horrible. She was very depressed, and she says that these things happen quite often. That policeman, BKS, is a beast.'

She looked at me and sighed, 'This place is not exactly what I had expected. There is not much hope, is there? Smita said that you had an idea to help get Neetu, her aunt, and Hukum out of jail?'

'Well,' I answered, 'I may have a little plan that could help...'

I explained how the discovery of my uncle's rifle made it clear that Neetu was not the culprit. Obviously, as long as I could not identify the rifle that shot the third bullet, it was technically possible that some other rifle belonging to Neetu had also been used, but it was highly unlikely. Still, the Captain was right, it would be better to identify the real murderer and the rifle he had used, but my discovery basically cleared Neetu. Unfortunately, I did not have the murderer, and only two shells. Something else bothered me. The Captain seemed genuine. But was he really trustworthy? How could I be sure? Pat thought for a bit, then said, 'There is a lot of corruption here, that is what everybody says,' she agreed. 'But, like everywhere, there must be some honest people. You should ask someone who is outside the picture, somebody who might be involved in all this for professional reasons but has nothing to gain. Someone not directly concerned with the murder.'

'Who?'

'I know,' she said. 'You should ask that guy, Ashok Kumar. From what you say, he is a regular lawyer. And he must know everything and everybody.'

Why not? Ashok Kumar didn't ooze energy, but he seemed honest. I decided that Pat deserved a kiss for this idea. I then turned to the Hukum problem. The pictures would help but they had to be used at the right time. And they had to be printed too. For that, at least, I had a clear plan. Pat would have to help me, though, and I explained what I expected from her. Basically, she would need to keep the owner of the studio busy while I discreetly developed the prints. She agreed enthusiastically, 'Tomorrow, I will first take a bath with Smita. Then, you and I will go to Chandausi. Let us see what we can do.'

Exhausted, I was closing my eyes when Pat added, 'And I must say that your generous decision to help Babu with his wedding is highly appreciated. I did not know that you were the type to get people married. One discovers something new every day when one lives with an interesting person.'

She pushed her body against mine, 'Apparently, I would be to Babu's taste, even though I am a bit too thin. What do you think?'

I was already drifting off, but Pat managed to wake me up again.

Chapter 18

Palanpur, 1984

We got up very early. As planned, Pat set off for the pond. I was curious to see how this would work. After taking care of my own bath, I quietly walked to the pond where Smita—and, long ago, Dukhi—had her bath, smiling at the thought of the commotion Pat had probably caused when she dipped in. I was right and the camera captured an unusually large group of men performing the ballet that had so often taken place at that spot, enraging the women, whether they were bathing or not. I did not smile.

As expected, Pat returned, furious, 'These guys are sick,' she said. 'Sick and frustrated.'

I nodded and expressed my empathy.

'I saw you,' she went on accusingly. 'I saw you with all of them. You were all looking. Even that stupid billy goat is looking at me right now,' she added, throwing a towel at the animal.

I pointed at the camera. 'I had just dropped by,' I argued. 'But it is true that you generated a lot of interest. I have the proof.'

She shrugged her shoulders, still angry. 'And I must say that when you wear a sari sticking everywhere, you are just irresistible,' I added.

Her eyes were still furious, but she smiled a bit, 'Shall we?'

I carefully placed the precious negatives of Smita's ordeal in a backpack so that my hands were free. We had decided to take the tandem and I had immediately agreed when she asked to sit in the front. That way, I would enjoy the view and I could operate the camera.

As we were cycling to Chandausi, Pat relaxed and started marvelling at the beauty of the fields. I smiled: Palanpur was growing on her. Forgetting all about the bath incident, she added, 'And people are nice in spite of their ordeals. You are lucky to come from this place. Don't you think?'

I replied that she was the prettiest addition to the landscape. She very gently shook her head as if to say no but, since that could also mean 'yes' in India, it was not obvious that she disagreed.

The shape of her neck was really nice, cute I should say. The movement of her hips was also very appealing. She was drawing an '8', horizontally. A sense of infinity.

'Stop looking at me like that.'

'I'm behind and you are supposed to focus on the road. How do you know that I'm looking at you?'

'I sense it.'

Her sensitivity was decidedly amazing.

'You know,' I said. 'I realize to what extent you girls beat us guys at everything. You are always ahead of infinity. Ain't it amazing?'

She waved her right hand. With so many bangles, we did not need a horn, 'Don't be silly. We are the infinity. Now, tell me where I should turn.'

Absorbed by the landscape, I had not realized that we had already arrived at the ADO's office. I went in, Pat following me. The ADO was not there but the BDO, no doubt impressed by my girlfriend, assured her that the school would be repaired within a month at most, the temple too and the road would be built within two months. It was just a question of meeting a few administrative requirements. In the meantime, the BDO would be delighted to keep Pat company while I waited for the ADO. Pat smiled nicely but said to a disappointed BDO that she would rather explore the local market. We agreed that I would meet her there one hour later and then we would go to the studio to try our luck with our plan. Since there was nothing to do and the BDO seemed less eager to chat with me than with Pat, I went back to my father's notes.

Palanpur, 1937

During one of his visits to The Perfumed Garden, Pitamber experienced an artistic revelation that would later prove disastrous. As a special treat for her regular guests and to test a new line of business, Ms Padma had organized a dance show with her three most agile hostesses. Pitamber was so impressed that, raising his glass of liquor, he made a solemn decision: one day, he would invite these dancers to perform the same show for his own guests. In truth, the girls' performance was a far cry from what Bollywood later came to be known for. They occasionally lost their balance, tended to giggle inappropriately, and the synchronization of their movements was not perfect. But to Pitamber, it was the pinnacle of choreography and, one day, he would have it all to himself. Once his special needs had been satisfied, he paid the price, some other costs, the general fees, plus the extras.

A few years had passed since Pitamber's retirement and his financial situation was slowly becoming precarious. Shobha had sensed it and she tried to hint that some luxury expenses could be curtailed entirely or at least reduced. Pitamber did not take it well: he was careful with every anna! He never spent unwisely! It was she, Shobha, who was careless. Did she want him, a retired colonel, to work in the field like Rajesh? It would be a disgrace. Was that what she wanted?

Shobha did not want that, but she gently suggested that gambling had resulted in some losses, careful not to mention the visits to Moradabad. The retired soldier got angry again. He knew from experience that gains and losses from playing cards or chaupar cancelled each other out, more or less, in the long run. In any case, he was a chief and knew better. In truth, Pitamber had a good but secret reason to remain calm about his finances: two months earlier, he had been approached by the zamindar—at that time, it was Tikam Singh, my father—who had an appealing proposition to make. The British had decided to expand the network of pucca roads in India and one such road would connect the different villages of the area. Firm believers in the virtues of decentralization, the colonizers had informed the zamindars—who would in turn inform the village chiefs—that the money would be made available to the local authorities who could then choose the roads that best suited their needs. There were some constraints on permissible expenses, but not that many, and verifications would happen after completion, which meant later. Much later.

Tikam Singh was very excited. He and Pitamber first talked about the quality of material to be used and that was soon settled. It would obviously be possible to save a lot while maintaining the highest standards—or close enough—and the difference would be shared with a pliable material supplier. That was basic but effective. As the zamindar was adding—or rather subtracting—the numbers, Pitamber started realizing that the gains would be substantial, even after being shared.

Then, Tikam Singh unfolded a map of the area that showed Samastipur, Pipli, and Palanpur. The road could take several routes. It could also take shortcuts.

'I don't understand,' Pitamber admitted.

The clever zamindar pointed at the map. 'The road is supposed to connect all the villages to Akroli but also go through each village.'

Tikam Singh paused and looked sternly at Pitamber, 'Is that really necessary?'

'Where else could it go, then?'

'Well, it's important that the Thakur side of Palanpur is connected, of course, but there may be other areas where a road is not essential.'

'Like the Murao area,' Pitamber exclaimed.

Even though they were alone, the zamindar cringed at hearing his scheme revealed so loudly, 'Let's say, if money is short, the Thakur quarters will be given priority. If money is not short, the road will also go through the Murao quarters. If there is more money than expected, it could even connect the Chamar households on the southern side of the village.'

Pitamber approved with a sly glance, happy to hear a ready-made line of argument that could be used in the village council. Tikam Singh smiled. The cake would be shared between more people, but it would be bigger and there would be more culprits, thus more confusion if the scheme were ever exposed.

Looking virtuous, Pitamber later explained to the village council the 'short of money' scenario. Just for information. It was unlikely and the council did not really need to look at it too seriously. In any case, the chief promised to share all the information with everyone in the spirit of full openness. There would be plenty of documents with all the information that would be available to all. The meeting had been chaotic but the proposal to re-examine the file in due course seemed reasonable and the Muraos sensed that further objections would be interpreted as bickering. They reluctantly let go. The Dalits were not consulted.

Finally, work started on the brick road. Soon, the contractor, a friend of Pitamber's and the zamindar, revealed that the money would be short. In spite of his best efforts and the slightly cheaper—but still quite good—bricks, the road would not go through the whole village. A village council was called. The first one had been chaotic. The second was tumultuous. Later, Palanpuris discovered that the road construction from Pipli hadn't even started while the segment from Akroli was already crumbling. The Muraos were so furious that Bhupal was sent with a few other henchmen to help reduce the tensions.

Although the scam was exposed, nobody was caught. Tikam Singh, Pitamber and a few others were lucky. The Independence movement was gaining strength and the situation in Europe was getting worrisome. The British did not want to create problems with rural folks because of a miserable road connecting—or rather failing to connect—a few small villages in the United Provinces or elsewhere.

Two years passed. A more financially secure Colonel Pitamber continued to take care of the farm and the village. He ruled with relative wisdom and, except for the occasional visit to Moradabad, with serenity. Under the protective eye of Shobha, Phool Singh and Rampal grew up, surviving the various illnesses, accidents, fights, snakebites, angry buffaloes and other risks inherent to village life. No small achievement.

About that time, Bhupal's long-term girlfriend had become pregnant. That was a shock for the henchman. Years earlier, he could have assumed that he was not the father. No longer. Despite a very adventurous youth, his girlfriend had become very faithful as she grew older. The baby lived. Bhupal sensed that his life would change.

This unexpected child needed to belong to a social group. Bhupal decided to talk to the Muraos and seek a suitable deal to rejoin what was, after all, his natural peer group. That was easier said than done. In spite of all the bribes he was ready to pay—and even paying some—the opposition was too strong. The henchman had beaten up and abused almost everyone. Besides, even as he was asking for a favour, he was unable to control his aggressive instincts. In the end, Bhupal, his girlfriend and the newborn son were rejected. They left the village and settled in Moradabad. The son was nicknamed BKS, for reasons that are off the record, and he later became a policeman.

These were times of major change in India and some percolated—mostly by train—to Palanpur. In 1936, the Indian National Congress held a conference in Bareilly under the presidency of Acharya Narendra Deo. It was addressed by Jawaharlal Nehru, M. N. Roy, Purushottam Das Tandon, and Rafi Ahmad Kidwai. None of these important people stopped at Jargaon station, but some passed through it, possibly without taking any notice. George even told a sceptical group of Palanpuris that he had seen in Chandausi a man who was touring the country in a truck. His name was Zulfiqar Ali Bokhari and he had made a series of long speeches on widow remarriage and untouchability. Most villagers—as well as most people in Chandausi—thought that the man was crazy, but his message had resonated with some, including George. Then, a poem appeared, seemingly from nowhere. Although not artistic by nature, Palanpuris were moved by it. Soon, some even knew it by heart. The poem was called 'Akashvani,' by a Bengali poet called Tagore. These seemingly unrelated events were transforming the minds and souls of Indians, including some in Palanpur.

Palanpur, 1984

This story certainly confirmed what Kishan Lal and Babu had told me about BKS. But I had to stop reading because the BDO informed me that the ADO had finally arrived. He looked—obviously for the first time—at all the documents I had left for his perusal two days earlier and nodded distantly. Finally, he asked to see the individual receipts that would account for all the contributions. I had left the receipt book in Palanpur and argued that this should not have anything to do with him: it was an internal matter. I also asked what the next trap would be. He smiled and answered that before anything further could be done these receipts had to be produced. A heated but useless argument followed, and it was finally cut short when I explained that I had no intention of coming back from Palanpur the next day to show the receipts. This annoyed the ADO who failed to see much benefit for him in this venture. He closed the meeting by saying that, under these circumstances, I should sort that out with the IDO.

Fuming, I went to the office of Ashok Kumar. He was quietly sitting at his desk and seemed pleased to see me. Now that I was sitting in front of him, I found it difficult to ask direct questions about the Captain's character. My convoluted approach did not seem to upset the lawyer and he finally seemed to understand what I wanted to know.

'The Captain is a very good fellow. His integrity cannot be questioned. He was even suspended for one whole year,' confided Ashok Kumar, who seemed to consider this an undisputable proof of honesty.

'This is good news,' I said, 'so you are sure I can trust him?'

The lawyer looked at me and smiled, 'Particularly you,' he said. 'You two have some connection, after all.'

'Well,' I said, surprised, 'yes, I suppose, in a way. We often meet in the train and he certainly seems to know a lot about Palanpur.'

The lawyer smiled again, 'Much more than you may think. Would you like some tea?'

I declined the offer and left the lawyer, reassured but suddenly less clear about who the Captain really was.

At the market, I immediately spotted Pat, surrounded by a whole group of fans. She had finished her shopping and was calmly waiting for me while drinking a cup of tea. At her side was a large bag full of indispensable stuff that I had not needed until then. I joined her for tea. As we enjoyed drinking and looking around, I suddenly saw something in the distance that made me jump off my seat.

'What happened?' Pat asked, surprised.

'I've seen a goat that I know well.'

'What?'

'The goat. I want to find that animal. And the guy holding the rope.'

But when I reached the place where I had seen the goat, it was no longer there.

'What are you doing?'

'I know only one goat,' I said—'personally I mean—and if that is her, that means that her owner is not working in my fields.'

'What are you talking about?'

'Babu is in the market, not in my field where he is supposed to be. Never mind. Come, it's time to go to the studio.'

Chapter 19

Palanpur, 1984

Pat and I had decided that the expedition to the studio had a higher chance of success if we pretended not to be together. I would enter first, and Pat would appear a little later, after the photographer and I had started operating the lab. The plan worked. The owner of the studio let me use his darkroom and he also offered to help. We had just started exposing the first sheet of an innocuous negative when a voice called. He went down, and I could hear Pat asking all sorts of questions, marvelling at his talent, and finally asking if he would come with her for a photo shoot. Not surprisingly, he immediately agreed. The photographer asked if I would mind being left alone for a little while and I assured him that it was fine. Off they went and I had the lab to myself. Pat and I had decided to develop ten copies each of the nine most revealing pictures. Just in case, the last ten sheets in the 18×24 Ilford box containing one hundred pieces would be used for duplicating some other negatives I had already shown to the photographer. I set to work as fast as I could with the Meopta. I was almost through when I heard Pat and the photographer coming back to the shop.

'Are you done?' he shouted to me from downstairs.

'Almost,' I replied. 'Don't bother, I can finish on my own.'

I heard Pat's voice but could not understand what she was saying.

'Okay, then,' the studio chap said in my direction, 'I will take care of a client.'

I was not too sure what 'taking care' of Pat meant, so I rushed through the last prints, rinsed them fast and arranged them in order to hide the hot photos. I looked around carefully. There was no trace left. I had taken the negatives and put them back in the plastic box. I placed the box and the ninety critical prints in the backpack and left the lab. I was ostensibly holding in my hands the ten prints that captured the landscape, a few trains, the Seed Store, the blind veteran, and Govindi.

As I came down the stairs, the photographer was answering Pat's technical question on the possibility of changing the focal length on a fixed focal lens. Curiously, the professional photographer did not mind the question and seemed eager to give her a full lecture. He also hinted that a dinner for two in a nice restaurant like Kallu Halwai would be a better place than a studio to discuss such things. Pat had obviously had a difficult time and, although we had agreed that we would pretend not to know each other, she exclaimed, as I appeared, 'Oh, but I know you. Are you also holidaying in Chandausi?'

'Do you know each other?' asked the deflated studio owner.

'We met in Delhi,' I answered. 'Thank you for allowing me to develop the pictures, they are good. Would you like to see them?' I asked Pat.

'Yes indeed,' she answered. 'Let us have tea and then you tell me what you're doing here.'

I paid the photographer handsomely, Pat thanked him profusely, and he promised to get her pictures ready very soon. We departed.

On the way back, sitting at the back of the tandem again, I briefed Pat on my failure at the ADO's office. She found it depressing. So did I and we started thinking of an alternative approach. We both agreed that it would be much easier if I could find my uncle's money and use it to fix the school. I also reassured Pat: the pictures were clear. We stopped in the middle of nowhere and Pat examined them:

'This is really a sad affair. What a nasty guy! Poor Smita. I will try to cheer her up.'

'Good idea!' I agreed. 'And I think there is enough here to put that police officer behind bars.'

'Perhaps, but Smita is right, we have to think about it a bit more. For the time being, hide the pictures and, tomorrow, we will deal with Neetu. That is the next priority.'

At the entrance of the village, still bothered by the goat I had seen at the market, I stopped at my fields. As I expected, Babu was not there. I could see that he had done some work, but that could not have taken him very long. Furious, I told Pat we should rush. I wanted to scold Babu at his own place. But there was no need to go to his house. As we approached the station, a train stopped, and I saw Babu and the goat get off it.

'See that,' I told Pat. 'This guy did not work in my fields and he took his goat for a ride.'

We had stopped. Pat was standing, her legs on either side of the tandem. She turned her pretty face towards me, 'He probably tried to sell his goat and failed again. Do you see the touching aspect of this?'

'I'm not even sure that he really wants to sell it,' I objected, still furious. 'He doesn't go about it the right way, the fool.'

She looked into my eyes with a lot of tenderness. With her left hand, she caressed my hair, 'For once, you banker may have a good point there. Maybe he does not really want to sell it. Just like you don't really care about your fields. Pay him for half a day and do not comment. That will be nice. He's worried about his wedding. And if you cared about your photography project, you would have taken a picture of Babu and the goat hiding behind that skinny tree.'

'All right, all right,' I agreed reluctantly, 'I won't scold him. Let's go home.'

When we arrived at my house, Pat said that she wanted to talk to more women in the village before the arrival of her PhD advisor. I stayed at home and, after hiding the pictures, I lit a cigar and was soon absorbed in the notes.

Palanpur, 1942

Pitamber was trimming his impressive moustache. As years went by, it had turned salt-and-pepper, but he still carried it with pride, for it stretched so far and so straight that it seemed to constantly challenge the laws of gravity. The moustache was a true symbol of chiefly authority and power, like the 'Smelly' Lee-Enfield, carefully placed on top of a slightly chipped Belgian mirror when not martially carried around. As was the red turban, skilfully arranged in the manner of fierce soldiers to make them look even fiercer by adding an inch or two to their height. But while the turban or even the rifle could achieve only so much, the moustache did not just contribute to Pitamber's proud appearance, it catalysed the effect of all the other attributes. In short, it was the jewel in the crown of the chief.

Every morning, this symbol of authority was the subject of great care by the bearer himself. One could not leave such an important affair to a common barber. Pitamber would trim his moustache in front of his mirror, ostensibly hung for this sole purpose, although Shobha also used it from time to time behind his back.

Despite the raindrops drumming furiously against the roof, Pitamber's trained ear detected his sister's footsteps along the thin mud wall outside. They were light and fast: she was trying to get to the door as quickly as possible to avoid getting wet. They were a little hesitant too because she had to avoid the numerous muddy potholes in a lane that had not been well built and was never maintained. After several years of cohabitation, Pitamber had learned to interpret the slightest variations in the rhythm of his sister's light walk. In this case, and in spite of the rain, it was a little too fast, too determined. There was a sense of urgency. The chief was slightly alarmed. He sighed, tried to put aside the uncomfortable feeling, and bent slightly to better focus on the critical task at hand. But nothing doing, the mirror sent back the sad image of a downward sloping moustache.

Shobha was furious. The rain had once more revealed the pathetic state of the lanes that ran through the village. If her brother had used the money he had earned from the road scheme to improve the condition of the household, that would have been one thing. But he had wasted much of it in Moradabad on illicit activities that Shobha knew enough about. She hated the looks the Palanpuris gave her when they got stuck in the mud. Recently, she had been scolded by the Bhatnagar family because the school had gone to the dogs. Finally, Shobha made it to the entrance of the pucca house. Or rather, of the house that used to be pucca. She passed between the buffaloes and ducked the rainwater pouring from a hole in the roof: a hole that was still not repaired because they did not have the money to do it. That further infuriated her. She charged loudly through a corridor. As the door opened violently, Pitamber jumped. His scissors cut through skin and a bit of blood came out.

'Kya hua?' asked Pitamber politely, trying to appear composed in spite of the trickle of blood. 'Is anything the matter?' he added soothingly.

Shobha was not soothed. She embarked on a litany of grudges that Pitamber listened to patiently while taking care of his small injury. To put a long energetic speech in a nutshell, Shobha was unhappy about Phool Singh's education and about the state of the roads.

Pitamber was not very receptive. Phool Singh had miraculously learned how to read and write. It was solely Shobha's doing, granted! Sending children to school was a women's fad, Pitamber had long maintained. But Shobha had pushed back hard. Her main reason—forcefully argued—was that since, as a chief, a man of importance, an alleged Colonel in the army, and a formerly rich landlord, Pitamber did not want his sons to work or play in the fields with other kids, they might as well be in school. Especially Phool Singh—Shobha's favourite boy—as Rampal was not so sharp. To preserve peace, Pitamber had finally agreed. That decision had a major impact on education levels in Palanpur. Chief Pitamber convinced the council that the school needed repair, that the salary of the teacher should be paid, and that the teacher should be present. For a while, things had worked. But the situation had deteriorated later. As for the road, Shobha gave another stern lecture. It made her feel better, even though she knew that nothing could be done in the absence of a new grant from the government.

Once Shobha was gone, Pitamber reflected on his situation. It was not brilliant. His sister's anger was one more symptom of increased uneasiness in the village about the current state of affairs. He could sense it everywhere. First, there was the anger in the Murao quarters. Pitamber's victory in the last elections had been achieved by cheating and everybody knew it. There was also a general resentment about the taxes that went to the British, and hence anger against the zamindar. Tikam Singh was not in favour and that was not good. The uneasiness also expanded beyond the village. George had reported more agitation than usual in the main stations, especially in Bareilly and Moradabad. At the same time, the number of trains had become fewer and fewer. Many of the engines and coaches were sent to Bombay or Calcutta, officially to be repaired in Britain or have their engines upgraded. But the locomotives were not coming back. Their drivers did, sometimes, sad and lonely without their machines. They revealed that Indian soldiers, and trains, were leaving India to help the British in their fight against the same cousins they had fought some years earlier, when so many Indian soldiers had died.

There were other outside influences. Some Palanpuris had heard a certain Dr Faruqui explaining on the radio that the Germans were stronger than the British and would defeat them for a thousand years. That seemed a very long time. And very much at odds with what the British were saying. But then, could the British be trusted? They were supposed to have crushed the Germans years ago and that was obviously not true. Again, but this time more openly, people started to wonder why the all-powerful British needed the help of Indian soldiers.

Locally, lower frequency of trains reduced the incomes in Palanpur, sometimes in unexpected ways. The dharamsala being located close to the railway tracks, some enterprising dacoits had thought of storing their loot there. It would be very convenient: being known to the police, their own home was sometimes searched, and it was hard to find a safe hiding place. They had approached Lakshminarayan, who was always ready to help fellow human beings in exchange for suitable donations. These matters settled, the dacoits expanded their business in the cities of Chandausi and Moradabad, and along the tracks. They would store the loot in the dharamsala, and all was well. Unfortunately, fewer trains meant less need for the dharamsala and that, in turn, limited Lakshminarayan's ability to donate to the gods.

Palanpur, 1984

Pat came back rather depressed. She had decided to talk to several women, including the wife of the blind soldier I had taken pictures of. Unfortunately, he had come home drunk the day before and had beaten her up so badly—shouting that she had not been able to give him a son—that the doctor had to be called. Quite often, one is disappointed to discover evidence of violence, vice, greed or hypocrisy in people and the stereotype of the gentle and wise old man is particularly misleading. But if the condition of women was sad, that of children was no better. Pat had visited the headman's house because she wanted to talk to Veena. There, she learned about the sordid death of Jagpal. He had had another violent encounter with the girl he had threatened earlier with the khurpi and she had been hurt very badly. After that, Jagpal was so scared of being beaten by his father that he swallowed some insecticide. He collapsed almost immediately but was still breathing. Rampal had gone around the village, desperately begging for a dunlop to transport his son to the government dispensary in Akroli. His own dunlop needed repair. He was able to borrow another one after two hours, and they left. Jagpal was still unconscious. By the time they reached Akroli, his body was cold. They wanted to avoid a police enquiry, so they returned to Palanpur and quickly buried the child's body. Having seen how Chunni and his wife had beaten their son, I could certainly understand how scared Jagpal had been. And he must have feared his father for a long time since Rampal had had to buy the special plastic bedsheets in Chandausi. The family was devastated: one son in jail and the other dead.

Pat had also run into Smita who was determined to arrange Babu's wedding ceremony as soon as possible after her aunt Neetu came out of jail. To speed up the wedding preparation, Smita had invited a friend of the future bride to come over and discuss the necessary arrangements. Pat and I were invited too as the generous employers and sponsors.

The girls had discussed other matters as well. Pat told me that she had informed Smita about the rifle. I looked up, annoyed, 'That means that the whole village will be on the platform commenting on my trip and the reasons for it.'

Pat did not think so. In any case, we would soon know.

In the morning, Pat woke me up with some difficulty. I had to get going. I packed the rifle neatly in a rectangular box. Nobody could tell what it contained. I had not asked Kishan Lal to accompany me, but he had things to do in Chandausi and would therefore come along. Nor had I asked Babu, who was busy with his wedding preparations. What concerned me most was that I had not spoken to the Captain about my plans. I had decided to trust him, and he could have provided some meaningful support. Unfortunately, my last few trips had been by tandem, not by train, so I had not met him. I could only hope that he would be on the train that day.

Chapter 20

Palanpur, 1984

Smita had not talked, after all, and there was no commotion—at least no unusual commotion—near the tracks when I reached the station. Kishan Lal was waiting for me and we were left alone. Unfortunately, the Captain was not in the train. Should I go ahead? I hesitated but decided to proceed. In Chandausi, we first went to see the lawyer. I had several things to tell him and I wanted to ask a little favour. I was immediately received. Kishan Lal stayed in the waiting room: there was no reason to expose him, it could be dangerous. I had announced my visit to Ashok Kumar, but without specifying the purpose. I placed the box on the table where the land register had been shown to me and opened it. The lawyer, who had not bothered to stand up when I arrived, sprang up on seeing the rifle and rushed to the door to make sure that it was bolted.

'Is this your uncle's rifle?' he asked.

'Indeed, it is. And the shells that I found at my uncle's place do not fit in it.'

'I'm not surprised. It is a very old rifle. With some history too. It's a nice piece, a very nice piece.'

I explained how I had found it in a hideout together with some documents and I showed one of the black notebooks containing my uncle's accounts. I then asked the lawyer if he could sign a paper certifying that I had shown him these things before I went to see BKS. He listened carefully, then said, 'Can you go back to the waiting room? I need to make a phone call. Leave the rifle here, you can take it back in five minutes.'

I agreed and went to the waiting room. There, to my surprise, I found Kishan Lal consulting some legal document, assisted by one of the lawyer's juniors. Kishan Lal was enquiring about the price of some piece of land in Pipli. This seemed strange, but the industrious farmer was probably looking for a productive use of his savings. I could not ask him what he was doing because Ashok Kumar was already calling me back to his office, 'What are your plans now?'

'I want to show this to BKS. It seems to me that this is a piece of evidence that exonerates Neetu.'

'Technically yes,' agreed the lawyer, 'but you may need a little help to clinch the matter.'

'What kind of help?'

'The help of someone who carries authority. You will be quite alone there, and that may not be a good thing.'

He paused for a while, looking worried, then asked, 'Are you going there immediately?'

'I don't think so. That guy is never in his office before 11 a.m. I will first go to the ADO.'

'Oh, yes, the proposal for a new temple.'

'For the school, Mr Kumar.'

'Yes, yes,' agreed the lawyer without much conviction. 'Yes, go to the ADO, then visit BKS. But be careful. I do not think that a paper from me will be very helpful, but if you want one...' He sat at his desk and wrote a short, official looking note with plenty of stamps and handed it over to me. 'Here it is. In the meantime, I will try to get you some help for your visit to the police station.'

'If you're sure that's a good idea,' I said after a short hesitation. Maybe he was right and the paper would not be necessary. Still, I pocketed it. 'You're the best judge.'

'No, I am only a lawyer,' replied Ashok Kumar, surprising me with a touch of humour that I would never have expected of him. 'But I will inform the judge that I have seen these items. Leave the notebook here and just take a copy of a few critical pages.'

I put the rifle back in its inconspicuous packing and went out, pulling a reluctant Kishan Lal away from the land register and his dreams of agricultural expansion.

The ADO was sitting at his desk when we arrived. He looked a little uncomfortable, and his cheeks were bulging on both sides like the stomach of a pregnant goat. Bending down, he reached for a small plastic bucket below his desk, spat a long jet of thick paan juice into it, then bared his red teeth at me, 'Welcome,' he said in an uncertain tone.

This time, I had taken the receipt book with the signatures of all those who had contributed. The ADO looked at the book, agreed that it was in order—it could not have been otherwise, the IDO had said that it was exactly what was needed—but he then came up with another demand: the traditional 'collection fee'. I learned that, in addition to the receipts, a 10 per cent 'collection fee' should be levied on the villagers and deposited on his desk in cash. I asked if he would give me a receipt for that, but he indicated that it would not be necessary since the collection charge was a well-established procedure. A tradition, in fact. A heated but pointless argument followed, finally cut short when I explained I had no intention of giving him any phony collection fee.

The ADO was obviously irritated, and he was past pretending, 'No problem, but in these circumstances, the proposal must go to the JDO. Do not come back until the collection fee is duly paid. The JDO will explain that himself.'

I collected all the documents and left, much to the dismay of the BDO.

On our way out, I wanted to lighten the atmosphere and asked Kishan Lal to explain what he had been doing at the lawyer's office. His answers remained evasive and I decided not to press him. So, we discussed the problem at hand and the number of hurdles we had overcome to take the gram panchayat proposal forward. They often occurred because we had not succeeded in seeing the right people at the right time. Then, there were the bureaucratic obstacles, and my resolve not to pay any bribes. Kishan Lal pointed out that, with their regular salaries, none of the civil servants we had met were supposed to be able to buy cars, TVs, Titan watches and such. And yet.... Kishan Lal, quite rightly, attributed that to their 'over-income', as it was known in the area.

I left Kishan Lal at the market to buy a few things for the farm, on the understanding that he would go back on his own to Palanpur. Then I went to the police station. On the way, I went past the post office. There was a telegram for Pat from her PhD advisor. I followed the Palanpur habit and read it: due to unavoidable circumstances, the Professor would only arrive a couple of days later, by the 10 a.m. train.

At the police station, the first thing I saw was the Mahindra with the twisted flag mast. BKS was there. I gave my name and the officer on duty went inside to announce me. He soon came back to say that BKS was extremely busy and that there was no way he could see me that day. I nodded and pretended to leave while shouting from the door, 'I'll take the rifle directly to the judge, then.'

A tornado came my way. I would never have thought that the fat BKS could move so quickly, 'A rifle? What rifle?'

'The rifle I found at my uncle's place. I also found something else, a little book of accounts,' I claimed. 'It points to a possible culprit. But you're very busy, I'm told, so I will come back later. The rickshaw is waiting for me to go to the district judge, don't worry.'

But BKS was obviously worried. 'I want to see that rifle. It's a piece of evidence in a police case.'

'I know, that's why I have to give it to the judge. I am sure that he will transfer it to you later. Actually, I already informed him that I was coming. He is expecting me and already has the book of accounts. I only brought a copy of a few pages, but they are interesting. You should take a look. I just dropped by to give you the good news,' I added, looking as angelic as I could. 'I also have a proof that I have deposited these things, I continued, showing the paper from the lawyer. BKS took it from my hand and crumpled it before dropping it on the floor. Ashok Kumar had been right, his paper was completely useless.

'Show me,' he barked.

I handed over the copies, holding the rifle close to my chest.

He glanced through and I showed him the last sentence, which read 'P getting greedy and aggressive. Could become dangerous. Has threatened me. B too.'

'All this plus the rifle seems to prove Neetu's innocence,' I emphasized.

'Who is Neetu?'

'The woman you are keeping in lock-up, whom you've accused of killing my uncle.'

'Ah, the Chamar woman. Her son is called Babu, isn't he? It starts with a "B", as in your uncle's book. He could be the culprit,' observed BKS. 'And this Chamar woman has resisted arrest. She has also been violent at times,' he added.

I ignored the mention of Neetu's violence to focus on Babu's possible involvement, 'I really doubt that Babu, who is always broke, could have received so much money from my uncle. It would have been noticed, don't you think?'

'Maybe,' he grudgingly agreed.

'Babu or Neetu could not have found my uncle's rifle, and Dalits do not own rifles, you know that. You cannot seriously argue that Neetu or her son might have kept a rifle at her place and brought it to my uncle's house. We now know for sure that he was killed by someone who already had a rifle, so....'

'I do not need you to tell me how to do my job,' he barked.

I nodded and made a pacifying gesture, 'Of course not,' I paused. 'Still....'

BKS did not like my tone. He glanced through the booklet. 'Your uncle was a crook, then,' he noted shrewdly, looking at me with mean eyes.

'I fully agree. But that does not make me one, does it? In fact, I can see that you are a little annoyed. Let me take this to the judge. That will be better.'

'There is no need.'

At this point, I expected BKS to become rude, perhaps violent, when I saw him look over my shoulder. His jaw dropped and he suddenly looked much less assertive.

'Indeed, there is no need,' said a calm voice behind me. 'The police will take care of everything.'

I was as stunned as the superintendent of police. The Captain was standing behind me, looking relaxed, 'I was about to release the Chamar woman,' BKS claimed. 'This man has just brought in a new piece of evidence.' While speaking, he had picked up the crumpled paper from the attorney and was smoothing it out on his desk.

'I know this young man. The nephew of Rajendra Pratap. I have just heard that you had found something interesting,' the Captain added, turning to me.

I managed not to look surprised, 'Hello, Captain, how are you doing?'

'I'm doing very well, thank you. I was just passing by and thought of paying a friendly visit to my old colleague BKS.'

BKS did not look all that pleased. He turned to the guard on duty, 'Get the Chamar hag out,' he shouted. Then, turning to me, he added defiantly, 'And you, leave the rifle and these papers.'

'Of course,' said the Captain.

A few minutes later, I was helping a very weak Neetu walk out of the police station. The sudden appearance of the Captain had surprised me. But I was truly startled by the presence of Babu on my tandem accompanied by several other Dalits and by Roshan.

'You should have told me that you were planning to do this,' whispered the Captain. 'You're lucky that I was informed. Please do not do such things again without informing me, it could be very dangerous.'

'Let me guess: Ashok Kumar contacted you,' I said, feeling rather clever.

'No, he could not have reached me. I was away. If you showed him all this, he probably tried. Anyway, I will see you later. Go back to Palanpur with Neetu. I have a few things to attend to.'

He walked back into the police station.

That was surprising: someone else who knew about my trip carried enough weight to move the Captain. I was lost.

Our return was triumphant. I was riding the tandem slowly, Neetu was sitting behind me and Babu was walking alongside, supporting his mother. Soon though, he said that he was tired and suggested that he would ride and Roshan could hold Neetu. That is how we arrived in Palanpur, Babu proudly driving the tandem with his mother at the back and I running behind them.

Everybody in the village was pleased, in particular Smita who emerged from the school building and came running towards us to greet her aunt. The only person who was not so pleased was the headman. He took me aside, 'So much effort for a Chamar,' Rampal grumbled. 'And you gave away the rifle, too. It was in my family before, you know. Anyway, why could you not do the same for my son?'

I could not really talk about my other plan with the pictures. At that stage, it was more a vague idea than a definite plan. Still, I tried to comfort him as much as I could. Finally, I managed to send him home and walked back to my place.

I was at home, quietly resting on my charpoy when Babu stormed inside, 'Anil sahib, come with me, quick!'

This was very unusual behaviour so I jumped and followed him. By the time I came out, Babu had already disappeared but I joined several others who were running towards the Seed Store. Something uncommon was clearly going on. Then we all heard the horn of a vehicle in the distance. People stopped running and gathered around Rampal's house. We did not have to wait long. Rampal's own dunlop emerged from around the corner, with Phool Singh standing on it and whipping the bullocks as hard as he could. He was followed by a tractor—the first that Palanpur had ever seen—and the driver, a Murao called Ganga Sahai, was blowing the horn.

For a minute, I thought that the arrival of the first train in the nineteenth century must have created a similar commotion. Of course, there was no zamindar in the crowd this time, but there was a headman and he was not looking very chiefly. Rampal's mouth was open and his bidi had fallen from his lips. His eyes were fixed on the unfolding drama. The whole village witnessed his humiliation: as hard as he pushed the bullocks, his brother, Phool Singh, was unable to remain ahead of the tractor. He was overtaken as they approached the Seed Store. Then, the tractor slowed down and crossed the Thakur area. It is not that Ganga Sahai was trying to show off, but there was no other route: the other approach to the Murao quarters was not wide enough for a tractor. And so it happened that Ganga Sahai, grandson of a poor Murao farmer who had struggled to make ends meet as a sharecropper of the zamindar, drove a tractor right past the homes and bullock-carts of the Thakurs. The writing was on the wall, and the affront would be hard to forget.

The tractor was not exactly brand-new, or the latest model. It was old and battered, but it was still a tractor. Ganga Sahai had competently steered his ship over the years. He had no brothers, and nor had his father. Thus, by the accident of demography, he had inherited his grandfather's entire estate: a full eighty bighas of fertile land. He could have lived an easy life off his property, but instead, like most Muraos, Ganga Sahai immersed himself in farming, spent in moderation and invested his savings wisely. With the cash of his early sugarcane crops, he bought healthy cows and she-buffaloes and fed them well. In the winter, he augmented his earnings by making gur from a kolu. He was often the first to acquire new farm technology: a pumping set, a thresher or flour mill, and now—a tractor.

Not all of Ganga Sahai's vast land was cultivable. The fallow patches were strewn with large stones and tree stumps that no one had ever been able to remove. Ganga Sahai went straight to his house, dropped off a few boxes and went on to his field. Obviously, he intended to make the best possible use of his investment. A few Thakurs had followed Ganga Sahai, hoping to witness his venture failing. It did not. Within an hour, the largest obstacles had been removed and the Murao was still working. He would clearly continue for a few more hours. I left, soon followed by Rampal, 'You see, Anil sahib, this is what happens when people try to rise above their station.'

'As headman, you should be happy,' I objected. 'This will improve living conditions in the village. Like the train in the old days.'

'It will bring wealth to Ganga Sahai, but the rest of us will suffer. These Muraos do not respect anything.'

I let him brood and went back home. On the way, I saw Kishan Lal going to his field. I called him, 'Did you not go see the tractor?'

'No, I'm busy. I also want to buy a tractor, but I have other plans first.'

'That is great,' I said.

'Yes, I want my farm to grow. When we expand our horizons, good things happen.'

Impressed, I left him. As I was walking back home, I almost bumped into Smita who was carrying a pair of women's shoes. She explained that her aunt needed rest and she herself had some business to discuss with Pat. That sounded mysterious and interesting, so I wanted to know more. I learned that, after the fiasco of the bath and the excessive interest displayed by Palanpuri men in her jeans, Pat had decided to confront the wardrobe issue head on. She had requested Smita to help her drape one of the many saris that she had bought in Connaught Place. Her Adidas shoes would not go with a sari, so Smita had brought a pair of sandals. I could stay in the house, but access to the dressing room—that meant the other room, since there were only two—was forbidden.

Smita and Pat went into the room. I could not see anything but I could hear. I figured that a few Palanpuris were also listening. The billy goat certainly was.

'Hold this while I fold the sari.'

'Shit, it's going everywhere.'

'No! Not like that!'

'Oh dear, it's all fallen out.'

This was followed by giggles but then some serious technical discussion took place.

'Of course, you can decide how low you want to wear it on your waist. Like, whether you want to show your navel or not.'

I decided to contribute, 'But you should look very annoyed if it slips a bit,' I yelled.

'Well, yes,' agreed Smita, in a serious tone.

I pushed my luck, 'And the strategy you adopt for the lower part can be enhanced by tactical movements of the upper part.'

'Can you just keep quiet?'

'But that's true, actually,' laughed Smita.

'Yes, I suppose that all these wardrobe accidents do happen in spite of our best intentions.'

'Naturally.'

This went on for a little while. Then the girls were finally ready.

When Pat emerged from the dressing room, I must say I was not totally convinced. Of course, Pat always looks cute, but just as I was not sure that Smita would have looked great in jeans, I felt that Pat in a sari did not look as great as she usually did. She immediately sensed that by seeing my reaction from the corner of her pretty eyes. Smita too.

'It's all very nice,' I said. 'You ladies look lovely. What's the plan?'

'Do you think we did all this just for you? Not at all! We are going out for a ladies' night.'

'That's impressive. A ladies' night in Palanpur? Would I be allowed to join?'

Pat turned to Smita, 'What do you think?'

'He is a foreigner, so that is fine,' she replied with a smile.

'Let's go.'

Pat was holding the pleats of her sari with both hands so that it would not interfere with her steps and would not get spoiled by trailing on the ground. It was practical if nothing else.

'They're going to teach me a famous song,' she continued. 'It's from a movie called *Ujala* and the title of the song is 'Ya Allah Ya Allah Dil Le Gayi'. It is the story of a nice guy called Ramu who is very poor and falls in with bad company.'

'Let me guess…. In the end, honesty and love will triumph. Because I bet there's a girl in the story.'

Pat looked at me suspiciously and shrugged her shoulders, 'Are you not happy that we girls are here?'

'Delighted,' I agreed.

By then, we had crossed the village and ended up in a house in the Murao quarters where a group of women were playing an odd game—if it can be called a game—to find out which one of two spouses would die first. The game consisted of writing both their names, converting the letters into numbers and performing some simple arithmetic operations to finally arrive at a number to be divided by three. The residual indicated the gender of the first spouse to die: 0 when it was not clear, 1 for the man and 2 for the woman. It all looked like mumbo-jumbo to me. All the same, trying the formula on a few cases of Palanpur couples where husband or wife had died recently, we got the right answer in every case.

While Pat was learning her song, I went out for a smoke and Chunni turned up. I offered him a cigar. After the first few puffs, he started coughing endlessly. Worried, I suggested that he should stop smoking but he replied that this cough had nothing to do with it: it was just that he had forgotten to chew sugarcane that day. After a while, the cough subsided, and we discussed the likelihood of there being prostitutes in Palanpur. Chunni thought that they generally did not exist in villages, but illicit sexual relationships did happen. Enlightened on this matter and with my cigar coming to an end, I went back in. The conversation was quite animated. The women agreed that 'some people' tended to discriminate, paying more attention to boys than girls. Two women said that girls were looked after more tenderly than boys, however, because they would have to leave the home one day while boys could enjoy the whole range of Palanpur pleasures all their life. One lady had some progressive ideas, arguing that they both needed equal love and attention. But she also agreed that one boy was necessary to manage the land and inherit the property. That was why she and her husband had spent so much time and money—six hundred rupees—on the treatment of their first boy who nevertheless died.

On the way back, I reflected on this mix of simple pleasures and terrible sadness that was everyone's lot. It was presumably true in London too, but Palanpuris had to live through the downs without any form of financial protection.

Chapter 21

Palanpur, 1984

It was already 9.30 a.m. and Pat was nervous, 'You understand, he is a great professor and has published plenty of papers. He has a PhD from the London School of Economics, and although he has spent all his life in Bombay and Delhi, I'm sure he has rural roots. So, he must know rural society, you see. And I cannot make his hypothesis work.'

She had been discussing her hypothesis with most women in the village, but without much success. The idea was clever and appealing though. It also fit with her own beliefs. According to the theory—not really hers, more that of the LSE-trained advisor with rural roots—women in Indian villages wanted to work outside the household in order to gain financial independence, but their husbands were preventing them from doing so. With Smita, she thought she had the perfect supporter. Over the first few days, being focused on Smita—and hearing stories of like-minded friends of hers in Moradabad—she felt vindicated. But while Pat wanted the proposition to be tested, Smita had warned her that gainful employment for women was an urban idea. It would hopefully extend to Palanpur, one day, but in a distant future. Pat wanted it to be true now. Unfortunately, and frustratingly, Pat had soon discovered that Smita was right: women in Palanpur preferred not to work outside the household. Those who did were forced to do so because their husbands were not earning enough to keep the household going. For them, giving up outside work would mean an improvement in social status. Conversely, those who did not work considered that they would go down in the social hierarchy if they were forced to do so. Pat's long explanations, translated by Smita, on the freedom that came with financial independence sounded strange to the women answering her questionnaire. Pat wasted several days pursuing that line of argument. There had been a glimpse of hope with the Bhatnagar family, where women agreed that their girls should study and have the option to seek employment. But even they added that if the girls could avoid exercising that option, it would be just as well. This was a major blow to Pat's academic aspirations. She desperately wanted to discuss the matter with her advisor, fearing that she had approached her topic the wrong way.

'Maybe that theory is just wrong,' I suggested cautiously.

'I should have taken the other topic, the one on sharecropping,' she continued, not really listening to me.

'What is that?'

'That is when a farmer rents land and pays the owner with a share of the crop,' she answered absent-mindedly.

'What is there to research about that?'

Pat looked at me, slightly irritated, 'Do we have to talk about that now? It is very complicated. It has to do with cooperative conflict, the Coase conjecture, and stuff like that.'

'Kishan Lal and Babu never mentioned any conjecture of that Coase guy, you know.'

'Can you just go away and keep yourself busy? I have things to do. And we can argue about who knows India better, but Professor Subramanian, I can tell you, knows it better than both of us together.'

One thing I have learned in life is that when your girlfriend explodes like this, you keep calm and make the best of it. For example, you can go fish or see friends with her blessings. In this case, Pat's outburst gave me a good excuse to read some more of my father's notes before the train arrived. She left to arrange for tea and biscuits for Professor Subramanian, alias Subbu, who would surely appreciate the attention after the train journey. She had already set up a table with a few chairs in the Seed Store with Babu's help. Since Subbu would spend one, perhaps two nights in Palanpur, arrangements had been made to erect a spacious tent with a real bed on the outskirts of the village. Everything was ready.

Palanpur, 1940–1944

For many years, Lakshminarayan had lived with a young woman called Preeti whom he had met in undisclosed circumstances. She was an orphan, smart and good-looking. He took care of her and she took care of his needs. All of them. It could have been a peaceful life for Lakshminarayan, but both Pitamber and Tikam Singh disliked him. That had reduced his income—

already battered by the reduced train traffic—in ways that soon proved incompatible with Preeti's material aspirations. Together, they devised a simple, innovative and rather lucrative scheme. Lakshminarayan would pretend to be looking for a suitable groom for his protégée whom, out of the kindness of his heart, he had rescued and taken care of for many years. In words that would have made a stone cry, Lakshminarayan would explain how miserable her childhood had been and how he had done all he could to give her his best. The time had come for Preeti to get married though. Lakshminarayan was sad to let her go but was taking comfort in the obvious: being raised in a devout atmosphere, she would be a good wife for the lucky boy who would marry her. Of course, he would humbly add, there could be no question of a dowry. They had no money: Preeti was used to a simple life and the holy person was content with the bare minimum. Still, the groom's family could perhaps make a little donation and contribute to the temple. Most families in and around Palanpur would have laughed at this story. But it had some traction in remote villages. Lakshminarayan would accept the donation and let Preeti go. The sight of the poor girl crying in the arms of her heartbroken protector-cum-uncle as she departed for her new home was very touching.

A month or two later, depending on how fast the generosity of the groom's family declined, Preeti would reappear in Palanpur, claiming that she was being harassed by her new in-laws and perhaps even in danger of being killed. Running for her life, she would seek protection from the holy man again. He would sternly receive the groom's family—they would usually arrive in the next train—and express his bitter disappointment at how his little gem had been treated. Talking about gems, the groom's family would explain that several necklaces and rings had disappeared at the same time as Preeti. An offended Lakshminarayan would scold the complainants and swear that he had not seen any of these valuables that they were talking of. On the contrary: the poor girl had come back with nothing but the clothes on her back—and in what shape, God! That was a scandal. Finally, feeling angry or confused depending on their nature, the groom and his family would leave. Lakshminarayan would happily resume his relationship with Preeti until—money having run out again—it was time to look for a new groom. As the years passed and Preeti grew older, they had to look for victims further and further away, but the trick still worked.

In the fullness of time, Lakshminarayan realized that he was getting older himself. He had felt it in his bones and seen it in Preeti's eyes. Earlier, his girlfriend would come back from her adventures rejuvenated. Her eyes were brighter. She had had fun and relished being part of a conspiracy. That feeling had faded. She still returned each time but now wondered where all this was taking her. She also found Lakshminarayan less and less attractive while the grooms seemed more handsome. Sensing this, Lakshminarayan decided that they had enough money and he took drastic action: Preeti became pregnant and gave him a son. They called him Brahmachari.

Preeti, however, was missing the eagerness of a new groom and was no longer content in Palanpur. She persuaded Lakshminarayan to play the little trick one more time. Reluctantly, he agreed. Brahmachari was sent away to some relative in Jargaon when the future in-laws arrived and Preeti left with them.

The groom turned out to be quite attractive. After minor failures due to lack of experience, which was compensated for by Preeti's abundance of it, the dazzled husband proved to be a good lover. The family was well off, the mother-in-law not too unpleasant, there were servants around and the house was more comfortable than Lakshminarayan's humble abode: the Brahmin had always been more reluctant to repair a roof than to wash his clothes. She decided to stay.

An alarmed Lakshminarayan took the train to remind Preeti of her duties towards him and their lovely Brahmachari. They met at night and in secret. She explained that her duties were now with her new family. What about your son? Preeti promised to come once in a while but she was pregnant again and would therefore have many other obligations. But she was not worried: the holy person would make a great father for Brahmachari. Not particularly interested in fatherhood on a daily basis, Lakshminarayan argued vehemently and the discussion degenerated. Still, Preeti did not agree to come back. The Brahmin lost his temper and hit Preeti hard, leaving her with a black eye and a few broken ribs. He also stole the necklace and bangles she was wearing before going back to Palanpur. At least, he had not lost everything. The groom's family lodged a complaint and urged the police to visit Palanpur: the black eye had forced the new wife to reveal the truth, or some version of it.

When the police visited Lakshminarayan, he cried, screamed and displayed all the signs of very deep distress, moving the policemen. He squarely put the blame on the groom's family. Unfortunately, he had been seen at the train station and denounced. Tipped off by Preeti, the police had searched his place and found the necklace and bangles. The evidence against him was strong and he was taken into custody where he soon died. Brahmachari stayed with the distant cousin in Jargaon who raised him. Preeti was too busy with her other children to look after him.

Palanpur, 1984

A familiar whistle got me on my feet. It was 10.05 a.m. and the steam engine was slowly approaching the station as if reluctant to stop. It finally did. Distressed by the tragedy that had struck his family, Rampal would not welcome the important visitor, in spite of Pat's insistence, so the welcome committee was modest.

Professor Subrahmanya Subramanian, dressed in a suit, had travelled first class. He immediately complained about the journey. Although there were only a few passengers in his coach, he had had the misfortune of sitting for the last hour next to some retired army man who kept asking all sorts of awkward questions. Fortunately, the man had finally got off, so the Professor had had some peace but only for a short while. He looked at the blazing sun, observed that it was hot and that there was a lot of dust. His new shoes might get spoiled. He bent down and dusted them.

Pat waited until Subbu stood up before expressing her delight at the prestigious visit. Would the great man care for some refreshment? The visitor raised his hand in horror: he would not have it, preferring to drink from his own thermos. He accepted a biscuit, however, and explained that the same unexpected complications that had delayed his arrival would force him to go back to the capital by the 3 p.m. train the same day. There was not much he could do about it.

'Oh,' exclaimed Pat, 'that's unfortunate. Are you sure? I was hoping you'd stay longer. We prepared a tent. I think it's important, you see, I found some interesting...'

Subbu looked offended, 'Of course, I'm sure. As I said, there is nothing I can do about it. If you have found something important, let us review your work now.'

'That is not what I meant,' answered a nervous Pat '...would you like to come to the Seed Store? We have set up a little table and...'

The Professor looked at his shoes, then in the direction of the Seed Store at the other end of the sandy path. 'Would it be possible to set up that table in the waiting room of the station instead?'

The request created a bit of a commotion but Babu was sent to bring back to the station the table and the chairs that he had carried earlier to the Seed Store, while Subbu waited impatiently. Finally, everything was ready, and the Professor agreed to sit on one of the chairs. For convenience, he chose to sit next to Pat rather than in front of her.

I chose to leave and spend the rest of the scholar's visit reading the last few pages of my father's notes.

Palanpur, 1955

One day, Pitamber came back from Moradabad, triumphant. After a thorough search, he had found a suitable bride for Phool Singh. Rampal could wait a bit, he was younger. There had been many interested parties, as expected. For one, the groom's father was a village chief as well as a famous ex-soldier. In addition, Phool Singh, although not a great student, had been admitted in a teacher training college pompously called Ideal Academy. Regular gifts of sweets and a little cash to the college teachers earned him a degree in English and History that his marks did not warrant. Among the brides on offer, Pitamber had selected Meena who came from a respectable and well-off Thakur background. The two families were distantly related, something both found convenient. Preliminary discussions had been arranged by an interested third party. It was followed by bilateral talks. Phool Singh had made an appearance at the bride's house. He did not shine, but that was attributed to shyness, and quite appreciated in view of his and his father's great achievements. That short encounter was enough for Meena's family, but Pitamber and Shobha took a long hard look at the future wife. They found her pretty, suitably shy and in good health. She had been well fed by attentive parents and her body would be able to carry a few strong sons. Her large eyes, fair complexion, round cheeks and smooth arms were all displayed. Her hair was modestly hidden by the pallu of her sari, but enough was shown to convey that it was very dark and looked strong. Meena talked very little and that was also highly appreciated. This legitimate curiosity satisfied, her parents sent Meena away and serious negotiations started on dowry and other practical matters. That took several visits to Moradabad, but everything was finally settled. It was also agreed that the ceremony would exceptionally be held in Palanpur, at Pitamber's request.

There was a reason for this. At the end of the last visit, after everything was agreed, Pitamber sent Shobha back to Palanpur. He stayed in Moradabad, on the pretext of some official duty. Shobha pretended to believe her brother and left. Pitamber rushed to The Perfumed Garden and, ignoring the immediate pleasures that Ms Padma obligingly offered, started making arrangements for the special party he had been dreaming about for so long. Those negotiations were less tedious than the marriage discussions, but costlier. In the end, there too, everything was settled. Ms Padma asked where the ceremony would take place. Pitamber smiled: for what he was planning, he would surely be more comfortable in his own place. He gave his address in Palanpur.

The big day arrived. For Pitamber, it was the greatest in his life. It also turned out to be his last, but he died in such blissful circumstances that, years later, old Palanpuris still sighed, hoping for a similar fate. Everything was grand, from the appearance of Phool Singh, who was sitting on a magnificent horse and carrying Pitamber's rifle, to the arrival of the bride, covered from head to toe, her pretty, plump hands beautifully decorated with henna. The dowry included shiny jewels and many other things that considerably impressed Palanpuris. The food was good and, perhaps more importantly, it was abundant—as a proud chief, Pitamber had invited everybody. Chhote Ram, who tried to demonstrate that laddoos were in short supply, had to give up with a major bellyache that made him run to the fields many times and kept him in bed for several days.

The main event took place in the evening. The incredible sight of three dancing girls—accompanied by Ms Padma who wanted to keep an eye on everything—arriving on a cart in the sunset eclipsed the rest of the ceremony. Nobody in the village had ever dreamed of so much beauty. And when they performed, the artistic quality of the show was a revelation. In Palanpur certainly, but possibly even in Bombay or Delhi, the villagers thought, such elegance, such depravity, such excesses, such beauty had never been experienced. The women of the village watched out of the corner of their eyes. The men displayed less modesty.

The best and the worst parts of the day were yet to come for Pitamber. Ecstatic, more immersed in the dance show than he had been in the marriage ceremony, and burning with anticipation, he discreetly called two of the dancers and they escaped to the fields. However, his exit was noticed by Chhote Ram who was still swallowing laddoos as fast as possible. He decided to follow the trio and was himself immediately followed by other curious villagers. Thus, it was a whole crowd that observed, with considerable interest, the lovely and fleshy bottoms of the dancers frantically moving around a slimmer Pitamber. One of the women suddenly realized that they were being watched and shouted angrily. While she did not appear particularly flustered, the impact on Pitamber was devastating. After a few more thrusts, clearly out of rhythm, he uttered a roar. Pitamber's cry was a paroxysm of agony and pleasure. Then, the chief stopped moving altogether and forever. The women hastily reached for their clothes.

Pandemonium ensued. The guests started running around frantically. The women ran to where the action was taking place, brushing aside their husbands' argument that the scene would not be suitable; and the husbands followed. All came upon a naked Pitamber. Despite angry shouting from the men, none of the women covered their eyes. A massive brawl erupted, started by some drunk guests who did not think that the party was proceeding as it should. Things became even more complicated when some men insisted on protecting the virtue of the escaping dancers from a large number of harassers.

Phool Singh had run, along with the others. Seeing his father dead, he stood still, not quite sure what to do. Meena arrived a little later owing to the heavy load of jewellery around her neck and arms. Rampal was already there. He took matters into his hands, 'We must deal with him and get these idiots to stop fighting,' he told a still confused Phool Singh.

Stoically, he covered the body.

Phool Singh was not quick-witted in spite of his education. His thoughts still on the wedding and his eventual return to Chandausi, he proved unable to grasp the implications of the tragedy. Two days later, he went back to college, ceding the reins to Rampal who became the head of the family. When Phool Singh returned, perhaps prompted by his wife, he tried to claim what he thought was his due. He even competed with his brother in the elections and the result was that a Murao was elected village head.

Angry, Rampal gave his brother hell. Phool Singh now sat at home without even reading any of the few books he had brought back from college. An obscure certificate stating that he had attended some classes proudly adorned a shelf in the main room, just under his high school degree. That one had been framed in more glorious days. Phool Singh drank tea, occasionally a bit of liquor, and played cards with the other Thakurs. The rest of the time, he took naps. He settled for a life of leisure and dignity under the cosy shadow of his hard-earned degree. All was well.

Rampal was not pleased, however, and he got Phool Singh a job as a teacher in the village school. He would at least earn some money. Phool Singh's liquor intake increased, especially after Meena's death, and that gave him an idea for a business. He decided to run the illegal alcohol store in front of the station and completely gave up on the school. Rampal rejoiced: his brother was finally contributing to the household.

Palanpur, 1984

Thus ended my father's notes, clarifying Pitamber's dubious reputation. It was nearly 3 p.m., so I decided to go to the station to check on Pat.

Chapter 22

Palanpur, 1984

It had taken Pat just a few hours to become less of a fan of her advisor. Apparently, he had turned down Govindi's lunch—I had paid for it—preferring to eat what he had brought in his own tiffin. Perhaps this was a good thing after all, since the food that had been prepared for Subbu was given to Babu who passed it on to Roshan. As he was eating his chicken sandwiches, the Professor gave a short speech about development issues in India, stressing the need for endogenous growth.

The Professor had also declined to visit the village. Being an expert, he already knew what to expect and feared that his shoes might not survive the walk. It would be better if the women interviewed by Pat came to him for a short triangulation. Unfortunately, some would not leave their house, whether it was because their husbands objected or out of their own will. That limited the scope of the interviews and implicitly confirmed that social change was best seen as a long-term objective.

Finally, the whistle of the 3 p.m. train, although still far away, signalled that the misery was coming to an end.

Just before departing, Subbu summed up his findings. He concluded that the hypothesis about women in the labour force was still correct but that Palanpur was not a representative sample: it was biased by the frequent influence of western ideas. Foreign visitors had spoiled things for economic theory and its application. He was sure that the hypothesis could easily be proved right in Pipli—just next door—for example, or anywhere else. He would be very eager to have Pat at his side while touring India to find more suitable sites for fieldwork. They could also work together on the model and include more explanatory variables. Did Pat care to accompany him? Pat quietly answered that she would consider the proposal but, unfortunately, was unable to leave right then.

I reflected a bit. Was Palanpur polluted by western influence? On the whole, I had found very little evidence of consumerism in the village. Perhaps a tradition of frugality was still influential, or people concealed their true purchasing power in a colourless peasant lifestyle, as Kishan Lal had once explained to me. I had seen no fancy clothes, no expensive watches, few radios, very few cigarettes—just bidis—and no items like expensive bags or shoes or silver plated lighters. According to Pat, who had visited some slums in Delhi, these things were quite common there. Was I guilty of importing western habits? I had distributed a few cigars, of course, but only good ones. And I would leave my two-in-one behind with a few cassettes, but I doubted that it would change mentalities. To be sure, I would take back the cameras.

I decided that Professor Subrahmanya Subramanian was an ass and Pat was also thinking along the same lines. We decided to go home and relax a bit. We did that and spent an hour resting. Suddenly, Pat stood up.

'I almost forgot! Smita told me that the family of the girl she had found for Babu wanted the ceremony to take place at the earliest.'

'Who is the lucky girl?'

'Smita did not give me the details, but we should get acquainted with marriage ceremonies. Don't forget that you are the main sponsor,' she teased.

It was true that the marriage season was in full swing. Following Pat's advice, we accepted Phool Singh's invitation extended the day before: one of his cousins was getting married to a girl from Rastampur, a village about 10 kilometres away from Palanpur. Pat and I were welcome to attend. We left on the tandem and joined the 'baraat' escorting the groom—a guy called Devinder—to Rastampur for the marriage ceremony. The event was quite impressive. The guests had come on six or seven tractors with trailers as well as a jeep, and there was an excellent band as well as a 'company' of entertainers and dancers. The premises were vast. Several Thakurs had brought their rifles and cartridges were available for free, despite costing—I was told—five rupees each. Everything went smoothly until a fight erupted. It all started during the 'dwarwar' ceremony. Earlier, Devinder's father, a landowner called Basant, had told the girl's family that he had no particular demand for the dowry. So, at the dwarwar, the bride's family gave Devinder the customary bicycle, a radio, a bed, two chairs, one small table, a watch, three bedside lamps, five pressure cookers, and two hundred rupees in cash. Unfortunately, some people in the baraat, realizing that the girl's parents were quite affluent, thought this was stingy. They commented that the girl's family had 80 bighas of land, a tractor, and, hypothetically at least, heaps of hidden jewellery. Basant—quite drunk by then—became furious and shouted that unless his future in-laws handed him 20,000 rupees on the spot, the baraat would leave. Phool Singh sided with Basant but didn't think that the baraat should leave. Modest as it was, the dowry was consistent with what had been agreed and the consensus was that Basant had been careless, missing an opportunity to demand a good amount of cash. Basant's fury ignited the fight. He even objected to the lewd performance of the 'company', although the show was being performed at some distance. As time passed, the risk that the food, cooked at midday, would go bad was increasing and tensions were rising. By 3.30 a.m., under severe pressure because the state of the food had reached tipping point, the baraat agreed to eat, signalling Basant's capitulation. An hour later, after this late dinner, Pat went to sleep for a couple of hours. Everybody else continued to drink and talk. I had stayed awake and that was how I heard confirmation that Phool Singh was involved in all kinds of schemes to sell liquor, organize gambling sessions, and—the chatter had become whispers—sell opium. My father's notes were accurate. A lantern used to be lit, I was told, when the liquor store in Palanpur was open for business. Unfortunately, crestfallen guests explained, all that was over. At 7 a.m., I woke Pat up and, too tired to cycle back home, we loaded our tandem on a dunlop headed for Palanpur. Small quarrels were still going on, but the issue of the dowry had not been raised again.

In the afternoon, as I was focusing on my book project, Pat came back from another tour of the village. She had talked to Veena again.

'She is an interesting girl, you know. A bit boyish in her ways, but very sweet. She is very disturbed by the fate of her brothers. Nothing can be done about Jagpal but I think that if Hukum could somehow be freed, she would leave Palanpur. She does not want to leave just now though because the family is already struggling.'

'Well, these are nice thoughts, but her future is rather easy to predict,' I said. 'Her parents will find a suitable boy and that will be it.'

'Why should it be that way? She is a capable girl and she was studying until last year. She is getting bored. She needs a good occupation.'

'Housewife,' I suggested.

'Stop it! No way, something more satisfying. I think she will do better than you think. She even said she had a plan.'

'We shall see,' I concluded doubtfully.

Pat had also learned that Pratap, one of Devinder's relatives in Palanpur, ended up selling two buffaloes to help with the wedding expenses. 'How is that possible?' I asked. 'And how are they going to cultivate their fields now?'

'They will borrow, I guess. They must pay because one of the guests, a nephew of Pratap's, took off from Rastampur with some of the bride's jewellery.'

'What?'

'Yes, that is what happened.'

'I told you there was never a dull moment in Palanpur. Now, let's rest a bit. Tonight we have another wedding and tomorrow, I must leave early to go to the JDO.'

'Oh, yes, I forgot to tell you,' exclaimed Pat, shaking her pretty curls, 'Smita and I are coming along to Chandausi. We have to buy stuff for Babu's wedding.'

'Really?'

'Yes, it is all arranged, my dear!'

Pat put a finger on my lips, 'Tomorrow, I want to sing for the village.'

'Oh gosh!'

She heaved herself up and looked angrily at me, 'What do you mean, gosh? I have brought my guitar all the way. Why should I leave it in the case? It will be a good change for everybody.'

'What will you sing? Nobody knows Herman's Hermits or Manfred Mann in these parts.'

She leaned back on her pillow, smiling, 'All these weddings, these love stories, have inspired me. Would you agree that everybody here talks about love, meeting the right person, and the rest of it? Essentially, they discuss all these things that are important in Palanpur and elsewhere?'

I had to agree, even though the scope for adventurous affairs in Palanpur was very limited, certainly compared to London.

'It's true that I could sense the tension when you were taking your bath. Love was in the air. A subtle kind of hush.'

She smiled again, 'Not so subtle. But it shows that the universal theme of frustrated love appeals to people here as it does elsewhere, isn't it right? I have chosen a song that invokes just that...with some adjustments.'

'And that is?'

'You will see,' she answered, kissing me.

That triggered a chain of actions that made it impossible to ask more questions.

In the evening, we went to Pipli to attend a wedding in the Murao community. There were no rifles and no fireworks, just a little band, and the groom arrived on a small horse. The dowry, however, was more substantial than the previous day and the presents included not only the usual radio, watch, etc., but also 600 rupees in cash. The Thakur wedding had ended in a fight. This one was dull. Some guests were just killing time as they waited for the food. I even caught Kishan Lal gambling with a few others. They were playing with beans and, knowing Kishan Lal, I was sure the beans did not stand for real money. The party finished quite early—everybody had a lot of work to do the next day.

The next morning, we met a peppy Smita on the railway platform. She was still very concerned about Hukum, but wisely explained that it was important to make the most of any happy moment. She was confident Hukum would agree. I agreed too and asked what the deal was with Babu, 'The girl I found for him started studying with me, but she did not finish. Still, she is very intelligent. A bit older than Babu, but that does not really matter, does it?'

'A lot older?' I asked as Pat discreetly stepped on my foot.

'A few years, but that does not prevent love, does it?' argued Smita, beaming.

'Of course not. And is she pretty?' I continued while Pat was—less discreetly now—pinching my arm.

'I would not say pretty, but she is a beautiful person with a lot of charm,' Smita answered with enthusiasm.

'And when will the ceremony be held?' I asked, and Pat relaxed a pre-emptive pinch.

'In two days. Things are more or less ready, but there is still a lot of work to do. Please do not be too hard on Babu. He has a lot on his plate.'

I promised with a smile, trying very hard not to roll my eyes or say something I might regret. Pat had stepped on my foot, ready to apply pressure if needed. At Chandausi, I accompanied her and Smita for a while as they went around buying a pair of new shoes, a watch, a shirt, and plenty of other essential items that Babu would never use after his wedding. I left the girls to themselves when they entered a shop selling cosmetics and silk handkerchiefs. It was time to go and see the JDO.

The meeting with the JDO was refreshing in a way. He made it clear that the work would not start any time soon if things proceeded through official channels. Less official ones would be much faster. He did not open his hand for a bribe. He was simply experienced. He suggested that I should see the KDO who could perhaps accelerate matters by doing the work in a sequential manner. I did not really understand what 'sequential' meant, but still rushed to the office of the KDO.

The KDO was a very friendly and respectable old man with grey hair. He explained that all the bureaucratic difficulties I had faced were just the tip of a huge iceberg that sadly obstructed rural development. He would help me. Feeling understood, I accepted a cup of tea and we chatted a bit. When I asked why the ADO could not better handle the law-and-order situation in the locality, he answered bluntly that there were plenty of guns in Chandausi and Moradabad. He pointed at a recent article in *India Today*, dated 30 September 1983, that said that any official in UP who tried to deal with corruption was quickly transferred. Indeed, when visiting the CDO—or was it the EDO?—I had seen the list of his predecessors and noticed the increasingly rapid turnover. As he was talking, the KDO drafted a letter that authorized the work to start. He signed it, stamped it, sealed it, and asked a peon to post it to Rampal as the village head. So much efficiency was unbelievable: the letter would be in Palanpur the next day.

I was in a cheerful mood when I joined the girls on the railway platform. Smita was also happy: Pat had told her about the pictures.

'This is really good news. We must make the most of it.'

I agreed, 'We need to think it through carefully, though. We have only one opportunity. We cannot afford to waste it.'

'I'm not sure what to do, but I will ask Babu for his advice,' Smita said seriously.

I tried not to laugh, helped by another hard pinch from Pat that left a mark.

'Excellent idea,' I managed to say, in a serious tone.

'But we should wait until after the wedding ceremony. The marriage is too important. He will take care of others afterwards.'

'Yes, that is better,' I agreed. 'Did you manage to find everything for the ceremony?'

Smita clapped her hands, 'Yes, we did. It is all so nice.'

I was quite well trained at patiently going through the full list of things Pat would buy on a Saturday shopping trip in London, and thus skilled at displaying signs of deep interest. Pat was not fooled but she expected me to make the right noises. These acquired skills turned out to be immensely useful in this situation. I went through everything, including a silk tie that would presumably be used each time Babu would be received by a BDO or CDO.

Back in Palanpur, we reminded everybody that Pat would sing that evening and we went home. The day was far from over though. I reached home to find Kishan Lal waiting for me.

'Come quick, they are destroying our houses.'

'Whose houses?'

'The houses in the Murao quarters. Maybe the Chamars' also.'

On the way, he explained that Phool Singh and his cousin Pratap—the uncle of the young man who had stolen the jewellery in Rastampur—had spent the whole day draining a pond using Pratap's diesel engine, hoping to catch a lot of fish. I immediately suspected that Pratap was trying to recoup the loss of his buffaloes by selling all the fish in the pond. To start with, the water pumped out of the pond had been used to irrigate the nearby fields and people were pleased. Soon, however, the fields were saturated, and the water went to waste. It started running down the path and had ended up against the wall of Kishan Lal's house. I tried reasoning with Pratap and Phool Singh, but my plea was not heard. Phool Singh argued that this was free water that the Muraos could use if they wished. For all he cared, they could also redirect it towards the Chamar quarters. But the Muraos did not want to inundate others.

With nobody able to control the flood and the Thakurs deaf to my arguments, the water finally destroyed a portion of Kishan Lal's front wall and continued towards the Dalit quarters where it flooded a few houses. But no one complained.

Since nothing could be done to stop the disaster, I took pictures and observed the scene. The draining of the pond had been a long affair, already going on for perhaps seven or eight hours. It had started in the morning, soon after I had left for Chandausi, and looking at the water level, the pump would still run for a good part of the night. I suspected that the engine would not survive this, but Rampal thought that it would. The children had fun, jumping in the dirty water, shouting and trying—without much success—to catch some fish.

Chapter 23

Palanpur, 1984

In the evening, the mango tree witnessed its largest gathering ever. Pat, dressed in a new sari, conservatively wrapped around her—the focus had to be on the performance—tuned her instrument.

'It's called a guitar,' explained Brahmachari.

'But where are the tablas?' asked Kishan Lal.

'There is no need. It is a western sitar that can also be banged with the hand. That makes a sound like the tablas.'

'She plays two instruments at once and she also sings,' exclaimed Babu, impressed.

Pat cleared her voice and started:

Mrs Brown you've got a lovely daughter.

Kishan Lal, who had learnt some English in college, obligingly translated for the audience:

'Auntie aapki beti kitni pyari.'

'Who is this auntie?' asked the shrill voice of a woman who had just arrived.

'It does not matter,' said Kishan Lal to Pat's satisfaction.

'But why is her daughter pretty?' continued the woman.

'She must have big eyes and long black hair,' suggested Smita.

'Maybe, and also fair skin,' said Babu.

'Naturally,' responded Phool Singh. 'This Brown name must be British. They are fair there.'

'Or maybe it is a south Indian name. Then she may not be so fair. Besides, I think that brown means dark in English.'

'Maybe she has green eyes, like Mandakini,' suggested Phool Singh who had been spending more time in the movie hall since he was no longer running an illicit liquor store.

Pat looked furious. She coughed and tapped on her guitar for attention.

'You were right, it is also a tabla,' agreed an impressed Kishan Lal.

Gradually though, the crowd settled into relative silence. Pat resumed her singing.

She is sharp, the sharpest I ever met.

Kishan Lal echoed: *'Itni smart-si ladki kaheen naheen.'*

'So, she is smart?' interrupted Rampal. 'I'm sure this girl will cause trouble.'

'Why should she not be smart?' asked Govindi's daughter who had discovered her feminist leanings after Smita arrived in Palanpur.

'Smart girls talk back to their husbands,' insisted Rampal while Govindi was energetically silencing his daughter.

'Perhaps it is just that this girl studied,' asserted one of the representatives of the Bhatnagar family.

'So what,' said Govindi, 'as long as she is obedient and keeps her eyes down.'

A stern look from Pat silenced everyone, but the uneasy crowd was clearly left with many unanswered questions. Nevertheless, she managed to sing two more sentences:

Why doesn't she love me?
She told me so and I am so very sad.

'I told you she would cause trouble,' cried Rampal, feeling vindicated.

'It must be God's will,' suggested Brahmachari.

'The father should beat her up,' advocated Mullo.

'Or the mother can do it,' recommended Chunni, who preferred to delegate such matters.

'Why should she not go with him? Love will come later,' said someone practical.

'Yes, maybe he should kidnap her,' ventured Babu whose desperation for a bride had accumulated over the years. 'She will love him afterwards.'

'Anyway, why is he talking to the mother?' asked Kishan Lal.

'That must be because the girl's father died,' answered one of the women.

Everybody seemed to think that this was the most plausible explanation and Pat took advantage of it to squeeze in two more lines.

She said she does not want my gifts and I can keep them.
But I really want her to keep them.

That was the tipping point in the show. Suddenly, the flood of questions could no longer be contained.

'Arey baba. The dowry is not going the right way,' exclaimed Rampal, stunned.

'Maybe it is like that in foreign places,' an adventurous and open-minded woman suggested wistfully.

'That may not be a bad idea,' reflected Mullo who had no son but many daughters.

'We should perhaps send someone to sort things out,' suggested Phool Singh who still had traces of his background as a teacher.

He turned to me, 'Sir sahib, do you think it is a good idea? Maybe I could go?'

'The boy must be very rich,' an envious Govindi reflected.

'If he is very rich, why should she not love him?' asked a woman, turning to Pat for an explanation.

Quite desperate, Pat tried to hurry along a few more lines:
Still, she is so lovely that,
Even in a crowd, I would notice her.
And I would go down on my knees

'If he is rich enough to pay the dowry the other way, what is she doing outside the house?' asked a Thakur woman.

That was when Pat abruptly ended the song, to the dismay of the listeners who were enjoying the unusual performance. She did it with a slap on the guitar that she probably would have liked to give to some people in the crowd.

'If you want to know what I think,' said Brahmachari as we were leaving, 'the built-in tabla is not bad, but I still prefer it as a separate instrument.'

I wanted to go back home with Pat but Phool Singh had another idea, 'Sir sahib, do you want to come check on the pond?'

I followed him. It was now completely dark and we could not see much. Still, it was obvious that a few fish were flapping around in the mud. Phool Singh went in, swearing as he slipped in the mud and landed on a fish. He collected as many fish as he could in a bucket as Rampal lifted a rather weak kerosene lamp to help him see. While Phool Singh was collecting the fish, Rampal explained that they had spent 34 rupees on diesel and would likely get about 10 kgs of fish. They would sell about 15 rupees of it and eat the rest at home. The venture was a financial and social disaster. Water had been wasted, a wall destroyed, some houses flooded in the Chamar quarters, and there would be no fish—and very little water—in that pond for the foreseeable future. Phool Singh climbed out carefully, carrying the bucket. He thought there could be a few more fish in the mud. He emptied the bucket and gave it to Babu, 'Go get the rest.'

But Babu objected that it was dirty water, full of slush and perhaps even 'women's urine' which, as I told Pat later, would indeed be terrible. Finally, he exclaimed—as he had done when I had asked him to clean the dirty corner in my room—that he might be a Chamar but that did not necessarily mean that he should do all the shitty tasks in the village. Brahmachari, who had joined us at the pond, hoping that some fish would come his way, looked very unhappy with Babu. He gave a short speech on the need for everybody to abide by their assigned role in society. Then, he made a fuss because it was not proper to use that bucket for such purposes: it was also used for bathing. Once Phool Singh had emptied it, he gave the bucket to Babu and told him to wash it thoroughly. Brahmachari told Phool Singh that he would purify it with Ganga jal after Babu had washed it.

Pat was asleep when I reached home, and I felt it was best.

Early the next day, a beaming Babu knocked at my door.

'You look happy,' I noted. 'Did your house survive the flood yesterday?'

'No, one of the walls is gone,' he said, looking unconcerned.

'This is terrible,' I said.

Babu quickly brushed away the flood just like the water must have brushed away the wall.

'Still, you are happy,' I noted.

He pointed at his belly. It looked a bit like the day he had stuffed himself at the sweet shop in Chandausi.

'They had left some fish at the bottom,' revealed Babu. 'That is why I refused to go with the bucket. They would have given me just one rupee and no fish.'

I gave him an admiring look, 'That was very clever,' I said. 'And were there many left?'

Babu tried to look modest but failed, 'So many that I invited Roshan. He ate very well too.'

I smiled. At least, all had not been lost.

'And I've taken some home. We will cook them for the wedding.'

Maybe I had been wrong about Babu after all. He had managed

this situation rather nicely.

A little later in the day, I ran into Pratap and Rampal looking depressed. They complained that no engine was available that day to irrigate Rampal's potato field. The field, located a little outside the village, had not benefited from the flood the previous day. Pratap's engine had broken down, adding a substantial repair bill to the already high costs of draining the pond.

Back home, I found Pat packing.

'What are you doing?' I asked.

'Can't you see? I'm packing.'

'I can see that, but why?'

'Because my place is not here.'

Then, the floodgates opened, and, half-shouting, half-crying, Pat let herself go:

'It is not what I expected...that Professor only wants to sleep with me and my research topic is no good.... They don't like my music.... I like theirs but I do not understand it.... Smita is nice but we are so different...and...and...I look terrible in a sari...'

We had a long conversation. No sex, just talk. In the end, Pat explained that she wanted to keep a little dust from Palanpur as a memory of the place where she had finally worn a sari and spent smelly nights, like in the book her friend had shown her years earlier.

'I don't know the book you are talking about, but I get the message,' I agreed.

She smiled, 'And speaking of smelly nights, please get rid of that billy goat and clean that dirty corner of the house before leaving.'

'Should I leave too?' I asked her.

'That is for you to decide,' she answered, looking at me indulgently. 'But before you go, you should visit the Dalit area again, I think. A bit more thoroughly. Babu and Smita have invited you.'

Maybe she was right. I never seriously explored it.

She added that she would wait for me in London, in case I cared to join her a little later. But she would only leave after Babu's wedding. In the meantime, she would talk to Veena a little more. Maybe that would cheer her up. She would also help Smita—very busy with Babu's wedding—with the school kids.

'Why don't you go to your fields and take pictures?' she suggested.

I took the camera and we left the house together. This was not a good time to disturb Babu, but I went to his place because I wanted to check how things were shaping up. Organizing the wedding just after Neetu's release was a good idea. It had given the old woman a sense of purpose. She also must have eaten well the night before. She was even humming a little song as she was cleaning the house with the help of Smita's mother. As for Babu, he was busy with a mysterious task. Sitting in front of a rickshaw, he was tying ropes and little pieces of wood to the main body.

'What are you doing? I did not know you had a rickshaw.'

'It's not mine. It's my cousin's who is working in Chandausi—he took you and Kishan Lal once—and I am preparing a surprise.'

'Tell me!'

'No, it's a surprise.'

I then pointed at his goat, busily munching some grass:

'No luck with the goat?' I asked, still upset about their stealth trip to Chandausi.

Babu looked at me with pride, 'Oh, but I have found a buyer. It is sold already.'

'Really?'

'Absolutely.'

A mysterious buyer and a surprise! I left Babu in peace after having taken a few pictures and proceeded to Kishan Lal's place. He was busy repairing his damaged wall and would probably be at it for the rest of the day. Thus, he was not free to work in my fields and he regretted it. They required more attention than I was giving them, he added reproachfully. I took a few pictures of the damage and of the empty pond with the 18 mm, then decided to help him bring sand from the dried riverbed outside the village. My fields could wait a little more.

Loading the sand had been hard work and we remained silent for a while on the way back. As we approached Palanpur, we saw a little group of men slowly leaving the empty pond, one or two of them with a shovel in their hands. There was no need to ask what had happened and a little later we learned that Mahender Pal's child had died during the night.

As we were passing by the Thakur quarters, the bullock cart got stuck in the mud left behind by the flood. It was deep and we had to work hard to free the cart. Quite a few people were sitting around, watching us and dispensing advice. They were not unsympathetic, but it was simply no one else's business. Kishan Lal did not mind and he was even joking with them once in a while. It was a form of individualism that was accepted by all. I took a few pictures of the scene before we managed to free up the cart.

Then, I went to see Rampal. Pat had been talking to Veena earlier but had soon left because three men had arrived from Akroli to see Rampal. I hung around a bit and, like a true Palanpuri, asked what was going on.

The men were well-dressed and one of them was a doctor. They were looking for a match for one of their daughters. While enquiring about suitable Thakur households in the area, they had heard about Hukum from one of his teachers. They found his background promising and wanted to have a chat with the family. When I arrived, Rampal had just accepted one thousand rupees as an advance on the dowry and was expressing his deep regrets that Hukum, currently travelling on some important business, could not meet the girl's family. He was so convincing that I wondered whether his troubles had put him out of touch with reality. The girl's family left and Rampal, elated, turned to Veena, telling her that her turn would come soon. This did not appear to enthuse the young woman, especially as Rampal added, 'The problem is that you are smart. Like the girl in that song. It will be difficult to find a willing husband, but I will try.'

'The real problem is that Jagpal is dead and Hukum is in jail,' she objected.

'Chup,' said Rampal.

He turned to me, urging me once again to do something about Hukum fast, so that the bride's family would not hear about what had happened. Keeping such a secret from the visitors was unwise, in my opinion, but I said nothing. The headman then turned to public affairs and handed over the letter from the KDO that had just arrived. Miracle: the projects were sanctioned, and the funds had been transferred to the panchayat account. I continued reading…

'WHAT?'

Chapter 24

Palanpur, 1984

At least the letter made it clear that, in spite of my Indian roots and recent Palanpur experience, I continued to fall prey from time to time to the most naïve anticipations. I had honestly believed that the KDO wanted to help with the school in Palanpur. Perhaps he did and was constrained by the system, but one could be forgiven for interpreting the letter otherwise. I also suddenly understood what he had meant by a sequential approach.

The letter stated that the projects were sanctioned, and that the money would reach the panchayat account soon. Unfortunately, the matching grant from the government would be small: 5,000 rupees only. The rules had recently been revised—earlier, the grant would have gone up to 15,000 rupees. That was the first piece of bad news. The second was that the government grant would come later and would only be disbursed after work had started as per the priorities of the village council. That meant the temple before the road, and the road before the school. Finally, the labour component of the scheme—the professional masons—was increased and the daily wage was fixed at 9.50 rupees. The authorities—through the KDO—therefore encouraged us to start the temple as soon as possible.

The letter also suggested inviting the local Member of Parliament to lay the foundation stone of the temple in a public ceremony. It did not mention the coming elections, but the connection was obvious. A date was proposed, rather strongly, as Netaji—as the MP was known—happened to be available that day. He would take the opportunity to demonstrate his commitment to rural development. Would it be possible to identify a destitute and deserving villager who could benefit from a 600-rupee loan? The money would be generously disbursed from Netaji's Fund for Dalit and Minority Empowerment. To finalize the arrangements, the ADO, who would also attend the ceremony with some of his colleagues, would appreciate seeing headman Rampal Singh and Mr Anil Singh the next morning at his office. Indeed, the proposed date for the foundation ceremony was just three days away.

Fuming, I argued that this was scandalous. First, the initial instalment of construction money would effectively be my money. Second, the rest of the money was coming mainly from the Muraos and the Dalits as well as the Bhatnagars, who all cared more about the school than about the temple or the road. Third, I had given an advance that was supposed to be reimbursed after the sale of the old panchayat tree. So far as I knew, the tree was still standing, and nothing had been done about felling or selling it. Fourth, if the school was not repaired soon, the roof might collapse. Finally, having a bunch of highly paid masons in the village would create problems.

Rampal remained very cool and he reminded me—as he had done before—that I had volunteered my donation in writing. I had also promised to go along with the decision of the village council. That I disagreed with this decision was my problem, not his. The panchayat tree would be dealt with in due course but there was no rush as it still displayed signs of life. Besides, the tree was a critical fixture of the village and provided shelter to the monkeys. How he could say all that while remaining serious was a marvel. He also regretted that so many people did not care about the house of God. It was shameful, and he would discuss that with Brahmachari a little later in the day. Finally, I should understand that the provision of 9.50 rupees per day for masons was meant to cover not only their wages but also other charges that would be borne by the contractor.

'Like bribes, for instance?' I asked innocently.

'I mean "other charges",' replied the headman sternly. 'The contractor is an important person who happens to be the cousin of the KDO and a friend of the ADO. I also know him personally.'

Would I nevertheless agree to accompany him to see the ADO, since we were both invited?

I reluctantly agreed. Still, I pointed out that it would be a miracle if the grant materialized within a year. The villagers who had donated for the road and the school would become restless. If all sorts of sharks swallowed their money along the way, that would really be bad, and I shrewdly added that Rampal might even lose the next elections.

The headman was not anxious. A loan from Netaji would help the recipient and also demonstrate how he, Rampal, cared for the poorest of the poor. A good electoral argument.

'So, who is that poorest person?' I asked.

'Roshan, of course,' answered the headman. 'Can you go and bring him here?'

I went to Roshan's house. It was a miserable mud hut squeezed between larger kuccha houses. Sakina Bibi, his wife—the woman some people, according to Kishan Lal, thought I was interested in—told us in a weary voice that he was sick and that they had no money for medicines. Babu had tried to help, but he did not have enough money. Her reception was very cold and, feeling sorry, I just wanted to leave. Still, Roshan managed to get up and agreed to follow me although we had to walk slowly. It was frightening to think that this man could die any day in the lonely darkness of his hut even as his neighbours were going about their business.

When we finally reached Rampal's house, Roshan was informed that he had been selected for a government loan. Despite his weakness, he flatly refused. He had just escaped from a debt trap that had made his life miserable for years. He did not want to risk that again. His objections fell on deaf ears. There was no way the simple-minded views of an illiterate Muslim could be allowed to ruin a solemn event like Netaji's visit to Palanpur. Roshan was cajoled, lectured, scolded, yelled at. Nothing doing, he did not want the loan.

The situation was becoming problematic. With Roshan ruled out, it was not clear who else could serve the purpose. Babu had a job with me and he was busy with his wedding anyway. Many others were certainly poor, but they were much better off than Roshan. I suggested sleeping over this, hoping that a solution would be found by the next morning.

Quite depressed, I went back via the school. There was not a chance on earth that any money would be left for it at the end of what promised to be a tortuous and corrupt process. I would need to find a way to help more directly. Although the wedding ceremony was only a few hours away, Smita was in the school and had made it a point to teach her class. Pat was assisting her. A dozen kids were sitting under the cracked roof and listening carefully. I took a quick look at their books and realized that they were memorizing sentences like 'I live in a house with six rooms', that too in English. That further depressed me. But Smita was smiling:

'They are already making good progress. And to think that the building will be repaired soon—how wonderful!'

I didn't have the heart to disabuse her, so I allowed her illusions to live on and enquired whether everything was ready for the wedding.

'Yes. It will be a nice ceremony with plenty of food and there is a surprise, you will see. Babu is working on it.'

I assured Smita that I loved surprises and went home, rather worried. Pat accompanied me. She finished her packing and I helped her. That welcome moment of tenderness was soon interrupted by loud knocks on the door.

'It is me, Rampal! Are you there?' shouted the headman whose outbursts of activity apparently had helped him put aside the worries of the day.

'And me, Babu.'

It was strange for those two to be together and I suspected that something unusual was happening. I opened the door. 'It is all arranged,' said Rampal.

'But no more than 180 rupees,' insisted Babu.

'For the loan?' I asked.

'No, for one goat.'

I was a bit lost and turned to Pat for help. She did not seem to find the conversation any more enlightening than me. Rampal explained:

'It's like this. I went to Roshan to convince him to take the loan and met Babu on the way.'

'I wanted to talk to Roshan about something,' explained Babu although nobody had asked him.

'I asked Roshan what it would take to make him accept the loan.'

'I told him not to take money,' said Babu.

'Precisely…' Rampal tried to continue.

'But to take goats. That is good value,' Babu said hurriedly.

'You mean to say he should receive goats rather than money?' I asked.

'As a loan, yes,' confirmed Rampal. 'But he should not owe more than 180 rupees for each goat. That is a fair price.'

'Yes,' said Babu. 'That is a fair price for a goat.'

'A bit high maybe,' conceded Rampal, 'but…'

'Not at all, I had a buyer for mine,' insisted Babu.

'Okay, okay,' I summarized. 'So, the deal is that Roshan should accept three good goats and 60 rupees in cash in lieu of the 600-rupee loan? We will have to convince Netaji.'

'That won't be a problem,' responded Rampal, for whom the ways of the rich and powerful did not seem to have secrets.

Once they were gone, Pat looked at me, 'I smell a rat,' she said.

'Me too, but what can I do?'

She smiled, 'I know. But you could start with something small.'

'Like what?'

'Like cleaning that mess over there and getting rid of that animal. It tried to butt me this morning.'

'Not now. We must get ready for the wedding. And you look lovely.'

'But I'm not ready yet.'

'I don't understand what you mean: you always look lovely.'

'Okay, go. I need time to get dressed.'

I decided to return to Rampal's place and go again over the important matter of that loan. Just as I approached the entrance, I overheard Brahmachari and the headman talking. I knew they had planned to meet, so that was not a surprise. I was about to enter when I heard something that made me freeze:

'Society is collapsing. Imagine, BKS dared to put my son in jail. The son of that bastard Bhupal. People were interested in Hukum as a groom and, because of BKS, I now owe them money. Ganga Sahai has a tractor. Besides, elections are coming. If things go wrong, a Murao may get elected again.'

'Yes, that would be terrible,' agreed Brahmachari. 'Better than having a Chamar as village head, but still bad.'

'We already have a Chamar teacher,' frowned Rampal. 'Remember that Babu refused to collect the leftover fish from the pond. The pond was dirty, he said. Society has become rotten, I tell you.'

'Yes, the pillars of society are crumbling,' Brahmachari added unctuously.

'You must find a way to make people come to their senses and comply with our traditional values. They must understand the truth.'

'The truth...the truth...' Brahmachari chanted. He seemed to be lost deep in thought and Rampal interrupted.

'What are you thinking?'

'Yes,' Brahmachari exclaimed, 'the truth! We should organize a procession.'

'A procession?'

Brahmachari clapped his hands, excited, 'The procession will take place just after Netaji lays the foundation stone. It will be led by a sacred bull. I have been to the South and I learnt how a sacred bull can reveal the truth.'

'Very good idea,' approved Rampal.

'I can ask a Brahmin friend of mine to come over. You know him. The sadhu who came a month ago from Haridwar and told us stories. He keeps a sacred bull. Of course,' Brahmachari added shrewdly, 'there will be some costs…'

'Naturally,' agreed Rampal in an understanding voice. 'A modest fee would suit me too. We will of course charge the project. After all, this is being organized for the development of the village.'

'Including the road and the school, of course, even if they are a bit delayed,' added the holy person devoutly.

'Naturally!' Rampal agreed again with a satisfied laugh.

I decided that I had heard enough and started walking out backwards so as not to be noticed, when a young voice whispered just behind me, 'Do you understand why I would rather not stay here?'

Veena had silently come up behind me. She looked sad once again.

'I can't take it anymore and I'm not sure I can stay here much longer.'

'What will you do?'

'I can take care of myself and I have a plan,' she replied, a touch of defiance in her voice. 'I just hope that Hukum gets out of jail soon.'

That evening, we attended Babu's wedding. Although I was quite worried, and sad about Pat leaving, I enjoyed myself. It was a small, simple gathering. The bride had arrived earlier in the day and had stayed with Smita and her mother. She did not have a large family—just one cousin who had come with her. There was a little band that did not play too badly. Babu appeared on a strange contraption, rather nicely decorated. It consisted of a huge and funny assemblage built around his cousin's cycle rickshaw. It was ingenious and colourful, and I took a bunch of pictures of a proud Babu sitting on top of it. I also took one or two when one of the wheels gave way as the groom was doing a little dance on top of the contraption. He fell to the ground but Smita, who had rushed to the rescue, reassured us: all was fine. Babu had received the usual gifts: some cash, a bicycle, a radio, a watch, the nice ties, and handkerchiefs that Pat and Smita had bought for him, and two pressure-cookers. The dinner was splendid. As expected, there was plenty of fish and...goat meat. It started to dawn on me that I was the buyer that Babu had mentioned: the 180 rupees were part of the lump sum I had contributed to the wedding. Pat winked at me:

'This goat meat is superb. When you pay the price, you get the quality. You should take a little more.'

I smiled and had some more. Everybody had great fun and ate abundantly. I heard later that some country liquor had also been served, but not in my presence.

The next morning, I escorted Pat to Chandausi. From there, she would take the express train to Delhi and then fly on to London. Rampal would come on the next train and join me for the meeting with the ADO. Pat looked sad but resolved. Her train arrived and I helped her with the luggage. She waved and I noticed that something was missing. Then, I realized, 'Your bangles,' I cried, 'you forgot them.'

She smiled at me, 'I will not need them anymore. I gave them to Babu's wife. The necklaces too. She was very happy.'

I smiled back, 'See you soon, Pat,' I said.

'Forget Pat. From now on, I am Jane again.'

The train left. I turned around and came face to face with the Captain.

'She's a charming lady. Shall we have tea, young man?'

'Captain, one of these days I'll stop being amazed when you turn up in front of me.'

The Captain smiled kindly, 'I know you have an appointment with the ADO, and I thought that we should have a chat before that.'

I decided to be frank. His integrity was now beyond doubt, 'Indeed. Perhaps you can help.'

I explained my problem: it was hard to identify the people mentioned in my uncle's notebooks. And, above all, I had not found the third shell. The Captain seemed surprised, then he laughed, 'You mean to say, all this time, you were looking for the third shell? This is amazing.'

I was irritated, so I said, 'Well, do you know where it is?'

'Yes, I do. Or rather, I have a very good idea. But I cannot get the shell. I would need a good excuse for that, and I do not have one. But maybe you're offering me one on a platter.'

'What do you mean?' I asked, flabbergasted. 'If you know where it is, let's go get it.'

The Captain smiled indulgently, 'It's a little more complicated than that, my young friend. But, tell me, there will be a big procession in Palanpur very soon, right?'

'Yes,' I answered. 'You know that.'

'It was a rhetorical question. I think as many people as possible should be invited. The time has come to clean up this mess. Netaji will be there, I will be there, and you would be well advised not to grumble too much about BKS's presence. Tell Rampal not to object either. It is important, we may need the police.'

'Okay,' I said. 'I suppose you know what you're doing.'

The Captain did not answer immediately. He smiled again: 'I know what I'm doing. I was asked to do it by my superiors and I also have a personal interest in all this. Sometimes, it is good for all concerned to be in the same place. The chemistry can produce surprising results.'

He looked over my shoulder, 'Now, go. Rampal has just arrived, and you don't want to be late for a meeting with the ADO.'

'He's always late.'

'He will not be late this time.'

I joined Rampal and we walked together to the ADO's office. The ADO was waiting for us and he started giving us a long speech on the importance of rural development.

'And,' continued the ADO, 'Netaji will make a generous loan of 600 rupees. Have you identified a destitute person who needs assistance?' he asked, peering at us over his spectacles.

'Well,' I said, 'we have someone, but he does not want the loan.'

The ADO leaned back in his chair and crossed his arms on his round belly, 'In these circumstances, we may not be able to proceed. This would be bad for the village and'—the ADO looked sternly at Rampal—'its headman. Even worse, Netaji's feelings might be hurt.'

'Wait,' I interrupted, 'Roshan does not want a cash loan but he would be willing to accept goats instead of cash.'

The ADO opened his arms and smiled, 'Oh, but this can easily be arranged. 600 rupees would pay for two or three goats.'

'More,' I argued. 'At 150 rupees per goat, it would be four goats.'

'The price is 180 rupees per goat,' Rampal interjected.

Finally, we agreed that Netaji would come with three goats valued at 180 rupees each, or a total of 540 rupees plus a 10 per cent fee, adding up to 594 rupees. The remaining six rupees would be given directly to

Roshan, in cash, by Netaji. The goats would be bought from a seller of good repute who happened to be a friend of the ADO. Netaji would arrive by train, accompanied by some important guests—including the goats. Being very busy, he would leave soon after the foundation ceremony. It would be nice if, in view of Netaji's generosity, Rampal could organize an appropriate welcome, including a meal.

This being settled, I let Rampal go back to Palanpur and went to see Ashok Kumar, 'So, you have finally agreed to sell your property,' he rejoiced.

'Yes, my project is over. You said you had a buyer. Is he still interested?'

'He is, he is, but he knows your property and believes it is not well maintained. He is very particular about a methodical approach to farming.'

'I guess that would reduce the value?'

'Just a bit,' he conceded.

We agreed on a date for the sale—that would be the day of my departure for London—and that I would clean up the house, perhaps paint it, in order to shore up the selling price.

As I arrived in Palanpur, I bumped into the three men who had expressed interest in Hukum as a possible groom. They looked furious and it did not take a PhD in psychology to guess that they had demanded their money from Rampal, who had not been able to return it. I decided that it was a bad time to visit the headman and, instead, went home to discreetly collect the pictures. I gave them to Smita, hoping for the best. Maybe a married Babu would know, somehow, what to do with them.

Chapter 25

Palanpur, 1984

The next day, prompted by the imminent sale of the house, I decided to clean up. Babu had been eyeing the billy goat for some time. So I handed him the end of the rope.... The billy goat immediately pulled Babu down and tried to gore him. Babu managed to avoid the horns and ran away, closely followed by the beast. Getting rid of the junk took more time. The animal had obviously lived in that corner for years and other billy goats had stayed there before. I had never come across this sort of sticky, smelly shit. Still, I finally managed to clean everything. In the afternoon, I lit a cigar and went out with both cameras, one equipped with the 135 mm and the other with the 18 mm. I had a fair idea about the pictures I had taken so far and wanted to complete the set with the missing places or people. This was an interesting expedition, giving me an opportunity to walk at my leisure in and around the village in corners that I knew less well. On the way back, I went past the school, but Smita was not there.

Once I came back home, I lay down on the charpoy and lit the second Romeo y Julieta of the day—a rare occurrence and that is why I mention it—before reflecting a bit. I would leave soon but had made little progress. Of course, Neetu had been freed, but I still did not know who had killed my uncle. The Captain seemed to know but he said he needed an excuse to find the third shell. What did that mean? How could the shell be somewhere else anyhow? And how could I get Hukum out of jail? My last weapon—the pictures—was in Babu's hands. Smita, Pat, and even the Captain seemed to think that it was a good thing, but I continued to feel that it was a scary proposition. There was decidedly too much that I could not control. By way of diversion, I decided to do some manual work. My eyes wandered across the house. All it needed now was a coat of paint and I had pots of paint, retrieved from the pile of junk near the billy goat. No more excuses. I had to get going.

Using an old screwdriver, I opened the first pot of yellow paint...

and could not believe my eyes. Inside the paint was a plastic bag with gold coins, jewellery, and a wad of banknotes. I laughed, realizing that I had just solved one of the mysteries of this whole affair. And I felt a moment of admiration for my uncle who had managed to have four hideouts that had remained undetected for years in a house where there were holes in the windows and just a few pieces of furniture. He had kept his wealth in a smelly corner guarded by a vicious billy goat. Nobody would ever go there. What a brilliant idea! But thanks to my deductive skills, worthy of Hercule Poirot—or so I would tell Pat in London—I had found Rajendra Pratap's loot. I was the Columbo of Palanpur, the Sherlock Holmes of Moradabad District. I carefully bolted the door and covered the holes in the shutter. Nobody could see me. Then I explored the plastic bag. There was quite an amount there. What should I do? I quickly decided to place everything inside the hideout in the wall. Then, I opened the doors and windows again and started painting the room as I was thinking. Soon I knew what I had to do.

Once I finished painting, overjoyed and feeling that the sky was the limit, I walked towards the school. Smita had returned and—truth be told—I started flirting a bit. At one point, Smita smiled at me. 'You say that I am pretty. That is very kind. But suppose I come with you to Britain, what would happen?'

'Well, you could...' I fell silent.

'You see? Besides, it is grey and cold there. You told me so yourself. When it rains, everyone grumbles. Here, there is sun, and when it rains, during the monsoon, the kids run everywhere, and people are happy.'

'We have fun there too sometimes,' I said.

'But this may not be the fun I'm used to, and you will be a little embarrassed by me, you see. Just as I'm embarrassed by you being here with me now. I like you, but we do not belong to the same world. Now think of you being here forever with me. It would not work. You should be with Pat, she is a lovely girl and very pretty.'

'She wants to be called Jane, now,' I interjected.

'Oh, that's great. We discussed that, you know. Her being called Jane again, I mean.'

There is so much that guys don't know about what girls talk about. Smita was right, of course, and a life for Smita and me together here did not make any more sense than a life together in London. My fantasies had come to a healthy end.

'Besides,' Smita continued, 'this is our own fight. I already told you that. We will do it our way, lose some battles, keep fighting, and perhaps win eventually. If there are failures—there will be, I am sure—they will be our failures. It will take time.'

'Talking about possible failures, are you sure you can trust Babu with the pictures?' I asked doubtfully.

She smiled again, 'He will do it his way. You'll see. Maybe he will fail, maybe not. Have faith.'

That is when I took my decision, 'You have faith too,' I said. 'You will get the money for your school, I promise.'

'I don't see how,' she replied sadly. 'Everything will be spent on the temple, there will be nothing left.'

'As a banker, I know how to rustle up money, you see,' I explained. 'I will arrange something, and you will receive regular instalments that you can use for the school as you see fit.'

She looked at me uncertainly, 'I don't know where this money will come from, but I know you enough to think that you mean it. I feel like thanking you, but you people owe it to us, really.'

The next day, I rushed to Chandausi and paid Ashok Kumar a visit. We discussed my idea. At the end, he smiled, 'Your girlfriend had told the Captain that you were unbeatable when it came to money.'

'Well, you know, I'm not sure....'

'She was right, your plan is good.'

I tried to look modest, 'So, it's okay then?'

'It will be done,' answered the lawyer. 'I suggest you come next Monday to sign the papers and transfer the assets. The buyer of your property will be here, so we can do everything in one go. Since the house is now painted, I shall bargain for a higher price on your behalf.'

A few days later, Palanpur was ready for the foundation event. Not exactly everybody because Babu, unconcerned, was going around like a spoilt child with his new bicycle, the watch, the radio at full volume and the beautiful red silk scarf around his head, that looked like a clumsily folded turban. But the rest of the village was eagerly waiting for the important visitors. As for me, I decided to participate, even though the event was a big burden on the project's small budget. And since the Captain seemed to think that something out of the ordinary might happen on that occasion, I took my cameras and slipped the two shells into my pocket before joining the crowd. They just might come in handy. I had not heard anything about the photos I had handed over to Smita and decided to trust fate as she was doing.

The first important guest to arrive was the CDO. In this election season, he had volunteered to give a short lecture to Palanpuris on how to vote in the gram panchayat elections. In front of a small crowd of local residents, he explained that it was very simple. The ballot papers would have several names with a square in front of each name. The voters had to blacken the square that was in front of the name of the person they wanted as their next village head. In the case of Palanpur, it would be Rampal, the incumbent, or Tajesh, a Murao, or some other candidate from the village if others were also interested. Up to that point, the CDO had been delivering the official line. Then, he added that for candidates other than the current headman, voters should also put a big mark on the other side of the candidate's name. Such was the rule for aspiring new headmen. Everybody listened carefully. Some questioned the procedure, but they were on shaky ground and the official looked very official indeed. I decided to stay out of it. As Smita had said, it was not my fight.

That was when the sadhu appeared. I remembered him from his last visit but had not paid much attention to his looks. This time, he did not go unnoticed. First and foremost, his wisdom was evident from a penetrating gaze, a heavily coloured forehead and a long white beard split in the middle to reveal a bunch of tulsi bead necklaces. He was wearing a long saffron gown that fell loosely over his thin body. The bull was even more impressive than his master. It was a formidable animal, beautifully caparisoned, its horns painted, with a bell around the neck. Brahmachari welcomed both visitors with a great deal of respect.

Meanwhile, the train had arrived and Netaji had disembarked, followed by the ADO, the BDO, the DDO, the EDO, the Captain, many other personalities, and three goats. The goats did not look in great shape. One was limping, the second seemed to have lost an eye, and the third one was suspiciously thin. But, even so, these three goats had some value. BKS had arrived too, by jeep, and he had left the vehicle near the old panchayat tree. He was proudly carrying a rifle that looked a bit like my uncle's Lee-Enfield, but more modern. Several Palanpuri Thakurs also carried rifles.

A meal had been arranged at the station for important guests and the refreshments were welcomed by all. Netaji bent graciously to receive a garland of flowers that had been prepared by Shakuntala herself. Then he made a speech about the importance of his Fund for Dalit and Minority Empowerment and Roshan was pushed forward to the front. One of Netaji's assistants handed him the three goats and told Roshan that he could go. But Roshan showed poor taste by insisting: he had been promised six rupees in cash. Netaji looked irritated, explored his pocket and could only find a one-rupee coin. He gave it to the assistant, asking him to add the rest. Unfortunately, the assistant did not have any cash either. Neither did the ADO, the BDO, the CDO, the DDO, the EDO, the FDO, the GDO, or the HDO (the last three had just arrived by car). Finally, I supplied a five-rupee note and Roshan agreed to leave, albeit slowly because of the limping goat. The delay had annoyed Netaji, who had other pressing engagements—related to women's empowerment—later in the day. So, we hurried to the temple, Rampal pushing aside anyone—including me—who was too close to Netaji's path. We soon reached the temple where Brahmachari, the sadhu, and his bull were waiting.

The foundation stone was laid, with due solemnity. Then Netaji gave an interminable speech, despite being in a hurry. Stirring words were also said by other important people, who congratulated each other for their respective achievements. Finally, everyone settled down and Brahmachari took the floor:

Mitron

Today is an auspicious day for Palanpur. The stars are well aligned, and Ravi has entered the house of Dharma. Let us bow to the son of Kashyapa, the enemy of darkness and destroyer of all sins.

Today I have come armed with the Prajnastra, the magic weapon that brings people back to their senses. Just as Dronacharya used his Prajnastra to wake his army from the stupefied trance caused by Dhrishtadyumna's Sammohanastra, I am unleashing the Prajnastra on Palanpur today to open your eyes and warm your hearts.

Look at yourselves. Think about Ram Rajya, the kingdom of Lord Ram, and how Palanpur fares in comparison. Theft, quarrels, gambling, fornication: that is how most of you waste your time. Fathers and sons are at loggerheads. Brothers despise each other and live separately. Weeds are growing in your fields while you play chaupar by the railway tracks. Daru flows like water down the Ganga. Monkeys are all over the place.

And what to say of the women? They have lost all respect for their husbands and in-laws. Pativrata and sati-savitri are all but forgotten. On the day of Karva Chauth, women nibble on biscuits on the sly. Some of them have even started moving around freely with their face uncovered. When I look at a child in Palanpur, I cannot help wondering whether his father is his mother's husband or someone else.

But my biggest sorrow, mitron, is how you have forgotten Varnashramadharma, the pillar of our social order. Today, the hand of the Thakur, instead of holding a sword, or at least a lathi, is on the plough, breaking a tradition that has served you well for centuries. Muraos are selling their cows' milk, instead of keeping it for their children and using it to make curd or ghee as was the custom. The barber has become a carpenter and the carpenter a blacksmith if not—God forbid—a butcher. The Brahmin is an outcaste and the thief is king. Chaos prevails and everyone has forgotten his varna, his dharma, and his parampara.

Even Untouchables have lost their way. Did Gandhi not remind us that Harijans were children of God? Indeed, manual scavenging is an experience in spirituality. Just as a priest cleans the temple every day before prayers, Harijans clean the village like it is a temple. The Harijan and the temple priest work and worship alike. But today, forgetting their noble calling, Harijans want to work as peons, if not clerks, and some even aspire to become teachers. One of them had the audacity to sneak into the position of village chief. Remember the chaos, the confusion, the corruption!

'Bravo, bravo,' interrupted Rampal, clapping.

Everybody looked at him disapprovingly. Rampal coughed and went silent.

Suddenly, a crumpled piece of paper landed on Brahmachari's nose. Taken aback, he was momentarily lost for words. The paper had rolled to the BDO's feet who unfolded it. Finding something scribbled on it, he read the text aloud:

Pothi padh padh jag mua pandit bhaya na koi
Dhai akshar prem ka padhe so pandit hoy

(The entire world is engrossed in reading scriptures, but no one has become learned.
The one who understands the two-and-a-half letters of love attains wisdom.)

There were murmurs of disapproval, but also suppressed giggles. I had lost the plot, so I whispered to Smita, 'What does this mean?'

'It is a popular doha,' she said. 'It means that the two-and-a-half letters of prem—meaning love—from the heart are worth more than all the scriptures.'

A Bhatnagar interjected, 'Some say that two-and-a-half also evokes the move of a horse on a chessboard. Meaning, one must be bold in love.'

'And you can forget the horse,' said Smita. 'The point is that when two persons love each other, they become more than two. But not quite three, because love is never complete.'

Meanwhile, it dawned on Brahmachari that someone was making fun of him.

'Who wrote this?' he shouted.

'Kabir,' said someone.

'Who is Kabir?' asked Brahmachari, annoyed. 'Let him dare to come forward.'

No one knew what to say, since Kabir had died in the fifteenth century, or thereabouts. Brahmachari drilled the crowd with fiery eyes, without being able to identify the culprit. Frustrated, he resumed his speech.

Mitron, this is the situation today. Palanpur is engulfed in Kali Yug, the age of darkness. You have forgotten the ancient wisdom of the Vedas, the glory of the Mahabharata, the tradition of Varnashramadharma, the laws of Manu, the joy of the Kamasutra.

But, today, you have a chance to make a new start, and rise from darkness to light!

To do this, you must abide by Ram Rajya. Just as your eye keeps tracking the plough and your hand guides it on a straight line, keep your eye on Ram Rajya and do not stray from the path of righteousness. Remember your ancestors, the sacred books, and

Lord Ram. Look at everyone as your friend, whether he is a Thakur or a Murao or a Chamar. Let everyone abide by their sacred duty and remember that everyone else is also a child of God. Remember, all those who belong to this motherland also share one race, one language and one culture.

And now, mitron, I invite you to celebrate the return of Satya Yug, the age of truth, by walking with me around the village behind Ashish, the sacred bull who had warned Ravana that his evil kingdom would be destroyed. If you know Sanskrit, you would be aware that the bull is a symbol of dharma, the path of righteousness. In the age of Satya Yug, the bull stands on four sturdy legs, but then he loses one leg at a time as the world goes through successive ages, until he's standing only on one leg at the time of Kali Yug. You, Palanpuris, are standing on one leg like the bull of Kali Yug. The slightest blow will make you lose your balance and bite the dust. So, let us get back to our feet. Let us take inspiration from Ashish, the four-legged bull of dharma, and restore the glory of Satya Yug.

The Thakurs, sitting right in front, clapped enthusiastically, led by Rampal and slowly followed by others in a growing crescendo. Brahmachari bowed. Netaji, who had glanced at his Titan watch a few times during the speech, whispered something to the ADO. The ADO turned to the BDO and whispered something. The chain continued until Rampal. The headman got up and signalled the start of the procession. Brahmachari had planned to go around the village, but in a short circuit that would avoid the school and the Murao quarters: there was no need to go there. There was also no question of going to the Dalit area at the southern end of the village even though the Muraos and Dalits were, of course, part of the procession. Smita had joined them, dressed in a nice red sari. The only discordant note came from Babu who, still happy about his recent wedding, was behaving like a child and zigzagging on his cycle near the front of the procession. The radio hanging from his neck was blaring but could not surpass the din of the historic march. People were freely mixing devotional chants and popular songs, accompanied by the rhythmic sound of drums and clapping hands of the little band that Rampal had hired. The crowd was in a joyful trance and sweets were being distributed liberally, but I could sense some tension in the air.

Still, the procession was moving forward. Babu was sometimes at the back, sometimes at the front. His cycling technique was not very convincing, his red turban slipping continuously. Several times, he brushed against the sacred bull, triggering reproaches from the sadhu and causing the animal to become nervous.

As we were nearing the burnt-down liquor shop, Babu lost control of the cycle, ran into the bull and fell on the ground. Dozens of photos came flying out of his pocket and showered the procession. The bull became very agitated, even more so when Babu's red turban fluttered in front of it. The animal started pawing the ground with its hoof and snorting furiously. Nobody cared: everyone was looking at the pictures. The procession had come to a standstill and the music had stopped. People were commenting on the pictures and exchanging them. The thin sadhu was the only person trying to calm the beast, but to no avail. The bull lowered its head. That was when Babu's red turban settled on the bull's head, covering its eyes. The bull, blinded, panicked and charged. Everybody jumped for cover, but without dropping the pictures.

BKS had immediately realized that the pictures exposed him as a rapist. Normally, that would have no consequences, but this was a bit too crude for the villagers. They felt an unusual sympathy for Smita and for Hukum who had courageously tried to defend her. BKS also heard people laughing at the more intimate shots. Ridicule kills, but he was mostly scared of the anger that was slowly gripping the crowd. He rushed to the end of the procession, took Smita by the arm and pulled her towards his Mahindra. The bull was now far away with Babu in front of it, running for his life, and the sadhu behind it, trying in vain to slow it down. I followed BKS and Smita. He pulled her behind the old panchayat tree and a part of her red sari tore as it caught in the bent flagholder of the jeep. Smita was struggling, but BKS pushed her to the ground. Then, he aimed his rifle at her, 'You dirty Chamar. I will kill you.'

I had just reached the tree. Smita was on the ground, shaking and crying.

'Don't do that,' I said.

The rifle turned towards me, 'Why don't you join your friend, you sneaky foreigner?'

With a rifle aimed at your chest, you obey. BKS loaded his weapon, ejecting an old spent shell, 'Which one first?'

Overwhelmed by fury, he did not hear the growing noise or Babu's cries for help. And yet, the rumble was becoming louder and louder. Suddenly, Babu appeared, still chased by the raging bull. He tripped and fell, his feet caught in Smita's sari trailing from the Mahindra. The bull, still blinded by the turban, continued straight on. The policeman finally realized what was happening. I saw an immense fear in his eyes as he tried to point the rifle towards the animal, but it was too late. With a loud, horrible noise of crushed bones and torn flesh, the beast rammed its horns into BKS and pinned him against the panchayat tree.

Confused and finally stopped in its tracks, the bull calmed down. Soon, the holy sadhu appeared. He took the rope attached to the nostrils of the animal who now meekly stood by his master. Then Brahmachari appeared, out of breath. He realized what had happened and seemed to enter in a trance, 'Oh Ashish! The bearer of truth. Truth is revealed. The sacred bull has revealed it!'

'Shut up, idiot,' shouted Rampal who preferred some part of the whole truth to remain concealed.

The sadhu did not seem impressed either by his friend's line and he was busy checking that no harm had come to the bull, especially to its legs. BKS was badly wounded and in agonizing pain. The Captain arrived, followed by a large group of Palanpuris. I noted that the group did not include Netaji, the ADO, the BDO or any other important guests. Busy with important affairs, they had preferred to hop on a train that had just stopped at the station. The Captain bent down and picked up something from the ground. He showed me the shell that had just been ejected from the policeman's rifle. 'I told you I had guessed where the third shell was, but I needed a chance to get it. Here it is.'

'I...don't understand,' I said, still confused by the situation. 'BKS was the murderer? Are we sure?'

The Captain nodded. 'Everybody knew it. Babu had seen him and had followed him through the village that night.'

Some secrets were well kept in Palanpur, at least from foreigners. The Captain opened his palm. 'Do you have the other two shells with you? I will show you something.'

I gave him both the shells, the Captain added the third one and showed me a small scratch on each of them. It was the same scratch, slightly off the center. 'You see, the same rifle shot all three bullets.'

He opened BKS's rifle and demonstrated that the three shells indeed fit.

'With an old Lee-Enfield,' he continued, 'it would have been even more obvious. But even this relatively new weapon has its own signature. You cannot miss it. The shell is expelled when you load the rifle, so if only two shells were found at your uncle's house, there was a good chance that the third one was still in the rifle. That was my hope.'

The Captain went to Rampal and took him by the shoulders, 'Hukum will be out soon, do not worry about him.'

Next to me, Smita was still shaking but she was also impressed. 'You see? Babu has done it. He has done it! Is he not awesome?'

Right then, Babu did not exactly look like a proud, heroic saviour. He had scratched his face in the fall, the radio was in pieces and the watch would need some work. But I had to agree, he had succeeded in efficiently using the pictures. Smita jumped to her feet and hugged her cousin. Roshan pointed out that Babu had all the qualities of a future headman. Should he not contest the elections? Babu said nothing, but I detected a glimmer of interest in his eyes.

The next day was the day of my departure. My bags were packed. At the last minute, I had hesitated whether to hand over the account books to the police or not. I decided against it. After all, I had already given one of them to the lawyer. Justice would have to make do with that. There was no use giving more evidence against the Palanpuris. So, I put the other booklets in my bag and left. There were quite a few people near the tracks waiting to say goodbye, but to my disappointment, Kishan Lal had not bothered to come. Rampal was not there either. Even though Hukum would be freed soon, he was depressed. I knew why: Veena had taken advantage of the commotion during the procession to run away. Nobody knew where she had gone. She had just left a note urging her parents not to worry—she would be fine—and expressing her regrets that she would not be present when Hukum returned home. Phool Singh took me aside, 'You know, Sir sahib, my brother is also depressed because Hukum will not be able to join the army. People who have gone to jail are not eligible. And he has no other son now that Jagpal is dead. He so hoped that someone in the family would join the army.'

'Yes,' I empathized, 'what a pity. And what are you going to do?'

'I will reopen the alcohol store. That is good business. And I will not need to share the money with BKS.'

I nodded and agreed that the business would be more profitable.

Babu appeared. He was proudly leading my two bullocks. I had given them to him so that he could start farming as a sharecropper. Smita had come along. She was as lovely as ever, but we had said to each other what was important. Roshan had not come, though. He was preoccupied because one of the goats was sick. But there was Mullo, Chunni, and many others. Still, Kishan Lal's absence upset me. I climbed onto the train and soon departed for Chandausi.

There, as I got down from the train, I heard a voice I knew, 'Hello Anil uncle.'

'Veena!' I exclaimed, 'what are you doing here?'

She was boarding the train I had just left. It was continuing to Bareilly. She had a small suitcase with her. She smiled, a bit sad, but also hopeful, 'I left yesterday because it was easy, nobody was paying attention. I spent the night with a friend from school. Now, I'm going to Bareilly.'

'What are you going to do there?'

'Join the air force,' she said. 'Girls are allowed, now. And I am a Thakur, you know that.'

The train was leaving. I waved. The time for my appointment with Ashok Kumar was fast approaching so I went to his office. He let me in, and I gave him the cash, the jewellery and the gold to set up a foundation for the school. He would keep a small portion of the money for the road, to be spent as per the gram panchayat resolution. The larger portion, for the school, would be made available to Smita in instalments, to be spent as she saw fit.

As we were finalizing the document, the peon came in to say that the buyer of my property had arrived.

'Let him in,' said Ashok Kumar.

Kishan Lal entered. I was stunned. I turned to the lawyer, 'But you never told me....'

'Why should I?' he replied. 'I must respect the confidentiality of my clients. Be it you or others,' he added importantly.

There was not much else to add, although I realized that I had paid Kishan Lal to improve the quality of fields that he was now purchasing from me. But in all fairness, I had paid him a fair price for everything. We signed all the documents. I expected Kishan Lal to leave with me, but Ashok Kumar said, 'Mr Kishan Lal, we have one more business together that does not concern Mr Singh. I understand that the other party has arrived.' Kishan Lal was decidedly doing very well. We said bye to each other with some vague promise to meet again in the future. Then he pulled out a bag of seeds from his pocket:

'Anil Sahib, since you have learned a bit about farming in Palanpur, maybe you will want to continue in your country. Take these seeds with you. They are very good and will help you start.'

I thanked him and, in exchange, offered the two books on farming in the subcontinent that I had carried all the way from London. I guess we were both wondering what use we would have for our respective gifts but, after all, this is almost a universal feeling. That is why it's the gesture that matters.

Then it was the lawyer's turn. He had been a great help and very reliable. Now, the future of Smita's school was in his hands. He promised to do everything properly and I trusted him. He did not disappoint me.

As I left the lawyer's office, a little wistful, I found Rampal in the waiting room. He looked embarrassed and I did not enquire. I presumed that he had come to sell some land to Kishan Lal so that he could return the money he had taken from Hukum's aspiring in-laws.

That reduced our 'adieux' to the bare minimum. But I realized I would miss seeing him and his gun appearing in the narrow lanes of the village.

I went back to the station, thinking that both Veena and Kishan Lal were doing great for themselves. There was hope. The train was due to arrive an hour later. I had time. On the way, I had stopped at the studio and collected the pictures the photographer had taken of Pat.

'She was such a lovely lady,' said the studio chap wistfully. 'Her name was Pat, I remember.'

'Not at all,' I said, 'her name was Jane.'

'Really?'

'You know, if a girl uses a false name, she cannot be that interesting. It is better to forget her. It's a question of trust.'

I left a very sorry studio owner.

As I was sipping coffee and contemplating the pictures in the waiting room at the station, I heard a familiar voice behind me, 'Can I join, my young friend?'

'Captain,' I replied, 'will you also be on the platform at Old Delhi

Railway Station?'

He assured me that he would not. We talked a little. 'There is still one thing I do not understand: what happened to the liquor store?'

The Captain smiled. 'BKS felt that his partners were cheating him and wanted to teach them a lesson. I don't believe that he wanted to burn it down. More likely, it was supposed to be a warning, nothing more. That's what Babu thought.'

'You know Babu very well.'

'Yes, very well. He is a relative.'

I tried to absorb this. The Captain paused for a while, drank a bit of tea, then continued, 'I have a favour to ask you.'

'Tell me.'

'Could you please destroy the series of booklets you found at your uncle's place? There is one in the hands of the police and that should be enough. It points to a few established businesses outside Palanpur. Palanpur residents would be difficult to identify based on that document only. With more booklets, it may become possible. I don't think that's necessary.'

I smiled and tapped my luggage, 'Don't worry about that. They are safe and I agree with you, it is not necessary to dig deeper.'

My train had arrived. 'I really appreciate you having come to see me off,' I said.

'That is natural for a relative, I think.'

I was mystified. 'What do you mean?'

He took out a small ring from his pocket.

Smita's great-uncle, George, gave it to me some time ago so that it would stay in the family. I have always kept it. Your family's misdeeds were many, but they also gave us an opportunity to meet each other and collaborate on something good. It is all settled now, I think.'

'Do you mean that you are also...'

The Captain looked at me with his penetrating eyes: 'Dukhi was rumoured to be beautiful and Smita probably inherited her beauty. But Dukhi also had a daughter called Babli that everybody has forgotten. She too was beautiful. She never married but she was abused by one of your ancestors and died while giving birth. It was a boy. He survived and made it to the army'. The Captain smiled and we shook hands.

Two days later, at Heathrow, Jane was expecting me. The first thing I noticed was her new hairstyle. It was shorter and suited her beautifully.

Epilogue

Palanpur, 1 January 1993

Dear Anil uncle,

You may not remember me, but we met about ten years ago at my parents' house in Palanpur. You had a cup of tea there and gave my father fifty rupees. My mother used the money to buy us pencils and notebooks for school. I was ten years old then.

Today I am writing to let you know that my former teacher Smita is no more. She was a model for us Dalits and we miss her dearly.

Let me tell you a little more about Smita. Although a trained teacher, she never had a formal appointment from the education department. She had heard that the village school in Palanpur was as good as defunct, so she decided to do something about it. The education department had no clue what was happening there, so no one interfered. Smita was very sharp and she put her heart and soul into teaching. I am well placed to know, I was her pupil for several years, until I joined a secondary school in Chandausi. We loved Smita. Inspired by her, we studied really hard. Without her, I would be working as a coolie in Chandausi today, as my father used to do. Many other children in Palanpur, girls and boys, owe much to her.

Unfortunately, Smita insisted on living with us in the Dalit quarters and exposed herself to squalor and disease. Much of the time, she was not keeping well. Even then, she used to come to school and teach us. A few weeks ago, however, she caught malaria. We did our best to look after her, but we had little money. In the end, we got her admitted in the district hospital. She died there last month, on 6 December.

Smita brought new hope into our lives, but I fear that that fire may not last. Her presence in Palanpur is unlikely to be recorded in the surveys conducted there every ten years or so by famous economists and anthropologists. The next one, by the way, is due later this year. We are told that a Belgian novelist will be part of the team this time.

Your antics in Palanpur ten years ago were a subject of endless gossip in the village. But we, Dalits, were not in a mood to laugh at that time. After Neetu was jailed, the Dalits united and organized a sort of underground resistance. They knew that they stood no chance with the police or the courts, so they looked for other ways of getting justice. They used to meet every day after dark, and some of them were in constant touch with Captain Jotiram, our mentor of many years. That is how he was so well informed. They also wanted to talk to you, of course, but they weren't sure if they could trust you, and in any case Captain Jotiram had advised against it. He had asked the Dalits to leave you to him. Still, we asked Babu to befriend you and that worked out well.

It was not a coincidence that Smita came to Palanpur at that time. Captain Jotiram had persuaded her to go there and join the resistance. Her meeting with BKS in the school was not an accident either. It was a kind of honeytrap. Aside from Babu, many other Dalits were hiding near the school that morning. I was also there. We knew that BKS would try to molest Smita, and our plan was to beat him to death on the spot. It is only because you appeared, like a devil out of a box, that the plan was scuttled. But, anyway, he did pay for his misdeeds. BKS miraculously survived the sacred bull's attack, but he was tried after that. Ashok Kumar, the lawyer, delivered a stunning speech at the trial and BKS was sent to jail for life.

I should give you some news of your friends in Palanpur. Some are doing well, others not. Rampal has retired from worldly affairs, and spends some of his time as a wandering sadhu. His brother Phool Singh reinvented himself as a fish vendor after his liquor shop was closed down by the gram panchayat. To top this, he managed to get appointed as manager of the local ration shop. Veena, Rampal's daughter, is a helicopter pilot. Kishan Lal and Ganga Sahai are still enthusiastic farmers and compete for the best yields. Inspired by the Muraos, many other farmers in Palanpur, even some Thakurs, are now growing multiple crops over the year and living a little better than before.

The social climate, unfortunately, has not improved. Remember the procession that took place in Palanpur when the foundation stone of the temple was laid? One of us had thrown the crumpled paper at the Brahmin. It was risky, but nobody saw who had done it. Smita had explained that text to us at school, just a few days earlier. We hated that procession. Many ominous events of this sort have taken place in Uttar Pradesh in recent years. Last month, some fanatics even demolished the Babri Masjid in Ayodhya, on the very day when Smita departed from this world. You must have heard about it. Things are still relatively peaceful in Palanpur, but who knows for how long?

I forget to tell you that Babu is alive and well. In fact, he became head of the village after you left. Not the first time he contested, in 1984: that year, he had the most votes, but many were not valid because the person who explained the rules had given wrong explanations. Or perhaps we misunderstood. Rampal was re-elected. Babu was elected the next time, in 1989, when the Thakurs fought among themselves. Incidentally, Rampal never went beyond the construction of the temple but Babu tried hard to get the road built. Unfortunately, despite his best efforts to bring everyone to a sensible agreement, the road could not be completed. The section coming from the south turned west towards the Thakur area while the section coming from the north did not connect with it and instead went east towards the Murao area.

Anil uncle, your ancestors have a lot to answer for, and we, Dalits, have suffered more than anyone from their misdeeds. But you are different, and for me, you are one of us. Enclosed is an invitation for my wedding next month. As it happens, you know the bride: Hafsa, Roshan's daughter. Like me, Hafsa was fortunate to be taught by Smita as long as she was alive. She learnt to read and write, and even studied until Class 10. Both of us have joined Ganga-Jamna Express, a media house in Moradabad.

We will be delighted if you can come for the wedding. The three goats Roshan received from Netaji ten years ago were a little anaemic, but thanks to your billy goat, they had many kids. That billy goat was a very strong animal. Even Babu had trouble handling it sometimes. Hafsa took good care of all the kids and she has a whole herd of healthy goats now. We promise some tasty meat at the wedding.

Please say hello to Pat auntie and bring her along if you can. We still remember that lovely song she sang for us below the mango tree. And we had such a good laugh when she impersonated you behind your back.

Jiten Ram

Acknowledgements

We would like to thank all those who have contributed in one way or another to the successive incarnations of this book from the original 1983 diary onwards, starting with the residents of Palanpur. For helpful comments on the manuscript, we are particularly grateful to Veena Baweja, Bela Bhatia, Abinash Dash Choudhury, Danielle Meuwly, Pierre Nicolas, Varsha Poddar, Tej Prakash, Aditi Priya, Naresh Sharma, and Aya Taketomi. We are also thankful to Sohail Akbar, Helen Andoque, Micael Castanheira, Benoit Descamps, Eddy Franssen, Anomita Goswami, Lisa Hobbs, Samir Jahjah, Raji Jayaraman, Aparna John, Reetika Khera, Pujitha Krishnan, Mathangi Kumar, Sharan Mamidipudi, Adrien Marnat, Benoit Moreau, Neel Mukherjee, Vandana Prasad, Kezang Penjor, Thierry Picquot, Simar Puneet, Maria Ralha, Pierre Regibeau, Tom Richardson, Kate Rockett, Melba Ruzicka, Kanika Sharma, Indira Unni, and Anumeha Yadav for helpful suggestions.

An interesting development took place as this book neared its completion. We were having last-minute doubts, about whether it was ethical to use the name 'Palanpur' in this novel. We wondered if some Palanpuris might take offence and blame us for ruining the reputation of the village. The question seemed all the more pertinent as we had initially stayed in Palanpur as researchers. Would an ethics committee approve of research material being turned, later on, into a novel without the consent of the 'subjects'?

Ideally, we would have liked to go to Palanpur and discuss the matter with our friends there. Alas, time was too short. By now, however, there are mobile phones in Palanpur, so we called Kishan Lal—yes, Kishan Lal is a living resident of Palanpur. He understood the issue immediately and agreed to convene a group discussion on this matter. True to his word, he called the next day to report, saying he had been asked to convey four points. First, the village in the novel should be called Palanpur. Second, nothing need be hidden, good or bad. Third, the novel should be translated into Hindi so that they can read it. Fourth, some Palanpuris were hoping that their name would be in the novel, and even wanted a WhatsApp number to send us their photo for the book!

So, we did not rename the village. And Kishan Lal remained Kishan Lal, as did Babu and Roshan, who are also among our best friends in Palanpur. Everyone else was renamed.

Alas, Babu and Roshan are no more. But some of their contemporaries, who inspired this novel, are still alive. We asked them to send us a group photo for the book. Here it is—we bow to their courage, wisdom and sense of humour.

Kishan Lal (centre), Mitra Pal, Udaivir, Sakuntala, Zahuran, and other Palanpuris who were young adults in 1984, with some of their children and grandchildren.

Photo credit Afzal Ahmad